M

Maria Beaumont used to be the bad-ass daughter of working-class Cockney-Greek immigrants. She has since reinvented herself as a respectable middle-class housewife living in a posh North London suburb, innit.

To find out more about Maria Beaumont please visit her website: www.letstalkaboutme.com

Also by Maria Beaumont

Marsha Mellow and Me

MissFit

Maria Beaumont

arrow books

Published by Arrow Books in 2005

1 3 5 7 9 10 8 6 4 2

Copyright © Maria Beaumont 2005

Maria Beaumont has asserted her right under the Copyright, Designs
and Patents Act 1988 to be identified as the author of this work

Arrow Books
Random House Group Limited
20 Vauxhall Bridge Road
London SW1V 2SA

Random House Australia (Pty) Limited
20 Alfred Street, Milsons Point, Sydney
New South Wales 2061, Australia

Random House New Zealand Limited
18 Poland Road, Glenfield
Auckland 10, New Zealand

Random House (Pty) Limited
Endulini, 5a Jubilee Road, Parktown 2193, South Africa

The Random House Group Limited Reg. No. 954009

www.randomhouse.co.uk

A CIP catalogue record for this book
is available from the British Library

Papers used by Random House are natural, recyclable products made from
wood grown in sustainable forests. The manufacturing processes conform to the
environmental regulations of the country of origin

ISBN 0 09 947874 9

Typeset by Palimpsest Book Production Limited,
Polmont, Stirlingshire
Printed and bound in Great Britain by
Bookmarque Ltd, Croydon, Surrey

This is 4 my people

THE FIRST BIT

The Bit Before I Turn Into Lydia

'*Shhuuushhh!*' Daniel hushes me with a shush loud enough to get him a job as an air-raid siren. 'They must be able to hear you giggling a mile away.'

What can I say? I'm nervous. Who doesn't giggle when they're nervous? I should think Eminem practically wets himself in the dressing room, pre-concert . . . Well, I bet Gareth Gates does.

'OK, whatever you do, *don't* sneeze,' he whispers.

Oh my God. The power of suggestion. I clamp both hands over my nose. It does the trick, but only because I can't breathe. I'm literally suffocating myself, but I'm too scared to remove my hands in case I'm beset by sneezes or giggles or both at the same time, thus sending the precious white powder into orbit. I'm dying here . . . Need . . . oxy . . . gen . . . It's me or the cocaine. Simple choice, surely? The coke looks like Canderel and came wrapped in a ripped-out corner of a page from last week's *OK!*, whereas I am a sensitive and beautiful human being (or at least I would be if I could only lose a tiny bit from around my hips). No-brainer. I win. I remove my hands and take a noisy, drawn-out breath that sucks so much air from the room I feel my ears pop from the pressure change.

'If you're that scared, let's just forget it, Charlie,' Daniel whispers irritably. 'And keep the noise down. If someone hears us we're dead.'

'Oh, stop being such a drama queen. No one's going to die. We'll only get sacked . . . and arrested . . . and imprisoned. Er, please tell me you locked the door.'

'Course I locked it. Now, for Christ's sake shut up and let me concentrate.'

I shut up and watch him concentrate. I've seen people do this in dozens of films. Take a little heap of white powder and transform it into a pair of perfectly straight lines with a couple of deft chops from a Gold Amex card. Daniel doesn't have an Amex. He doesn't even have a TOPMAN card. He's using the edge of his index finger, which is trembling (so his lines are more like wiggly worms) and sweaty (so more coke is sticking to his finger than is on the desk) because, like me, he's shitting himself.

Being a drug virgin is *so* uncool. I'm twenty-four and I've never even had a drag of a joint – or a cigarette, come to that. Daniel's ahead of me. Slightly. He snorted his first line last night and came into work this morning raving about it. He also came in with that little bit of *OK!* in his pocket and he's been going on at me all day to try it with him. That's why we're locked in our boss's office now.

We're on the seventh floor of The Zone, London's most prestigious fitness centre. So prestigious that we're not allowed to call it a fitness centre. No, it's a Total Body Emporium. Apart from my own breathing, the only sound I can hear is the plinky-plonk of the piano wafting along the corridor from the ballet studio. Total Body Emporium, classical piano, ballet; these are *not* things usually associated with drug culture. Add to that The Zone's zero-tolerance policy . . . We must be out of our minds.

Daniel's lines are getting wonkier and he's looking seriously stressed. I thought drugs were meant to be

4

fun (well, apart from when you've turned into a desperate junkie who's reduced to selling everything from your Walkman to your ulcerated body in order to score the next fix). What we need here is some light relief. I've just had a thought that definitely comes under the heading of *light* so I try it on Daniel. 'Hey, this is good: Charlie's doing charlie. Get it?' I proceed to laugh a little too hysterically because, as I've explained, I'm shitting myself.

'Shut up,' he snaps, clearly impressed by my dazzling wit. 'Here, gimme some money.'

'I said I'd pay you for my half later.'

'Not for that, you prat. We need a note to suck it up through.'

'Oh . . . Yeah . . . I knew that.' I fumble in my pocket and come up with a fiver that's seen better days. It's limp from over-use and as I unfold it I discover it's held together with Sellotape. I hand it to my drug buddy.

'Is that all you've got?'

'Sorry. I told you I need to go to the bank.'

'It'll have to do.' With quivering hands he tries to roll it into a tight tube, but after several attempts it's obvious it isn't going to happen.

'How about a Post-it?' I ask, spotting the yellow pad on the desk.

'Don't be daft. The coke will stick to the gummy bit at the top.'

We look at each other, deflating audibly. Looks as if the seventh floor is as high as we're going to get today. 'Tell you what,' Daniel whispers, perking up. 'Let's do that thing where you rub it onto your gums.'

Excellent idea . . . *Not*. I know how this stuff gets into the country. I've seen those documentaries showing terrified African women sitting on toilets waiting to poo out condoms of the stuff. And he wants me to stick it in my mouth?

He doesn't wait for my answer. He dabs his finger-tip at the powder, but, unlike a few moments ago when he couldn't get the stuff off his hands, it doesn't want to stick.

'Use a bit of spit,' I suggest, remembering what I used to do with my Sherbet Dip when I was younger. (OK, last week.)

He licks his finger and tries again, this time getting a generous splodge of powder to stick. Without a moment's hesitation he thrusts finger into mouth and rubs vigorously – like he's at a mate's for a sleepover and forgot his toothbrush.

'*Euughhh!*' he squeals, rapidly withdrawing his finger.

'What?' I squeal back, registering the terror on his face.

He can't speak. He stands rigid as white foam begins to dribble from the corners of his mouth. *OhmyfuckingGod*, he's OD-ing. Or he's scored a batch of pure, uncut something or other. Or . . . Or . . . I don't fucking know. *I'm a drug virgin.* But whatever's happening, I'm sure it can only be a matter of minutes – *seconds* even – before he slumps into a coma, his heart goes into arrest and he becomes another tragic statistic in the terrible war on drugs. Gotta do some-thing because the dribbles of foam have turned into fizzing, popping bubbles that are practically exploding from his mouth. Do *what*, though? I've passed a fully accredited first-aid course, but – believe me – we *never* covered oral effervescence. His arms are flapping in a desperate plea for help before his body shuts down. I respond by – *obviously* – flapping my arms right back at him. He tries to speak, but it comes out as an incom-prehensible bubbly gurgle. I lean forward, because if these are going to be his final words I'd never forgive myself if I didn't catch them.

'Bastard,' he groans at last.

'C'mon, Daniel,' I urge, gripping his shoulders firmly. 'Talk to me. Hang on in there.'

'The fucking *bastard*,' he splutters, a fresh torrent of bubbles spilling from his mouth. 'This isn't coke—'

I *knew* it. He's bought a batch of rat poison!

'—It's Alka-fucking-Seltzer.'

'Uuueeh?' When I'm nervous I giggle. When I'm confused, words come out as strange noises.

'That fucking *con* artist. Fifty quid I gave him . . . for fucking hangover relief. Charlie, it's *Alka-Seltzer*,' he says, his mouth fizzing merrily to emphasise the point. Before I can show my relief by laughing in his face, we're immobilised by the sound of the door – the one that Daniel *swore* he'd locked – clicking behind us.

'What the hell are you two doing in here?'

We turn to see Lydia, hands on hips, left eye looking at me, right eye staring at Daniel. She has the world's freakiest squint, which right now is an asset because it means she can glare at the both of us simultaneously. Luckily we're standing in front of Jamie's desk and blocking her view of the mess of white powder behind us.

Oh boy, are we in trouble.

'Sorry, Lydia. Philip was complaining that his piano's out of tune,' I grovel. 'Just came upstairs to have a listen.'

Wow, I'm quick on my feet. I'm the queen of instantly improvised excuses. Put Philip the ballet teacher's constant whingey whinges about his piano together with the fact that we *can* actually hear the thing from here (sort of) and – *bingo*! – we have a possible get-out.

7

'In case you hadn't noticed, Charlotte, the ballet-studio piano is in the ballet studio, *not* in Jamie's office.'

Well, I only said it was a *possible* get-out.

Next to me Daniel is swallowing like he's never swallowed before (and, let me tell you, that's saying something) in an effort to deal with the ongoing fizz before he says, 'Obviously we came into Jamie's office because the acoustics in here are *excellent*.'

'Daniel, what in God's name do you know about mus—'

'*Shh* . . . Hear that?' he says as fresh notes cascade along the corridor. 'Perfect D sharp. Isn't that the most gorgeous note on the scale?'

Daniel wouldn't know D sharp from dog shit, but he has stopped Lydia in her tracks. For a moment anyway.

We should leave now. Walk out the door and *run*. But if we move she'll see the white powder and we'll have a fresh heap of excuses to think up. So we stay put. We stare at her nervously while she stares back, her spooky eyes swivelling independently like a pair of department-store security cameras. Her right one settles on me while her left hovers in the vicinity of Daniel's groin. And although it's strictly a no-girl zone (Daniel doesn't *do* girls, hence the swallowing comment earlier), I'm not surprised because I've done my fair share of staring at it today. He's wearing a pair of spray-on Lycra shorts which contain what appears to be a salami squashed between two grapefruits. Company cars, corporate health-plans and profit-share schemes? *Pah*. Daniel's is what *I* call an impressive package. If aliens were looking down, it's the first thing they'd see. '*They peel them with their metal knives and . . . What the fuck is* that *between his legs?*'

Tragedy, then, that it remains off limits.

Suddenly Lydia's eyes widen in alarm. 'What on earth is *that*?' she demands.

'What?' we reply in unison.

'On Jamie's desk . . . Is, is that what I think it is?'

Shit and fuck. We now have confirmation of what we've always suspected. It's official: *Lydia's mutant eyes can see around corners*. No *way* could a normal-sighted person have spotted it through two bodies pressed tightly together for the sole purpose of concealing it.

Daniel and I turn and look at it, feigning surprise. Then Daniel leans over and makes a play of careful forensic examination. 'You know what I think it is?' he says after a long pause. 'Alka Seltzer. Jamie did seem a bit hungover this morning.'

Lydia isn't going to buy it in a hurry and she pushes between us. She too leans over it and takes a slender metal nail file from a pocket. In a move she must have seen in a cop show she scoops a tiny cluster of granules onto the tip and brings it up to her mouth. She transfers it to her tongue and we listen to it fizz gently.

'*Hmm*,' she murmurs, unable to hide her disappointment that the bust isn't going to happen. But she isn't done yet because the eyes set off again. '*My God*, Charlotte! What are those on your socks?' she shrieks.

Her eyes are still swivelling in several directions and I briefly look over my shoulder to check there isn't another Charlotte standing someplace behind me. But I know what's going on here. *My socks*.

I've broken the First Commandment: *Staff shall exclusively and solely wear attire that bears The Zone logo*. I really should have known better but they were the only clean ones I could find this morning. I spent ten minutes carefully pushing the illegal ticks on the side into my trainers, but near the end of an eight-hour shift they've obviously had enough of being hidden

9

away and they've ridden back up my ankles – *just bloody do it*.

Ironic, isn't it? She can't do me for the liberal scattering of suspicious white powder on Jamie's desk, but *really*, I could lose my job because of the wrong sodding socks. I feel Lydia's eyes (well, one of them anyway) drill into me and I hope to hell she doesn't have x-ray vision and can't see the adidas stripes on my bra top. I'm sweating. And are those my legs trembling? My own father – five feet five of hair-covered muscle, ruler of my universe – doesn't have this effect on me, but he isn't Lydia. She's the Fitness Führer. And she *sees* things. Not just dead people, like the kid in that Bruce Willis film. She sees *ticks* on *socks*.

'Remember, I've got my eye on you, Charlotte—' Singular *eye*, that's about right '—Now, take them off immediately and get back to reception while I clean up this mess.'

As she turns towards the desk, we run.

'Ugly freak,' Daniel says when we're out of earshot.

That's not fair. She's nowhere near ugly. She's five-eleven with the figure of Beyoncé and her face is stunning. Physical perfection in other words . . . Except, I'm afraid, for that squint. Which there's just no getting past. Which makes her a freak.

We stop briefly to peek through the ballet-studio window. Philip's pianist is playing something really fast now – like the classical equivalent of drum 'n' bass – and his dancers are scurrying around like mice on acid. Philip pauses and gives Daniel a coquettish wave.

'Please, tell me you haven't had him,' I say.

Daniel smiles inscrutably – which can only mean that, yes, he's had him – and we set off towards the lift.

*

10

We arrive back in reception. Rebecca's there, frozen exactly where we left her half an hour ago. Literally. As we departed Daniel said, 'Just off upstairs, Becks. Don't move.' Well, she hasn't. I doubt she's even blinked. I check her eyes for puffiness. They look all right. No disasters then. Rebecca's only seventeen and not good with stress.

'Everything OK, Becks?' I ask.

She nods and says, 'A man phoned. Wanted to know if we had any Steps . . . I thought they'd broken up.'

'I think he probably meant step *classes*, sweetie,' Daniel says.

'Oh, like aerobics,' she says, blushing, suddenly remembering what we do here.

'Never mind,' I say. 'You got his details, yeah?'

(The Second Commandment: *Staff shall obtain every caller's details in order to ply them with membership info*. And they mean *every* caller, even those phoning to sell *us* something.)

'I didn't think,' she mumbles. 'I said he should try Tower Records.'

She's been here for six months and it's Daniel's and my job to teach her everything we know. She doesn't seem to have picked up much and it occurs to me now that maybe it isn't her fault; we haven't been the world's most conscientious teachers.

'Don't worry,' I say soothingly. 'Tell you what. Nip up to the caff and get us a drink. A Tango and a Co— Make that two Tangos.'

'OK,' she bubbles, chuffed to be given a job she can handle.

As she scurries off, Daniel says, 'She'll screw up, you know.'

'I know. I should've written it down for her.'

Seconds later the automatic doors swoosh open and

11

Jamie strides into the foyer as if he owns the place. Well, how else is he going to stride? He owns the place.

'Hi,' I call out. 'I thought your meeting was an all-dayer.' (Which was the reason Daniel and I felt brave enough to turn his office into a drug den.)

'Change of plan,' he says briskly. 'Where's Lydia?'

'She was in your office a few minutes ago,' Daniel says, unable to prevent a last maverick bubble escaping from his mouth.

'Good, I need to talk to her.'

As he steps into the lift, Daniel gives me a look. 'Jesus, it's only just sinking in: how close we came to getting totally busted up there. Thank God for Alka-Seltzer, man. I should find that bastard rip-off merchant and kiss him . . . with tongues.'

I flop into one of the chairs behind the reception desk, unlace my trainers and peel off my illegal socks. Then I sit back and put my slightly sweaty feet up on the counter. I look up at three fifty-inch plasma TVs on the wall. They're tuned into MTV Base. Nelly's gyrating on the screens. *Mmm*. I could so do it with Nelly. Just let him phone up with an enquiry about the Pilates timetable. That's what I love about this job. OK, Nelly isn't likely to call anytime soon, but Craig David was in a couple of weeks ago. And Daniel Bedingfield is a member. Not exactly A-list gyrators, but how many other jobs are there where I could meet real pop stars and in-between-times sit with my feet up watching MTV? Even the fact that I have to dress Zone is a plus. It's cool gear, every bit as funky as adidas and Nike. OK, it's still a uniform, but it's about as far from a McDonald's nylon smock as you can get. Yes, this job is just about perfect.

If only we could get rid of Lydia.

Daniel and I spend roughly an hour a day trying to

think of ways. We haven't come up with one yet, but it's surely just a matter of time.

'Have you really done it with Philip?' I ask, believing it but not wanting to.

'Twice,' he tells me. 'Once in Lydia's office and once in the Mile High Club Lounge.'

The Mile High Club Lounge is on the seventh floor – the only other room up there besides the ballet studio and Jamie's office. It's hardly a room, actually, more of a broom cupboard. It's only ever used by Daniel and the cleaners and I reckon he's in there more than they are. I don't know how he does it. It's dark and cramped, and more to the point it's only a few feet away from Jamie's office.

'I'd have thought Philip's a bit sophisticated for your dirty old broom cupboard,' I say.

'You're kidding, aren't you? You should see him on all fours. He's a dirty little *dawg*.'

'Who's a dog?' asks Rebecca, back with the drinks.

'Lassie,' Daniel says.

'Oh, yeah, right . . . Who's the Sprite for?'

'Neither of us,' Daniel replies, taking the cans from her and handing me the Lucozade.

I hate Lucozade. Wish I'd written it down for her.

'Turn the telly over,' Daniel says as he pops his can. 'I hate this.'

He's talking about the Kelis video that's kicked off.

I pick up the remote and flick to Box. Nelly again. He's everywhere today. Like a horny, hip-grinding virus. I carry on cruising through the fifteen music channels, getting brief snatches of Girls Aloud . . .

'*Ugh*, girls,' Daniel declares.

. . . Marilyn Manson . . .

'People that ugly should *not* be allowed to make videos.'

. . . Evanescence . . .

'*Yeuch*! Weirdo Christians.'

. . . Limp Bizkit . . .

'*Aaagh*!' Daniel wails.

I stop flicking because the phone's ringing. I pick it up, then immediately hold the receiver two feet from my ear. I can still make out every word that Mr Angry is yelling at me, even over Limp Bizkit.

Mr Angry: Steve the gym manager. That man is always shouting. So aggressive. Daniel puts it down to the steroids. I put it down to the fact that he's just an aggressive bastard. I once saw him pick a fight with an empty chair in the caff.

I don't have to listen. I know why he's phoning. He hates it when Daniel and I channel-surf. That's because the screens in reception aren't the only tellies in The Zone. They're all over the place. There are ten dotted around Steve's huge gym alone, all linked to the remote I've got in my hand. A few weeks ago one of the cyclists demanded a full refund on his membership. He claimed to have slipped a disc when Daniel flicked the TV from a soppy Will Young ballad to some speed garage.

'Sorry, Steve,' I say, bringing the receiver back to my ear. 'Shall we stick with the metal or find something else?'

'I don't give a flying fuck,' he barks. 'Put it on the fucking Shopping Channel for all I care. Just stop fucking changing it.'

As I hang up, I see Lydia. Stomping towards reception.

Shit.

She must have been in the gym when Steve called. I am in *big* trouble.

I brace myself, but when she reaches us she doesn't stop. She carries on down the corridor to the side of

14

the counter and a moment later we hear her office door slam shut. Daniel and I stare at each other, lost for words. Lydia never misses an opportunity for a bollocking. In the past, she's had us for walking too slow, breathing too fast, smiling inappropriately or not smiling enough. Whatever we do, however we do it, it's never quite right. Right now, for instance, she could have had us for not striking the correct poses. In quiet moments she likes us to go through gentle stretches or to stand straight-backed and erect like we're psyching ourselves up for an Olympic long jump. The Third Commandment: *Staff shall at all times look like fitness professionals*. My sweaty feet are still up on the desk. I don't look like a professional anything. I'd give a minicab office a bad name.

'What's with her?' Daniel mouths.

I shrug.

The first of the ballet dancers spill into reception. It must be eight o'clock. Our cue to shut up shop. The last classes are finishing. The gym and pool will be closing. The beauticians have performed the day's last massage/wax/facial. After a day of helping London's finest on their way to achieving Optimal Physical Outcome – well, having a laugh with Daniel and watching MTV – I'm ready to go home too.

'Fancy hitting Billy's when we're done?' Daniel asks.

Billy's Bar. Our local. Being at the Piccadilly Circus corner of Soho it's a pretty funky local. It usually has someone for everyone. Well, for Daniel and me. Gorgeous, empty-headed boy-band types for me and . . . er . . . gorgeous, empty-headed boy-band types for him.

But not tonight.

'Can't, Daniel. I've been using *the excuse* too much lately. Dad will go mental if I stay out again.'

'Surely not? After a smash as bad as Sasha's you could be helping with her rehab for months yet.'

I blush at the thought of my lies. Of course Sasha isn't in a wheelchair after a horrendous pile-up on the M25, and of course I'm not helping her defy the doctors and take her first tentative steps, but the thought that I am is making my parents very proud, proving, therefore, that lying can actually be a really good thing.

'God, you're twenty-four, girl,' Daniel says. 'I don't know why you still live at home.'

I know. Because it's warm and comfortable and I don't have to pay rent and . . . um . . . because my dad would kill me rather than see me leave – unless I happen to be wearing a white dress with a twenty-foot train and I'm tossing back the bouquet for my kid sister to catch.

The phone rings. Daniel's putting on his jacket and says, 'You get it.'

I pick it up and announce, 'Good evening, this is The Zone, Charlie speaking, how may I help?' . . . If you're still there after all that.

It's the way we have to answer the phone – the Fourth Commandment. I'm surprised we don't have to add on the time, date, temperature and a full rundown of what's on at the Leicester Square multiplexes before the caller gets a chance to speak.

'I'm Julie Furmansky at Mission Management,' the caller says in a nasal voice which makes her sound as if she's either got a very bad cold or she's just incredibly snotty. 'Can I speak to the studio manager, please?'

That would be Scary Lydia – last seen heading for her office with a face like thunder. Do I really want to be disturbing her now?

'She's left for the day,' I say. 'Would you mind calling back tomorrow?'

I should have said *Is there anything I can do?* but she might have replied *Yes, there is* and I could have been stuck here for hours – I just want to go home.

'You want me to call *back*?' she says, as if I've just asked her to clean out my toilet with her tongue. 'Do you know who I am?'

'Not exactly,' I tell her truthfully, suppressing a weary sigh.

'I act for Blaize,' she tells me. Four little words that immediately put me in my place.

Blaize is a big deal. At this year's *Smash Hits* Awards she got Best Newcomer, Best Single, Best Video, Best Snogger . . . No, made the last one up, but you can bet that if they'd offered it, she'd have won it. Yep, she's a big deal all right and normally I'd be thrilled to be speaking to her manager . . .

But I just want to go home.

So I tell her, 'I'm sorry, but the studio manager will be in at seven thirty tomorrow. You can get her then. OK? Bye now.' I say this in my jolliest voice so I can't be accused of being unhelpful. Then I hang up.

I head down the corridor as the phone rings again. Sod it. I'm ignoring it this time. I reach the locker outside Lydia's office and get my coat out. Her door is open a crack and I hear her pick up the call. I hope it isn't Ms Snottynose at Mission Management. I stand still and listen.

'A girl you say . . . ? Rude and unhelpful . . . ?'

Shit. It's her . . .

'. . . Well, she was wrong. The studio manager *hasn't* left . . .'

. . . And I am *fucked*.

'. . . I'm here, but I just don't give a shit. Goodbye.'

Lydia slams the phone down and I squiggle my

17

fingers in my ears because I can't believe what I just heard.

Lydia doesn't give a shit?

Lydia's whole point is that she gives a shit about *every*thing. She's the queen of giving a shit. I peer through the crack in the door. I can make out a cardboard box on her desk. She's chucking stuff into it.

Is she leaving?

She couldn't possibly be leaving.

Could she?

Right, I don't care how scary she is; I don't care if her wonky eyes give me migraines. I've got to know. I tap on the door and push it open. She looks up at me (and at the shelf to my left), but doesn't speak. Her face is streaked with tears.

'Sorry to bother you, Lydia,' I say nervously, 'but someone from Blaize's management just rang for you. I thought you'd gone home.'

She still doesn't speak.

'Is everything OK?' I ask.

'No . . . No, it is not OK,' she snaps. 'I'm leaving.'

Yeeeeeeessssssssssssssssssssssssss!

'My God, that's terrible,' I say, trying very, *very* hard to sound like I think it's terrible. 'Why?'

'Good question. Why don't you ask Jamie?'

He fired her? Oh, Jamie, I fucking love you, man.

'He didn't . . . you know . . .'

'Fire me? That's exactly what the bastard did.'

Tears are rolling down her cheeks again. I'm shocked. Not because she's crying either, but because her tears are running completely vertically. Shouldn't they be falling in opposite directions? *Ah shit*, now I feel really bad. Mostly because I've been longing for this to happen and now that it has I feel guilty.

'Why?' I ask. Stupid question because suddenly I

18

think I know. 'It wasn't the . . . er . . . you know . . . on his desk?'

'The Alka-Seltzer? Don't be silly. He fired me because I—I think I'll save the answer to that one for my lawyers. I'm going to have that bastard. I am *so* going to have him.'

'Is there anything I can do?' I ask, because it seems like the thing to say.

'I very much doubt it,' she replies, flinging more stuff into her box.

'I'm sorry . . . I'll really miss you . . . We all will.'

This is the biggest lie I've ever told in my life – bigger even than the Sasha-in-a-wheelchair one – but it also seems like the thing to say.

'Bollocks, darling,' she answers with her usual charm. 'By tomorrow you lot will be dancing on my grave. Now, are you going to stand there all night?' she asks. Is she talking to me or has someone else just walked in? A quick look over my shoulder tells me there's no one there. 'I wouldn't mind some privacy right now.'

I shuffle backwards and mumble, 'Of course, Lydia. Sorry. Look, goodbye and . . . um . . . It's been . . .'

What has it been?

Hell?

A nightmare?

Like having open-heart surgery without anaesthetic?

'. . . fantastic.'

What else can I say?

As I walk out, I feel very weird. Not sure whether to dance with joy or slash my wrists. I should probably go with the joy. God knows what our next boss will be like, but he/she/it couldn't possibly be worse than Lydia. Even if he turns out to be the Butcher of Piccadilly. '*I need to check your heart rate for our new*

19

research paper. Best to remove it first. Now, just lie still, girl, close your eyes and you won't feel a thing.'
At least I'll know for sure he's talking to me.

I arrive at reception to find Daniel putting the phone down. He has a frighteningly serious look on his face. Rebecca stands, cowering, just behind him. 'What's up?' I ask, bursting to tell him the news, but desperate to know why he looks so spooked.

'That was Jamie,' he says. 'He wants to see you.'

Oh, shit.

With knobs on.

The Bit Where You Meet My Dad
(Good Luck)

As I put my key in the lock I check my watch. Nine forty. Not *too* bad. Dad might yell a bit, but when I tell him my news he'll be thrilled.

Won't he?

'Hi, only me,' I call out as I open the door.

'Shuuussshhh!' Dad hisses. He's on the phone in the hall. He's listening intently with his head cocked angrily to one side.

'I don' care aboud thad,' he says after a moment. 'This is twenty century. Everybody is *delivering*. Even the women is delivering the babies in the home these days and the bluddy Griks cunt even be delivering the food!' He looks at me triumphantly, stabbing the air in front of him with his finger, a sure sign that he's had The Final Word. But whoever he's talking to (a) can't see the victory finger and (b) doesn't know that Dad *always* has The Final Word. He or she carries on the debate, unaware that my father is going from crimson to even crimsoner.

Dad's having a row. So what's new?

Think I'll go see if Mum's home.

Where else is she going to be? And there she is, right where she always is: in front of the TV. It's on RIK, the Cypriot satellite channel. Strange. She can't speak

21

a word of Greek. Why didn't she take advantage of Dad being on the phone and flick over? Next to her on the sofa, Emily, my kid sister, is asleep. Nothing odd there.

'Hi, Mum. Who's he shouting at?' I ask, nodding towards the hall.

'Oh, he fancied a kebab so he's calling Vrisaki.' She answers without moving her eyes from the screen. Outside, Dad sounds like he's building up to his climax.

'*No*, ukchew-ally, I don' spik Grik. You should learn spik Inglish!'

He's angrier than I've heard him be for . . . oh, about a week.

'Wotchew mean I sounding Grik? I don' sounding nuthing like the Grik! I bluddy Inglish and you stop changing subject. Now, are you gonna bring me the bluddy kebab or no?'

Not that I want to put money on it or anything, but from the look on his face, I think the answer was no.

'You bluddy ignoran' . . . I gonna, I gonna, you know what I gonna do? I gonna . . . Hey, don' you bluddy hanging up on me!'

Mum looks at me and rolls her eyes as Dad walks into the room. 'Jimmy, can I have the remote please?' she says.

So that's why she's still watching RIK. He walked out with the TV remote. Dad tosses it to her and she immediately flicks channels to something . . . What is that? Who cares, it's English.

Dad plonks himself into his favourite armchair in the corner. 'Gor blimey. How you calling yourself a food estublishment in this days if you no delivering?'

'You've got yourself a scooter now, have you, Dad?' I ask, imagining him bombing about Covent Garden,

22

Jamie Oliver style, delivering Jimmy Specials to his regulars. Dad: the fourth emergency service.

'S'nod the point. I want I picking the phone up and gedding whad I want. Thad teaching me to phone the Griks. Nex' time, I call for Chinese. I love Chinese peoble. They genius you know. Who woulda think of putting the sweet *an'* the sour together? Anyway, why you late again? They make you bluddy in charge or something?'

'Well, actually, Dad, now you mention it . . .'

I am the new studio manager at The Zone, London's flashiest, swankiest, Total Body Emporium.

Me.

Charlotte Charalambous.

Twenty-four.

Still living with her mum and dad in Nicosia N22 (AKA Wood Green).

In charge.

That's what Jamie wanted to see me about. Not to bollock me for the channel hopping. Or for using his office to snort hangover relief. Or for the wrong socks.

He wanted to give me Lydia's job.

'The Zone is a vision, Charlie,' he said, leaning back in his big leather chair. '*My* vision. The thing is, are you ready to take your place in it?'

It was like a scene in a movie. Jamie, the hot, young-ish entrepreneur in his massive office with its New York-ish view of Piccadilly-neon through the massive window behind his massive desk. Charlie, the young, sexy-ish innocent being offered the world – a place in his vision. Jamie would be played by Brad Pitt and Kirsten Dunst would be Charlie. *Just* like a movie.

Except I hadn't read the script and was struggling to keep up with the plot.

'What do you mean, Jamie?' I asked nervously, just about suppressing the urge to giggle.

'Lydia's . . . sort of . . . She's decided to move on,' he said.

Not exactly how she put it, but it didn't feel like the time to nit-pick.

'She was . . . er . . . First Phase of the Vision. Did an *amazing* job, but we're Second Phase now. Time for a managerial transition.'

I looked at him blankly.

'All right, all right . . . You want the truth, Charlie? Lydia was a good manager. *Fucking* good.'

Not exactly how I'd put it, but like I said, it wasn't the time.

'It's just those bloody eyes. Totally weirded me out,' he went on. 'My neck muscles have gone into permanent spasm; you think she's talking to you but you're always having to check behind you first. Way too freaky.'

I was in shock. I couldn't believe that Jamie, our lord and master, was bugged by the same stuff as Daniel and I were. I mean, it wasn't just seven floors that separated us plankton from Jamie the great white shark. He has been on the cover of every fitness mag, as well as *Management Today* (for being Entrepreneur of the Year) and *Heat* (for getting a snog off Ulrika – mind you, who hasn't?). Also, he spends more on suits than he does on Daniel's and my wages. All that money, power and influence, and Lydia's eyes still weirded him out.

'Anyway, Charlie, the upshot,' he said next. 'Are you ready for it?'

Ready for what, I thought.

'I . . . think . . . so,' I said.

'Good, 'cause I've been watching you. You were a

kid when you joined us, a mess. But look at you. You've really sorted your shit out.'

Have I? Well, I've got longer hair now – courtesy of Sheena at Hair We Go in Finsbury Park – and maybe a few less spots, which I can more or less hide completely since I discovered that brilliant Clarins concealer, but I wouldn't exactly call it a radical transformation. I didn't think it was the time to argue though. I tried to smile, but God knows what I must have looked like. My facial muscles were paralysed. Nerves again.

'I should've done this ages ago,' he went on. 'You're Zone to the core. You're Posh Spice without the snout. Angelina minus the trout lips. Yeah, you definitely *look* the part. Now let's see if you can play it.'

Did he mean Angelina Jolie? Me? As Lara Croft? The comparison threw me and I wondered if maybe he was talking to someone else – a result of working with Lydia, I suppose, but I turned round to check anyway. No, there was just him and me in the room.

That's when it finally clicked. All those years of pretending to be doing a great job whenever Jamie or Lydia were anywhere nearby had made it appear that I really had been doing a great job. I couldn't believe it. I've never had an ambitious bone in my body, and here I was being offered the top job. And now that I was, I'd never felt more made up about anything my entire life.

As Jamie's words sank in, I began to scream inwardly with excitement. Actually, not all of it was quite as *inward* as I would have liked. A few years from now, when I'm being crowned Businesswoman of the Year and I look back at the moment I took my first tentative step with this little promotion, I'm going to forget *totally* that I launched into the stupidest, most childish, prolonged screaming fit *ever*.

'The Zone is everything to me. Thank you so much, Jamie. I won't let you down,' is what I wish I'd said.

'Arrgghhh! I don't believe it! I *am* Lara Croft!' is what came out.

'I'm glad you're happy,' he smiled. 'It's a lot of responsibility. A fuck of a lot. But I've been asking around and the punters love you. Besides, I've got a hunch you can handle it.'

I knew about Jamie's hunches. He was one of the few that made a fortune in the dot-com boom. According to legend, he'd had a hunch it was all going to go pear-shaped. He sold his shares the day before it crashed and walked away with fifteen million. Then he had another hunch: that the fitness market was ready for a Total Body Emporium. It would be more than a flash gym – though it would have the flashiest gym. It would hire the best teachers in every discipline – t'ai chi, yoga, kick boxing, you name it. It would also offer beauty treatments and alternative health stuff – you know, all that herbal and crystal-healing bollocks that I manage to sound really sincere about when people phone up for info.

And it would offer dance. Jamie saw the boom in urban music and the street dance that went with it. He reckoned that if he could nick a few teachers from the dance world and get some Nelly-style gyrating going on alongside the boring old fitness stuff he'd give the place an instant injection of cred.

He was right – big time. The Zone got massive quick. Jamie made the fees astronomical, but, cleverly, he slashed them for Equity members. This and the fact that he'd managed to poach the top teachers and choreographers attracted the dancers in droves. It wasn't long before they were joined by the pop stars who wanted somewhere cool to rehearse the routines for their videos and tours. And, of course, it attracted the thirty-something media execs who wanted to do a couple of miles on the treadmill, but quite fancied the idea of rubbing shoulders with the Blue boys and the Mis-teeq girls while they were at it.

Yes, Jamie was good at hunches.

And if he had one that I could make an instant transition from mucking about with Daniel to running the place, then who was I to argue?

'You'll be in at the deep end, I know, but you've got Daniel to help. You two are best mates, right?' he said.

'Absolutely.'

'Good. There are certain things Lydia and I didn't . . . er . . . see eye to eye on, if you know what I mean. But I think you and I are going to get along fine. Just remember, The Zone is my baby, Charlie, and I don't like surprises. Any whiff of anything you can't handle, come straight to me and I'll help sort it out. *Capisce?*'

He said this with his widest smile, but there was no hiding the menace in his voice. And isn't *capisce* Sicilian for *screw up and I'll break your fucking kneecaps*? I left his office not feeling quite so Lara Croft.

'Dad, didn't you hear me? I've been promoted. I'm the studio manager,' I say, having given him the low-down.

'*Hmmph.* You own the place?'

'No, but I'm in charge. I—'

'See? You don' own the place. You're no in charge of nuthing. You still werk like bluddy idiot for *other* peoble.'

The Sandwich Bar King has spoken. It's a scratched record that would put any DJ to shame.

'I come Inglan' over thirdy years ago with five pounds in my pogget.'

27

Or Madonna even. Didn't she say she had a twenty on her when she hit New York?

'Now look at me. My own sun'widge bar, no mortgage. Me and your mum, we having nuthing when we—'

'Give it a rest, Jimmy,' Mum yawns. 'Charlie, love, do us a favour and stick the kettle on.'

She's just as bad in her own way.

'Mum, haven't you heard anything I've said?' I wail. 'I've been *promoted*. I'm *in charge* now. You know, the *boss*.'

'That's great, sweetheart, I'm really happy for you. Will you just stick the kettle on, though? I don't want to miss the beginning of *Sex and the City*. They're rerunning the entire first series, you know.'

Bloody parents, eh? They're chalk and cheese, mine.

Feta cheese in my dad's case – he's Greek, though that much should be screamingly obvious by now. Mind you, if you suggested as much to him (as the bloke from Vrisaki discovered), he might possibly reply, 'Grik? Wotchew tokking aboud? Am *Inglish*.'

Then again, he might say, 'Course am bluddy Grik, stoobid. You ever see an Inglish werk this bluddy hard?'

Or perhaps, 'I belong no one country. Am citizen of the *weld*.'

There really is no telling with Dad. He's definitely the most opinionated bloke, or make that *block*, I've ever known. The trouble is the opinions change from hour to hour. Second to second sometimes.

As much as I can figure him out, it's about going against the flow. Stick him in a church and he's an atheist. Take him to a Chinese and he'll ask for a kebab. Fly him to Cyprus and he'll develop a sudden urge for chow mein. He loves to be controversial. I remember a Greek wedding when I was eleven and Dad standing up and booming, 'I tell you my fevorit jok. Why is all Grik men have moustaches?' He paused as two hundred Greek men thoughtfully fingered their moustaches. Then he said, 'So they look like their *motha*!' Dad laughed like a hurricane, more than making up for the four hundred people who didn't. We weren't invited back to the christening.

Apparently he caused a stir when he married Mum. She's not a nice Greek girl. She's London Irish. She was Maeve Connell back then, more commonly known as Maevou now – Greek rule number one: add an 'ou' to everything. And while Dad is hands-on, in charge and has an (ever-changing) opinion on everything, she's so laid-back she never seems to have an opinion on anything much.

I used to think Mum let Dad get away with laying down the law because she was too lazy to argue. She's definitely the laziest person you'll ever meet. That must sound *terrible*. I honestly don't *expect* her to do stuff around the house the way mums on the telly do, honestly I don't. But the thing is, I work sixty hours a week, Dad does eighty and Emily is a spoilt brat who never lifts a finger unless it's to whack some nail polish on it. That leaves Mum, whose only job is sitting on the sofa monitoring daytime TV and acting as unpaid quality controller for Doritos, Pringles and Golden Wonder. She should be the size of an elephant, the way she packs it away, but Mum eats what she likes and stays stick-thin.

What was my point? That's right: Mum isn't exactly driven; but no, she's not being lazy when she lets Dad lay down the law. It's a tactic. She lets him rant until he's blue in the face because she knows that if she lets him have the last word, he'll *think* he's won. But then she'll take no notice of a thing he's said. Life carries on as before, but Dad's happy because he's had The Final Word (as well as The First and All The Ones Between).

I return to the living room with tea for Mum and Dad and Diet Coke for me. Mum is engrossed with whatsername from *Sex and the City* having sex in the city. Emily is still asleep. Dad is tutting. 'Cunt we watching something decent?' he says.

That's rich. The last time I checked out his favourite soap on RIK, a sweaty bloke with a handlebar moustache was leaving his wife and kids for a donkey. OK, my Greek is pretty crap, but that's what it *looked* like.

'She got no shame? You seeing everything,' he continues.

'Shush, Jimmy,' Mum says. 'They're in love.'

(For Mum, apparently, having a sweaty shag in a dirty alley behind a New York bar is a sign of true love. That'll do for me.)

'If he love her he wait till they marry before he do thad filthy rubbish,' Dad pronounces.

The Final Word because Mum stays silent.

Satisfied, he turns to me and says, 'So, this new *in-charge* job . . . They giving you pay rise?'

Shit. He's got a point. Jamie didn't mention money and I was too excited/scared/busy being Lara Croft to think about details.

'Of course they did,' I say.

'Good. You cleva girl, Theglottsa,' he says.

This is the closest I'm going to get to praise and I take a celebratory sip of my Coke.

'You're cleva like chip off the old bloke. Is true. I'm clevarest man I know!'

He probably is. That's no compliment by the way. You should see the people he knows.

After a pause he says quietly, 'Course, if you're rilly cleva, you doing what Soulla done.' He gently rolls this thought across the carpet like a grenade and it takes a second for its full significance to explode in my face. What on earth would ever possess me to want to do anything my boring, pregnant, sister-in-law has done? Past experience tells me this conversation can only be heading in one direction.

'What do you mean?' I say, trying to keep my alarm in check.

'Well, you see her run round werking her fingers up to the bone for *other* peoble? No, she marry your brotha, stay home, have nice life. Is your *brotha* who run round doing werk, werk, werk.'

I look to Mum for intervention, but she's still super-glued to the TV. Besides, why would she disagree – she who lives on the sofa while some bloke runs around doing work, work, work to keep her in potato snacks?

I don't know why I'm panicking, actually, because we've been here before. In the mad whirlwind of Dad's ever-changing opinions, his view on women is the one constant: Girls should be *nice*. Nice means long flowing dresses (not skimpy Zone crop-tops), two earrings (not five) and big hair (which, as my dad will tell you, was invented by the ancient Greeks and not the stars of *Dynasty* as Mum would have it).

There are two stages of Nice Girl. The first is the trainee, AKA the Gorry Girl. Stupid expression. Gorry is Greek slang for girl, so it literally means Girl Girl . . . Then again, not so stupid because a Gorry is about as girly as you can get. Emily is a Gorry. Jet-black hair, dark skin, huge black eyes and lips so plump they take half a tube of gloss to cover. Much as I hate to give the irritating brat credit for anything, she's devastatingly pretty. At least, she has been since she was old enough to handle a pair of tweezers and figure out that, ideally, eyebrows shouldn't meet in the middle – hair in inappropriate places, the cross we Greek girls have to bear. Any spare time she has she dolls herself up and heads for Wood Green Shopping City, where she hangs out with her Gorry mates. They keep themselves busy looking at boys, swapping texts and ringtones, looking at boys, deciding between Pizza Hut and McDonald's, looking at boys and looking at boys.

Not a groove I ever got into, and I'll never be the other stage of Nice Girl either – i.e. a fully trained, grown-up Gorry – i.e. my Soulla-in-law.

'You're so busy doing stoobid career, you're missing the boat,' Dad says.

He's talking about the Love Boat. Like all Greek girls (OK, I'm only half-Greek, but according to Dad it's been scientifically proven that the Greek half always dominates) I was born with a marry-by date. It's probably spelled out on my scalp like Damien's 666.

'It's OK, Dad. I meet plenty of guys at work,' I say.

'They all bludy poofs,' he says. 'And how many of them is Grik?'

As far as he's concerned, dancing isn't a pastime, let alone a profession, for a Real Man – unless of course it's Greek dancing, in which case it's about as manly as joining the SAS.

'At least you needn't worry about me coming home pregnant,' I say.

'Hey, you think I werk like dog all these years for you to go and be pregnant slut living on filthy council estate?' he shouts, rising to the bait.

I hit back. 'Look, you're the one who's desperate for me to get married and have kids.'

'*Egg-saggly*! Get *marry*. Like your brotha.'

'What's the hurry? He and Soulla seem to be making enough babies for the lot of us.'

Soulla is fit to burst with number two. The rate she's expanding, she'll soon be bigger round the middle than Dad.

'Soulla an' *Andonih* make me proud.'

'And what do I do, Dad?'

'You driving me up to the wall.'

'Will you two give it a rest? I'm trying to watch,' Mum says, forgetting that she saw Sarah Jessica Parker et al. the first time over, and that she'll be watching them for years to come on endless satellite reruns.

'Bluddy TV. Your dotter waste her life and you wanna watch TV? I try to make her understand,' Dad says. 'She has to get the priorities.'

Mum rolls her eyes. *Take no notice* that roll means, so I don't.

'Maybe I gonna get that boy over,' he mumbles.

I continue to take no notice. I'm going to have a bath, but before that I *must* delete Harvey's texts. We split up over a month ago, so why am I still hanging on to them? It makes me look like some sort of lovesick puppy, which I *so* am not – honestly, I was just about to dump him, only he got in there first. Anyway, Emily was snooping and read a couple of them and ever since she's been—

Hang on, what boy?

'What boy?' I ask.

'Jimmy, I said be quiet,' Mum hisses.

But he hasn't answered the question yet. I'm really panicking now.

'What boy, Dad?' I repeat.

'His a doctor and if we no doing something soon—'

33

'Right, that's it, shut up,' Mum announces. 'I told you I don't want to hear about the bloody doctor *now*. You know I love this show.'

'*What* doctor?' I ask.

'Who's a doctor?' Emily echoes sleepily, the rise in tension having woken her up.

'That's right, who's a doctor. Doctor Who,' Mum laughs, obviously hoping she can create instant peace with the stupidest joke in the history of the world (or at least since my *Charlie doing charlie* line, which suddenly feels like a million years ago).

But Dad's on a mission now. 'Theglitsa, I gonna arrange for you to mit this boy,' he says.

'No way,' I say loudly and very, very firmly, because hearing him put the words *arrange*, *meet* and *boy* into the same sentence is having the same effect on me it always does. Panic. '*Mum*, tell him to leave me alone,' I beg.

It's not like this is the first time we've had this conversation. Ever since I turned twenty, Dad's been desperate to get me married. Constantly reminding me that he did the smart thing by marrying young, raising his family and still having his whole life ahead of him. Mum usually tells him to get off my back. She wants her daughters to enjoy their freedom. To have fun while we can. She always reminds him that she could have had several more carefree years of being able to watch whatever she wanted before getting hitched and having to take someone else's programme choices into consideration. Oh, the things she sacrificed for love.

'Leave her alone,' Mum repeats automatically, transfixed again by the TV.

'Mum, I'm serious,' I yell at her now. I want her fighting for me like she usually does. For my right to live a life of debauchery in the free world as opposed to being slave to a peasant (OK, a peasant who happens to be a doctor) in some backwater with no mobile phones or glossy mags, at the end of the beaten track in a faraway land called Cyprus.

'Stop yelling,' Emily yells. 'Anyway, Charlie, you need help. You know you can't get a *decent* bloke on your own.'

This comment couldn't be more loaded if it was a gun. Harvey and I went out for about six months and he was very big on texting. Rude texting. When we weren't having sex he was sending me messages about how much he wished we were – he was better at texting than he was at the sex. I thought it was a great laugh at the time, but how I wish I'd pressed delete as soon as I'd read them. How could I have been so stupid not to know that the moment I left my mobile unattended Emily would read them? She may be too young to understand half the texts he sent (I hope), but the blackmailing little snot-rag has been using them against me ever since.

I ignore her and yell, 'Mum, tell him.'

'Why you screaming?' Dad's shouting now too. 'Shuddup and lissen. His fatha and me, we bin friends when we kids, but we losing touch. Then, juss like magic, he come in sun'widge shop. He don' know is my shop. Is like mirigol. We reggognise each other and is juss like the old time again. I telling you, he doing very well for himself. His a big deal in fushion. His got fucdory in Fonthill Road.'

A big deal in fashion. I've got to stifle a laugh at this point. Fonthill Road in Finsbury Park is about as far from the catwalks of Milan as you can get without actually leaving the planet. Far from running up sensational little numbers for the likes of D&G or even M&S, Dad's mate is probably turning out marquee-sized frocks for the, erm, proportionally challenged (if you live in Islington), or fat birds (if you don't).

'Anyway, we inviding them for dinner on Sunday,' he continues. 'You say hello, pleaze to meet you, bye-bye. Simble. No big fuss.'

'Jimmy, I'm not making dinner for anyone I don't know, especially not this Sunday.'

That's funny. Mum rarely makes dinner for anyone she *does* know, i.e. us, never mind what day it is.

'Yes, I phone tomorrow. Invide them Sunday,' Dad says, taking part in a completely different conversation to the one the rest of us are having.

'Well, let me know what time they're getting here so I can make sure I'm out,' I mutter.

'Bluddy women,' he mutters back. Then, as if the whole argument never happened, he perks up. 'Hey, guess what I bring from cush and curry today . . . No, you wait. I go get from the van.'

He jumps up and heads for the front door.

I look at Mum, who's returned to the telly. She doesn't look particularly disturbed, but she wouldn't let him get away with it, would she? I've got to talk to her. Make sure she isn't going through some sort of weird menopausal thing that will end in her siding with Dad in his plans to sell me off in a marriage deal.

Thass my final word. Fifty goats and the girl is yours. Go on then, fifty-five.

Before I can say anything, Dad reappears and announces, 'Who wanna piss off cake?' He follows this up by producing the most stupendous chocolate covered *thing* I've ever seen.

'Not me,' I say grumpily.

Ten minutes later only half of the monster cake is left on the coffee table. The rest is rapidly disappearing down the throats of Mum, Dad and Emily. Chocolate covers their faces and they look like toddlers who've just ram-raided the pick 'n' mix counter. The *bastard*. He knows how much I love chocolate. I can't keep this up. I reach forward and surreptitiously slide a slice onto a plate. Dad spots me and gives me a wink. 'Is delicious, eh?' he grins as I take a bite.

Delicious? It's fucking divine. It should have songs written for it, streets named after it.

'It's OK,' I reply. This translates as *By accepting this chocolate cake I in no way give up my right to refuse your shabby attempts to flog me off to the first bloke to come along with Doctor in front of his name.*

The Bit Where I Breeze Through My First Day In Management
(In My Dreams)

As I take my seat and strap myself in, a computerised voice announces, 'Blastoff in fifteen seconds . . . Unauthorised personnel must evacuate the area . . . Blastoff in ten seconds . . . Unauthorised personnel must—'

No, I'm not on a spaceship. That would be ridiculous. I'm catching the tube to work. Wood Green to Piccadilly Circus. Twelve stops. What the voice is really telling us is that there's a broken-down train at Caledonian Road and we can expect delays – again.

But this journey – home to work – *feels* as if I'm travelling between two planets. My two lives couldn't be more different if everyone at The Zone had pointy ears and spoke Klingon.

Work: seven floors of polished wood, marble and macrobiotic menus.

Home: two floors of mess, more mess and vast chocolate cakes.

Work: enough state-of-the-art exercise equipment to get every overweight American in Disney World Florida into a size eight.

Home: a clapped-out Hoover that hasn't been emptied since 1998.

Work: glistening men on exercise bikes talking on their hands-free mobiles: 'Tell him to make it a three-album deal and we'll sign in Cannes.'

Home: a sweaty man on a sofa: 'I drive very hard bargain on slice white today. Am telling you, no one is beating me in deal.'

For the past three and a bit years this has been my life. Shuttling between these two very different worlds. It's not just the journey that does my head in. It's the complete personality change I have to go through. From Theglitsa to Charlie in twelve mind-boggling moves. Sigourney Weaver had it easy. She may have had an as yet undiscovered alien to discover, but at least she didn't have to reinvent herself between planets.

As the train starts moving again I try to get my brain into Optimal Physical Outcome groove. Everything's changed. I'm not just a worker any more. Today I'm the boss, the studio manager. Top Dog.

And let me tell you, it's shitting me right up.

I stand on the corner of Brewer and Glasshouse Streets and gaze upwards. The Zone's glass walls are like a mirror from the outside. If I look straight across the road I can see myself, distorted so I seem seven-feet tall and super lean. Nice touch by the architects. Everyone walks in thinking they've already got the body of an athlete and they just need to pump a few weights/do a couple of sessions of cardio-kick to move up to Olympic class. Actually, that's probably true for most of our members.

Now I'm in charge, you can make that *my* members.

The automatic door slides open with a swoosh. In front of me, across twenty feet of shiny floor, is mission control. The marble reception desk. *My* reception desk.

Suspended on steel cables above it is another slab of white marble, cracked and ragged at the edges, as if it's been pulled from a Roman ruin. Carved into it is the announcement YOU ARE NOW IN THE ZONE.

My Zone.

Seven springy floors of hi-tech, ultra-modern, get-fit-or-get-fucked machinery. No idea what half of it does. Who cares? The point is it's all mine. OK, not mine exactly. Jamie's. And I'm not in charge of half of it. All those complicated machines are Mr Angry Steve's responsibility. And the swimming pool, the beauty salon and the alternative therapy suites, they all come under the swimming, beauty and alternative therapy people. But I'm up there with them. And when anyone walks through the door, who's the first *in-charge* person they'll see? That's right. *Me*.

And that, to be honest, is what's shitting me up. I wish I were spending my first *in-charge* day hidden in the basement's Aqua Zone, with the pool and sauna lot. Or tucked away in Daniel's Mile High Club Lounge on the seventh. I could handle that – learn the management ropes by being in charge of the broom cupboard for a bit. But, no, I've got to do my learning in full public view, with half a ton of marble hanging over my head – which is probably rigged to a remote in Jamie's office so he can drop it the moment I screw up.

Despite the delay on the tube, I'm early. Could have something to do with the fact that I set my alarm for five this morning. We don't open for twenty minutes yet. Those eager office beavers have to wait until seven thirty before they can swarm in and justify the three-hour lunch they're going to have later on.

Apart from the last of the cleaners dribbling out, I have the place to myself. I walk past reception and on to Lydia's— no, *my* office. I put my bag on the floor and sit at her— no, *my* desk. I haven't had my own desk since junior school. On top of the big diary there's an envelope with 'Charlie' scribbled on the front. I peel it open and a badge falls out. Underneath The Zone logo it's printed with CHARLOTTE CHARALAMBOUS – STUDIO MANAGER. There's also a note:

> Charlie – You don't want to know the trouble I had getting your tag printed up tonight, but I didn't want you turning up on your first day and forgetting I'd promoted you. Anyway, can't be with you to hold your hand. 2-day fitness convention in Loughborough. Can't miss it. I've checked the schedules and they look OK. Sure you'll be fine. Just don't fuck up or you'll wish you were home with Lydia – J

Lovely ending, Jamie – a perfect balance of good-humour and warmth to fill me with confidence. Not. I gaze at my new name-tag. A cheap plastic rectangle, but it's proof of my success. Only twenty-four and look at me. It's here in black and white – Zone blue and Zone green, actually: CHARLOTTE CHARALAMBOUS – STUDIO MANAGER.

Wonderful.

Amazing.

Fantastic.

But the more I look at it . . . It's horrible. *Charalambous*. Bloody foreign names. At least he could have made it *Charlie* Charalambous. That's what everyone calls me. Except for Dad, but that's another story. Lately I've been thinking about changing my surname to Charles. A bit less of a mouthful. And less of an eyeful – Charalambous goes on forever.

Charlie Charles. Would that be silly? Affected, even?

My pop-star name.

My studio-manager name.

I'll give it some thought. Later. It's seven twenty-five. Time to hit the front desk. I pin the badge to my Zone top, stabbing myself in the boob.

No, this is *not* a bloody omen, all right?

Eight ten: so far so good. What on earth was I worrying about? I can *so* do this job . . . At least as long as it involves doing exactly what I've been doing for the last forty minutes. That is, nothing much apart from smiling warmly at clients as they arrive, none of them needing any help from me because they're all regulars and know exactly where they're going.

The doors swoosh open and Daniel leaps through the gap. He's ten minutes late. Lydia would have used that time to type up a written warning, ready to hand to him the moment he arrived. But I'd never do that. Although maybe I ought to at least look meaningfully at my watch as he dumps his bag behind the desk.

Before I can do anything, he drops to his knees, lowers his head to the floor and stretches his arms out in front of him, as if he's a Muslim and I'm Mecca. *Ha*! He knew I was going to try it on with the boss thing, so he's pulling the cheap trick of making me laugh. He leaps to his feet. 'I, Daniel Conrad, am here to serve my mistress in any way that pleases her,' he announces.

'Shut up, you camp bastard, and get us a coffee.'

He smothers my laugh with a sloppy kiss on the lips, before disappearing to the caff.

The phone goes. I pick it up on the second ring, corporate greeting at the ready – well, I have to set an example even though there's no one around to see it. 'Good morning, you're through to The Zone, Charlie speaking, how may—'

'Enough,' Jamie snaps.

42

Don't know what his problem is – they're *his* rules.

'Hi, Jamie. How's it going?'

'I'm on the M1,' he snaps, 'it's chucking down and there's a great big fucking lorry trying to drive up my arse. Anyway, everything OK?'

'Brilliant,' I reply.

'Good. Something I forgot to mention. There's a producer from Channel Four coming by today or tomorrow. I want you to give her the maximum schmooze.'

'What's she want?' I say, trying not to sound too excited. His first bit of delegation and it's something to do with the telly. I *love* my new job.

'She's making a documentary about the fitness biz and she wants to give the place a once-over. Give her the full tour. Charm the tits off her,' he says with a leery snigger.

'No worries.' I'm still sounding blasé, so as Daniel arrives back with the coffee he doesn't even bother to earwig. 'What's her name?'

'Can't remember. But you can't miss her. She's a big girl – fucking *huge* . . . Don't let me down, right?'

'Of course, don't worry, I can handle it,' I say, immediately regretting it because isn't there a bit in every disaster movie where some idiot says *Don't worry, I can handle it* immediately before the scary music starts and everything goes pear-shaped?

'OK,' Jamie says. 'Just so long as you know, she's very impor— Shit, cop car. He's spotted the mobile. Got a fucking blue light on my arse now. Gotta go.'

'Bye, Jamie,' I say, but he's hung up already.

Daniel gives me my coffee and asks, 'What did he want?'

'Nothing for you to worry your pretty little head about,' I say. 'Daniel, do I look like Angelina Jolie?'

'Well, you've got the big, fat gob, I suppose,' he says.

43

'Fuck off.'

'I'm kidding. Actually, you do look a bit Lara Croft.'

'Really?' I say, trying to stop my eyelashes fluttering.

'Well, about an hour into the movie when she's been beaten up a bit.'

He sticks out his leg and teasingly pulls up his tracksuit bottom until I can see the adidas logo on his sock. 'Go on,' he says, 'I dare you. Fire me.'

'Fuck *off*, Daniel.'

He pulls down his waistband, revealing the Hilfiger label on his boxers. 'Read it and weep, baby,' he teases, sticking his arse in my face.

'That's it, you are *so* fired,' I say, pinging an elastic band at him and shoving him so he falls over. He staggers to his feet and gets me in an arm lock. I try a back-kick to his balls but miss, so I twist round and pull his hair. He screams and . . . So my first day in management has begun.

There are three phases to a Zone day. First, the superkeen pre-work mob who think nothing of running/swimming/rowing five miles before a hard day's deal-making. Then there's the daytime lot, which is a weird mix of the idle rich (mostly women, it has to be said) who come for the treatments and to lounge around the pool flashing their boob jobs, and professional dancers who come for the advanced classes. Finally, there's the post-seven-p.m. lot who are turning up now. Thirty-something execs here to sculpt the perfect pec, alongside teenage and twenty-something girls here for the street dance. This has been a thoroughly bog-standard day, just members coming and going, so apart from muck about with Daniel, I haven't done much of anything.

'You gonna do Jenna's tonight?' Daniel asks.

He's talking about Jenna Mason's Street Sweat. That's one of the perks of working here – a free run of the place, including all the classes. You wouldn't catch me dead in one of the daytime professional sessions, mostly because, funnily enough, they're full of *professionals*. If you were as rubbish as me, you wouldn't want to be standing too close to any of them when the music kicks off. I can usually just about keep up with the happy-hour evening classes though. It's just unfortunate that Jenna is teaching tonight. I can't stand her.

'Yeah, I ought to,' I reply.

'Mmm, you are looking a bit lardy round the middle at the moment. The exercise'll do you good,' Daniel says pinching my waist.

I push him away and suck my stomach in. 'Get lost. I'm going because Sasha asked me to keep her company.'

'That girl can't move without you beside her these days. I'm surprised she doesn't need you to hold her hand in the shop too.'

Sasha works in Zone Clone – the bit where we sell our merchandise. Daniel's forever taking the piss out of her. Reckons she'd use up all her lifelines on the £100 question on *Millionaire*. He's such a bitch. She isn't stupid, she just needs to have more self-belief. Sasha used to teach aerobics here full-time until her classes fell out of fashion. She only does two a week now. Hardly enough to pay the rent, but I managed to get her the job in the shop. She's such a sweet person. We don't get too many of those around here, so I wanted to help. Selling Zone gear may be a bit of a comedown after teaching, but at least it means she's still part of the place.

Her complete lack of confidence can be bloody infuriating. Sometimes I want to give her a good shake and scream, 'Pull yourself together, woman,' but I know that would just finish her off. OK, she may never have the bottle to be the world's best teacher, but she's an excellent dancer. But try telling her that. Try telling her that she could audition with the best of them. If you ask me, she's every bit as good as Jenna, but she won't even do her class unless I'm there too.

I'm always fighting Sasha's corner and I'm about to do it again, when two people I've never met before walk in from the street. He: tall, fit, grinning, a dead-ringer for Nelly. She: dark hair, unsmiling, a dead-ringer for someone really fat. She must be twenty-five stone (and that's being kind). I don't think they're together.

'*Jeez*, Biggie Smalls reincarnated,' Daniel whispers. 'Do you wanna call Overeaters Anonymous or shall I?'

I stamp on his toe under the desk, but he's got a point. We'll have to handle this one carefully. It's not written down anywhere and it's definitely not talked about, but there's an unspoken policy on . . . God, what's a polite way of putting this?

There isn't one. The Zone doesn't like fat people. There, said it. It's not my fault. I only work here. Blame Jamie. His obsession with making money is only rivalled by his obsession with physical perfection. He doesn't like *the wrong sort of body* messing up the place. I know, I know, people with weight issues should be applauded for their commitment to getting into shape. We should welcome them with (very) open arms, but Jamie would prefer them to piss off to some faraway church-hall aerobic classes until they've slimmed down to an acceptable size. The Zone exists to make the fit fitter. Everyone else need not apply. Because, if I'm going to be completely honest, Jamie is a body fascist. He proved it last night when he made squiffy eyes a firing offence. Only perfection will do.

Nelly and Biggie walk towards the desk, him strutting on long, lean legs and her wobbling like a mobile jelly. Daniel and I smile our best *Welcome to The Zone* smiles. Inside I'm thinking *Bet I get Biggie* and inside he's probably thinking *Bet Charlie gets Biggie*, because, well, that's just the way it always goes.

Daniel and I started in the same week. On day three or four the phone rang at the exact moment that Sting walked through the door. I got the phone – a sales pitch from a company trying to flog super-absorbent bog rolls – and Daniel got to show Sting to his rehearsal studio. OK, star sightings in The Zone are ten a penny, but that was my first one and I wanted to have a good gawp. (I don't gawp any more. I've learned to use my peripheral vision. Well, you've still got to *look*, haven't you?)

Daniel always gets the breaks.

Not this time, though.

This time I'm the boss.

'You take *her*, I'll handle *him*,' I whisper just as *she* makes for me.

Oh yes, I'm the boss all right.

Using my highly trained peripheral vision I look enviously at Daniel. Nelly is all ears as Daniel takes him through the various membership options he could take up now (yes, *now*!) for *no* money off and – get this! – *no* special concessions (unless Nelly can show him a good time and/or an Equity card).

Meanwhile, I'm dealing with *her*. She isn't letting me get a word in edgeways, which is probably a good job because, actually, how could I possibly say 'My boss would sooner turn down a dream date with both Miss

Bodily Perfection 2004 and her twin sister, Miss Financial Whizz-kid 2005, than let me enrol you' without offending her? Didn't cover that one in basic training. Bloody Jamie. Bloody Lydia. This unspoken-rule thing we've got going, now I think about it, is going to be a bloody nightmare to deal with. How can I bring it up with anyone? It's *unspoken*! Daniel and I were never allowed anywhere near anyone who walked in wearing anything over a size ten. Lydia used to handle all the 'difficult' enquiries. Oh, how I wish she was here this minute. Just for this minute, mind.

Jacqueline – 'Jacqueline, darling, *never* Jackie' – is doing all the talking, mostly about her weight, in a very loud voice and I'm thinking that if she is a member of OA then there's nothing very anonymous about it.

'. . . No fats, barely any protein, basically carbs. And kiwi fruit,' she explains. 'I've lost four stone in as many months.'

Ah, that'll explain the booming voice. She's feeling proud. And so she should be, I guess. *Four stone*. That *is* something to shout about. But it still doesn't come anywhere close to getting her a membership card.

I've just figured out why this is freaking me out so much. It's not because of the nightmare politics and it's not because I've got a problem with fat people. How could I have? My life is stuffed with overweight cuddly types. My *home* life, that is – Dad's family doesn't carry the slim gene. The Zone is the place for super-fit hardbodies and seeing Jacqueline here is all wrong. It's my two worlds colliding – as if she snuck on the carriage with me on my inter-planetary tube journey this morning. And now it's my job to get her back somehow.

'Now, before I join . . .'

Join? Who says you can join?

48

'. . . I expect a full tour of your facilities. What about your changing rooms?' Jacqueline booms.

Oh God, what do I say? I wonder what Jamie would do if he were dealing with her? Or Lydia? God, must stop thinking about Lydia, I'm in charge now. Think, Charlie. You've got a brain, use it. I wonder what Daniel would do. . . ?

'Your changing rooms,' she repeats.

'Sorry,' I say. 'Yes, changing rooms. We've got those.'

'Of course you do, but I'd like to inspect them. At Cannons – I was a member there before they treated me so rudely – they didn't have . . .'

I'm not listening. I've got to get her out of here. I steal another peripheral glance at Daniel, still seducing the Nelly lookalike into falling for his smooth sales-talk/him. And I steal a glance at the clock. Jenna's class starts in a few minutes and I'm stuck here, literally wedged in by Jacqueline.

'Why don't you take our brochure up to the café?' I say, hoping she'll see the outrageous membership prices and (more importantly) the glossy pictures of perfect bodies and maybe get the hint.

'I don't want to go to the café. I want to talk to you.'

'Yes, but you can relax up there. Sit down, take the weigh—'

Yikes! Don't go there.

She's still looking at me. Of course she is; I'm mid-sentence.

'Take the *way* . . . the way to the lifts. They're just over there. They've got lovely food up there. Low cal— Er . . . *Local.* Yes, that's right. Local produce, loads of it.'

What am I talking about? Local produce? Peaches from the orchards of Leicester Square? Prawns and lobster freshly caught in the sewers beneath Shaftesbury Avenue? God, the hole I'm digging for myself is so deep I can't see daylight any more.

'Are you trying to be funny?' she snorts.

'No, not at all. What I meant was, you can get a feel of how big we are . . . Er . . . That is, how large the place is in a square-feet-type way . . . Not big as in . . . Um . . .'

I trail off as she glares at me. Then she snatches the brochure from my hand and heads for the lift. I slump with relief before sucking my stomach back in where it belongs. I've just realised that all this time I've been pushing it out as far as it would go. An unconscious bid to make her feel at home, I guess.

Daniel is still locking eyes with the Nelly-alike. He must be gay. Just my luck. I turn to grab my gear for Jenna's class, but the phone rings. I'm about to answer it when I remember who I am. 'Get that, would you, Daniel?' I say slightly bossily. He glares at me, but does as he's told. As he answers it, Nelly-alike looks at me and smiles a twenty-four-carat smile – literally, because he has the most gorgeous gold tooth in the corner of his mouth. 'Big lady,' he says, nodding in the direction of the lift where Jacqueline is struggling to squeeze in. *Max capacity: 10 people* it says on the plaque, so I guess I'll be calling the engineers any second now.

'Was she?' I reply, fluttering my lashes in what I hope is a normal, this-is-how-I-always-blink type of way.

He laughs, then sidles along the desk towards me. Daniel glares at me from the phone. If looks could maim, I'd be on my way to A & E now.

'So, you're in charge, I see . . . Charlotte Chara . . .'

He strains to read my name – or is it just an excuse to look at my chest? Maybe I'll have to revise my view on Nelly-alike. Perhaps he isn't gay.

'Just call me Charlie,' I tell him in what I hope is a normal, this-is-how-I-always-talk type— Who am I kidding? I sound like the female equivalent of Barry White. Must calm down, repeat, *must calm down.*

He extends his hand and says, 'I'm Karl.'

'So . . . you're interested in membership?' I ask, keeping the huskiness firmly in check this time.

'Yeah. I'm looking for some fresh inspiration.'

'We do fresh. Has Daniel taken you through the timetable?'

'Uh-huh. Got a question, though.'

'Fire away.'

'When do you finish?'

'Well, the last class ends at—'

'No, when do *you* finish?'

Wow. Definitely not gay, because unless I'm completely stupid he's asking me out. OK, must answer with something a little elusive. Don't want to appear too available, do I? 'Seven o'clock,' I tell him. Oh yes, I'm on top form tonight.

'Can I buy you a drink, then?' says Karl.

I look nervously at Daniel who's hanging up the phone. I'm treading on his toes here. OK, it seems Karl isn't in the camp camp, but that wouldn't mean anything to Daniel. As far as he's concerned, all men are gay – it's just that some of them need a little coaxing before they can appreciate their true selves. One of these days, if I should ever want to see Daniel dead, I'll get him to try that theory out on my dad.

'You off to Jenna's class now, Charlie?' Daniel says with an I-know-exactly-what-your-game-is smile.

Bastard. On two counts. One, if I say yes to the drink now, Karl will know that I'm changing my plans for him. And two, I don't want the tastiest guy I've seen in ages hanging around to watch me jumping

51

about like an over-aged idiot in a class full of funky, streetwise sixteen-year-olds. OK, twenty-four doesn't exactly qualify me for a free bus pass, but it feels that way when I'm standing next to fifty-odd teenagers. And *I'm* the one with acne.

Karl looks at the timetable. 'Jenna Mason. I know her. Never seen her workout though. I might stick around and watch . . .'

Aaaaaggggghhhhh!

'. . . Then maybe we can have that drink.'

He'll be gone in less than ten minutes.

I know my luck.

'It's . . . good . . . to . . . night,' Sasha says between pants.

She's right. Jenna's routine is good. It's sensible at least. Not one that has us jump-splitting in the air or spinning on our heads or doubling over backwards – moves that everyone else seems to be able to pull off without breaking sweat while I usually come close to breaking my neck. I really wouldn't want to be doing that in front of Karl.

I wouldn't say I have a lot of luck with men. Yes, I've been out with my fair share, but there's never been anyone who meant anything. And since Harvey, there hasn't been anyone full stop. Even when we were together, our texts were more fun than the actual relationship. And I hardly think I'm going to get any – by text or otherwise – with Karl. He's way out of my league. Fit, gorgeous and horny as hell. Even if he's unbendably straight, Daniel would probably still stand more chance. But you can't knock a girl for dreaming, can you?

I think he's still watching. My peripheral vision caught him checking us out through the window at the far end of the studio. Since then I've been trying very hard not to overexert myself. I've only had these hair extensions in a few days and I'm not sure how frizzy my roots will go if I get drenched in sweat. I've also been struggling not to look over at the window. Cool and laid-back. Oh yes, that's me.

'Why do you keep looking at the window?' Sasha asks.

'I don't,' I reply, looking away quickly.

I haven't mentioned Karl to her. If she knew there was a fanciable bloke outside she'd be way worse than me. She couldn't *not* look if her life depended on it. No, really, if I said, 'Don't look now, but there's a psycho outside and he's aiming a gun at your head and he's going to shoot if you so much as twitch,' she'd go, 'Where?' as she whipped her head round.

Jenna has split us into two groups. Her classes are too big for everyone to dance at the same time. Sasha and I join our lot at the side and watch the other half go through the routine. They're all so young. Not one of them can be over twenty. And they're all princesses. They must be to have daddies who can afford the fees for this place. They're the sort who're given pink RAV4s – not for passing their tests, but for booking their first driving lesson.

And they love Jenna. They pack out her classes. Partly because she's an older version of them – a twenty-six-year-old princess in trademark baby pink. But mostly because Jenna's so hot at the moment you could fry burgers on her. She's choreographed for Kylie, Holly Valance and Girls Aloud. I have to say she's very, very good – I don't know anyone else who could get Jay Kay to dance like he doesn't have Parkinson's.

I also have to say she doesn't half get on my nerves. Christina Aguilera came in a few months ago to tape an interview for MTV. She was everything you'd expect of a super-talented, super-successful American pop star. Spoilt, diva-ish, the business.

But compared to Jenna Mason she was an amateur.

Jenna acts as if she owns the place. Jamie, who actually does own the place, doesn't strut about like her. God, I've even seen him suck up to her. And *Lydia*. Lydia grovelled to no one. Unless, of course, she wore baby pink and answered to the name of Jenna. If she expects me to do the same just because she packs out the house, she can get lost. I'm no groveller. OK, I may have done the crawly-bum-lick thing with Lydia . . . Sometimes . . . A bit. But that was different. You *have* to grovel to your boss, don't you?

'I *love* Jenna,' Sasha gasps as we clap the girls from the other half. They get to have another go, and as Jenna stands to dance with them she gets a huge round of applause. I am in a definite minority in my opinion of the Pink Princess. 'If I had half her talent, maybe I wouldn't be working in the shop now.'

'Sasha, will you *please* stop putting yourself down.' It's one of those so-frustrating-I-could-shake-her moments. 'You're a brilliant dancer. Look at you, you're—'

'Oh, they've finished. Come on, our turn.'

Even if we weren't in the middle of a packed class, she wouldn't listen.

We launch into the routine and my mind wanders to . . . Karl. I wonder what he's like . . . you know . . . in bed. God, girl, wash your mind out with soap. No, sod it. Guys wonder this stuff all the time. Why can't we? I asked Daniel about it once and he said it was usually the case that while he was shagging someone he'd find himself wondering what they were like *out* of bed . . . Or the broom cupboard or wherever.

As we finish Sasha leans into me and whispers, 'I'm in love.'

'Really?'

I'm stunned. She's usually so fussy about men; blokes actually have more chance of winning the lottery than of getting a *second date* out of her. Now she's telling me she's in love.

'His name's Ben,' she says dreamily. 'I think he might just be perfect.'

Lucky Ben, because Sasha is very pretty as well as very choosy.

'Have you done it yet?'

'Charlie! You're so rude,' she shrieks, not answering the question. 'Listen, do you mind if I give tonight a miss?'

'Tonight?'

'We said we'd try that new bar on Beak Street, remember?'

I nod, giving her my sad, really disappointed face. She doesn't need to know I'd totally forgotten.

'It's just that Ben might call and I don't want to, you know . . . be out.'

'It's OK, Sash. I might just go out with Daniel,' I fib – still too soon to mention Karl. 'Actually, do me a favour. Don't call me at home tonight, will you? If they ask why I'm late, I'm going to give them *the excuse*.'

'OK, sure,' she says. 'Just in case it ever comes up, how am I doing?'

'Oh, the physios are really impressed. You should-n't even be able to wiggle your toes, but with *my* help you've taken three steps to date.'

'I'm amazing, aren't I?'

'A bloody miracle, girl.'

'Thank you and goodnight,' Jenna yells, and the room explodes. The standard applause plus whistles, cheers and whoops. They beg her for an encore and after some half-hearted protests she gives in – as any idiot would have known she would. That's the thing with encores. You always know there's going to be one, so why do singers and bands (and Jenna) make such a show of pretending they're finished?

'OK, one last time,' she shouts, putting the music back on. 'Five, six, seven, eight . . .' and they're off.

'You're not going, are you?' Sasha sees me eyeing the door.

'I know I should stay. I'm feeling really bloated today,' I say, looking down at my stomach and remembering Daniel's dig at me earlier.

'Don't be ridiculous! You're a *rake*. Not like me. God, I'm getting so fat, Jamie's going to ban me soon,' she says, trying to pinch an imaginary spare tyre round her waist.

'That's called skin, Sasha,' I tell her. 'You know, the stuff that stops your internal organs falling onto the floor.'

Listen to the pair of us. We sound more like twenty-five-stone Jacqueline than two size tens (although I'm not certain my clothes labels aren't lying). But I guess if people can't obsess about their weight in a *Total Body Emporium*, where can they?

Sasha runs off to take part in the final, final go at the routine. My cue to grab my gear and slip out. It's become so steamy in here I am getting seriously worried about these extensions. OK, they say you can lead a normal life, but after what I paid for them I don't think I should take any chances.

Outside, I casually look around for Karl. No sign. I walk along the corridor to the café and, even more casually than before, give it a quick circuit. Simply checking everything's OK in my capacity as studio manager. I scan every table. All surfaces shiny and clean. Absolutely nothing to do with seeing if Karl might be waiting here. He's not; though I hardly even notice because the thought that he might be had barely crossed my mind.

I head down to reception and find Rebecca and Daniel. 'How was class?' Daniel asks.

'Oh, the usual,' I say, not wanting to give Jenna any credit. 'Did he join then?' I add very, very casually because I really couldn't care less.

'Who?' he asks, frowning.

'You know, that Nelly lookalike you were giving the spiel to earlier.'

'Oh, him . . . No. He went ages ago.'

'Never mind,' I say, because I really, *really* don't mind.

'He left this for your though.' He hands me a Post-it with a number on it and *Call me – Karl* scribbled beneath. 'Poor sod's deluding himself he likes girls. You gonna call him then?'

'Nah,' I say, which isn't a lie because I'm not going to call him . . . tonight. Maybe tomorrow.

The doors open and Jamie walks through.

'Hi, Jamie. Thought you were in Loughborough,' Daniel smiles, snapping himself into an erect welcome-to-the-home-of-the-perfect-body pose.

'Waste of time. Can't stand the fit-pro mob.'

I know Jamie is Mr Fitness Industry, but he's so not fitness industry. Underneath the three-grand suit is a body that hasn't been exercised since its last compulsory PE. He talks the talk when he has to, but he's not in it to make himself any fitter. He's in it for the money.

'So how's your new boss, Rebecca?' he asks.

Poor girl doesn't know where to look. Numero Uno is actually addressing her by name and that's way too scary for her.

'Don't worry,' Jamie says. 'You can tell me what a bitch she is in private.' Then he turns to me. 'Let's step into your office.'

I do my best to ignore Daniel's sneery look and follow Jamie into *my* office. He plonks himself on the edge of the desk and says, 'Well then, how's Day One been?'

'Fine, thanks,' I say. 'Brilliant. No problems.'

'Good. I knew I could trust you. You're gonna be a star, Charlie.' I smile and blush simultaneously. I only wish I could bottle this moment.

'So, did she show?' he goes on.

'Who?' I ask.

'My bird from C4.'

OhmyfuckingGod.

My mind flashes back to Jamie's call first thing this morning. How did he describe her? 'She's a big girl – fucking *huge*.' Brain fast-forwards to the only fucking *huge* person I've seen all day: twenty-plus stone of her quivering at the desk. 'Give her the maximum schmooze,' Jamie had said. 'Charm the tits off her.' Well, I think I may have managed to offend the hell out of her. 'Give her the full tour,' he told me. Does sending her up to the caff with a brochure count? I think not.

'No, she didn't show,' I say, my heart sinking into my stomach.

'No worries. She's only coming for a look round – she was pretty vague about when that would be. Hopefully she'll show tomorrow,' he says, standing up and heading for the door.

Something occurs to me. 'Jamie,' I say, stopping him in his tracks, 'don't you mind, you know, with her being so big and everything?'

He laughs. 'Why should I mind? It's not her fault, is it? It's all in the genes. What is this? One of those bitchy, girly things? Didn't have you down as the type, Charlie.'

'No way! I'm no bitch,' I splutter.

'I believe you. See you in the morning.'

God, I am confused now. Maybe I got him all wrong. That's the trouble with unspoken rules – you can never be too sure of the finer details because they're bloody well *unspoken*! So, maybe Jamie isn't the fascist I thought he was. That is definitely a good thing.

On the other hand, it looks as if I've fucked up big-time on the big-lady-from-Channel-Four front.

And that is not a good thing at all.

The Bit Where You Find Out Just How Clever My Mum Is

I don't feel any better by the time I get home. Worse, if anything.

Dad is glued to RIK. Mum has her head in a TV mag, swotting up on upcoming soap plots. I don't know why she bothers watching them. She knows what's going to happen before the actors do. No sign of Emily. She must be upstairs doing her homework – I can hear her hairdrier.

'Hi, Charlie. How's work?' Mum asks without looking up.

'It was a nightmare, actually. I—'

'Shuddup,' Dad says. 'Is a good bit. Is *him*. His a bluddy shit.'

He points at the telly. A man has walked onto a set that wobbles with his every step.

'His having an affair with his own *sista*,' Dad explains. 'Can you beliv it? Disgusting. You should watch. Is brilliun.'

'How can it be brilliant if it's disgusting?' I ask, flopping onto the sofa next to Mum.

'Because, stoobid, he don' know she his sista.'

Well, *duh*, obviously.

We watch the TV, the silence broken only by the sound of Mum turning pages. 'So, how's the job go,

Thaglotta?' Dad asks during a lull in the incest.

I'd better explain the Thaglotta/Theglottsa/Theglitsa thing. Dad's got a thousand different names for me – well, eight to be exact – and he calls me by a different one according to his mood. How it came about is the best example there is of Mum's cunning strategy of letting him feel he's had The Final Word.

It says Charlotte on my birth certificate. Not very Greek, is it? I'm not the oldest. My brother Tony is twenty-nine. Tony might not sound very Greek either, but he was christened Antoni (or *Andonih* when Dad says it). When he was born, Dad decided to wear his course-am-bluddy-Grik hat and demanded his right to do the traditional thing and name him after *his* dad. Mum went along with it and over the years *Andonih* became Tony. When I was born, the course-am-bluddy-Grik hat got another airing and Dad decreed I be given his mum's name. Theglou.

That's right. *Theglou.*

No way was Mum standing for that. She let Dad announce to anyone who was interested that he had a little Princess Theglou and when it was time to register me she told the clerk to stick Charlotte on the certificate. Dad wasn't paying attention, apparently – he always lets her get on with the boring stuff like form-filling. He exploded when he found out, but calmed down when she explained that the name Theglou originally came from Charlotte. She told him that it would be right there in black and white in any book of names that he cared to look at (knowing full well that he wouldn't bother). Then she went through the evolution for him:

Charlotte,
Charlotta,
Chaglotta,

61

Thaglotta,
Theglottsa,
Theglitsa,
Thegla,
Theglou.
Staring you in the face when you think about it.

And here I am: *Charlotte* (thank God): living, breathing proof that (a) with a bit of forethought Dad can be suckered, and (b) when it really matters Mum is in charge round here.

It didn't end there. Emily arrived nine years after me. 'Our little accident,' Mum once let slip with a smug grin, which translated as *Get this: me and your father, still having sex, eh?* Way too much information. I can see from the mountain of photo albums in the cabinet that they were a couple of ravers in their time, but I really don't want the gory details of their possibly ongoing sex life, thank you.

Mum's attitude to the Greek naming thing had softened by the time she had Emily. Knackered by a forty-eight-hour labour and a screaming newborn, she wasn't prepared for another battle and she drew up a list. All Greek; Androulla at the top. 'Wotchew tokking aboud?' Dad yelled. '*Androulla*. Stoobid name. My baby, she Inglish rose. We calling her Emily.'

I don't answer Dad's question about my day, but only because I know he's not really interested. He's just being polite – for him, anyway.

'Come on, tell me,' he prods. 'Whass happening?'

But I need to tell someone about my hell, so I give it a go. 'It was terrible, Dad. You'll never believe what a stupid mistake I made. Jamie told me to look out for this producer from Channel Four, but . . .'

I trail off because no one's listening. Mum and Dad

62

are each lost in their worlds of televisual entertainment, neither of them giving a shit about my problems.

I look at Dad slumped in his armchair, his gut so firm and round he can rest his coffee mug on it. And Mum on the sofa with her *TV Quick*. I can't quite equate her with the bird in the old photo albums – pictures of a woman wearing shiny cat-suits and with silly hairdos who wanted to be the dark one out of Abba. Now she's happy to sit in front of the TV and relive her youth by watching untold reruns of every-thing on UK Gold. Twenty-four years ago she came up with an unbeatable anti-Theglou strategy. Today, the only plots she's interested in are the ones in her favourite soaps. What happened to her?

Is this going to be me in twenty-four years' time? Will I have my father's tum and my mother's TV habit? Will I have kids who won't quite be able to believe that their mum once fancied herself as Lara Croft?

Sitting up close to her, I can see her roots. She's never going to be the dark one out of anything any more.

'Cup of tea, Mum?' I ask.

'That'd be nice, sweetheart,' she says.

The Bit Where You Find Out
Just How Rubbish I Am

Terrible night last night. Fucking abysmal morning after.

I hardly slept for worrying. Didn't get me anywhere. I didn't come up with a single useful idea for saving Jamie's TV deal and, with it, my job. I am so fucked. It's just a question of time. How long have I got before he wonders why Jacqueline hasn't shown and gets on the phone to her? Bet I'm back home by lunchtime, P45 in my pocket.

'Just been fired, Mum.'

'That's nice. Stick the kettle on.'

What I need is a quiet start to the day; time to get my head together, engage my brain and come up with a way out of this mess. I check my face in the mirrored glass at the front of the building and walk up the steps. The doors slide open and I'm greeted by . . .

Mayhem. Absolute screaming pandemonium. It's only seven fifteen. The place isn't even open yet. What the hell's going on?

I focus on the mob filling the foyer. It only takes a second to figure out they're all dancers. The bandannas, sprayed-on vest-tops, oversized trousers hanging off every set of oh-so-narrow hips are a slight giveaway. Let's face it, unless there's been an overnight change in the world's dress code, they're not chartered accountants here for an audit. But why are fifty-plus dancers chok-ing reception at seven fifteen in the morning?

I fight my way through them to the desk, where I find Rebecca. Amazingly, her eyes are still dry. God knows how she's managed to keep it together amid this chaos. Best handle her gently. I take a deep breath, smile sweetly and say, 'What the fuck are this lot doing here, Becks?'

'One of the girls said they had a call,' she whispers.

'What, a casting call?'

I didn't know about any casting calls booked in for this morning.

'I thought she meant, you know, a phone call,' Rebecca says. 'What's a casting call?'

'It's a . . .'

What's the point? Right now, Rebecca couldn't be more useless if she was on eighty grand a year as Executive in Charge of Complete Uselessness. But I've only got myself to blame. I'm supposed to be in charge of bloody training her, aren't I?

Deep, deep breath. Stay calm. Together, we're going to sort this out.

'OK, Becks, go to Lydia's— *my* office and call Daniel. See if he knows what's going on.'

She sets off, but stops and says, 'Oh, I almost forgot. Julie something from something management is wait-ing for you in the café.'

What's she on about?

Hang on, it's all falling into place. Like a fucking landslide.

I remember a Julie Something from Something Management calling a couple of evenings ago and telling me in a horrible nasal voice that she represented Blaize. Blaize is a pop star. Pop stars require dancers. I'm putting two and two together and getting an audition. But auditions don't just happen like something in a Cliff Richard movie – *'Let's do the casting call right now, and let's do it right here!'* They require organisation, phone calls, the booking of a studio. So why the hell didn't I know anything about this? I'm the bloody studio manager, in charge of bloody *studios*. You can bet a thing like this wouldn't have slipped past Lydia's attention.

Jeez, I'm even more rubbish at this job than I thought.

As Rebecca sets off to phone Daniel, I decide to see what I can find out. I sit down at the computer, try to shut out the din and go to bookings.

And there it is. The seventh-floor studio blocked out in the name of Mission Management from seven thirty till five. This would be fine if it wasn't the personal property of the precious Philip and his piano. He's got his usual five ballet classes in there today. Then there's tap at three. Fuck, this is a double-booking nightmare from hell. I scan the schedules to see what else is free. Nothing. Everything's wall-to-wall.

What to do, what to do?

Hyperventilate? Bad idea. Giggle? Could prove useful. Not.

Got it. Studio Four is empty all day (which might have something to do with the fact that the aircon is broken and we're waiting for the engineers).

Sorted.

Stick them in Four and round up a couple of electric fans to prevent suffocation. Failing that, get Rebecca up there flapping a bit of cardboard.

Fuck, I am *brilliant* at this job.

Kiss my arse, Lydia.

I smile to myself and set off through the mob to find Julie Something, but she finds me first. I hear her before I see her, that nasal whine slicing through the buzz of at least fifty hyper dancers. Then I see her. Small, slightly dumpy, wearing Prada and a pair of Anastacia specs that don't make her look anything like Anastacia. I fix my best smile to my face and thrust out my hand. 'Hi, you must be Julie.'

'And you are?'

'Charlie, the *new* studio manager,' I reply, putting extra emphasis on the new to make it clear that I'm *not* the rude, unhelpful bitch that hung up on her a couple of days ago (and hoping she doesn't clock my voice as that of the other rude, unhelpful bitch who'd hung up on her a couple of minutes before that). I've put you in Studio Four,' I smile. 'It's on the third floor.'

'The *third* floor?' she replies. 'I was promised somewhere private on the seventh by the boy who took the booking.'

What boy? Could only be Daniel. I'll bloody kill him.

Later. Got to dig myself out of the shit first.

'Oh, the seventh-floor studio is completely overlooked.' (It's *true*. Rooftop pigeons – biggest hazard for pop stars since paparazzi were invented.) 'You'll find Studio Four is far more discreet.' (Well, it will be once I've sent Rebecca up to shut all the blinds.) 'Madonna was very happy with it when she used it.' (Slight change of tense never hurt anyone. She *will* be happy with it, if and when she ever uses it.)

'If you say so,' Julie says grudgingly before clapping loudly. 'Ladies and gentlemen, Studio Four, third floor. Let's get this show on the road.'

She spins on her heel and heads for the stairs. The dancers throng behind her like she's the Pied Piper. As she reaches the double doors she turns her head and yells, 'Tell the choreographer where we are.'

'Who's the choreographer?' I call out, but she's gone.

The foyer empties. I collapse into a chair and take a deep breath. I'm thanking God it's all sorted and enjoying the relative silence, when the doors slide open and Jamie sweeps in.

'Morning. Everything cool?' he asks.

'Cool,' I reply as he disappears into the lift.

And I feel anything but as my head spins in panic. Top priority: find a way of getting hold of Jacqueline.

Rebecca reappears. 'Daniel says sorry, but he forgot to mention the Blaize thing. He says not to worry though because he's sorted them out with the ballet studio.'

'Well, I've put them in Four. I want you to go up there now and make sure all the blinds are shut. Then go and find some fans and put them in there. Reckon you can handle that?'

'Blinds and fans,' she says with a nod before scurrying off.

I sit back and try to get my mind off dreaming up imaginative ways of murdering Daniel. I need to calm down and think about Jacqueline. Maybe she'll come back. Or maybe she'll call with a question about the sauna. Aren't you supposed to be able to sweat pounds off in there? The phone rings. Maybe God has answered my prayers. Maybe it's her.

I pick it up. 'Good morning, you're through to The Zone—'

'Stop, stop, it's only me.'

'Hi, Sasha. What's up?'

'Listen . . . I'm really sorry, but I think I'm going to give today's class a miss. Would you mind putting up a cancellation notice for me?'

My heart does a little dive. She only teaches two

68

classes a week and here she is cancelling one of them. But she sounds awful. Poor Sasha.

'Sasha, you can't blow it out now. Your classes have just started to pick up,' I say.

'That's not true. We both know I'm just wasting my time.'

'They have,' I insist, because technically it's true. Her last aerobics session had four people in it – a massive *one hundred* per cent increase on the one before.

'Oh, stop being nice and admit it, Charlie,' she says with a deafening sigh. 'It's a complete waste of time.'

Poor Sasha. We've all got insecurities, right? For instance, my nose is too big, my stomach pokes out, I trip up over my own two feet and my hair is frizzier than all of Beyoncé's afro wigs put together. But I have got nothing on Sasha. *Nothing*! If you asked her to make a list of her faults and failings, she'd write you a novel – and not a slim one either. Madness. How can anyone so pretty, so cute and so *brilliant* at dancing – think Justin Timberlake with boobs – be so low on self-esteem?

I despair that she'll ever make it because confidence is actually slightly more important than a sense of rhythm in this business. Take Jenna. She's good, but she *believes* she's amazing and that's what counts. When she graduated from dance school she walked straight into a gig on a Boyzone tour, then a Kylie video and then some show with Will Young . . . On it went, and now she's no longer just dancing with the pop stars, she's doing their choreography as well – and somehow finding the time to pack out six peak-time classes a week at The Zone.

By contrast, when Sasha left college she was immediately freaked by the audition process. She had a string of rejections, while dancers with a fraction of her ability got the jobs simply by walking into the room and looking the part – chests out, shoulders back, noses raised. After a while she developed audition phobia. That's how we met. She was hanging about outside Studio Two, too scared to go in for whatever commercial they were casting inside.

We talked and it didn't take long to work out she was in a bad way. The poor girl wouldn't even have been able to get a slot on a cruise ship; high-kicking in a feather headdress for bingo-playing pensioners who wouldn't know a head roll from a bread roll – in other words, the bottom of the barrel for any professional dancer.

I wanted to help her, but I wondered what I could do. Jenna was already here, and we had plenty of others who were teaching hip-hop and locking and body-popping. (Don't ask. They're just the technical terms for impossible dance styles invented for weirdo double-jointed types.) She was all set to jack it in, but I thought she was giving up too quickly. That's when I suggested aerobics.

Asking a dancer to switch to aerobics is a bit like asking a Greek to sing the Turkish national anthem. Actually, that would probably be easier. They don't like each other much, the dance and aerobics mobs. They're not exactly feuding like the East and West Coast rappers in America, but I reckon that if you gave them Uzis you might have a Biggie/Tupac scenario on your hands.

STEP TEACHER SLAIN IN DRIVE-BY BLITZ – POLICE SUSPECT DANCERS

Having said all that, given Sasha's bubbly personality (outside of an audition, at least) and her talent, I could really see her making a go of it. We had a gap in our schedules, and after I'd convinced her it was the right thing to do, I persuaded Lydia to fit her in. With unspeakably bad timing, Sasha's first class coincided with the exact second that aerobics went out of fashion.

Spinning seemed to have completely taken over. *Spinning*. I ask you, what is that all about? Idiots peddling exercise bikes to a techno soundtrack and disco lights. I shouldn't really knock it because it makes this place a fortune, but, I mean, if you must ride a bike, why can't you go for a spin round the block?

It's just a fad and it'll pass like all these things do. Aerobics will make a comeback . . . Won't it?

'Sasha, it's *not* a waste of time. You've got to give it a bit longer,' I say now. 'Try to stay positive.'

'I've had enough,' she says. 'It's just too depressing. My life is *crap*.'

'But it's not all bad,' I say, trying to sound perky. 'What about your new boyfriend? The one you were telling—'

'Don't even speak to me about him!'

'Hang on, Sash. Something's come up.'

Jenna has just walked in. What's she doing here at this time of day?

'Morning, Charlie,' she singsongs. 'Where've you put them?'

'Put what?' I reply dumbly.

'My dancers, silly.'

Her dancers. So she's running the Blaize show. I should have guessed. 'They're in Four,' I say.

'Four? You've had the aircon fixed? Excellent!' she says.

I watch her skip towards the lift – the cat with the

71

double cream, whipped and topped with a big fat straw-
berry – and I hope to hell that Rebecca finds some fans
or my life won't be worth living.

'Sorry, Sasha,' I say, returning to the phone. 'Look,
come in today. Just teach your class and we'll have a
proper chat afterwards.'

'I'm not coming and that's that. I'll talk to you later.'
And she's gone.

As I hang up I make a decision. Sasha's been going
nowhere for too long now. She's too talented to waste
her time teaching a class she doesn't have her heart
in (plus, I don't know how much longer I can keep
lying to Jamie about her attendance figures). And as
for working in the shop, well, it hardly needs stating,
does it? I'm going to convince her to get back to dancing. Sort her out somehow. I have the power to do
that now – change people's lives. I am the Studio
Manager.

Not for much longer, mind, if I don't get hold of
Jacqueline.

Before I can think about what to do, the phone rings
again. I grab it and say, 'Good morning, you're through
to The—'

'—Zone, I'm Charlie, how can I help?' Daniel finishes
for me.

'*Daniel*, I'm going to kill you,' I hiss. 'Why didn't
you tell me about the Blaize thing?'

'Because I took the booking after you'd left yesterday. I phoned you at home to tell you about it, but
your dad said you were in the bath. What he actually
said was, "She in bath. You wanna tok about werk,
you save it for bluddy werk".' His impression of my
dad is so good it's scary.

'Daniel, don't be so rude,' I say testily. No one's
allowed to take the piss out of my family except

me. 'Anyway, it's cool now. I put them in Studio Four.'

'Four? They'll fucking melt in there. That's why I swapped them with Philip. I told him that if he was prepared to spend a day sweating to death in Four he could have a piano tuner *and* one of my special blowjobs.'

Maybe Daniel should be doing my job – at least until I can add special blowjobs to my list of man-management skills.

'Anyway, can't hang around chatting to you all day,' he goes on. 'Gotta get to work. If I'm late my bitch boss will kill me.'

I put the phone down and take a deep breath. Alone at last.

Time to think. I've got to find a way of getting out of this mess I've created. What am I going to do about Jacqueline? Maybe Daniel spoke to her? And maybe he got her number while she was here? You never know, stranger things have happened. Just as I'm about to call him back, my peripheral vision catches a woman walking through the automatic doors. My peripheral vision can hardly bloody miss her, actually. She's got the biggest tits I've ever seen. They're jostling for attention beneath her jumper, as if her bra is playing host to the world sumo championships. As she reaches the desk I force myself to look into her eyes and say, 'Hi, how can I—'

I don't get to finish because the doors leading to the staircase fly open and half a dozen sweaty, irate dancers spew through them. 'Fucking *bitch*, man,' screams one, a mixed-race guy. 'This is a complete fucking stitch-up.'

'Too right. I should've given her a slap,' one of the girls agrees.

They reach the desk as one, knocking Big Boobs off to the side. I look at her apologetically, but she gives me a *don't-mind-me* gesture and sensibly steps out of the firing line. I quickly scan the dancers and spot a face I recognise – a girl I've seen doing Fenton's Garage Jam class. 'Why don't you tell me what the problem is?' I say in the soothing voice I learned at a customer-care seminar Lydia sent me on last year. (Golden rule: to hear is to understand; to understand is to empathise; to empathise is not to roll your eyes in total boredom – at least not when the customer is looking. OK, I added that last bit myself, but it's an important point.)

'I'll tell you what the fucking problem is, Charlie,' garage jammer yells. 'It's that fucking lying slag.'

'I'm sorry, but which fucking lying slag are you talking about?' I prod gently.

'Jenna, man. Who the fuck else?'

Charlie to mission control – we have empathy.

Before I can ask what she's done the doors crash open again and another group of angry dancers spill out. At the same moment two guys holding toolboxes step in from the street. They walk straight up to me, slamming their gear down on Jamie's beautiful marble desk.

'Morning, love. We're from Southern Airways,' one of them says, seemingly oblivious to the irate mob around him.

I look at him blankly – (a) why are airline pilots carrying toolboxes and (b) what the hell are they doing here?

'Come to fix your aircon,' he explains.

Oh, *that* sort of airways.

Jesus, I'd forgotten for a moment. They must be

near meltdown up there. Where the hell is Rebecca? Just how long can it take to get a couple of electric fans?

'I'm sorry, you won't be able to do it today,' I say. 'The studio's busy. You'll have to make another appointment.'

Another feisty group of dancers bursts into the foyer – the rate it's emptying, maybe the studio won't be busy for much longer.

But Aircon Bloke doesn't move. Why would he? He's surrounded by a bunch of ultra-fit dancers, fifty per cent of them women and all of them displaying generous bits of midriff and cleavage, as well as the odd glimpse of thong. Now he clocks an unexpected bonus – the biggest chest he's likely to see today unless Jordan is cooking his tea tonight. No, he and his mate are going nowhere in a hurry. They're jostled to the side so that they're standing next to Big Boobs.

I spot Rebecca. She's moving towards the lift. 'Becks,' I shout, 'have you sorted the fans out?'

'Doing it now,' she calls back.

An angry girl with dreadlocks pushes her way to the desk. At last, a face I know by name.

'Charlie, you've got to do something about this.' Her name is Courtney and you should see this girl dance. She is amazing. Hard to think why she didn't make it through Jenna's audition.

'Bit rowdy in here, isn't it?' Aircon Bloke says. 'Want me to step in? I used to do crowd control at Wembley.'

I ignore him and turn to Courtney. 'What's happening up there?'

She doesn't answer because her attention turns to the double doors, which are flying open – *again*. This time only the one dancer tumbles through them, but she's making enough angry noises for ten.

'*Kristine*! Not you as well,' the mixed-race guy screams as she's swamped by a dozen comforting hugs.

'Oh dear,' Big Boobs mutters to Aircon Bloke, 'not Kristine as well.'

That's it. I've had just about all I can take.

'Everyone, SHUT UP!' I yell at the top of my voice. Bugger the soothing customer-care voice. How the hell can I hear/understand/empathise when I can't even hear myself think? It works like a dream. I have absolute silence.

'OK, Courtney,' I say, switching back to soothing, 'tell me.'

'It's Jenna. We get the call yesterday,' she tells me, 'to turn up at the crack of dawn.'

'And she doesn't even wanna see what we can do,' says another.

'Call that a fucking audition, man?'

They're all chipping in now.

'And guess who the chosen ones are.'

'Who?' Me, Aircon Bloke and Big Boobs ask in unison.

'The same ones she picks every time.'

'The arse-kissers she picked for Blue—'

'And that crap Lisa Maffia vid—'

'And Christina Milian—'

'It's a fucking scandal,' Aircon Bloke says, angry now and looking at me while he says it.

'Jesus, I could've been at the Robbie call this morning,' the mixed-race guy groans. 'At least Fenton would've got me to dance before he told me to piss off.'

Suddenly, it all makes sense. So there's a Robbie

76

Williams audition this morning and it's being run by Fenton Brown. He teaches here too and Jenna hates him, mostly because he's a threat. What better way of fucking him over than hogging all the best dancers on the day of his call? She never had any intention of using ninety per cent of them – she just wanted to make sure he didn't get them. The politics of dance are something else.

I really don't know what I can do. Even if I did, right now I don't have a chance. Julie from Mission Management is striding up to the desk.

'Excuse me, but what business do you have authorising members of the public to attend a *private* audition?' she demands in a voice that could freeze the Med.

'I'm sorry, I'm not with you,' I say, completely baffled.

'Your assistant just dragged some *oiks* off the street and brought them into our studio.'

'But I asked her to get you some . . .'

Round up some fans, I'd said. Fuck, which of us is more stupid? Rebecca for totally misunderstanding me, or me for not knowing that Rebecca would totally misunderstand me?

'I'm really sorry. It's been a silly misunderstanding,' I say as my good old peripheral vision catches a tear-streaked Rebecca herding a bunch of spotty teens back into the street where she found them.

This is all my fault. I should have explained it to Rebecca *properly*, with diagrams if necessary.

'As I said, I'm sorry. What can we do to put things right?' I say. If grovelling is what is required here, then I'm ready to kiss arse for England.

'You can get the aircon fixed. It's like the Black Hole of Calcutta up there,' she says, spinning on her heel and heading back to the lift.

I look beseechingly at Aircon Bloke.

'Say no more, love,' he says, grabbing his mate and his toolbox and setting off after her . . . but not before he's exchanged hugs and handshakes with half a dozen dancers. Shit, he's doing The Handshake – the one that involves intricately choreographed wrist, finger and thumb moves. I've worked here for over three years and I still can't do it. How the hell did he master that in the last ten minutes?

I close my eyes. When I open them again the place seems to have calmed down. The dancers are ripping Jenna to pieces a little more quietly, and while they shouldn't really be messing up my wonderfully calm reception with bitch vibes, I'm way past caring.

I look at Big Boobs. She smiles at me pleasantly and I thank God for her patience. 'I'm sorry,' I say. 'What can I do for—'

The phone rings for the tenth time since all this kicked off. Where on earth is Rebecca? She must be sobbing in the loos by now. I'm really going to have to make it up to her. But later.

'Sorry, but I'd better get this,' I say.

'Go ahead,' Big Boobs says, still managing to sound pleasant.

It's Sasha. Again.

And she's crying.

Really crying.

'What is it, Sash?' I ask gently.

'I didn't tell you everything earlier,' she sobs. 'You know, about Ben.'

'And you want to tell me now?' I prompt, trying to sound like I've got all the time in the world, then giving up. 'Is that it? Because now isn't exactly the ideal moment.'

Big Boobs is still at the desk, hanging on every word.

'Tell me, Sash. Preferably quickly.' I try to sound as if I'm joking.

'It's all right for you. You get every bloke you ever go after. I'm so bloody . . .' I miss the last bit because she's blowing her nose down the phone.

'What did you say?' I half shout.

'He's dumped me!' she wails.

'Dumped you?' I wail back.

'He's dumped her?' Big Boobs mouths at me, managing to look almost as upset as I feel.

'Why?' I ask. 'I thought this was true love.'

This triggers a fresh wave of sobs and she doesn't answer.

I shake my head disconsolately at Big Boobs. 'Sorry, Sasha, but, you know, you haven't been seeing him for that long, so maybe it isn't the end of the world—'

'I knew you were going to say that!' she cries. 'Ever since you got those hair extensions and this stupid promotion, you've really changed. You think everything's so easy. Well, it's *not*.'

That's unfair. The extensions are only five days old and the promotion is just two – hardly enough time for a radical personality change.

'OK, listen. We're going to have a long chat, when you get in to work. Er, will you be teaching today?'

'He's *dumped* me, Charlie. Don't you get it?' she bawls.

'OK, so you're not teaching. Right, we'll meet for lunch. At Billy's. Talk then . . . yes?'

Muffled sobs. I'll take that as a yes.

'See you there. And *don't* worry.' I slam the phone down because I've just seen someone walk through the automatic doors and I'm climbing over the desk to get to her.

'I'll come back when you're a bit less . . . pressurised,' Big Boobs says.

'Whatever,' I reply because, nice as she seems, I really don't care any more. I'm over the desk now and I'm pushing my way through the dancers towards salvation . . .

Towards *Jacqueline*!

She's turned up with a kit bag and she's wearing a revolting purple and yellow tracksuit with matching wristbands, and she's the most beautiful thing I've ever seen.

I reach her just as the lift door opens and Jamie steps out. Terrible timing – I could have done with a chance to grovel shamelessly to her first – but I'll just have to make the best of it. I grab her arm and steer her towards Jamie.

'She only just got here,' I pant as we reach him.

'Who did?' he asks, puzzled.

'Jacqueline,' I reply, looking at my angel from Channel Four. She seems to be just as confused as Jamie.

'Who the fuck's Jacqueline?' he says, looking her huge frame up and down in horror.

'Your producer? From Channel Four?' I add, though I say it very quietly because I'm beginning to sense my most monumental fuck-up yet.

'I'm not from Channel Four,' Jacqueline says, eyeballing me contemptuously.

'No, *she's* from Channel fucking Four,' Jamie hisses. He points angrily towards the street – towards Big Boobs who's now climbing into the back of a black cab.

But, of course, I knew that already.

The Bit Where I Find Out
What Those Handles
In Disabled Loos Are For

Sasha's late.

I'm sitting in Billy's Bar with a bottle of wine. I'm not going to wait for her. I pour myself a glass and take a sip . . . Then a gulp . . . Sod it, drain the glass, pour another. God knows I need this. No one could be more amazed than me at the way things went.

Jamie and I stared open-mouthed at Claire Eastman's cab as it drove off. You know, *Claire Eastman*, as in Big Boobs, as in Jamie's top producer bird from C4.

Bye-bye, TV deal, he was thinking.

Hello, McJob, I was thinking.

Daniel walked in then and he actually did say, 'Hiya, have I missed anything?'

Jamie glared at him, then at Jacqueline, then at me and snarled, 'You've got five minutes to hand over to Daniel, then get your arse up to my office.' Then he stormed off.

I was rooted to the spot, feeling the life drain out of me. How could I have been so stupid? Why hadn't I realised that when Jamie said, 'You can't miss her. She's *huge*,' he was talking about her tits. He's a bloke. What else could he have been referring to? 'Charm the tits off her,' he'd sniggered. Well – *duh*! – it finally clicked that he was being literal. I was still clinging to Jacqueline's arm, but only because I knew that if I let go, I'd collapse. Luckily Daniel sensed the desperation and moved in. He peeled my hand off her and said, 'You'd better get a move on, Jacqueline. Your yoga class will be warming up already.'

As she waddled off I managed to whisper, 'She's a member?'

'Signed her up for full Platinum Membership last night when you were doing Jenna's.'

'But—'

'Know what you're thinking. She's not exactly Zone-shaped, but she let slip that she's an opera singer. Jamie loves all that bollocks – and she was buying Platinum – so I thought I could make an exception.'

Jamie and opera? It's a flashy wide-boy thing. Probably something to do with the prices. If the Royal Opera House was like the Odeon – tickets for under a tenner, popcorn by the skip-load – he'd probably hate it.

As Daniel led me through the loitering dancers and back to the desk, he said, 'What the fuck's been going off here? It looks like the Equity enclosure in a refugee camp.'

'Jenna's been at it again.'

'Is that what Jamie wants to bollock you about?'

'I wish,' I said as I headed for the lift.

Less than a minute later I was standing in front of him.

'Jesus Christ, Charlie,' he said. Then nothing for a bit. He just shook his head. Then: 'Jesus *fucking* Christ.'

'Sorry,' I mumbled.

'Sorry? *Sorry*? It was Baghdad on a bad day down there. I've seen more fucking order at a Sex Pistols gig. And you let her watch it all?'

'Sorry,' I whispered.

82

'And then you just let her walk out of the fucking door.'

I didn't say sorry this time. There didn't seem much point. Besides, my entire cowed body was screaming SORRY in thirty-foot neon letters.

'Do you have any idea what you've just blown?'

I shook my head – well, he hadn't told me anything about it, had he? Then he said, 'Maybe I fucked up. Maybe I was mad to promote you. Jesus, I never thought I could miss Lydia.'

Something we agreed on, then.

'What are we gonna do?' he asked.

I didn't think he was including me in his *we*, and all I could imagine was that *we* were going to fire me. But then the phone rang and saved me. I don't mean it gave me a few minutes' breathing space. I mean it literally saved my life. He picked it up and I listened to his half of the conversation: 'Hullo . . . Oh, hi, Claire . . . I'm really glad you rang because I was gutted to miss— . . . Yeah, saw you climbing into a— . . . Look, I've got to apologise. You caught us at a really bad time. Honestly, it's not normally that chaot— . . . Oh . . . Oh, really? . . . Exactly what you're looking for? . . . Well, yes, when I say it's not usually that mad I mean it's . . . um . . . madder . . . Yeah, the place is full of characters . . . Egos, yeah, we got those in spades . . . Uh-huh, The Zone definitely thrives on tension . . . Charlie? What can I say about Charlie? . . . Yup, she's amazing, isn't she? She's definitely got something, I dunno . . . *special* . . . You saw it too? Well, great minds and all that . . . *Fantastic*! That's wonderful news. I can't tell you how thrilled— . . . Absolutely . . . Yup, call me when you've got your diary in front of you. Look forward to it . . . Bye for now . . . Bye.'

The phone went back down and he stared at me for a few seconds that seemed to stretch into weeks. He looked shocked, dazed, as if he couldn't figure out why the dog turd he'd just stepped in smelled like Chanel No. 5. I couldn't quite work out what had happened either, but I did know this much: I was safe.

'Seems I owe you an apology,' he said at last. 'She loves you. Fuck knows how you swung it, but you've clinched the deal.'

'What do you mean?' I asked. I was pretty sure he meant we were getting the gig, but I had no idea what the gig was.

'Prime-time doc on Channel Four about the posh end of the fitness industry, featuring . . . *us*. That's like a whole *hour* of free advertising, Charlie.'

He stood up and pulled at a panel on the wall that hinged open to reveal a fridge. He took out a bottle of champagne. 'Fancy a glass?' he asked. It wasn't even eight thirty, but I nodded. As he eased out the cork, he said, 'If this was just an average celebration I'd be opening a bottle of crappy old Lanson. This is Krug, Eighty-nine, over a hundred quid a pop. And I ain't even had breakfast yet. She had it down to three. Cannons, the Third Space and us. Thanks to you, we're in, baby. We are gonna be famous!'

This time, when he said *we* he definitely meant *we*.

When I got to Billy's I was still a bit pissed from the breakfast champagne. Now well into my second glass of wine, I don't know how the hell I'm going to keep a clear head for Sasha.

Sasha.

What am I going to do about her? For some reason, I seem to think of myself as her surrogate mother, which is crazy. I can't cope with my own problems, never mind anyone else's. And by the sound of her

84

earlier, it sounds like she's going to need some major sorting out.

'Didn't think I'd see a familiar face in here,' says a voice behind me. I look round and see Nelly, and I want to sing about how hot it is in herre and how I've got an uncontrollable urge to . . . I dunno . . . take off all my clothes. Or something. OK, it isn't *the* Nelly. Just the next best thing.

'Hi . . . Karl, isn't it?' Of course I know his name, but I don't want him to get the impression that I've been practising saying it in front of the mirror or anything.

'Lunch hour?' he asks.

'Yeah.'

'Alone?'

'I'm meeting a friend.'

'Mind if I sit here while you're waiting?' He plonks himself beside me before I can answer, but, hey, was I really going to say no? 'Male or female?' he asks.

'Who?'

'Your friend.'

'Female,' I smirk, because, well, he's just told me he's still interested – I can't have looked that spazzy in Jenna's class last night.

It's a good job I'm not one of those people who don't like having their space invaded because he's sitting as close to me as he can without sitting on my lap. Actually, I *am* one of those people, but I'm making an exception because he's gorgeous. He's so big too. All tight white T-shirt over tight black muscle and it's as much as I can do to stop myself from wondering what's going on elsewhere if you know what I mean, which, of course, you do.

'What are you doing here?' I ask.

'Same as you. Meeting a mate,' he says, nodding

towards the bar. It's crowded and I wonder who he means – and are they male or female. But I don't ask, which just goes to show that I *can* be laid-back when I want. 'Listen, sorry about last night,' he goes on. 'I don't usually rush off without explaining, but something came up.'

'No big deal. These things happen,' I say coolly, like I'd forgotten he existed by the time my class had finished and I didn't really spend half an hour scouring the premises for him.

'Anyway, I'd like to make it up to you . . .'

And I'm thinking, *That's nice. Drink, dinner, maybe a club . . .*

'. . . I'd really like to fuck your brains out.'

What was that? Did he say, 'I'm going to have to go or I'll miss my train', or, 'My mum's doing broccoli tonight – my favourite', because surely he couldn't possibly have said—

'I mean it. I've got to fuck you. Now.'

OK, so my ears weren't deceiving me, but he can't mean me. This is the sort of thing that happens to sex bombs. Not me. I'm not going to explode with Cameron Diaz-ness any time soon. I'm plain and ordinary and I've got to pull my stomach in all the time and my surname is Charalambous. But he does mean me because his eyes are drilling into mine and he's definitely not glancing absent-mindedly in my direction while he has a conversation with Cameron Diaz on the next table. I do what most girls would do in this situation (apart, that is, from the ones who'd slap his face and reach for their rape alarms). I giggle nervously, but I can't take my eyes off his.

'*Now*,' he repeats, very, very insistently.

So I say—

*

Can I just make a few things clear at this point?

- I'm not the sort of girl who does this – i.e. agrees to screw a bloke she's barely met just because he asks.
- I'm not the sort of girl who has quickies in her lunch hour.
- Not even with proper boyfriends.
- I'm just not that sort of girl.
- Honest I'm not.

So I say, 'Where?'

Which somehow stops short of being *yes*, but not by much.

'Come with me,' he says, and he takes my hand and pulls me to my feet. And – fucking *hell* – I let him. But . . . But, well, you just wouldn't believe how *dee*licious this bloke is. And his voice! It's like listening to Barry White – try hard to imagine the Walrus of Love with cheekbones and decent muscle tone (oh, and alive) and you're there. He pushes his way slowly through the smoke, the laughter, the glasses being held by people who aren't going to get laid until tonight at the very earliest, until we get to the door at the far end of the bar. He opens it and pulls me through. Now we're on the dark staircase that leads down to the loos and the kitchens and I'm wondering – in between listening to the deafening thumps of my heart – whether he has a Daniel-style broom cupboard in mind. It seems not because we've reached the basement and he's pulled me to the end of the corridor where the bogs are. I'm thinking, *Please, God, not the toilets – I can't do it in a bloody cubicle*. We pass the door with the bloke symbol, then the one with the girl symbol. Now we're in front of one with . . . Is that a wheelchair? I'm wondering how the hell the owners think a disabled person is supposed to get down a steep, narrow, badly-lit staircase but I can't dwell on it for long. Karl pushes open the extra-wide door and drags me inside. As he locks us in I look around. It's quite big. And – rare for a loo in a Soho bar – it's clean. Rarer still (and I can't believe I'm noticing this), there's a full roll of toilet paper. But of course there is. A disabled loo at the bottom of a staircase? I bet it hasn't been used since the grand opening.

He turns and we stare at each other. The silence makes me aware that I'm panting. Am I breathless from that short jog down the staircase? Or is it out of guilt because I'm remembering it's bad manners to take advantage of the less fortunate (the way I feel when my dad nicks the disabled parking space at Asda)? Or is it because I'm gagging for it? He grabs me, pulls me into him and kisses me, and I admit to myself that I have never been more gagging for anything in my life . . . And I realise that he's panting too.

The kiss goes on . . . And on . . . And on. In fact, I think we only stop because we realise that if we don't we'll suffocate and die and never get to do what we came down here for in the first place. He turns me around and I stumble forward. My hands reach out and grab hold of the two bright yellow rails to either side of the loo. He yanks down my Zone ra-ra skirt and my grip on the handles tightens until my knuckles are white . . . And I can't help thinking how bloody useful they are.

I'm standing in front of the mirror, wishing I had some make-up so I could dust over that *just fucked* look. I watch Karl come up behind me. His arms go around my waist, his face nuzzles my neck. 'Gimme your mobile number,' he says. 'We've got to do this again.'

'Got a pen?' I ask.

'No need. Photographic memory.'

As I recite my number I'm thinking, bullshit. No way is he remembering it. He's just being polite. And while I'm thinking that's a shame I'm also kind of glad – I mean, I'm not sure I want to see the man I've been *this* bad with again.

'Better go,' he grins. 'People will talk.'

He turns and unlocks the door and I nearly wet myself. Wouldn't you know it? There's a bloke in a wheelchair outside. 'You finished? Only I'm busting,' he says very matter-of-factly.

'Sorry, mate,' Karl says as he pushes past him. I follow, but I can't help pausing and looking at him. He doesn't have any signs of a recent run down the stairs – cuts, dislocated limbs and so on – and I ask, 'How did you . . . You know . . .'

'Get down here or lose the use of my legs?'

'The first one,' I mumble, embarrassed now. *Ha*, like I *wasn't* before.

'There's a lift,' he says, nodding towards the lift door that I hadn't noticed before. 'Now, would you mind? I really am gonna piss myself.'

'Sorry,' I mutter, getting out of his way and following Karl.

I'm back at my table. Alone. Karl left a couple of minutes ago – mission accomplished. My legs are demurely crossed, I'm taking a ladylike sip of wine and I reek of sex. The guy in the wheelchair reappears and rolls to a table on the far side of the room. He raises his beer bottle in my direction. I look away, squirming. I can't believe what I've just done. I'm really NOT THAT SORT OF GIRL. I feel disgusting, filthy, cheap . . . I'm also feeling an amazing tingly sensation sparking through my whole body because, though the entire experience ran to less than ten minutes, it was the best sex I've ever, ever had. And that's the scariest thought of all.

'Sorry I'm late,' Sasha says breathlessly.

I look up at her and cringe. She *must* be able to smell it on me – *l'Air d'Orgasm*. I feel awful now. She's depressed, she wants comfort and hugs and mumsy advice from a friend who just happens to have had a frantic shag with a virtual stranger in a disabled loo.

She sits down, grabs the bottle and fills her glass. I look at her and she doesn't seem to be any of the things she was on the phone a few hours ago. Where are the red, puffy eyes, the chewed nails, all the symptoms of ongoing hysteria?

'You OK, Sash?' I ask gently.

'God, how stupid am I?' she shrieks. 'Such an idiot.'

Well, that's what they say, but I've always stuck up for you.

'Why? What's happened?'

'He called me as soon as I hung up on you. How mad am I?' She's laughing now, the despair of earlier vanished without trace.

'So . . . um, he hasn't dumped you?'

'No! God, I am so out of practice with men. Last night, he'd called to say he couldn't see me and I assumed he meant he couldn't see me, like, *ever*, but he just meant he couldn't see me *today* because something had come up. He called me just after I spoke to you in fact.'

'Right. I see. What was it that came up?'

'Oh, he didn't say. Whatever, everything's fine now. In fact, better than fine. Everything's *beautiful*.'

So mumsy advice is off the agenda. I breathe a sigh of relief. 'Look, Sash, I wanted to talk to you anyway, about your career.'

'What about it?' she says taking a sip of wine, still beaming.

'You're wasted in Zone Clone. I don't think you should give the teaching up.'

'Why not? I'm a bag of nerves in front of a class. Look at Jenna. She's so together. I can't compete with her.'

'Stop comparing yourself to her. She's a couple of years older than you anyway, so she's got a head start. If you just give it another go, who knows? I think you should teach dance. It's what you're good at. I'm in charge now, so I can make a space for you in the timetable without crawling to Lydia. I had a thought. Why don't we take it back to the traditional style, good old-fashioned jazz dance? No one's doing that any more and I reckon it's going to make a comeback soon, what with . . .'

Why am I bothering? She isn't even listening. She's miles away, rooting through her handbag. It's like talking to my mum and dad, and there isn't even a TV in here for distraction. God, maybe it's me. Maybe I'm really boring or something.

'Anyway, as I was saying,' I continue. 'I think you should teach S&M ballet. You know, rubber tutus. And studded codpieces for the blokes. Whaddya reckon?'

'Yeah, maybe,' she says dreamily, emerging from her bag with something wrapped in tissue. 'Do you like this?'

I peel away the paper and look at the shiny silver thing inside. 'It's lovely,' I say. 'Er, what is it?'

'It's a business-card holder. It's for Ben. Look, it's got a B on it. I saw it on my way here and I just *had* to get it for him. He is so amazing, I can't believe how lucky I am.'

'That's great,' I say and I mean it. She's got a lousy

track record with blokes, which is surprising given her looks and her general levels of sweetness. I just hope she isn't running ahead of herself with this Ben guy.

'Anyway, we've got to sort you out now,' she continues. 'Get you someone new so we can do all that icky double-dating stuff.'

I think of telling her about what happened with Karl, but I can't. Not yet. I barely know him, but I suspect he's not the icky double-dating type. And Sasha definitely isn't the doing-it-in-a-disabled-loo type. No, she'd only ever do it in a bed with fresh white linen, scented candles and Enrique on the stereo. She'd be horrified if I told her and I'd die from shame. Best save this one for Daniel. Filthy sex in public places is his speciality. Instead I tell her about my nightmare morning. About the riot and the appearance, then disappearance, of a woman from Channel Four.

'Channel Four?' she squeals. 'We're not gonna be on telly, are we?'

Oops. I'm not supposed to tell a soul. Jamie swore me to secrecy. On pain of death he'd said. So I say, 'Yeah, we're going prime-time!'

I tell her all about *The Fit Factor*. About how C4 are doing this special on how far the fitness industry has come since Jane Fonda marched her way onto our TV screens all those years ago. And I'm going to be the centre of attention. Well, I'm studio manager, *and* a senior producer at Channel Four *loves* me. If it were a proper film J.Lo would play me. Definitely.

'That's incredible, Charlie,' Sasha gasps. 'Can I be in it?'

'Of course. We can all be in it. But you can't tell anyone yet, right?'

'Would I?'

'Yes.' Sasha isn't famous for her discretion. Like I am.

'My lips are sealed. I swear.'

'Anyway, what about this new boyfriend?' I ask. 'Tell me about him. Where did you meet?'

'He's a dancer, believe it or not. Remember when I snuck off to Danceworks last month to try out that new class. I met him there. He's—'

She stops because my mobile beeps. It's a text.

```
CUM 2 MINE 2MORROW. 8.
DNT HVE 2 DO IT IN BOG ...
UNLESS U WNT 2 ... K
```

'Who's it from?' Sasha asks.

'Just a friend,' I tell her as I concentrate on the little blue screen. I mull over my reply. I need something enigmatic, elusive, mysterious, sexy, slightly cryptic, clever, cool . . .

NEED ADDRESS

That'll do for me.

'I just did it,' I whisper to Daniel as I dump my bag behind the desk.

'Did what?'

'*It*. With the Nelly lookalike.'

'You filthy fucking whore. Where?'

'In the disabled loo at Billy's. I didn't even know they had a disabled loo.'

'I did. Had it sussed as soon as the place opened. Those handles are such a godsend, aren't they?'

The Bit With The Long Goodbye

I slide my key into the lock and turn it quietly. I've slipped into the house unnoticed loads of times. Usually at gone midnight. Not so often at seven thirty in the evening, but I have my reasons. I feel filthy, as if I've been surrounded by a smoggy cloud of slutty sex all afternoon. I'm paranoid Mum and Dad will smell it on me, so I'm going to bypass the living room and head straight up for a bath. It's bound to work. I've timed my entrance to coincide with the start of *Coronation Street. Corrie*, in Mum's expert opinion, is The Best Soap in the Whole Wide World (Ever) and she gives it the respect it's due by watching it with the volume turned up to Ayia Napa rave levels.

I step through the front door and freeze.

Why is it so quiet? Where's the deafening din of people speaking Manc? Maybe I've got the wrong house, but a quick scan confirms that I'm home. The silence isn't total. I can hear voices on the other side of the front-room door. My parents, socialising? During the week? Never. Must be something else. Double-glazing salesmen perhaps. Or Jehovah's Witnesses – Dad always gets them in for a good row.

I stand very still, listening. I can hear Mum. She's got her posh voice on. 'Tea or coffee, Maroulla? And George, another beer maybe?'

Who the hell are Maroulla and George, apart, that is, from very obviously being Greek?

The door opens and Mum comes out into the hall. She spots me and says, 'What are you doing, hiding out here?'

'Who's in there?' I whisper, ignoring her question.

Mum grabs me and pulls me into the kitchen. She closes the door behind her and hisses, 'I could kill your father. I'm missing *Corrie*, you know.' (I know.) 'We're supposed to find out who the burglar is tonight.'

I don't know why this bothers her. Having read every TV mag in existence, she knew who the burglar was several weeks ago.

'Who's he got round here?' I ask.

She ignores me and puts the kettle on. Then she turns to face me. 'Look at you. You're a mess. Go and comb your hair and put some lipstick on or something. You look like you've been—'

Aagh! Fucked to within an inch of my life in a locked toilet?

'—dragged through a hedge backwards.'

Phew.

She still hasn't answered my question. 'Mum, who's in there?' I ask again with extra urgency.

'Look, don't go getting all silly. Your dad's just invited some old friends round, OK?'

I hear alarm bells. 'It's those bloody doctor people, isn't it? I thought he wasn't dragging them round till Sunday?'

She doesn't answer, but her expression does it for her.

I'm completely thrown now. Since Dad mentioned the doctor a couple of days ago I've been planning my escape route with meticulous care. Sunday was going to be the day I took the tragically crippled Sasha to meet the Texan faith-healer who was only going to be in London for a fleeting visit. But Dad must have read

95

my mind. That's why he's ambushing me with a mid-week visit. The crafty *bastard*.

'*Mum*! Why did you let him bring them? I'm not going through with this. *Get rid of them.*' I must sound a bit hysterical. Why not? I feel it.

'Calm down,' she says firmly. 'Actually, they're really nice people. It won't do any harm just to pop in and say hello, will it?'

'Yes, it will.' I'm picturing Dad lying in wait in the front room with a Greek priest primed to perform an instant ceremony – '*OK, I holding her down, you marrying her. Ignore the screaming. It mean she happy.*'

'I can't believe you're going along with this, Mum.'

'I'm not going along with anything. All we're doing is having a chat. Anyway, Dino isn't with them.'

'Who the hell's *Dino*?'

'He's the doctor.'

Dino the Doctor. Dino the bloody Dinosaur more like, because he'd have to be prehistoric to go along with the ancient ritual of selling daughters off to the highest bidder.

'It's just his parents,' Mum tells me. 'Nothing sinister's going on.'

I don't understand why Mum's humouring Dad and I can only hope that she's got a wicked plan up her sleeve, one even slyer than the turning-Theglou-into-Charlotte scheme. She's spent her entire marriage resisting Dad's occasional explosions of Greekness. She's also, thank goodness, spent the last four years throwing scorn at Dad's ongoing attempts to raise the topic of My Wedding. But I'm sensing a slight shift in her attitude here. I'm damned if I know what's changed, but something clearly has.

'C'mon, love,' she says, giving me a nudge in the

direction of the living room. 'They'll be going in a minute. It'll be fine.'

I decide to smother my panic and force myself to stay calm. What choice do I have?

'Look everyone, Charlotte's here,' she says as she steers my rigid frame into the room.

'Ah, Chaglotta,' Dad booms, 'you're home at last. Come mit George an' Maroulla Georgiou.'

They rise as one and I fix a smile to my face as I shake their hands. And I look at them. They're both tiny and round. With matching moustaches. Some gene pool. What hope for Doctor Dino?

We sit down and look at each other awkwardly. It's now that I notice Emily. She's squashed up on the sofa next to Maroulla, but now she stands to pour tea. She's playing the golden child to perfection, but she can't resist slipping me a sly smirk. She's loving this.

'So, you werk in gym?' Maroulla asks, managing to say *gym* as if it's down there with *brothel*. 'You late *every* night?' This question is loaded. Being late home is at the very bottom of the list of qualities required of a suitable wife – above being HIV positive, but below smoking crack.

'Oh yes, I'm late most nights,' I say, happy to create a lousy impression.

'Theglitsa in charge,' Dad announces, suddenly brimming with pride at his career-girl daughter.

'Dino be in charge soon,' George says, rising to the challenge – the irresistible *my-kid's-better-than-yours* routine. 'Betchou any day now he running whole of bats . . .'

Bats? What's he talking about? I thought he was a doctor.

'. . . Yes, they lucky to have him at the moment, Bats Hospital.'

Oh, he means *Barts*. I should have got that. I've had twenty-four years to work out this accent.

'The hours he werk,' George continues. 'Blimey. Still, they got lot of peoble to save, eh?' He sits back, smiling – obviously thinking he's won.

But he doesn't know my Dad: the man that has *never* lost an argument. At least not in his own mind. 'You think Charlotta's not saving the lives in gym?' he asks the room in general. 'If huff the peoble in hospital went gym, they woulden ending up in the hospital, would they?'

He's overcompensating wildly for all the years he's ridiculed the importance of staying fit. He shifts his huge frame as he polishes off the last pastry on his plate. 'She like Soobagirl! She chip off the old bloke. One day she gonna chenge the weld,' he proclaims, grabbing what he hopes to be The Final Word with both hands.

If you've spent any time with Greek dads, you'll know that this could go on. And on. But Maroulla pipes up, reminding us of the real reason they're here. This isn't a cosy get-together; it's a job interview. 'If she so busy chenging weld,' she says, 'how she gonna cook for family?'

Dad, of course, has the *final* Final Last Word already prepared: 'She so cleva she gonna do *both*.' He laughs and chinks glasses with George.

I should be bursting with joy at all this praise . . . But I'm not. My dad is acting like a car salesman and – guess what – I'm the car. Dad is lying about my mileage and talking up my features while George and Maroulla walk around me and kick my tyres. I feel as if I should have a big vinyl sticker plastered across my forehead proclaiming me DEAL OF THE WEEK.

'So, is big, this gym?' George asks.

'Is mussive,' Dad replies for me. 'Is very posh, very high-tegnical.'

I don't know how he's so informed all of a sudden because he's never visited me at work. This fact, by the way, is worth mentioning because his sandwich bar is in Covent Garden – ten minutes' walk from The Zone. Obviously he's never dropped in because he doesn't actually give a shit. Mind you, I can't complain. I hardly ever call in at his. 'Whass wrong with my food?' he asks on a regular basis. 'You no wanna taste the best chiz and piggle in the weld?' *Well, Dad, put like that . . . No.*

I listen to him doing a better job of selling The Zone than even our ultra-glossy brochure manages. Think I might leave now. Reckon I've sat here politely for long enough – don't want to give George and Maroulla the impression that I'm actually interested in their stupid son. I stand up as Dad starts on the complexities of yoga. His version anyway. 'Is no good for you ukchewally. Why you think Indian peoble funny colour? The yoga making their skin yellow.'

'I'm going for a bath,' I announce. 'Lovely to meet you.' No one's listening. They're too fascinated by Dad. Ordinarily, I'd stay for a laugh, but this is too good an opportunity to get the hell out of here.

I tiptoe out of the room, watched only by Emily.

I'm up to my neck in bubbles. The bath is the only bit of this house where anything like peace can be found. But even in here I can't escape completely. I can still hear them.

The door clicks open and Emily slides through the gap.

'Get lost, will you?' I yell as I rearrange a triangle of bubbles. 'God, can't anyone get any privacy round here?'

'Mum and me worked our butts off to get this place

tidy before they got here. *Without* your help,' she says as she sits down on the toilet.

She's got a point now I think about it. The place is incredibly tidy. What's going on? Because Mum and Emily never tidy.

'I didn't ask you to,' I say.

'Is Sasha walking yet?' she asks.

Sly bitch. She *knows*, I can tell. But it could be a bluff; I don't want to risk blowing my best ever cover-story by challenging her, so I just say, 'Piss off downstairs and suck up to Dad or whatever it is you're doing.'

'You should be down there getting to know your future *in-laws*.'

'Oh, go away you silly little—'

'Oh, now would you just look at what I've got here,' she says slyly. She's taking something out of her jeans pocket. 'Oh, look, it's your mobile. And, hey, look at this text.' She reads from the screen. '*Don't have to do it in bog*. I wonder what it could possibly mean?'

The sly, evil, conniving bitch!

She's got me. She has well and truly got me.

'Give me back my phone, you cow.' I have to use every ounce of willpower to stop myself from screaming.

'Sure,' she says, dangling it over the bath. 'So what exactly do you do in the bog? You gonna tell me or shall I go and ask Dad what he thinks?'

'If you drop that phone, I'll kill you.'

But I have to admit defeat when she's holding my life in the palm of her hand over a bath full of bubbles. She's won. *Again*. Why can't I ever learn?

'What do you want, Emily?' I say wearily.

'I'm a bit broke,' she says. 'A tenner would do.'

'In my purse.' What else can I say? She knows too much and ten quid for her silence is cheap.

100

'You're a star,' she says. She puts the mobile on the side and leaves as quietly as she arrived.

What a mad, stupid day.

I shut my eyes and sink into the water until I'm up to my nostrils. I wish I could shut out the noise. Why do Greeks have to shout everything? It's louder now because they've moved into the hall. At least that means they're leaving. 'Your house is so clin,' Maroulla is saying. 'How you keep so tidy? Inglish no' usually so clin.'

'Thanks, Maroulla, we try,' Mum replies, choosing not to mention that (a) she isn't technically English and (b) she doesn't try at all, as a rule. 'You've got to keep your standards up, haven't you?'

Excuse me, what standards? What's going on? Usually when Dad invites people round and suggests that Mum might, you know, pick up a duster, she gives him a weary *They can take us as they find us*. It's as if she's actually out to impress these people. Why would she want to do that?

It doesn't bear thinking about, so I don't. Instead I cast my mind back to lunchtime and the best shag in the history of sex. This works a treat until the gorgeous Karl transforms into the son of George and Maroulla Georgiou – i.e. Danny DeVito junior, only shorter, rounder and minus the charisma.

I snap my eyes open . . . And see a tiny chink of light.

Doctor Dino's non-appearance.

The no-show must mean that he thinks the idea of an arranged marriage is totally shit.

Well, I can only hope.

The water's cold now; my lovely, frothy bubbles have disintegrated into scum; my skin's so wrinkled and baggy that I could get two of me in it. But I can't get out of the bath because they're still at it in the hall and I don't want them to see me dart from bathroom to bedroom wrapped in a skimpy towel.

What is it with Greeks and goodbyes? They take even longer to bugger off than they do to arrive (and that can take an eternity). As soon as the coats go on hundreds of fresh topics suddenly materialise from nowhere. This one's been going on for at least an hour. By the sounds of it, Dad and George are making up for their years apart by reliving every second of their childhoods in our cramped, narrow hallway.

What's wrong with these people? Haven't they heard of those really handy phrases, like *It's been great catching up* and *Must do this again some time*? Don't they know I'm catching hypothermia up here?

Still The Bit With The Long Goodbye

Aaaaaaaagggggggggghhhhhhhhhhhhhhh!

It's gone two o'clock and *they're still at it.*

At least I'm in bed now – managed to escape from the bathroom without being spotted by doing a commando-style crawl along the landing. But there's no way I can sleep, not with Dad and George still reminiscing in voices loud enough for all our neighbours to enjoy the anecdotes.

I know Greek goodbyes always drag on, but this is ridiculous. At least they're no longer shouting. I can't hear every word but I'm picking up enough of a vibe to figure out that these guys *love* each other (and I mean that in a wholesome heterosexual way, of course. Actually, let me make something absolutely clear at this point: *there are no Greek homosexuals.* Got that? *None whatsoever.* George Michael? Wicked lies).

They're still talking about their schooldays. I reckon they're up to the age of twelve. Now, I know they lost touch when they were fifteen . . . Only three years left to cover, then. Perhaps they'll be done by four o'clock . . . Maybe five if they give us another telling of the absolutely *hilarious* one about cutting down their neighbour's olive tree. Please, God, no; we've had it three times already . . .

'. . . Thad remine me,' Dad booms, getting excited

all over again. 'You remembering the time I gedding the axe and we chobbing down Stavri's olive tree . . . ?'
Aaaaaaaaaaaaaaaagggggggggggggghhhhhhhhhhhhhhhh!

The Bit Where I'm Definitely *Not* Going To Do It

It's a well-known fact that Victoria Beckham wanted to be more famous than Daz. (Or Persil Automatic, or Ariel, or Tesco own label. Not sure which, but that's not the point.) Madonna was just as focused in her ambition: world domination, pure and simple. Two of the most successful women on the planet have one thing in common (apart, that is, from sexy husbands, cute kids and more money than they could burn in a very big bonfire). They both made a plan and *stuck to it*. Well, I thought, if they can do it . . .

This was *my* plan:

One: arrive at least fifteen minutes late. In the end I was only ten minutes behind schedule, but he still said, 'You're late,' as he opened the door. *So far, so good*, I thought.

Two: sit down and engage him in conversation. I'd prepared a variety of topics on the tube to South Ken. Dancing, pop music, his job (whatever that is), films, anything. I didn't mind.

My thinking was: finish the date we started yesterday lunchtime. Yesterday we did it arse about face – we did the end of the date bit first. Today we were going to go back to the beginning and do the pre-amble – the let's-get-to-know-each-other-before-we-rip-our-clothes-off stuff.

It worked brilliantly . . . Oh, for all of five minutes.

While he went off to the kitchen to get us a drink I sat down on a white sofa and admired the minimalism of his flat. Minimalism, my arse. More like can't-be-bothered-to-buy-any-furniture-ism. Even so, it was a pleasant change after the clutter of home.

He appeared after a couple of minutes carrying two glasses of something chilled and fizzy. 'Very flash,' I said, trying not to sound too impressed. I was impressed, though. Those daft, overpaid L'Oréal girls are so wrong. A glass of expensive champagne is what I'm worth, never mind a poxy bottle of shampoo.

As he sat down next to me I felt a sudden gush of self-consciousness. I was hardly dressed for a date. I was still wearing my work gear – Zone T-shirt and jogging shorts. The top was quite nice – tight and white with a sort of pink *Powerpuff Girls* logo on the front – but, like I said before, it's still a uniform. As he looked me up and down, I said, 'Sorry, I've been so busy I didn't have time to change out of my work stuff.'

That was when the plan went pear-shaped.

'I don't give a shit what you're wearing,' he said. 'Fucking *hell*, you really turn me on.' Then he was on top of me.

My head was saying, *Whoa, let's talk, find some areas of mutual interest other than shagging*, but my heart (not to mention this bit somewhere in the middle of my pelvis) wasn't agreeing.

So did I resist him? What do you think?

And here I am. Not resisting anything much.

And what I'm thinking is *so what?* This man not only has the most fantastic body I've ever seen, but he also knows exactly what to do with it. What else do I need to know? How many dates have I been on where I've pretended to be interested in his job in IT/the offside rule/that mad time he had with his mates in Ibiza, and then got back to his place and realised what a waste of time all that *being interested* was because he's too small/too quick/too rubbish for me to ever want to see him again? Because it doesn't matter what we say – forget the eyes, the personality, the sense of humour – the only thing that really counts is *thedoingit*. I make a vow: never again will I put myself through the job description/offside rule/Ibiza rubbish because this is what you really call *getting to know you*.

As we *get to know each other* a bit more, I'm tensing my legs so they feel as firm as possible. I'm also pulling my stomach in and squeezing my bottom tight. I swear, from now on I'm going to use all the facilities at work to transform my body into a temple – one that Karl will come and worship at any time he damn well likes.

'What's that for?' I say, involuntarily releasing all the clenched muscles I've been trying to impress him with. It's standing in the corner next to his wardrobe. A tripod with a camera fixed to it. Seen those before, but never in a guy's bedroom.

'What?' he asks, not stopping what he's doing.

'The camera.'

He gives me a little laugh, and it's as if he's laughing at me. 'I film myself sometimes.'

'Doing what?' I ask, getting an unpleasant feeling.

'I train in here. See those weights?' He points at some equipment in the other corner. 'And I rehearse in here too. Filming myself means I can play stuff back and see what works. That all right with you?'

'Sorry. Just took me by surprise, that's all. Are you

107

an actor or something?' *Now you're trying to get to know him?* I ask myself.

'Or something,' he replies, but we're not going to be doing any more talking because his mouth is otherwise engaged. And, actually, I couldn't give a damn what he does for a living as long as he doesn't stop what he's doing right now.

The Bit With The Long Shiny Poles

Zone Check. Whose crap idea was that? I hate it. It makes me feel like a traffic warden. I'm doing it now, walking round the entire building with a checklist, putting ticks in boxes. Towels in sauna? *Tick*. Loo roll in loo? *Tick*. Pool guards in attendance? Ditto gym instructors? *Tick, tick*. Basically, I'm a spy for Jamie. Not exactly covert operations. I mean, CIA blokes didn't sneak around Baghdad with great big bloody clipboards. Suicide bombers? *Tick*. Weapons of mass destruction? *Er, tick it anyway*.

Actually, I know whose idea Zone Check was. Lydia's. For a control freak like her it was the perfect opportunity to catch people out. The days she came back from her tour with half a dozen scalps dangling from her clipboard were the times she was truly happy. She once fired this poor trainee lifeguard for walking around the pool deck with splash marks on his trainers. I ask you . . .

Lydia!

My God, how that woman has turned. From Jamie's obedient spy to the woman that wants him dead. And from the bitch that loved to make my life hell – she even picked on my *socks*, for Christ's sake – to my new best friend. I had a call from her yesterday. It went like this:

'Charlie, I had to call and tell you how pleased I am for you.'

'Really?' I couldn't keep the surprise out of my voice.

'*Absolutely*. I know we didn't always see things the same way . . .'

No one on this planet sees things quite the same way as you, Lydia.

'. . . but if anyone deserves my job it's you.'

'Really?' I couldn't help repeating. Let that be a lesson, people. The next time your boss is bollocking you for the wrong attitude/posture/socks/whatever, remember, they're only doing it because they see *ideal management material*. A definite sign that you're on your way up, and *not*, as you might have suspected, because you're completely shit and they totally hate you.

'Obviously, I'm devastated about the way things ended,' she went on, 'but I bear no ill will towards you, Charlie. Congratulations. And good luck . . . You'll need it working for that bastard. How could he be so cruel? Firing me . . . for my . . . *condition*.'

I felt terrible at that point. Remember, I'd spent all the time I'd worked with her making jokes about her . . . *condition*. 'I'm sorry, Lydia,' I mumbled as she sniffed slightly dramatically.

'I'll be OK,' she said, pulling herself together. 'I've got a very good lawyer. Between you and me he says he's never seen a clearer case of discrimination in the workplace.'

'Really?' I said – *again*. I didn't know what else to say. She was right. It wasn't fair. Much as I hated her, you can't go round firing people for being cross-eyed. If Jamie had told her she had to go because she was an officious, snotty-nosed bitch, well, *that* would've been perfectly reasonable, but not for her . . . *condition*. But I couldn't tell her she was right because Jamie was still my boss. Besides, he'd never done me any harm.

Just the opposite; he'd thought I was *ideal management material* – or at least the closest he could get the night he sacked Lydia.

'Let's be honest, Charlie,' she said. 'Jamie's prejudices are way beyond a joke. Remember Fiona?'

Poor Fiona. How could I forget her? She used to look after the sauna. One day she turned a tap the wrong way and got a blast of steam in the face. It left her with a big scar on her cheek that we all found hard to look at. Except for Daniel. He couldn't take his eyes off it. He reckoned it was shaped like Italy – he wanted to get a felt-tip and do a little dot for Milan.

'Jamie flipped when she came back after the accident,' Lydia went on. 'Ranted about how members would desert in droves when they saw her. You have no idea how hard it was to persuade him not to sack her. In the end it was only my determination to do the right thing that kept her here. Face it, Charlie. Jamie's attitude stinks.'

Silently I had to agree with her. For all his good points – and I could think of at least . . . one – Jamie is appalling. He can't bear any kind of . . . er . . . *disfigurement*. Scars, rolls of fat, missing limbs, whatever. In his ideal world everyone in The Zone would be a perfect ten. In the real world he can't tolerate anyone less than an eight.

'Just pray nothing ever marks *you*, Charlie,' Lydia concluded.

I nervously fingered the zit that had erupted on the side of my nose and wondered if it was a firing offence. 'Maybe I can work on him,' I said optimistically. 'Try to sort of re-educate him or something.'

She snorted down the phone.

'Well I don't know what else I can do, Lydia.'

'There is something,' she said quietly, and I had a

sudden suspicion we were getting to the real point of her phone call. 'There's an email he sent me at the time of Fiona's accident. It was shocking – all his prejudices laid out in black and white. I never trashed it. It's still on the Mac in my— *your* office . . . You could run it off and send it to me.'

'I'm sorry, I can't do that,' I said.

'Oh.' She sounded both surprised and disappointed. 'Look, would you have grassed him up when you were here?'

'That's not the point—'

'I'm really sorry,' I said lamely. I was desperate to give her something, though. Let her know that I wasn't simply a spineless flunky in Jamie's fascist regime. Well, not *just* that anyway. I'm multi-dimensional. Sort of part spineless flunky, but part funky studio manager changing the world in small steps type of person too. 'Look, Lydia, there are things I can do,' I said firmly. 'I'm in charge now. Daniel and I are changing things already. We signed up this really fat girl the other day.' Like it was a deliberate policy decision.

'Good for you,' she said with a heavy sigh. Then, 'If you won't . . . *can't* help me, I won't waste any more of your time. Good luck, Charlie. And don't take it too badly.'

'What's that?'

'The fact that everyone ends up hating the boss, i.e. you, eventually.' Then she hung up.

I felt like shit. All these years I'd been going along with Jamie's body fascism, tittering with Daniel at anyone that wasn't Zone-shaped and not giving it any serious thought at all. I decided I had to see this email. I sat down at the computer and searched through the folders. It didn't take long to find.

```
Lydia — thoughts on the Fiona situ-
ation. I can't run the risk of her
suing but we can't have her scar-
ing the punters either. People don't
bung us 2 grand a year to look at
a runaway from a serious-burns unit.
More to the point, I don't want to
have to look at her when I go for
a steam. Couldn't we shift her to
some backroom job? Preferably a room
where the light stays off — Jamie
```

Lydia was right. It was shocking.

But Lydia wasn't being entirely straight with me. As I recall, not long after the accident Fiona did get moved to back-of-house. OK, it might have been Jamie's idea, but Lydia must have made it happen. Jamie doesn't get his hands dirty with stuff like that. Cruel as Jamie is, Lydia was just as bad, and it was a bit late for her to get all preachy about it – just because she'd been the victim of the Fiona treatment herself.

I swore, there and then, that there was no way in the world I would ever, ever do a thing like that.

As for her snidey little dig about everyone inevitably hating the boss ... Well, that was just a snidey little dig. Not even worth thinking about.

It's early afternoon now and I'm finishing my second Zone Check of the day. Jamie's orders. Everything has to be immaculate, he says, because we've got the C4 production team coming in to give the place a once-over – see where they can stick their cameras, stuff like that. That's not all. We're having a visit from royalty. Not Prince Charles or Wills or anyone. The real deal. Pop Royalty. Also known as Blaize.

As I get back to reception I see the first of her dancers – the chosen few – drifting into the building. They'll spend an hour or so warming up in Studio Four before Her Royal Blaizeness arrives.

'Ticked all your little boxes?' Daniel asks.

'Uh-huh,' I say. 'Signed up any you-know-whats while I was gone?'

'No, but I did do a heavy sell on a really ugly bloke with a false hand. He'll be in later with his credit card.'

'Excellent work,' I say. 'Keep it up.'

'Yes, oh mistress.'

I flinch. Ever since Lydia's remark, I feel a slight sting every time Daniel makes a *you're-the-boss-and-I'm-the-slave* dig. If I think about it, I'm getting them all the time these days. He never seemed the least bit ambitious, but why shouldn't he want the top job? After all, we're the same age and we started at the same time. Perhaps if Jamie had chosen him rather than me, I'd be feeling miffed now . . .

No, no, *no*, I'm being paranoid. This is Daniel we're talking about, the piss-taker supreme. He's my best mate; he couldn't possibly resent me.

The doors slide open and Jenna Mason makes her entrance, sweeping towards us regally – reminding us that if Blaize is the princess then she is the queen. 'Hi, Jen,' I call out chummily, knowing full well she hates being called that. 'You're in Four again. Some of your dancers are already here.'

She doesn't even stop. 'Just pray the aircon doesn't conk out again,' she says. 'Today I'm gonna make them *sweat*.'

I remember the near riot in reception not so long ago. All those dancers dragged in at the crack of dawn just to satisfy Jenna's massive ego. 'No worries, it's fixed,' I say, adding, 'you spoilt cow', just as the lift doors close on her. 'Daniel, if you ever catch me kissing her arse, do me a favour and kill me.'

'Happily . . . Talking of arses and kissing, how's it going with Superschlong?' he asks.

'Oh, you know, fine,' I say, dreamily thinking back to last night – and I used to think multiple orgasms were invented by journalists to flog women's magazines.

'So, tell me about him. What's he do for a living?'

Damn. I wish he hadn't asked that. I'm still not sure how Karl earns a living. I've been to his flat five times since D-Day (Disabled-loo Day to you and me) and we still haven't *talked* as such. We've made plenty of noise at his flat, but not much of it was what you'd call making conversation. God, I still don't even know his surname.

'He's . . . He's . . .'

'You haven't a clue, have you?'

I shake my head.

'You're getting as bad as me. Once, I was seeing this guy for over a month and after we finished I realised the only thing I knew about him was his phone number. I couldn't even describe his face, but I could still draw you a map of the veins on his knob.'

'Thanks, Daniel. I think you'd have made the point just as well if you'd stopped at the phone number.'

The lift opens and Rebecca steps out. 'Steve wants the sound up on the tellies,' she says. 'Reckons he can't hear a thing up there.'

'Tell him to stop yelling then,' Daniel says, picking up the remote and raising the volume on VH1's Kylie special to disco levels.

The doors open and a deliveryman comes in. 'We're here to fit these poles,' he says, sauntering up to the desk.

Just as I say, 'Sorry, what poles?' the doors swoosh open and reception fills with more deliverymen. Each is carrying a ten-foot pole-shaped thing between them that's covered in that protective stuff you just have to get your hands on in order to spend the rest of the day popping. Their leader peers at his clipboard and reads, 'Three-metre chromium rods to be erected and secured by end of play. Studio Two it says here,' he shouts, straining to be heard above Kylie's 'I Should Be So Lucky'.

I don't believe it. Pole-dancing classes. It's got to be. Jamie didn't mention it, but I'm discovering that as the person, you know, *in charge* round here, I'm the last one to find out anything. Pole dancing is all the rage. The best thing since the last new thing. At least until the next new thing comes along in about . . . oh, a couple of weeks. God, I'm getting cynical, but I've seen more exercise fads come and go than I have useless boy-bands. Personally, I can't see the point of coiling your legs round a chilly metal pole and slithering up and down like a circus contortionist, wearing only thigh-length boots and a minuscule thong . . . *Duh*! What am I talking about? Of course I can see the point – there are men out there who are happy to part with a month's mortgage to gawk at a metal pole, just so long as it comes equipped with a semi-naked woman displaying her fallopian tubes.

'You'd better take them up,' I say. 'It's on the first floor.'

The man thrusts his clipboard at me. 'Whack your signature at the bottom, would you?'

As I scribble my name, I feel as if I'm signing Sasha's death warrant. But why am I worrying about her when she doesn't seem to give a shit? She's only taught two classes since we met for lunch and they each had just three people in them. I've been nagging her to do something with her dance training, but she's not interested. It's all Ben, Ben, Ben. Any ambition she may have had has been refocused on him. Now Kylie's crooning 'Can't get you out of my head'. That's about the size of it. Oh well, at least she's happy.

Maybe I should show some enthusiasm for her job in Zone Clone. OK, so it's only a clothes shop, but at least it's at The Zone. Yes, maybe I'll do that and encourage her to draw a line under her classes. After all, who's going to want to do boring old aerobics now there are poles to be shimmied up?

'Look who's here,' Daniel says, snapping me from my contemplation.

I look up and immediately look back down, checking my top for juice stains, my bum for VPL, my fingers for missing nail-extensions. Then I take a deep breath and attempt to look the coolest, couldn't-care-less-est I've ever looked in my life. 'Hi, Karl,' I say. 'This is a surprise.'

The cool thing is quite hard to maintain because inside my heart is doing 'The Locomotion' along with Kylie. *I knew he wouldn't be able to keep away, I just knew it!*

'Yo, Charlie,' he says, but just as he's about to vault across the desk, sweep me passionately into his arms and give me a full-on mouth-to-mouth kiss (because I'm *certain* that's what he wants to do), he's distracted by the commotion behind him. Blaize has arrived.

Wouldn't you just know it? Bloody pop stars. Always turning up when they're not wanted.

She's surrounded by her entourage. There's Julie with the Anastacia specs, a bloke the size of a football stadium who could only be a bodyguard (or possibly a football stadium) and a couple of squirrelly little things who I suppose must do the scurrying around. I can just about make out Blaize in the middle of them. She's prettier in real life. Shorter, but definitely sweeter.

I feel torn now. Part of me wants to gawk, but another part – the ultra-professional bit – is telling me I have to deal calmly and efficiently with her every pop-star whim, while yet another bit of me wants to grab Karl and drag him off to the nearest disabled bog for . . . You know what for. Best go with the ultra-pro bit for now. Karl will wait. Hopefully.

I walk round the desk and stand in the middle of reception as she approaches. 'Hello, welcome to The Zone,' I say, shoving my hand towards her. 'I'm Charlie, the studio manager. I'll take you up to the—'

I stop because she's ignoring me. My hand is left dangling in midair. What am I? Invisible? I glance in the mirror behind me to check I haven't suddenly mastered the art of miraculously disappearing. The dumb, open-mouthed expression looking back at me tells me not. Blaize sails straight by, dragging the entourage behind her, until she reaches Karl. What's going on here? I know he's pretty irresistible, but even I didn't stare dreamily into his eyes the first time I saw him. Now what's she doing? *Fuck*. She's *kissing* him. Hang on. She must *know* him. He never mentioned that he knew any pop stars.

But what did he mention? I ask myself.

Smooch over, she finally looks at me. 'It's OK, Karl can take me up.' She slips her arm through his and says, 'You know the way, yeah?'

'Yeah, we're in Four, aren't we?' He looks at me for confirmation and I make a strangled *nnngg* noise that's supposed to be *yes*. So much for being cool and professional. I'm standing here with my jaw hanging open like a total pillock. But – I'm sorry – *what the hell is going on?*

They turn towards the lift and all I can do is stand and watch.

Just before the lift door shuts, Karl winks at me.
Bastard.

That was fifteen minutes ago.

'Where the fuck's Rebecca?' I snap.

Being the consummate professional, I sent her to Studio Four to get a refreshments order . . . OK, I sent her to spy.

'I don't know why you bothered,' Daniel says. 'I'm telling you, he's one of her dancers. He *must* be.'

He's almost certainly right, but I still want confirmation. And, of course, I want to know if he does more than just dance with her.

The lift opens and Rebecca scurries out.

'Well?' I say.

'They definitely know each other,' she says.

'That's pretty bloody obvious. What's he *doing* up there?'

'He's standing next to her and he's doing these moves.' She wiggles her hips and jerks her arms about a bit. 'And when Jenna says *five, six, seven, eight* he's the first one to—'

'Told you,' Daniel says.

Knowing it doesn't make me feel any better though, and I slump on the desk. I feel Daniel's arm go around my shoulder. 'Look, don't worry,' he says. 'All that touchy-feely stuff doesn't mean anything. It's what pop stars and dancers do. Anyway, she's not nearly as pretty as you.'

'Bollocks. She's fucking gorgeous. And she's had *two* number-ones.'

'Right, I've got a plan,' he announces decisively. 'Get a pen and paper, Becks. You'll need to take notes.'

Rebecca grabs a Zone pad and stands ready.

'OK, it's two thirty now. If we're quick we can just about do this . . .'

Rebecca looks excited. And I must admit I'm a tiny bit intrigued.

'First, Charlie, you have to cut a demo. There's a cassette player in the office. We'll use that . . .'

Oh, it's one of his stupid plans.

119

'. . . Then Becks can run the tape over to Simon Cowell's office. You'll have a deal by teatime, you can record the single tomorrow, *Top of the Pops* on Friday, number one on Sunday. Blaize won't know what's hit her.'

'That's *brilliant*,' Rebecca whoops. 'What song are you gonna do, Charlie?'

I didn't get to see Karl again. He left when I was busy with the C4 people. I had to take them round the building and pretend to anyone who was curious that they were in to measure up for new air conditioning – the TV documentary is still Jamie's and my big secret.

I did send Karl a text:

HUNG LIKE A DARK HORSE

Pretty clever, I thought, and a little bit rude without so much as a hint of desperation. He didn't reply. But I'm honestly not bothered. *Honestly*. If he calls, he calls, and if he doesn't I'll survive. It's not like he's Mr Right or anything. Well, actually, he might be. I still don't know his surname, do I?

It's drizzling outside Wood Green tube station as I set off for home. I hope this rain doesn't make my roots frizz.

Talking of Mr Right, there hasn't been any more mention of Doctor Dino since his parents visited. The planned Sunday lunch never happened. Didn't even get talked about. Maybe Dad has gone off the idea or perhaps the Georgious couldn't stand the sight of me. Either way, it suits me fine.

It's seven twenty-five. I'm early tonight. Plenty of time to have a shower before *Celebrity Millionaire*. How sad. Saturday night and I'm in for a night of nonstop TV. I must be turning into my mother. Oh well, that's not so bad. It's when I start turning into Dad I'll need to worry.

I open the front door and I'm hit by the sight and sound of Dad screaming on the phone. He's having another row. He holds a *halt right there* hand out at me so I can't move. He wants an audience for this one.

'Wotchew mean, *spik Inglish*? I um spikking Inglish! I telling you I want the order *delivering*. Whass wrong with you? This twenty century, even the women delivering the babies at home and you cunt even—'

His great line about home births is cut short and he drops his free arm as he stoops to listen. Apparently, stooping enables you to hear more easily, and he's almost doubled over now. He looks up at me and points at the receiver as if he's talking to an idiot and we're in on this together. *Leave me out of it, Dad,* I'm thinking as I try to find an escape route. *If you want to go picking fights with the local Greek restaurant, that's your prerogative. I just want to watch TV for a bit before I go to bed.*

'You lissen to me . . . No, you *lissen* . . . Spik *Inglish*. I don' understand a werd you bluddy saying. I juss want you bring the Chow Men to my home. Is it too much to be usking?'

So it's the Chinese's turn tonight. Whatever. I'm done listening and I squeeze past him and head into the front room where Mum's making her way through a tube of Pringles. 'Will you please go and tell your father I've got twenty leaflets for Chinese, Indian, Pizza, Greek and bloody Lebanese takeaways that *do* deliveries in the bottom drawer in the kitchen? He's giving me a bloody headache.'

I don't have to (not that I was going to) because Dad has slammed down the phone and is stomping back into the front room.

121

'Stoobid bluddy peoble today. Anyone thinking they don' wanna making money. Bluddy forenners. They huven't godda cloo.'

'Oh, says Jimmy Englishman,' Mum quips without taking her eyes from the TV.

'Of coss am Inglish. If I was forenn, I'd be lazy, stoobid bustudd like the rest of 'em.'

'I told you the Jade Palace doesn't deliver,' Mum sighs. 'I know you. You're just in the mood for picking a fight.'

Dad sits down next to her and slides his arm round her shoulders. 'Who telling you I in the mood for fighting?' He gives her a sloppy kiss on the cheek. She pushes him away, pretending to be straining to watch the telly, but I can tell she's loving it. *Eurrgghh*. Do they have to?

I turn and trudge upstairs. Aren't girls supposed to see their boyfriends on a Saturday night? There hasn't been any word from Karl. But then, is Karl my boyfriend? My shag-mate? What is he? I have no idea. I definitely, *definitely* wouldn't call it love, but I do know I'm thinking about him all the time. That hardly a minute goes by when I don't picture his face and dream about the last time I saw him.

Up in my room I take my mobile from my bag and will it to flash up a text from Karl.

But that has nothing to do with love.

Got that?

Nothing.

The Bit With The Greeks
Bearing Gifts

Mmmm, Sunday morning.

I love waking up on a Sunday.

Looking at the alarm and not caring what time it is.

Stretching my arm across the bed and touching—

Aaggh!

How did that huge, naked man get in my bed?

And why doesn't this look anything like my bed?

Shit, it's all coming back to me now.

Last night. Sitting at home with Mum and Dad. Watching *Pop Idol* and listening to Dad contradict everything Pete Waterman said. Obviously it was *Dad* who'd masterminded a string of hits stretching back to the mid-eighties, while PW had spent the time cutting sarnies.

What was I doing there? Young, free, single (ish, if you consider Karl) and at home with Mum and Dad on a SATURDAY NIGHT? Even Emily had managed to escape. OK, only as far as the Shopping City where she'd be trying to work out if she had enough to go to the cinema *and* buy popcorn, but it beat what I was doing. Anything would beat having to listen to Dad say, 'Whass he tokking aboud? She sing beaudiful. Like the voice of the angel. *Ah beliv ah can flyyyyyyyyyyyyyy*,' after a performance that would have been jeered at a deaf-school karaoke night.

Then my mobile rang. I lunged for it, not caring who was calling. It could have been Lydia asking if I could help her with eyeball practice and I'd have seriously considered it. I stood up and took the call in the hall.

'Who was that?' Mum asked as I came back into the front room a couple of minutes later.

'Sasha,' I replied. 'I've got to go and see her.'

'What, you're helping her with physiowhatsit on a Saturday night?'

'No . . . She's . . . er . . . stuck.'

'What do you mean?'

'At the bottom of her garden. She went for some fresh air in her wheelchair and got kind of stuck . . . It's boggy. Don't wait up. She says she's sunk in quite deep.'

Ten minutes later I was dressed to murder. Tiny top, tinier mini and boots pointy enough to have your eye out if you're daft enough to be crawling around on the floor when I'm anywhere near. I ignored Mum's 'Are you sure those are suitable for digging?' as I flew out of the door.

Of course it wasn't Sash on the phone. It was Karl. After his pop-star snog right in front of me, I should have told him to go fuck himself. But there I was sprinting for a tube to South Ken, where, with any luck, Karl fucking *himself* would not be necessary.

So *he's* the huge, naked guy lying two feet away from me now. Obviously. But why am I still here in South Ken at – check bedside clock – ten twenty-seven in the morning? This wasn't supposed to happen. Must have drifted off when we finally got finished.

When we finally got finished. What time was that? Who cares, because it was incredible. Like we'd just invented sex and we didn't know what it was for, but we had to do it and do it and do it in case we never got to do it again.

I look at Karl asleep beside me. Exhausted? I doubt it. The man has *stamina*. I climb out of bed and head for the bathroom. God, I don't even know where it is. I walk down the corridor and try the first door I come to. Locked. Ooh, very mysterious. I try another and I'm ambushed by a stack of fluffy towels that tumble off a shelf. That'd be the airing cupboard then. The next door I try is the bathroom. I go to the wash-basin and run the tap. But I'm reluctant to wash. Like a fan who's just had her hand shaken and resolves never to clean it again. Only he did a lot more than shake my hand. I'm being soppy. Gotta clean up. I splash water onto my face and armpits. My mouth tastes horrible. No toothbrush, though. I look for Karl's . . . And that's when I spot it. A Louis Vuitton make-up purse on a shelf above the sink. I grab it and look inside. It's crammed – lipstick, eyeliner, mascara, foundation; a full girly set. Unless there's a side to Karl's sexuality that he hasn't yet revealed, this can only mean one thing.

How does it make me feel? It shouldn't bother me, should it? It's not as if we've made any promises to each other. We're not even officially *going out*. Love has got nothing to do with this . . . So why do I feel terrible?

I've got to get out of here. I head back to the bedroom. Karl is still asleep as I pick my clothes up from the floor. I dress silently, not wanting him to wake. Finally I'm done – tiny skirt, tiny top and tiny knickers; designed to go back on as quickly as they came off. I pick up my boots and bag and tiptoe towards the door . . . And a phone rings. It's coming from my bag. Karl rolls over, opens his eyes and looks

125

at me. I get my phone out and look at the display: HOME. Of *course*. I can always rely on my family to interfere with my personal life. I smile awkwardly at Karl and gesture that I'll take the call outside. I turn and scurry into his living room, where I press *answer*. 'What?' I snap.

'Where the hell are you, you *slag*,' Emily says.

'I'm at Sasha's. Where do you think?'

'Oh, I believe you. Millions wouldn't.'

'Look, Sasha's really ill. You've no idea how much help she needs.'

'Yeah, yeah, yeah. Anyway, you'd better get home. We're leaving for your nouna's soon.'

Shit. I'd completely forgotten. Lunch at my nouna's – that's Greek for godmother. Nounas are a big deal if you're Greek, a responsibility closer to the Don Corleone *Godfather* thing. You may wonder why, at the age of twenty-four, I don't just say *sod it* to Sunday lunch at hers. But you know what? I might spend my life making jokes at their expense, but there's a part of me that loves the Greek thing. The fuss, the noise, the outdated opinions, the mispronunciations, the whole lot. What can I say? It's in my genes. Well, half of them anyway.

And how could anyone not like it? They're warm, generous people and there's always tons of good food and, well, at the very least, a Greek Sunday lunch gives me loads to laugh about with Daniel on a Monday morning. And it could be worse. They could be dragging me off to meet Doctor Dino. Mercifully, there's been no mention of my . . . er . . . husband-to-be for a while. Obviously Dad has projected forward and pictured himself leading me up the aisle. I'm hand-cuffed to his wrist, a gag in my mouth, and he's realised it's not an *ideal* scenario. I knew he'd see sense.

I hang up on Emily just as Karl joins me in the living room. He's still naked, and from where I'm sitting his thing is waving at more or less eye level. It's almost impressive enough to make me forget that not only have I just found a make-up purse of dubious origin, but also that during the twenty minutes of conversation we managed to snatch between other stuff I *didn't* get to the bottom of his relationship with a certain pop star. The one who's had hits with 'Big Love' and 'Do It Like This'. When I was still a young innocent – ooh, all of a couple of weeks ago – those songs didn't hold much meaning, but now when I play them in my head all I can imagine is Karl, naked, glistening and bearing down hard.

Blaize and Karl.

Karl and Blaize.

Hmmm.

'How do you know her?' I managed to ask – fairly casually – as he set to work on me last night.

'Who?'

'Blaize.'

'Known her years. I danced on her first video,' he said, his mind not entirely on the conversation.

'Are you . . . um . . . close?' I asked, immediately wishing I hadn't.

'Quite,' he said with a golden grin, 'but she's never let me do this to her.' I yelped out loud at that point because I'd never let anyone do *that* to me either.

I look at him now and feel myself flush at the memory.

'Breakfast?' he says.

'No . . . I'd better . . . I'm supposed to be having lunch with my . . . With someone.'

He throws me a look of mock devastation and says, 'Tell me there isn't another guy.'

Hardly – though my nouna does have the facial hair.

'No, it's just, you know, family.'

He flops onto the sofa beside me. He pulls me towards him and kisses me, and I must admit, it's very, *very*— But, no, not now. I'll be in enough shit when I get home as it is. And then there's the make-up purse. That bothered me more than I want to admit. And now I think about it, it looked familiar. Where have I seen one of those before?

But why am I doing this to myself? It's not as if he's my *boy*friend. We're what Daniel would describe as fuck buddies. Of course he's had/has other women. The question is *when*? Last month? Last week? A few minutes before I arrived last night? The thought makes me feel nauseous.

I pull away from the kiss and say, 'I've got to go.'

'Shame.'

'I'll call you, yeah?' I pick up my bag and head for the door.

'No need,' he says. 'I'll be at The Zone virtually every day next week – the Blaize thing.'

Of course, how could I forget?

The Blaize thing.

I'm sitting in the back of Dad's Mercedes. All his life he's wanted a Merc and he finally got one about six months ago. It's over ten years old, rusty and rattly, and the radio doesn't work. But it's got a Mercedes badge on the front and that's all that matters. A couple of months ago we were driving to a wedding in Southgate and it broke down. While thick black smoke poured from the open bonnet and we waited for a tow truck, Dad, in his best suit, leaned debonairly on the roof, watching the passing traffic with a smug expression – '*Look at me. I godda Mercedes-Benz.*'

Not that he's looking smug now. I keep catching his

eye in the rear-view mirror. He's not a happy bunny.

Well, I was out all night, wasn't I? And when I crashed through the front door I wasn't dressed like his idea of a physiotherapist.

'Where you bin?' he yelled. 'We bin worry sick. Your mum, she want me to call the pliss.'

Mum, of course, couldn't have looked more relaxed if she'd swan-dived into a vat of ingredients at the Valium factory. The idea of her worrying about the whereabouts of her daughter when there's good stuff – or even complete rubbish – on the telly is plain ridiculous. The only reason she'd call the police is if her *TV Quick* went missing.

Dad hasn't said much since. This is the way it always goes. He knows I've had boyfriends and can probably guess that the times I say I'm staying with *a friend* are lies. He doesn't like it and would prefer it if we didn't talk about it. He *will* give me the silent treatment for a bit, though, just to let me know that he isn't happy.

He's doing the glaring thing now. Emily sits next to me. Every time I glance at her she mouths *you're in trurrrr-bull*, which makes me pinch her thigh really hard, which makes her kick my shin, which makes me mouth *piss off*, which makes her mouth *piss off yourself, fatso*, which makes me bend her little finger back until it almost touches her wrist . . . And so on. Because of the nine-year age gap we missed out on fighting in the back of the car when we were little. We're more than making up for it now.

We're driving through Friern Barnet on the way to Whetstone. Boring North London suburbs full of Greeks who've moved up from scuzzy old Wood Green. Like my nouna. She's a widow and she bought herself a three-bed semi when her husband died. She reckoned it was proof of His existence. God had provided her with a home in her time of need. She didn't mention a thing about the life-assurance policy. We're coming up to her turning now . . . and sailing straight past.

'Where're we going?' I ask.

'To see your nouna,' Dad says.

'You've missed her road.'

Silence. I'm smelling a rat.

'Dad?'

Silence. I look at Emily. She's smirking.

'*Mum?*'

'Your nouna's not at home today, love,' Mum says quietly.

'Where is she?' I ask, and I'm thinking hospital. I can't stand hospitals. Not because they're full of sick people; I'm not that cold and heartless . . . OK, it's because they're full of sick people.

'She at George and Maroulla's,' Dad snaps. 'We see her there. Whass the big deal?'

Emily is laughing openly now and I realise that I've been well and truly stitched up. 'I'm not marrying him, you know,' I yell. 'I'm not even going to talk to him.'

'Will you calm down,' Mum says. 'We're just going for lunch. No one's talking about *marriage*.'

'Why all the secrecy, then?' I demand.

'Is no secret,' Dad says. 'Change of planning, thass all. We gedding call last night when you go out . . . Dress like a *putana*.'

If he thinks calling me a prostitute is going to shut me up, well, he's right. Staying out all night was a *big* mistake on my part because he's got one over on me now. If I carry on this argument it's going to get extremely messy. Best to shut up and get the day over with.

*

130

We've pulled up outside a huge detached house in Totteridge, an area full of Greeks who've moved up from scuzzy old Whetstone. George's frock factory must be doing all right. They've got one of those crunchy gravel drives with room for six or seven cars. It's full already so we have to park on the street. I'm wondering who else has been invited as Dad opens the boot and takes out the dishes that Mum *made*. A pavlova and a black-cherry cheesecake. The only preparation she did was to take them out of the boxes Dad brought them home from the cash and carry in. He hands Emily and me the rest of the gifts we've brought. As he passes me various boxes of chocolates I get a whiff of him. He's drenched in Old Spice. When I got home this morning he was emptying the entire bottle onto his torso. I should have twigged then – the desserts, the gift mountain, the cologne – that this was going to be no ordinary day out at my godmother's.

I look at my watch: one fifteen. We're a respectable forty-five minutes early. It's a Greek thing. When you absolutely, positively have to be on time, you always, *always* arrive late. When it would be polite to arrive a few minutes on the late side, you get there the day before.

'I can't stay too long, you know,' I say. 'I'm supposed to be going into work later to help upgrade the computers.' This is rubbish, but I've got to give myself a get-out for when Dad settles down for his fiftieth game of backgammon and it looks as if we're actually moving in with the Georgious.

'Bluddy *werk*. Thass all I ever hearing from you,' Dad shouts. 'Why you cunt be like the other girls and be interesting in normal things?'

Are there really parents out there who actually *encourage* their daughters up the career ladder? Mine

131

have got me by the ankles, yanking me firmly back down, and I'm barely off the first rung.

Mum puts her hand on my arm and says, 'Go easy, Charlotte. Maroulla's been through a difficult time lately. Her dad had a stroke a couple of months ago.'

'Did he?' I say, feeling bad. 'How old is he?'

'Ninety-seven, I think.'

'Oh, right. So let me get this straight. A man of ninety-*seven* has a stroke and that's a big shock, is it?'

'*Charlotte*,' Mum hisses.

Weighed down like mules, we set off through the gate and up the drive. Emily's behind me. She's humming 'Here Comes the Bride'. I stop and bring my heel down on her toe really, *really* hard. Then I hiss, 'Just remember, *Gorry*, when all else fails I'm still bigger than you and I'll smack your stupid head in.'

She pokes her tongue out at me. *So* mature.

Dad rings the bell and I nearly die when the door opens.

'Mum, Dad, you're here.' It's my larger-than-large, pregnant Soulla-in-law. Georgina, four years old, hangs from her mother's thigh, scowling at us. That child's so spoilt she actually believes Disneyland Paris is her personal property and she only lets other kids go out of the kindness of her heart. Tony, my brother, stands behind them simpering. It looks as if he's going through every stage of his wife's pregnancy with her – well, he's matching her for weight gain, that's for sure. Poor Tony. He definitely inherited Dad's size and shape, and standing side by side they're more like twins than father and son. I can't believe how much Tony has aged since Georgina was born. More pertinently, I can't believe they've been invited as well.

My entire family surrounds me, happy to be here. As ever. I'm the odd one out. It seems that wherever

I go, whatever I do, I'm *always* the odd one out. I'm half of one thing, half of another and all of nothing. At home, I'm supposed to play the dutiful Greek daughter, but as dad will confirm, I'm rubbish at it. At work, I'm meant to be ultra-professional and in-control, but I feel as if I spend the whole time trying to catch up with the latest crisis. The Zone used to be a laugh: hanging out with Daniel and the girls, taking the piss, mucking about. But now I'm supposed to be the boss, I feel as if that's all changed. Ever since Lydia's they'll-all-end-up-hating-you barb, I've been getting increasingly paranoid. I'm scrutinising everyone now, working out if they stop talking when I enter the room because, obviously, if they do they must have been talking about *me*.

'Come in, come in,' Tony says as if he owns the place.

'Sorry we late. Traffig terribol,' Dad mumbles as we go into the hall and are joined by George and Maroulla, who more or less literally fly out of the front room. They're quickly followed by more people, mostly old, mostly women, all dressed in either head-to-toe black (the widows) or shiny, brightly patterned frocks (*'My husband's still alive – na, na, na, na, naaaa'*). A happy Maroulla begins with the introductions. 'This my sisters, Yirgoulla and Yianoulla . . . And thass Yianoulla's two dotters, Sodiroulla and Vasoulla.' Why add an ou when you can stick on a whole oulla?

I'm suffocating beneath the tidal waves of hugs and kisses that seem to be coming from all directions. When the introductions are finally over, the bodies move back and a space clears around us. It's Handover Time. The giving of gifts is a crucial part of the ritual of Greeks visiting Greeks. It almost requires a drum roll. You have to do it so it looks nonchalant ('Honestly, it's nothing . . . *really*') and at the same time employ a little bit of showmanship ('Though *obviously* I did go to quite a bit of trouble'). It's a tricky bit of body language and takes years of practice to get right.

Mum goes first, presenting the desserts to Maroulla with all the flair of a natural-born Greek. Emily's next with the potted chrysanthemums, plus two mixed bouquets (bought at a petrol station on the way, just in case only *three* plants made us look cheap). Then Dad with four bottles of wine, a carrier bag of beers and two three-litre barrels of Diet Coke. Finally it's my turn and I hand over the Milk Tray, Ferrero Rocher, Black Magic, Quality Street and Terry's All Gold.

Never let it be said we Charalambouses go anywhere empty-handed. If we were invited to a piss-up in a brewery, we'd still arrive with the contents of an off-licence.

'Thank you, thank you, you shoulden have,' Maroulla gushes, obviously impressed. She looks admiringly at the pavlova. 'Is lovely, Maev*ou*.' (Giving Maeve its original Greek pronunciation.) 'You muss tell me how you keeping your mering*ou*—' (Oh yes, the original Greek again.) '—so white. Mine is always going bluck.'

Mum bats away the compliment with an Oscar-winning 'It was nothing.' Gwyneth Paltrow could take lessons from her.

We're led into the front room, which is massive. A good job too because it's packed in there. This means another round of introductions. We're taken over to what looks like the oldest couple in the room, who have somehow been lowered into the squishiest sofa. Their eyes are half closed and their hands are clasped together on their laps. Are they even alive? No, really, I think someone should check. 'This my motha an' fatha,' Maroulla announces proudly, 'Yianis an' Eleni.' Mum gives me a shove towards them and I bend down for the kiss. They already smell of formaldehyde and she's got spiky hairs sticking out of her chinny-chin-chins. It's like kissing an embalmed tarantula. I can't take my eyes off her as Maroulla grabs a few more people to introduce us to.

Weird. In the last five minutes I've met every member of the Georgiou family, plus various hangers-on and – who knows? – possibly a couple of perfect strangers, but I haven't yet been introduced to The One.

No, silly, not Keanu (I wish).

Doctor Dino.

I'm wondering if the half-dead lady on the sofa might be the Oracle and she could maybe give me a quick prediction, when I see a bloke walking through the French windows that open onto the garden. This couldn't possibly be him. How can I be so certain? Well, he's over six-feet tall for a start and he's good-looking enough to actually be Keanu. His body couldn't possibly contain a single gene from the barrel-shaped George and Maroulla. So unless she nicked him from a pram parked outside the supermarket, this man is *not* Dino Georgiou.

You can imagine, then, that I'm just a little taken aback when Maroulla grabs him by the arm and drags him towards us. 'Dino, where you bin hiding? Come mit Theglitsa.'

Yup, she definitely called him Dino.

I'm not the only one in shock. I look at Emily, who has fallen into some kind of a swoon – the sort you see ten-year-old girls going into at Gareth Gates concerts. *Pathetic.* I don't care how gorgeous he is; you wouldn't catch me going dizzy over a bloke. And before you say *What about Karl?*, that's different. Completely not the same. At all.

Dino seems to be as embarrassed by all of this as I am. We stare at each other like a pair of idiots while Maroulla, George and my dad beam, radiating pride as if we're already married and have just announced we're expecting triplets. He smiles awkwardly and sticks his hand out, shaking mine firmly. 'Hi,' he says. 'So they finally got us in the same room.'

'Looks like they got everyone they know into the same room,' I say like the idiot smartarse I am. My words hang in the air like daggers pointing at his parents, and I feel like such a bitch. I try to smile, but it isn't happening. My facial muscles, as well as Emily's heart by the look of her, have gone into arrest.

'Oh, you know how it is. You're Greek, aren't you?' he says a little defensively.

'Only half,' I mumble.

'Yeah, but science has already proven the Greek half always dominates.'

He winks at me, and before I can deliver the wittiest punch line in the history of punch lines (because I *so* have one ready), he gets ambushed. He's being accosted by one of the -oullas I met earlier. 'Ah, Dino,' she says seriously, 'I wanna show you something I worrying aboud.' She reaches down, hikes up her billowing skirt and displays a bloated ankle. 'Is my leg. My doctor say is water inflation, but his a forrener. You cunt truss the forrreners. I think is maybe a *condishon*.'

That's the thing about Greeks; they've all got *condishons*, invariably terminal, and if they spot a doctor they're on him like a rash. Go to a Greek wedding and naturally you'll see a throng around the bride and groom . . . but if there's a doctor among the guests, the queue from *his* table will probably stretch out of the building. Dino bends down and prods a squishy

136

ankle that looks like it's retaining enough water to fill a paddling pool and I'm grateful for the chance to escape.

I turn away, but jump as a hand grabs my arm. It's George. 'Come with me. I wanna show you something,' he says excitedly. As he leads me from the room and up the staircase, I'm panicking. Really panicking. What's he thinking of, taking me upstairs alone? Oh God, oh my God . . .

. . . I think I'm going to be sick.

How disgusting can you get?

'Wotchew think?' George asks excitedly.

'It's . . . very . . . *colourful*,' I say, looking at myself in the bedroom's full-length mirror. Actually, apart from my head I can hardly see myself. My body is hidden by the vast shiny dress that I'm holding against it. It's pink, lilac and sunflower-yellow, fresh from George's factory. And now, well, it's *my* dress.

'I juss knowing you like,' he says triumphantly. 'I see it on rail at fucdory and I thinking *this is Theglottsa . . .*'

It may be Theglottsa, mate, but it certainly isn't Charlie.

'. . . When you bin in fushion as long as me, you gedding the eye. Is like sick sense. Go on, puddidon!'

'Oh, I think I'll save it, thanks . . . For something really, er, special.'

'*Ah*, very sensibull. No showing everyone or they oll wanting one!'

He whips the dress away from me and I jump as I get a jolt of electricity. God knows what it's made from, but it's so charged with static that my extensions are standing on end.

'Come, lez go huv dinner,' George says, taking my

137

arm again and pulling me towards the bedroom door. 'So, you like Dino?'

'He's . . . um . . . very . . .'

'I juss knew you hitting it off. When you being a fatha as long as me you knowing these things. Is like sick sense.'

Sick sense? *Hmm*, that's about right.

We get downstairs to find a team of the youngest, fittest male guests attempting to heave the two corpses – sorry, Maroulla's parents – up from the sofa. Outside in the hall there's a convoy of women scurrying from the kitchen with dishes of food. Even Emily, the delinquent teenager from Planet Lazy Arse, is helping. The food – tons of it, like Greek famine relief – is going onto the huge dining table at the far end of the open-plan living room. Beside it is a smaller table decorated with a Fimbles cloth. Funny, I haven't seen any children yet and they're essential for any Greek gathering. But now the French doors crash open and a dozen plump, dark and hairy tornadoes storm the room. Whose kids are they? Who cares? The way I feel right now, I just want to leave. I wonder if anyone would notice me sneaking out?

Before I have a chance to put the thought to the test, Maroulla grabs me and points to a chair at one end of the table. 'You sitting there,' she tells me. 'Next to Dino. First, you come help me in kitchen. We bring the chiggen and turkey and the lumb. And the biff. Also you helping me fix the potato salad and we see if the *maccaronia* is cooked . . . Oh my God, I hope I doing enough food.'

The talk round the table is loud and merry. To my left Dad is sounding off about my brother's celebrity

138

connections: 'Tony – his an accoundan you know.' *Yes, we bloody know.* 'His doing the books for the guy thad is selling the car to the guy thad is driving Terry Woggan into the Bee Bee Cee every day. Can you beliv? Terry *Woggan.*' This makes me seethe. I mean, never mind knowing a bloke who knows a bloke; I've probably *met* virtually everyone who's been in the charts in the last three years. I've arranged massages for two-thirds of the Sugababes and looked after Geri Halliwell's stupid dog while she was rehearsing. I've made tea for Sir Elton bloody John, close personal friend of both Lady Di and George Michael, Prince of the Greeks. Was Dad impressed? 'Elton John? Bluddy poofing bustudd.'

To my right, Mum and Maroulla are talking food. Mum feigns interest in Maroulla's recipe for stuffed vine-leaves and then heads for a patch of dangerously thin ice by saying, 'I must treat you to some of my Chinese chilli beef one of these days.' Dangerous because her recipe for Chinese chilli beef goes:

1. Pick up phone.
2. Dial Hong Kong Garden.
3. Order number 24.

At least I'm not having to make polite chit-chat with Dino. He's a safe ten feet away at the other end of the table. As I was staggering into the room under the weight of a turkey that was the actual size of Turkey, Emily was slipping surreptitiously into the seat designated for me. I'm looking at her now, gazing wide-eyed at Dino like the winner of a *Smash Hits* 'Lunch with Robbie Williams' competition. You know what? I could kiss her. Actually, *eurgh* to that. Maybe just shake her hand.

God knows what they're talking about. Dino catches me looking at him and gives me a smile. I wonder what the hell he's doing this for. Going along with his parents' Cilla (or should that be Coulla?) Black-style attempt to fix him up with a complete stranger. We can rule out the too-ugly-to-pull reason. So we're left with just two possibilities:

a) He's completely thick to the point of being educationally subnormal. The medical degree? Obviously bought for a few hundred quid from a made-up university in Texas or somewhere.
b) He's in the closet.

I look down at my plate and feel depressed. I usually enjoy these big lunches and accept them as an important part of my family life. I might not feel like I fit in as such, but at least the people are always welcoming and generous. And Dad can be a laugh when he's on form. Put him with a bunch of Greeks and he'll good-naturedly ridicule the lot of them. (And he wonders where I get it from?) It's always been OK because I've always had the other half of my life to escape to. The Zone is the place I go to have fun and good-naturedly ridicule everyone there. But since the promotion I don't seem to be having much of a laugh there either.

Still depressed, I look down at my plate and realise that, actually, I can't see it. It's hidden by a mountain of food. One of the -oullas ignored my protests and constructed Mount Everest for me. Where do I begin without starting an avalanche? I reach forward and nervously pluck a small black olive from the top of the heap. As I remove it I relax – there was a slight wobble, but no food in lap. I bite the olive in half and hear a sudden hush descend over the table. Everyone's staring at me.

'Whass wrong?' Maroulla gasps, gazing in horror at the tiny fragment of olive that's still held between my finger and thumb. 'You no like my cooking? . . . I go make something else. Maybe I pob some fish in the grill? You a vegetationist? You telling me and I making for you.'

'No, this is *lovely*,' I yelp, grabbing my knife and fork. If I don't want to be accused of having an eating disorder, I'm going to have to go for it. I pack my cheeks with food until I resemble a human hamster and attempt to chew . . .

This is going to be a long day.

I. Can't. Move.

Total paralysis the fast way: consume ten thousand calories in under fifteen minutes. Greeks don't savour their food. Eating is a race and was probably an Olympic event in ancient times.

Unable to do anything else, I half listen to my dad and George talk pregnancy with Soulla. A fine example of two old boys from the village effortlessly transforming themselves into New Men? Hardly. 'Is gonna be boy this time,' Dad says. It's not a hope; it's a demand.

'To be huving the boy very impordant,' George agrees. 'The one who carry the name. If you gedding it right you huving the boy first.' He looks at Georgina who is now a splattered mess of food on the kid's table. 'She juss pragdice, eh? Now you huv *boy*.'

'I really don't mind so long as it's healthy,' Soulla says through gritted teeth. Normally she's a vision of smarmy creepiness, so it's weird to see her irritated. Must be the hormones, plus the fact that it looks as if she's smuggling Maroulla's eighty-pound turkey down the front of her dress. Who invented pregnancy? What a crap idea.

'Of coss. *Healthy*,' Dad booms. 'A healthy boy.'

I feel someone slide into the empty seat next to mine. I look round to see one of the -oullas. 'My sista rilly liking you,' she says with a nod towards Maroulla who's stacking up plates. 'And Dino like you too.'

Really? I've barely spoken to him; what would give her that idea?

'You liking him?' she prods.

I look at his now empty seat – as is, for that matter, Emily's – and say, 'Yes. He's really . . . er . . . tall.'

She beams as if this translates to *I love him with a passion I didn't think possible* – and, God, my Greek is lousy so who knows? 'You liking children?' she asks.

'Um . . . No, not really. Can't stand them to be honest.'

Now, this obviously translates to *Yes, I can't wait to lie flat on my back and pop out babies* because she clasps my arm warmly and says, 'Good, good, the children is very impordant. How old you?'

I can almost see her mentally calculating the state of my ovaries. Next, I imagine, she'll expect me to stick my legs into a pair of stirrups and submit for a full internal. I feel sick. Really sick. I need to throw up for so many reasons, not least because I have enough food to stock a corner shop sitting in my stomach.

'You'll have to excuse me,' I say. I force my legs to work and haul myself to my feet. I stagger from the room and up the stairs. I reach the top and see the open bathroom door at the end of the long corridor. I set off towards it, but stop when I hear voices coming from a bedroom. Not just any old voices either. It's Emily and she's being shushed by someone. Then: 'I think we'd better go back downstairs.'

We? Who's *we*?

'OK, you go on. I'll just clean up . . . Be down in a minute,' says Dino.

That's right. *Dino*.

What the—

Before I can move the door opens and my sister and I are face to face. She looks stunned to see me, but the girl is good – I'll give her that – because she pulls herself together in an instant and says, 'Spying on me? You sad old cow.'

'What the hell are you playing at?' I ask, making a good job of sounding shocked. Inside, I'm thinking *Oh yes, this is all the ammo I need*.

'Nothing,' she says. 'Just got a bit of a headache. Came up for some peace and quiet, but you've spoilt it now.'

'*Liar*,' I hiss. If I know her, she's been doing her flirt routine on Dino and it looks like it might have worked. She's somehow managed to get him up here alone. And don't think I haven't noticed a distinct lack of the Passion Red she smeared over her fat lips in the car. I'm no detective, but it's a fair indication of what probably just took place in there. How could he? She's just a kid for God's sake.

Behind her Dino sits on the bed looking remarkably relaxed for a pervert. 'How's the head now, Emily?' he asks. 'The cranial massage usually works pretty quickly.'

Cranial massage. I thought that in my time I'd managed to come up with every lie possible, but that's a new one. As Emily simpers at him I don't know what to feel. Joy that she's got me off the hook – well, I'm hardly going to let Dad lumber me with a virtual paedophile, am I? – or disgust because my baby sister has been seduced by, well, a virtual paedophile.

Emily pushes past me and I'm left staring at Dino.

143

'She, er, had a headache,' he says awkwardly, rising from the bed.

'Yeah, right.'

'Look, don't blame Emily for what's happened.'

'What *has* happened then?' I ask.

'She . . . Look, it's not my place to say. You should talk to her. She's your sister, you should—'

Why am I still standing here? I don't want to hear this. I turn and flee to the bathroom. It's definitely time to throw up.

'So, you enjoy?' Dad asks as he starts the car. He doesn't wait for an answer. 'Lovely peoble. And Dino, very intelligen man. You like him, Charlotta?'

'I think he's going to be a big hit with our family,' I say, looking at Emily. Now that I've emptied my stomach I feel so much better. Never again will my sister be able to blackmail me, and judging by the slitty-eyed glare she's giving me, she knows it.

'Good, I knew you hitting it off. I telling you to truss me,' Dad says. 'I gedding you together again soon. You hardly huving the chance to spik to him today.'

'Oh, I got to know him plenty,' I say. 'By the way, I didn't see Nouna. Where was she?'

'Wotchew tokking aboud? Your nouna no invited.'

Why am I not surprised? Now that he thinks Dino and I have taken our first steps down the petal-strewn path leading to the altar, he feels he can abandon the big lie that got me here in the first place. He puts the car into gear and flicks the windscreen wipers on; it's chucking down. As he's about to pull away, someone bangs on my window. It's George, standing outside in the rain in his shirtsleeves, drenched. He's clutching a big carrier bag with a bit of shiny pink, lilac and sunflower-yellow fabric spilling out from the top.

144

'You forgedding your dress,' he pants, leaning in through the window.

OK, so it's never going to be up there with any of Halle Berry's red-carpet numbers, but George's smile is so sweet that now I feel like the most ungrateful, mean cow ever for hiding it behind a sofa.

The Bit Where Daniel Does It With The Director And I Do It With Forty-Five Northern Women

'Just leave the tray there, thanks, and shut the door on your way out,' I tell Rebecca the way Jamie usually tells me. Moving slowly, a trembling Rebecca carries the tray of juice and pastries across the room before lowering it carefully onto the table. When it goes down without a hitch she can't help giving me a triumphant smile – *yesss!* – she did it. She's rooted to the spot now, having forgotten the leaving-the-room bit of my instructions. I shoot her a look and she makes a hurried exit.

We're in the ground-floor meeting room. The one next to Zone Clone. Jamie is beside me while around the table sit half a dozen people from HyperReality, the production company that's making the documentary for Channel Four. All eyes move from the croissants and danishes to me like I'm Businesswoman of the Year. I've never been in a high-powered meeting before, let alone *chaired* one. But as Jamie said in the lift a few minutes ago, 'You're the studio manager, Charlie. It's your show.' So this is Girl Power. I *am* Management Spice.

I'm so excited I can hardly speak . . .

But I'm chairing this meeting so – *damn it* – I have to.

'Right, OK,' I say assertively, 'why don't we . . . er . . . kick things off by . . . um . . . Who wants a croissant?'

Oh yes, Anita Roddick herself couldn't have done it any better.

'So, tell us, Charlie,' says Big Boobs (oops, *must* start thinking of her as Claire Eastman, v. important producer bird), 'a typical Zone day.'

I think back to the morning I met her – the riot, the tantrums, Sasha's 'dumping' – and I wonder if it was typical . . . *Hmm*, probably.

'We don't have a typical day,' Jamie cuts in smoothly. 'But whatever happens, you can usually trust Charlie to fuck things up.'

Cue blushes (me) and laughter (everyone else).

We're an hour into the meeting. We've discussed pretty much everything: camera placement (everywhere except for Jamie's office and Daniel's broom cupboard), release forms (to be signed by everyone who crosses the threshold on filming day), pop stars (will there be any?) and my trailer (as in the one I'll be retiring to, in between my close-ups. Well, a girl can dream, can't she?)

Things are starting to break up now and one of the blokes – I think his name is John . . . or Jack – scrapes back his chair and says, 'I'm going to have one last recce, check out the best vantage points. Come on, Marco.'

Marco? I thought he was Michael. *Must* pay more attention in future.

Marco and John – or Jack – leave, and Claire leans across the table towards me, her breasts arriving several seconds ahead. 'This is going to be fantastic, Charlie, *amazing* . . . One thing I'd like you to do, though.'

147

'What's that?'

'Have a word with the staff. People tend either to freeze when they're being filmed, or they behave as if they're auditioning. They've got to block out the cameras, pretend they're not there,' she continues. 'Can I rely on you to keep things as real as possible?'

'Oh, I'm the real-est person you'll ever meet,' I say. 'After J.Lo, anyway.'

Despite the fact that it's not the funniest crack I've ever made, it gets a bigger laugh than Jamie's gag – even from Jamie, who only ever laughs at his own jokes. You can't blame the man for being excited. We might be used to stars using the place like it's their local corner shop and having camera crews trailing around after them, but there's never been anything like this. Now his *personal vision* is about to get the Hollywood treatment and he's gagging. Good for him. I am too.

'I take it you've organised security for the door?' Claire says.

I look at Jamie. Have we? Is that my job?

'However tightly we control things, word that we're filming will get out,' she explains. 'In our experience security is the only way to keep the influx at a manageable level, otherwise you are going to be inundated.'

'It won't be anything we can't handle,' Jamie tells her.

I picture Daniel and me ripping our hair out as Rebecca flees in tears. Six million people are in reception, clamouring for membership of the most famous fitness centre (sorry, Total Body Emporium) in the world. And Jamie stands in the middle of them yelling 'We can handle this!' to anyone who'll listen. It's going to be pure insanity, I know it, but I don't care; we're going to be *famous*.

'Thank God you're back,' Daniel says as I arrive in reception. 'Someone new to talk to at last.'

It's three thirty, the quietest time in a Zone day.

'Bored, are we?' I ask.

'I wish,' he says. 'It's Sasha. I don't think I can take any more. She's more loved-up than a Celine Dion album. If she leans on this desk and sighs *"Ben"* one more time, I don't know what I'll do.'

'C'mon, give her a break,' I say. 'She's in love; she's happy for once.'

He grips me hard by the shoulders and stares into my eyes. 'Read my lips, Charlie. I. AM. GOING. TO. HAVE. TO. KILL. HER. It's sick the way she gets so obsessed with people. First Jenna, then you, now it's flippin' Ben. *Je-sus.*'

I know Sasha isn't his favourite person, but it's not like him to be nasty. Well, not *this* nasty anyway. He does have a point, though. Sasha may not have been the world's most dynamic teacher, but at least she showed a hint of ambition back then. Since she met Ben, her only purpose is to get through a day in Zone Clone, then go home and wait for his call. It doesn't seem to bother her that her teaching career is dead. Her love life is alive and kicking and that's all that matters.

'You know her track record with blokes,' I say, feeling obliged to defend her again. 'Aren't you at least a little bit pleased that she's finally met someone?'

'Yes, yes, I'm happy for *everyone*. You've got your promotion, she's got her man, *great*. The Zone is one big, happy family. Hoo-bloody-rah!'

I feel my paranoia kick in. He hates me for getting Lydia's job, I know it. Lydia's comment is coming true.

Even though I'm trying really, really hard not to be bossy – not to be like her, in other words – everyone is going to despise me, starting with my best friend.

I can't bear it. We've got to talk about this. *Now*.

'Daniel, can we . . .'

I stop, feeling a lump in my throat. Got to fight it. Mustn't cry. I've got to have a proper grown-up conversation with him about this. The only thing that matters is sorting things out with the people you care about, and that takes open, honest discussion.

I start again. 'Daniel . . . er, I . . .'

And stop again.

'Oh God,' he says. 'I've upset you, haven't I? Come here.' He grabs me and hugs me so tight I can't breathe. 'I'm sorry. Just ignore me. Got out of bed the wrong side, that's all. Friends?'

'Friends,' I repeat, relieved.

I knew I could sort this out. Open, honest discussion. Works every time.

'So, aren't you going to ask me how the meeting went?' I ask.

'Darling, there's nothing you can tell me that Jerry hasn't already,' Daniel says with a camp yawn.

'Who the hell's Jerry?'

'The director, you pillock. The one you spent an hour having a *high-powered* meeting with.'

Must be the one I thought was John . . . or Jack. I don't know how Daniel does it. Is there anyone he doesn't get intimate with in less time than it takes to boil an egg?

'What did he tell you?' I ask.

'More like what didn't I tell him . . . I showed him the Mile High Club Lounge. I ended up giving him a demo of the room's possibilities . . . Just in case he's ever scouting for porn locations.'

'You did it? With the director? But he didn't look gay.'

'What do you expect, Charlie? Handlebar moustaches went out with the Village People.'

'I wish someone would tell Dino's mum that.'

Dino.

Nothing much was said about him when we got home yesterday. I'm sure Emily was up to something with him. Not sure what. Innocent flirting? A snog? It must have been something, otherwise why would Dino say I should talk to her? I'd have had it out with her if she hadn't stayed glued to Dad's side until bedtime. Still, I'll get my chance. When Dad casually tossed 'So, you wanna see Dino again?' into the conversation, I just smiled, shrugged and gave my sister a knowing wink. She looked terrified and hid behind Dad, while he took the fact that I wasn't putting up a fight as a clear indication that it must be love. He spent the rest of the evening with such a smug look on his face. But do you know what? So did I. Well, when it comes out that my *fiancé* is a child molester – and not just any old kid, but Dad's precious *Inglish Rose* – I reckon we might just be calling the wedding thing off. God, I'm so evil . . . But at least it'll teach him not to meddle in my life.

'I could lend her my Gillette Mach3,' Daniel says. 'It's the best an old Greek bird can get. Says so on the ad.'

'What are you on about?' I ask, my attention distracted by Sasha who's rushing towards us looking flushed. Please, Daniel, be nice to her.

She collapses onto the desk, panting. 'Charlie, can you come up to the caff for a quick herbal tea? I need a drink to calm down.'

'What's the matter?'

151

'I've been having telephone sex.'

'*Disgusting*,' says Daniel. 'Please tell me you moist-wiped the receiver when you finished.'

'Not sex *with* the telephone, stupid. Talking . . . you know . . . *dirty*.'

I'm too shocked to speak. What's happened to the girl? Not long ago she considered sex in a bed with the lights off to be a little bit pervy. Now she's doing it on the phone. This new bloke of hers must be very persuasive. I need to find out more and I look pleadingly at Daniel. 'Do you mind if I nip off for ten minutes?' I ask.

'You don't need my permission, boss lady. Go on up.'

Was that another little dig? No, I'm being paranoid. We just did the *friends again* thing, remember?

'How many times?' I ask quietly.

'Five . . . No, six,' Sasha replies.

'In how long?'

'Just over eight hours.'

'*Jesus*. I don't mean to get personal, but doesn't it hurt to walk?'

'Terribly,' she whispers, screwing up her face.

I've just sat through the tale of Sasha's Sunday. While I was getting stuffed with four different roasts and a wide selection of Greek side dishes, she was, well, getting stuffed . . . six times over. I know I was a bad girl on Saturday night, but she's making me feel about as wanton and hussy-like as Minnie Mouse.

'I just can't get enough of him,' she gabbles, blushing now and desperate to justify herself. 'Ben's completely opened my eyes.'

That's not all he's opened, girl.

'Anyway, my shift's over, so I'm going straight over there. He's really busy but he said he's just got to see me this afternoon.' She sighs and gazes into the distance. Then she says, 'It's definitely love. And you know what? I don't even know his surname yet!'

You're not the only one, I think. Karl *who*? This would be the ideal moment to tell Sasha about him and I'm just about to when I see HRH Baby Pink heading our way.

'Ooh, Jenna,' Sasha coos, going from lust-struck to star-struck in one smooth move. 'I hope she sits with us.'

Personally, I hope she sails straight past us and marches out of the window. But I put a smile on my two-faced face as she does indeed sit with us.

'Hi, girls. Gotta take the weight off. *Ex*hausted,' she says wearily, popping a can of Diet Coke. 'You wouldn't believe my day. Been talking to the Gurly-Wurly people.'

'*Wow*,' Sasha gasps.

'Who?' I say.

'New girl-band. Gonna be huge. It's their first *TOTP* next week and they need a routine.'

Gurly-Wurly. I ask you. Are there highly paid panels of experts at every record company whose sole job it is to dream up the most ridiculously mis-spelt names for these groups? Well, I've got some for them. How about Ph'ked? Whanquers? Jysem? Or what about Kantsing? Pratz? Wunminitwundas? And that's just off the top of my head.

'You're rehearsing them here?' I ask in my coolest professional voice, putting all thoughts of a career in the record biz from my mind. 'We're tight on studio space this week.'

'Not rehearsing them at all. Turned 'em down.'

'*Wow*.' (Sasha again.)

'I've got *way* too much on already. I've got to get Ms Dynamite back in shape and there's the Steps reunion thing and now there's Blaize . . . And of course there're my classes. I couldn't let my little girls down, could I?' she says, pinching a lump of Sasha's cheek.

Sasha, of course, giggles. I, of course, retch.

'You're *sooo* in demand, Jenna. It's *amazing*,' Sasha gushes. 'You're just the best teacher ever.'

'That's sweet of you, but teaching's the easy bit.'

I flinch on her behalf, but Sasha doesn't bat an eyelid.

'It's fitting everything in that's the nightmare,' Jenna goes on. 'Believe me, sweetheart, you do *not* want to be in my shoes. I don't know whether I'm coming or going half the time.'

Well, going would be preferable.

'And the Gurly-Wurly people have given me so much grief, but hey, it's just too bad. More important things to worry about,' she says dismissively before looking at me with her serious face. 'Charlie, Blaize is back in tomorrow. Can you *please* double-check the sound system?'

Of course, your majesty. Luckily I brought my toolkit in today just in case I should be asked to carry out technical checks on various bits of electrical equipment.

'The speakers were dodgy last Friday – made a horrible buzzing noise. I want everything *pumping* tomorrow. You should see the routine. Blaize *loves* it. Mind you, she's good. Picks things up so quickly. And she's got fantastic chemistry with her dancers. Her and Karl Benjamin. I know they're shagging in real life, but you should see them dance. You can practically see steam coming off them.'

Hang on, rewind, *rewind*. What did she say? The bastard *is* screwing Blaize. I *am* sharing a bloke with a *Smash Hits* readers' poll winner. I feel as if I've been whacked in the stomach with a baseball bat.

Something else. She said his surname is Benjamin.

Karl *Ben*jamin . . . Could it be? No, can't be possible. Too much of a stretch. As Jenna goes on about her fabulous choreography, my head is spinning. I look at Sasha who is simultaneously cooing at Jenna and scrabbling around in her bag, looking for something. After a moment she finds it: a small Louis Vuitton make-up purse.

I *knew* I'd seen it somewhere before.

This is too much.

Karl and Blaize. Sharing a bloke with a pop star. It's too surreal to get upset about, isn't it? Besides, in all the magazines I've read I have never come across advice on how to react when you discover your boyfriend is having it off with this month's chart sensation. It's way off the radar.

But Karl and *Sasha*. The girly mags have plenty to say about your boyfriend doing it with one of your mates. You're supposed to be devastated. Mad as hell. But I'm feeling very confused here. Did anyone say he was my boyfriend? I didn't even feel I had a right to ask him about the make-up purse when I found it yesterday.

God, my head's in a mess. I think back to yesterday morning. Me rolling out of his flat; half an hour later, Sasha rolling in. *Fuck*, what a piece of work. Did he even bother to shower between shifts? Disgusting. *Totally* disgusting.

What am I going to do about it? Well, I'm not going to see him again. *Obviously*. And I have to tell Sash . . . I suppose.

Or maybe I don't. I look at her chatting to Jenna, completely oblivious to the bomb that's just exploded right in the middle of us. Maybe I can just stop seeing him and never mention him and me . . . And him and a pop star. And him and God knows who else. No,

155

no, no, Sasha's my friend. I've *got* to tell her. But she'll go mad, won't she? After all, she was with him first and why would she believe me when I say that I had no idea? She'll most likely hate me. But it's got to be done.

Now would be the perfect opportunity. Jenna's just getting up to go. *Oh no,* Sasha's leaving too. For his place. *Fuck.* I'm lost for words – totally gobsmacked – as the pair of them blow me kisses and walk out of the caff. Got to pull myself together. Think, Charlie, *think.*

OK, first off, I'll talk to Daniel. He's had plenty of experience with complicated multiple-partner-type scenarios. He'll know how to handle it. Yes, I'll take a few deep breaths, and then find Daniel.

'Where the fuck have you been?' he snaps when I get back to the desk. 'Ten minutes, you said. It's been going mad down here.'

Reception is empty now and there are no bodies on the floor, so any insanity's been capably dealt with. But his mood is as black as it was earlier. 'Sorry, but you won't believe what's just happened,' I say.

'You've got to hire some extra staff,' he says, ignoring me.

'I'll talk to Jamie about it. But listen, I've got to tell you what's going on. You'll never believe—'

'Later, Charlie. There's something we've got to talk about.' He's gone from snappy to awkward. What's happening? 'We've got to find a way to deal with the Batley Weight Watchers.'

'The what?'

'There're forty-five of them. They're coming in for the five o'clock high impact.'

'That's Sasha's old class. It's cancelled.'

156

'I know. That's the problem.'

'Hang on. You've lost me. Who the hell are the Batley Weight Watchers?'

'Some women who're watching their weight and who come from Batley,' he says casually. 'It's near Leeds, I think.'

'And why are Weight Watchers from near Leeds coming here?'

'Because I booked them in.'

'Why?' I ask, completely baffled now.

'Remember the plan? Fill the place with blobbies and mutants. It was your suggestion, as I remember.'

'Yes, but the idea was to do it with *subtlety*. Not fifty at a time.'

'Look, it's only forty-five—'

Oh, that makes all the difference.

'—and they'll only be here for an hour. They're on a day trip, coming straight from Madame Tussaud's and off to the theatre afterwards so they can't hang about. Anyway, if Jamie spots them, tell him they're paying the full day-membership, plus the class fee, so he'll be well over a grand better off. That should ease the pain.'

'That's the least of our problems. We haven't got a bloody teacher. When did you take this booking, Daniel?'

'Couple of weeks ago, a week, can't remember.'

'Why didn't you tell me?'

'I'm sorry. I forgot all about it until the group leader called for directions ten minutes ago.'

'So you told her we didn't have a teacher, yeah?'

'No . . . Rebecca took the call.'

'Fuck,' I say. I look at my watch. Four thirty-five. They'll be here soon. 'Have you phoned round the relief list? There must be a spare teacher somewhere.'

He shakes his head.

'*Fuck* . . . Well, you'll just have to find a way of letting them down when they—'

I stop because Jamie is strolling up to the desk.

'What are you two looking so panic-stricken about?' he asks.

'Nothing,' I say, a touch too breezily. 'Just checking the schedules.'

'Good. The pole classes kick off tonight. What are the numbers looking like?'

I check the computer. 'Not bad. The studio's booked to capacity.'

And it is. Twenty-eight women who want to get fit the porn-star way.

'I knew it was an excellent idea,' he says, mentally doing the sums. Money, money, money – his three favourite words. I think of the Batley Weight Watchers and Daniel's reasoning. This gives me an idea.

'Anything that gets people in here, eh, Jamie?' I say. 'Keep revenues up and, er, all that.'

Daniel sees where I'm heading and gives me an encouraging nod.

Jamie laughs. 'That's exactly why I made you studio manager, Charlie. You've got the killer instinct of a natural-born entrepreneur.' He watches my face bleed of colour. Some killer instinct I've got, and he knows it. 'Now, I'm going to take Claire for a drink. Don't fuck up while I'm gone.'

I'm breathing a little easier now, because at least he won't be here when the coach arrives. What happens next is almost – but not quite – as bad. As he heads for the lift, the foyer doors swish open and Jacqueline sweeps in. What is it with her timing? It's as if she hides in the street, waiting for Jamie to appear before she makes her entrance. She bowls past him and waddles up to the desk. Jamie freezes, staring at her huge frame in disbelief. I glare at Daniel, who's trying to blend in with the wall behind me. 'You handle her,' I hiss. He comes forward meekly – because he's got so fucking much to be meek about right now – and fixes his face with a weak smile. Meanwhile, Jamie recovers his composure and heads back to the desk. For a moment it looks as if he's going to grab Jacqueline and march her off the premises, but he doesn't. Instead he glares at me and says, 'Can I see you in your office, Charlie?' The look on his face tells me that he's the only one round here with killer instinct.

'In case you'd forgotten,' Jamie snarls through clenched teeth, 'this is a Total Body Emporium. Not a fucking fat farm for the endangered fucking whale population.'

'She's an opera singer,' I say feebly. 'Quite famous, I think.'

'I don't care if she's the Three fucking Tenors in drag, I want her out of here. *Now*.'

'We can't kick her out. She's a member.'

'*Excuse me?*'

'Full platinum,' I add, hoping an appeal to his bank account will save my life. As his face heads towards purple I realise I'm a dead woman. Just as he's about to erupt, my office door swings open and two breasts come into the room, followed a moment later by their owner. 'Hi, the guy on the desk said you were in here,' Claire says cheerily. 'I'm not disturbing anything, am I?'

Only my execution.

'No, of course not,' Jamie says, switching from murderous to oily like a true pro.

'This place is amazing,' she gushes. 'I've just been watching the martial-arts class upstairs. It's like the set of *Kill Bill* in there.' She must mean Master Stan Lee's (*honestly*, that's what he calls himself) Tai Kwan Do session. 'We've *got* to get that on tape.'

'He's a class act is Master Lee. He could fell an oak with those deadly palms of his,' Jamie says, smiling but still managing to glare at me. 'One of my *better* hirings. C'mon, Claire, let's get that drink.'

I follow them back to reception and watch them walk out of the door. And as they disappear down the steps I breathe a mighty sigh of relief because – *finally* – something has gone right today. A great big coach is pulling up outside, and from the way it's sitting low on its suspension it can only be full of Batley's Weight Watchers.

But, God, I am such a fucking loser. It's occurred to me that if I'd known about this just fifteen minutes ago, I could have stopped Sasha from leaving and she could have taught this class. But, oh no, she's gone on a *love rendezvous* with that sneaky, conniving, three-timing snake-face.

Daniel is still at the desk with Jacqueline, who, judging from the flirty beam that's lighting up her face, clearly loves him – fat fag hag. 'Looks like you'll have forty-*six* for your high-impact class, Charlie,' he says breezily. 'Jacqueline will be joining you.'

'What do you mean, *my* high impact?'

He pulls me aside and whispers, 'I had this idea. You could teach it.'

I can't think of any proper words with which to answer this, so instead I just go 'Eurghh?' and raise my eyebrows really, really high.

'Look at them,' he says, gesturing towards the mob that's squeezing into reception. 'They've come all the way from Yorkshire for this. We can't turn them away. They'll be gutted.'

'Are you stark raving mad? I can't teach a class.'

'Course you can, Charlie. I've seen you strut your stuff. You're a natural. Anyway, it can't be *that* difficult.'

I want to kill him, but maybe, just maybe, Daniel's right. It can't be that hard, can it? I know what aerobics instructors do. They stand at the front and yell instructions in a happy, motivating manner. I can do that.

Can't I?

I'm in Studio Three. I'm trying to sort out some CDs while behind me the room fills up with several acres of acrylic and Lycra leisurewear. I'd better not get them involved in anything too thigh-chafing because the resulting static overload could be lethal.

I could so murder Daniel right now.

But first, I'd better try and get my head round what exactly I'm going to do with these ladies. I've been doing some of that deep-breathing nonsense Maya teaches in her yoga class and it seems to have calmed me down. I now have a plan. We'll start with some simple marching. Chuck in a bit of slow grapevine. Faster with the grapevine. Throw in some knee-lifts for variation, then back to a march for cool-down. Beginners' stuff.

Couldn't be simpler.

Easy-peasy.

Who am I kidding? I'm shitting myself. I found Sasha's old microphone headset thing and I'm wearing it now; feeling like Britney. I wish. If I had any of her moves, I wouldn't be standing here trying to remember exactly how the grapevine goes, would I?

The CDs are a mixture of old and new. I haven't a clue what to use. I'm about to slip one into the player and try to find something suitable when I feel a presence

161

at my shoulder. I turn round and see the adidas marquee containing Jacqueline. 'I do hope you'll be starting *soon*,' she says, looking up at the clock on the wall.

As she turns and walks away I look up too: five past four. *Shit*. Better get this show on the road. Sod trying to find something suitable. I put the first CD that comes to hand into the player and turn around.

And there they are. My forty-five milling, slightly excited Weight Watchers from Batley, plus one opera singer. It is the weirdest sight. How did this happen? Somehow, all these women, the sizes of whom are more commonly found in my other life – my family life – have found themselves in the privileged position of crossing over to the other side. My work life.

They're looking at me expectantly and I'm engulfed by stage fright. I feel like one of those poor idiots on *Pop Idol* quivering like a leaf before the judges, except I'm a thousand times worse off. While they've usually had the sense to do some basic groundwork and memorise a song, I have NO FUCKING MATERIAL! I could *so* rip out Daniel's liver and feed it to a pack of hungry, slavering—

There he is now, peeking through the window to my right. The bastard is *loving* my pain. I look at my women, who look back at me agog, like I'm Jane Fonda herself and we're about to give this thing called aerobics its very first try-out. 'One moment, ladies,' I say and march purposefully to the studio door. I pull it open and stick my head through the gap. 'What the fuck are you doing here?' I demand.

'Thought I'd watch for a bit. See the mistress at work,' he says with a smirk.

'You've left Rebecca on her own?' In other words, *fuck off, Daniel*.

'Becks'll be fine. Anyway, I thought you might need

me more.' He can't suppress the titter – anyone would think he was deliberately trying to destroy me. 'Hey, they're looking restless. Isn't it time you started?'

I give him my best evil look, then spin round and walk back inside. I reach the CD player and try to compose myself. I'm distracted by the banter behind me.

'A *proper* aerobics studio. Beats keep-fit in the church 'all.'

'All these mirrors – just like in your and Frank's bedroom, Sal.'

'I never knew you 'ad mirrors, you saucy cow.'

'It's nowt like that. 'E likes to be able to see 'imself on 'is rowing machine.'

''Ere, look at your arse, Lynn. Forget your thong, did you, love?'

Lynn twists round to inspect her knicker-line in the mirror and her forty-four mates dissolve into giggles. I don't think they get out much. I smile to myself and . . . relax. I mean, how hard can this be? It's not as if they're a bunch of LA hardbodies, honed to perfection by the finest personal training money can buy. They're from *Batley* – which may or may not be near Leeds, but is definitely *not* in California – and they usually do it in a church hall. It's going to be just fine.

I turn the headset on and tap it for sound. A screech of feedback fills the air. It makes my ears hurt, but at least it silences the room. Must remember: avoid feedback by speaking normally; DO NOT SHOUT.

Right, Charlie, stomach in, shoulders relaxed, and for God's sake smile. 'OK, ladies, first off, anyone with any injuries?' I'm impressed with myself. I remembered the question every teacher asks before a session.

'Not yet, dear,' squeaks a voice from the back, 'but give it time!'

163

Cue laughter.

You wouldn't catch any Zone pros coming out with that one and expecting to get a laugh – far too cool. No wonder Jamie has such an elitist attitude to our client list. God, listen to me. I haven't even started the routine and already I think I'm Paula bloody Abdul. That's OK, at least I've relaxed. Even my hands have stopped shaking. I could easily give Daniel the finger now. He's still peering through the window but now he's not the only one. He's been joined by one or two others, including Ruby the spin teacher. So what? Let them gawp – they might even learn something.

I press *play* and 'Cha Cha Slide' explodes from the speakers. *Perfect*. Must be a good omen.

'OK, some marching on the spot,' I call out. 'No, not yet, wait for the beat . . . Hold on, in a sec. I think the beat goes— Yes, now. *Now*!'

And we're off! Ninety-four knees pumping up and down, romper-stomper style. An army waging total war on cellulite.

Fantastic.

I'm doing it.

I'm teaching a class and it's going to be *brilliant*.

'Knees *up*, everyone!' I'm not even having to force a smile – I'm actually enjoying myself. Even Jacqueline – who looks like Mount Everest with adidas stripes down its sides – is managing to keep up. Amazing – they're all keeping perfect time. *Oops*, I'm not. Find the rhythm again, little shuffle of feet and . . . That's better. Good, no one even noticed.

Actually, those two to my left did. I didn't spot them before. I assumed everyone in here was rubbish, but now I can see them in action some of these women are pretty good. The one in the front row dressed in black could be the Northern Area Aerobics Champion for all

I know. She's even doing that professional breathing thing – goldfish lips, inhale, exhale.

Damn. Too much silence. Proper instructors yell peppy motivational advice every four beats, don't they? 'Keep breathing,' I call out. Then, without meaning to, I look at Lynn with the VPL as I say, 'Stomachs in.'

'It *is* bloody well in,' she shouts, and they all laugh and I do too. *Shit.* This makes me lose the beat again. Got to get it back quick. Stop marching, listen . . . Start again. Miss Northern Champ spotted my mistake again and she's giving me a bit of a sideways look. Mustn't be paranoid. She's standing to my side; how else is she going to look at me?

How long have we been marching? The track seems to have changed without me noticing. Fat Joe and Ashanti are asking us what love's got to do with it and I'm thinking this is a bit bloody slow. I'm still marching to the beat of 'Cha Cha Slide'. Some of the women are keeping time with me and others are following Ashanti. It's looking like two separate classes. Got to get us all doing the same thing at the same time, but, *God*, this music is r-e-a-l-l-y s-l-o-w. And I've got to keep shouting things out, haven't I?

'Fantastic, keep going,' I yell, and Sasha's headset drowns me out with a shriek of feedback. Smiles fade as several women make a big show of covering their ears and wincing – instead of, like me, politely pretending not to have noticed their eardrums being punctured.

Through the window, Daniel, Ruby and the rest of my growing audience are giggling behind their hands. No time to worry about them because Fat Joe and Ashanti are fading out and the next track is mixing through, which means we've been marching on the spot for around eight bloody minutes. Now it's Britney's 'Toxic', and – wouldn't you know it? – it's the sodding remix, the one that goes at a million miles an hour.

I catch myself in the mirror and, Jesus, I'm sweating. *Drenched*. It's pouring off me. God knows what this is going to do to my hair extensions, but I reckon that's the least of my worries. Everyone else seems bone dry, but I guess they're not stressed and on the verge of nervous breakdowns on account of not having a fucking clue what they're doing. Which idiot said this would be a doddle? It's my very worst nightmare.

My women are still marching, trying to catch up with Britney. I can hear their legs rubbing together and I can smell smoke from the friction. I'm going to have total meltdown soon. Better do something. *Quick*.

But what? Stop and find another track? How crap would that look? (As if I've spent the last ten minutes looking *professional*.) I'll just have to go along with Britney as if she's part of my master plan.

'Let's do something,' yells a panicky voice from the back.

'*Anything*,' adds another as sniggers wash round the studio like a Mexican wave.

'OK, any second now we're going into a grapevine,' I shout above the music, giving everyone another screech of feedback.

And suddenly we're all doing the grapevine. This is sort of a good thing . . . And also a bad thing because I forgot to tell them whether to go to the left or the right. They're all going in different directions and colliding like fairground bumper cars. Shit, what a *mess*.

'OK, OK . . . Let's all just stop . . . I said STOP . . . And pick up the grapevine again. This time to the *right* . . . Wait for the beat . . . hold on . . . OK, *NOW*!'

But I don't go with the beat, do I? No, I'm so busy yelling directions I set off too slow. Some of them are keeping time with the music, some are in time

166

with me. It's a total mish-mash in here and they're still colliding with each other, worse than before in fact. I can't look. Instead, my eyes are on Miss Northern Champ to my left and I'm trying to keep up with her because at least she looks like she knows what she's doing. My heart is pounding, my legs are killing me and I can't remember what to do with my arms, which are glued rigidly to my sides. I look ridiculous.

I glance at the wall clock. We've only been going eleven minutes. How the hell am I going to get through the next forty-nine? My mind is a total blank. The motivational bollocks has dried up and I can't even force myself to smile any more. I steal another glance at the window. Daniel has given up trying to hold it in and has collapsed into hysterics. Beside him, Ruby looks very, very worried.

Hang on. Why is she so concerned? Because as well as teaching spinning, she's a top professional aerobics instructor, that's why! Graduated first in her class at the bloody YMCA – probably got a doctorate in Step. So why is she out there looking *concerned* while I'm in here making a total bloody idiot of myself?

'Keep going everyone,' I call out, before turning and heading for the door. I pull it open and stick my sweat-soaked head into the fresh air outside. 'Ruby, can you please get your arse—' It's only when I hear the *arse* word reverberate around the studio behind me that I realise I'm still wearing the headset.

Ruby gets the message. She snatches the mic from my head and swings into action, stepping into the hell that is Studio Three. I collapse against the wall outside and listen to Ruby do her thing. 'OK, how are we doing, girls? Ready for hamstring curls? Follow me, after four, three, two, one . . . Good. Let's go, eight more and eight, seven, six . . .'

OK, so that's how you're meant to do it. I knew that, of course.

Daniel can't speak for laughing. Fat tears are rolling down his cheeks. *I* should be the one crying.

'You *bastard*, Daniel. Why didn't you tell me Ruby was free?'

'I had no idea she was coming in early. *Honestly* . . . Come here, your G-string's gone all wonky.'

As he bends down and fiddles with my arse I hit him hard across the back of the head and set off down the corridor. Behind me Ruby's cheery, confident voice easily drowns out Daniel's cries of pain. 'OK, *fan*tastic . . . Now try this. Shuffle *and* step *and* jump *and* turn. *Again*, shuffle *and* step . . .'

Who does she think she is? Paula bloody Abdul?

The Bit Where I'm Horribly, Wickedly, Unforgivably Bad

I can't believe I'm confessing this.

It did cross my mind to miss it out. We're only talking about one little evening, so it would only leave a small gap. Tiny really. Who'd notice? No one, that's who.

But then I thought that what I've done is so horribly awful, if I lie about it I'll feel even worse.

But I can't just come out with it either. Maybe if I explain it from the beginning, put it into some sort of context, it won't seem so bad. Still pretty bad, admittedly, but not *burn-the-witch!* bad.

So, from the top:

After the aerobics disaster I had a shower. It didn't wash away the bad vibe, though. I was steaming mad, literally. With Daniel, of course. After what he'd just put me through, he'd better be afraid. *Very* afraid. He'd never have dared pull a stunt like that on Lydia. Jamie was right about all that killer-instinct stuff. I decided that I was going to get myself some, even if it, well, killed me.

My mood grew worse when I got back to reception. Jarvis, the Zone Clone manager, was waiting for me: 'Hey, great class. I've got a brilliant title for your work-out video: *Charlie's Spaz-robics*.' Bloody hilarious. Good to know The Zone grapevine was thriving, unlike the one I'd just been trying to demonstrate.

It was only five thirty. I was supposed to be on till eight, but I threw on my jacket and made Daniel cover my late shift. 'This is just the start, matey,' I hissed as I left.

My plan was to go home and think. Firstly, about Sasha, me and the snake-face. And once I figured out how on earth I was going to handle that dog's dinner, I needed to come up with a way to sort out the mess with Daniel. I was convinced the aerobics class wasn't an accident; he wanted to crucify me. Why? Lydia's words were echoing round my head like an evil curse. Daniel – my best friend – *hated* me.

When I walked out of The Zone my rage grew worse. I was thinking that if I was still mad by the time I got home, then Emily had better watch out. That girl had so much explaining to do. *Cranial massage*. I ask you.

Just as I was about to dive down the steps into Piccadilly tube, my phone went off. I looked at the display: SLEAZY, SERIAL-SHAGGING SHIT-HEAD WHO THINKS THE SUN SHINES OUT OF HIS ARSE. All right, it didn't say that. It just said KARL, which is the short version. I was tempted to turn the phone off, but I was in the perfect frame of mind for a confrontation and who better to get it in the neck than Karl Benjamin? I pressed *answer*.

Three minutes later I was on the tube, heading towards South Ken rather than Wood Green. I wasn't going to Karl's for sex. Got that? I had Blaize on my mind. But only Blaize. You see, the fact that Karl had phoned more or less convinced me that he couldn't be doing it with Sasha. After all, hadn't she left work this afternoon and gone straight round to Ben's? If Ben was Karl, Karl would have been with Sasha and therefore he wouldn't have wanted to see me. Slightly confusing, but as the tube rattled along I was pretty sure I had it straight: Karl Benjamin and Ben Whatever were totally different people. For sure. Hundred per cent. Ninety, at least.

That didn't mean I wasn't still cross with him about Blaize.

I made things clear the moment he opened his front door. 'Karl,' I announced in a serious voice, 'we've got to talk.'

'Yeah,' he replied, rubbing his forehead in a serious sort of way, 'we do. There's some stuff I need to tell you.'

Now, this kind of threw me. He wanted to *talk*? He didn't do talking and he certainly didn't tell me stuff.

I followed him into his living room and sat down while he went to get us a drink. 'Coffee, please,' I shouted as he disappeared into his kitchen – I intended to stay sober.

He reappeared with a bottle of champagne. What is it with him and bubbly? Most single blokes keep a fridge full of beer (with a tiny space for a pint of sour milk and a microwave curry), but his was stocked like he expected a wedding reception to drop by at any minute. He popped the cork and poured us each a glass. Then he sat down and poured out his heart. Well, not exactly, but compared to his previous form, believe me, he poured.

'I wasn't upfront with you the other day, Charlie,' he said slowly. 'You know . . . about Blaize.'

He told me everything. He's known her for a year and they see each other (casually shag) whenever their schedules permit. He said he's sort of her personal trainer (casual shag) and that despite the pressures of *the biz* they've managed to stay incredibly close (when casually shagging).

OK, so maybe he didn't tell me *everything* and I had to figure out the bits in brackets by myself, but, hey, she's a star and he'd never betray a celebrity confidence, right?

When he'd finished he looked at me, waiting for me to pass judgement. I wasn't ready for that. His confession had knocked the wind out of my sails; I just didn't feel that angry about it any more. To be honest, I wasn't quite sure what I felt apart from slightly tipsy, so I played for time by asking, 'So, what have you been up to today?' I figured that if he had been shagging Sasha, that moment – with him being in a confessional mood and everything – would have been the time to tell me.

'I've been working out some choreography,' he said. 'I had an emergency call from some A&R guy at Sony. He wants me to get his new girl-band into shape for *Top of the Pops*. Bunch of useless kids.'

'They're not called Gurly-Wurly by any chance?'

'Hey, how d'you know that?'

I raised an eyebrow and said, 'I know more than you could ever imagine.'

He raised his right back at me. 'Right, so do you know how much I think about you when I'm not with you?'

I'd drunk a fair bit by then and was starting to float anyway, but when he said that – *damn it!* – I could hear my heart racing, birds singing, choirs of angels . . . I had to get a grip. I had to ask him the big one. I took a deep breath and said, 'Is there anyone else you want to tell me about?'

I was willing the answer to be no.

'No,' he said firmly.

I gave him the most sceptical glare I could manage after the best part of a bottle of champagne.

'*What*?' he protested. 'I've told you everything, I swear.'

The fact that he was letting me grill him without

telling me to fuck off was a good sign, wasn't it? Did it mean we had actually come to mean something to each other? Or was it that I was just too drunk to read anything right any more? I let him pour me another glass and had a final think. What evidence did I have? There was the make-up purse. I know LV is a bit more exclusive than M&S, but I figured that Sasha didn't have the only one in the world. There must be . . . oh, millions if you count all the really good fakes you can get. If I'd been a cop and Karl had been my prime suspect, the make-up purse wouldn't have been nearly enough to get a conviction.

But then there was his surname. *Ben*jamin. Obviously, I was just being stupid to have thought anything of it. But just to be absolutely, positively positive – as he poured me yet another glass – I asked, 'Does anyone ever call you Ben?'

'Why would they do that?'

Of course. Why would they? His name is Karl. How could I have been so dumb to think that anyone would call him Ben?

And that's when he made his move. He sat down next to me and put his arm around me. And, let me tell you, I was torn. A full-scale debate was raging inside my head. Part of me was screaming, *Don't let him do that, you slut. Aren't you going to at least say something about him shagging the pop star?* Another bit was saying, *Chill, man. It's been a stressful day and you don't know for sure he's shagging her anyway?* And yet another bit was giggling drunkenly and cooing, *Ooh, that's nice*, as he gently chewed my neck.

And as he worked his way up from neck to mouth for the snog, I remembered the other snippets of circumstantial evidence: the fact that both Karl and Ben were dancers; the evening he watched me do Jenna's class and

173

disappeared (because he saw Sash in there with me?); the
. . . the . . . I was sure there were some other things that
I couldn't quite remember in the heat of that particular
moment.

By the time his mouth was on mine, I'd completely
lost the plot (as well as two buttons on my top, which
had pinged across the room in the clinch) and that's
when I . . .

Oops, I did it again.

The Bit With The Rodent

'Cheap slag, cheap slag, cheap slag, cheap slag, cheap slag . . .'

That's what the wheels of the train are calling me as they clatter rhythmically over the track. They're dead right. This evening I've been the cheapest, slaggiest slag *ever*. You see, just to reassure myself that I hadn't done anything wrong – although I was *completely* certain that I hadn't – I called Sasha's mobile before I dived into South Ken tube.

'Hi, Sash, this a bad time?' I asked, hoping I was disturbing her and Ben at an intimate moment.

'No, I'm watching telly.'

'Oh, I thought you were round at Ben's,' I said, my heart sinking.

'I left hours ago. He had an appointment. But, Charlie, he is amazing. Even half an hour with him is, like, *out* of this *world* . . .'

As she went on about the wonder of Ben, I felt suddenly, horribly sober, my cosy theory that Karl and Ben were two completely different blokes shattered.

The train is slowing into Wood Green station and a murderous headache is beginning to pound at my temples. I pull myself out of my seat and check my watch – ten to nine. I'll be home in five minutes. Mum and Dad will be watching TV and Emily will be . . . I wonder where she'll be? Thinking about her sneakiness

175

yesterday makes me feel slightly better. At least I'm not the only Charalambous behaving badly.

As I slide my key into the lock I wonder who Dad is going to be arguing with tonight. How many more restaurants can he fall out with before Mum *has* to learn how to cook? But it's calm in the hallway. I take off my jacket and chuck it on top of the two coats hanging over the banister. Hang on, why are two huge and expensive coats that definitely don't belong to anyone living in this house hanging over the banister?

Well, it's screamingly bloody obvious, isn't it? Rather, it is when I go into the front room and see George and Maroulla.

'Hi guys,' I say. 'Long time, no see.'

'We was thinking juss the same,' chirps Maroulla. 'So we pobbing by for a piss of your fatha's delicious chogg'ledd kegg.'

Her not getting my razor-sharp wit – OK, my out-and-out sarcasm – makes me feel bad so I try to smile. 'Where's Em?' I ask, looking forward to a spot of therapeutic torture – her room or mine; I'm easy.

'She gone Ulisha's house doing the revishon,' Dad says as he slices into the world's biggest and stickiest chocolate gateau.

Ulisha— sorry, *Alicia* is Emily's best mate. She is also my sister's standard excuse. Homework at Alicia's is her equivalent of my physio at Sasha's. Complete bollocks, in other words; a cover-story. I wonder what the sly cow is up to.

'Thad girl ollways doing the homewerk,' Dad says proudly. 'She gonna be very cleva one day. Shame she nod a block, eh?' He winks at George who winks back – as if they've got some secret sexists' code going on.

'*Dad*!' I say, putting my foot down. Why should he

176

get away with his chauvinistic crap? Once upon a time Mum would have whacked him for a crack like that, but she's gone soft. 'You'd better watch it, Mum,' I tell her. 'He'll have us in yashmaks soon.'

'Go and stick the kettle on, will you, love?' Mum says with a smile. Like she'd give a shit about having to wear a yashmak – just so long as she could see the telly through the slit.

I've inadvertently nudged Dad's memory with the yashmak remark and I leave the room as he launches into his Arab story. You don't want to know, believe me . . . OK, some nonsense about this Arab woman who used to be one of his regulars. He was convinced that – like most of his female customers – she fancied him because she was always winking at him through her veil. Of course, her husband must have found out and had her stoned to death because Dad hasn't seen her since he slipped some extra prawns into her bap. And that's one of his more believable stories.

I'm taking my time in the kitchen. More flicking through *Hello!* and scoffing biscuits than making tea. I'm in no rush. I've listened to all of Dad's stories at least a hundred times. Besides, I need to be alone with my guilt. I hear a crash, but I ignore it. He's probably telling them the one where he chased the three (or four or five, depending on how much he's had to drink) masked raiders out of his sandwich bar and halfway down Long Acre – he always re-enacts that one with noisy sound effects. But I can't ignore the kitchen door flying open and Maroulla stumbling through, her face white with shock. 'Chaglotta, *quig!*' she yelps. 'Your fatha's huving the hutt uttugg!'

'Having the *what*?'

'The *hutt uttugg*,' she repeats, this time clasping her

hands to her chest and miming some kind of seizure.

'Jesus, a *heart attack*?'

She nods and I push her out of the way in my rush to get to him.

And there he is. In his favourite chair, droplets of sweat breaking out on his forehead, his hands clutching his chest. He's in serious, serious agony by the look of things. My *dad*. Having a *heart attack*! This can*not* be happening. He's too young. And so fit. With so much to live for. OK, that's what everyone says when they think they're going to lose someone they love, but I can't help it. Of course he's neither young nor fit, but . . . *he's my dad*. Why is this happening? It must be God paying me back for being such a disgrace of a daughter.

Mum is by his side, for once completely oblivious to the TV and only concerned about the love of her life. I see the tears streaking her face and they jolt me out of my frozen panic. All the first-aid training I've had at The Zone and I'm standing here like a plank.

Got to act.

And fast.

'Don't move, Dad, just sit tight,' I say as I try to remember what the hell I'm supposed to do in a situation like this.

'Wotchewtokkingaboud? I no moving. I *cunt* move,' he yells, massaging his chest as if he's trying to rub away the pain.

'Someone call an ambulance,' I say, finally getting my act together.

'Umbulunce teg too long,' Maroulla wails. 'He be dead before they gedding here.'

'Well, we don't have much choi—'

I'm cut off by George. 'I know! We teg him Dino's flut. Is only few minutes from here.'

178

'Thass brilliun idea. His home tonight. He fix *everything*,' Maroulla whoops.

And I have to say I agree. The bloke two doors down from us fell off a ladder and broke his leg a few months ago. The bone had virtually healed by the time the ambulance arrived.

'Right, OK, we'll go in your car, yeah?' I say to George.

'We cunt. Is full of frogs . . .'

I furrow my brow. Why on earth would he keep amphibians in his car? Or Frenchmen for that matter.

'. . . You know, sambles from the fucdory.'

Oh, it's full of *frocks*. God help me – now is *not* the time to be practising my translation skills.

'We'll go in Dad's,' I say, snatching the keys from the sideboard. 'You two come with me, show me the way. Mum, you'd better stay here in case Emily gets home.' Oh yes, I'm in charge now.

Wood Green to Highgate in six minutes. That's some going, especially as I haven't been behind the wheel of a car for months. Dad never lets me drive the Merc, but he's hardly in a position to protest about women drivers tonight. As we screech to a halt I look at George sitting beside me, his fingers digging into the dashboard, his eyes wide with terror. Dunno what his problem is – I only jumped five red lights. I glance in the mirror at Dad, who's calmer now, but still clutching his chest. Maroulla is next to him, mopping his brow with a tissue.

'His on the ground floor,' George says, pointing at the tall terraced house we've parked outside.

'OK, let's get him in.'

As we heave Dad out of the car and across the pavement I feel terrible; wracked with guilt. I should have

179

picked up the signals. He has been very tired lately. And irritable. Well, more irritable than usual. And he's been, er . . . OK, I'm not exactly sure what the other signs are that someone's about to have a heart attack, but whatever, I should have spotted them. His body is slumped between George and me and I feel tears sting my eyes as I imagine the agony he must be in. I've never seen him do *silent* pain before. He's taken everything the attack has thrown at him. This man is my new hero. Amazing. All this time my dad's been a hero and I never knew it. But now that I do, I'll never, ever forget it. If he can just be all right, *please* . . .

Maroulla hammers at the bell and a moment later Dino appears, a look of annoyance on his face. It quickly dissolves into concern as his mother eggsblains— Sorry, *explains*.

'Right, quick, get him inside,' he says, translating *hutt uttugg* far quicker than I'd managed. We stumble through to his living room, which is light and airy and, er, not empty.

On the sofa. A girl. A blonde girl. Don't know why I'm mentioning her hair colour. Certainly not because they supposedly have more fun or anything. Who cares? About the more-fun theory or the fact that there's a woman in Dino's living room. I've got more important things to worry about, like keeping my dad alive.

'Where shall we put him?' I ask Dino, looking from the blonde to him to the blonde again.

'Lie him on the sofa . . . Would you mind?' Dino says to the blonde.

She stands up grudgingly. I'm putting Dino's irritation at our arrival together with her obvious annoyance now and I'm getting a *situation*. Wonder what we're interrupting?

We lay Dad down on the sofa and stand back as

Doctor Dino goes to work. 'How's your breathing, Jimmy?' he asks as he kneels down beside him and unbuttons his shirt.

'I breathing . . . juss aboud,' Dad pants.

I watch Dino place his hands on Dad's chest and feel up and down with a firm touch. His manner is cool and professional. Whatever we were interrupting, his training has kicked in smoothly and I'm impressed . . . As well as slightly weak at the knees. No, it's nothing as ridiculously girly as feeling safe in the presence of the strong, handsome doctor. It's because I've got weak knees anyway and the struggle from car to living room with half of Dad's bulk on my shoulders hasn't done them any good at all.

'When did this kick off?' Dino asks.

'About twenty minutes ago,' I reply, as my peripheral vision picks up the blonde thrusting her arms into her coat.

Dino spots it too and he interrupts his examination to say, 'Coral, please wait. Don't go.'

'Corro?' Maroulla says. 'Who Corro?' These are the first words she's spoken since we got here. I look at her and it's apparent that she's lost all interest in my father because she's staring in horror at Coral the blonde.

'Mum, this is a friend of mine,' Dino says wearily, obviously weighing up whether to tend first to my father's coronary or his 'friend's' frostbite, because from where I'm standing that's what she seems to be suffering from.

'No need for introductions, Dean. I'm going,' she says, grabbing her handbag.

'Din? Who Din?' Maroulla says, looking from Coral to Dino.

'You know whad? I think I cun breath a bit more

181

now,' Dad says, trying to push himself up on his elbows in an attempt to get a look at Coral. Now she's picking up – and this is the most bizarre thing – a metal cage. The sort you keep rodents in . . . And yes, there it is. A small brown furry thing snuffling in some straw at the bottom. *Weird*. This does *not* strike me as the pet mice kind of household. 'I'll collect the rest of my stuff later in the week,' she says as she pushes past us. 'Nice to meet you all.' She doesn't look as if she means it, but who cares? Definitely not Maroulla who is staring open-mouthed at the door as it slams shut behind her.

'Bluddy hell, I think is gone. I think is OK now,' Dad says with an audible sigh of relief. He's sitting upright and rubbing at his chest happily.

'*Please*, lie down, Jimmy,' Dino says, flustered now as he tries to shift his head from girlfriend nightmares back to his patient. 'Heart attacks don't *just go*. I'm going to have to take a proper look at you. I'll go and get my stuff.' He stands up and leaves the room.

Dad lies back on the sofa, the colour returning to his cheeks. George, Maroulla and I look at each other awkwardly.

'Who Corro?' Maroulla repeats. She seems to be more traumatised now than she ever was when Dad appeared to be at death's door.

Dino returns with a black medical bag – and I thought they only carried those in sitcoms and soaps. He kneels down beside Dad again, pulls out a stethoscope and says, 'OK, breathe as normally as you can.' He listens intently as Dad takes the most unnaturally deep breaths I've ever heard. 'Well, you've got a good, steady heartbeat there,' he says after a moment. 'Tell me, Jimmy, where exactly was the pain?'

'Oh, *every*where. It was rilly bad, like the hot

niddles,' Dad explains, his eyes widening. 'But oll's well thass ending well, eh?' he adds cheerfully.

A bit *too* cheerfully, if you ask me. I know my father and he's never been one to cut a drama short. Once, he sliced through his thumb at work and for weeks we had to listen to him tell us how he was 'this close—' (holding his finger and said thumb about a millimetre apart) '—to *ambudation*.' He's getting over this *heart attack* a little too quickly. I smell a rat, and I don't think it's the rodenty thing that left a couple of minutes ago with Coral the blonde.

'I need you to be specific about the pain,' Dino presses. 'We need to know what we're dealing with here: a mild heart attack or something else – angina, indigestion, something stress-related perhaps . . .'

'OK, is hurting here,' Dad says, stabbing at his heart . . . Or rather, where he thinks his heart should be.

'There, you say?' Dino repeats.

'Yeah, thass right. *There*,' Dad says with a triumphant beam.

'And where else? Did the pain extend down your arm?'

Dad nods.

'OK, which one?'

'This one,' Dad says, holding up his right arm.

'That's the wrong arm,' Dino says flatly. 'And *that*,' he adds, angrily pointing to the area of hairy chest indicated by his patient, 'is *not* where your heart is either.'

Dad's face falls. But only for a second – he's quick, I'll give him that, and now I know where I get it from. 'Hey, so whad?' he exclaims. 'This arm, thad arm, whass the diff'rence? The good news is I ain't gonna die!'

Yes you bloody are, mate. Just you wait till I get you out of here.

Dino stands up now and he looks less happy than

at any point since we arrived – seems he's reaching the same conclusion that I am. He glares at his mother who shrivels before him. But she, like my dad, has rapid powers of recovery and says, 'As we here, anyone like a drink? Cock, Theglottsa? Diet Cock?'

'Don't worry, Mum. I'll put the kettle on.' Dino stomps from the room.

Oh yes, I could kill my father all right. This was a set-up from start to bloody finish. I thought the ruse to get me round the Georgious' on Sunday was sly, but this is the best yet. I can picture him hatching it:

1. *Doing the hutt uttugg (easy 'cause I seeing them oll the time on* Holby City).
2. *Gedding my Theglitsa to drive me round Dino's.*
3. *Dino saving my life and showing my dotter his most brilliun doctor in the weld.*
4. *Theglitsa falling into his arms.*
5. *Booking the church, ordering the cake, Bob's your bluddy ungle . . .*

The only question is how many of them were in on it? My mum? The Georgious? Dino himself? Probably not. Coral the blonde certainly didn't know anything, but who can bloody tell with this lot?

I am *seething*. I glare in turn at Dad, George and Maroulla. Dad's miraculous recovery is apparently complete. The heart attack is forgotten and they're killing the time until Dino reappears with tea (or, more likely, a shotgun, judging by his mood when he stormed out) by putting the world to rights.

'I don' like their sort,' Maroulla says. 'You cunt truss them.'

'I having them at the fucdory and they ollways the ones I catching stealing,' George says.

184

'You're right,' chips in Dad. 'You cunt truss them. And you seeing more and more of them every day. We never having so many in the ol' days.'

What do you think they're talking about? Blacks? Asians? Gays? Lesbians? No, they wouldn't be that obvious.

They're talking about blondes.

I can't listen to this a moment longer without exploding, so I do a Dino and storm from the room.

I find myself in the kitchen with Dino. Or is that Dean? It wasn't the plan. I meant to head for the bathroom or something, but I don't know my way around this flat, I'm slightly blinded by rage and here I am. He ignores my arrival, preferring to work out his fury by clattering mugs together. Poor mugs . . . Or were they in on it too?

'Sorry,' I mumble after a few seconds. 'I couldn't stay there and listen to them. I'm so, *so* angry, I could . . . Er, need any help?'

He looks as if he does. He seems lost, as if he can't remember where the milk lives and when he does he's forgotten where the fridge is. Then he stops, turns and glares at me. 'Were you in on this?'

'God, *no*. What do you think—'

'You know what? I have no bloody idea what to think. *Jesus*, I know my parents are mad about you, but this is ridiculous.'

'Really?' I can't believe he just said that. Nobody's parents have ever been mad about me before – not even my own. I can't help but feel a little glow somewhere deep, deep down.

'You're all they've talked about lately. I've had it up to here, to be honest.'

Huh! Who the hell does he think he is to have had

it up to *anywhere* with talk about me? And there I was beginning to feel sorry for him . . . And thinking that, yes, he really *is* a bit tasty.

'Well, if honesty's what we're doing, I'm sick of having to listen to stories about you too,' I snap. 'And if you'd just been honest enough to tell your mum you've already got a girlfriend, we wouldn't be in this mess, would we?'

That told him. And if he dares to come back with anything smart-arse, I might just give him a bit of a grilling about what, exactly, he was up to with my baby sister at his mum's. A man his age, in a bedroom with a kid her age, it's not decent. It's Whacko Jacko territory.

He sighs deeply, slumps over the counter and says, 'I think you mean I *had* a girlfriend. She's gone . . . It's over.'

'I suppose you're going to blame us lot for that as well,' I say, and top it off with, 'eh, *Dean*.'

'I wish I could . . . No, it was my fault. All my sodding fault.'

I could kick myself. He's obviously devastated and here I am, shooting my big, fat mouth off. Ironic, huh? Ever since his name first came up I've flinched at the very mention of the guy, and now here I am feeling . . . What? Sorry for him? Yes, I think I am. The poor bloke looks broken . . . And, um, quite tasty.

'Do you love her?' I ask gently.

'It's not love. We'd only been seeing each other for a couple of months, but it could've turned into something . . .' He trails off pathetically. God, now he looks *really* delicious.

'What happened?' I ask, going for the full-on Samaritan effect.

'It's crazy. You wouldn't believe it.'

'Try me,' I nudge 'It could hardly be any madder than anything I've already seen tonight.'

'It was the gerbil.'

'The what?'

'You saw the cage she left with? It had a gerbil in it. They're rats, basically. Come from North Afri—'

'I know what a gerbil is. Go on.'

'She was crazy about it. She called him Nelson – only had one eye, you see? Nelson the one-eyed gerbil . . .'

A disabled-rodent-loving blonde. Tonight, I truly *have* seen everything.

'. . . Anyway, she went away on a course for a few days. Left Nelson with me.'

'That's a big responsibility,' I say, immediately regretting it because it sounded sarcastic and I don't want to be. Not when he looks so gorgeously vulnerable. I can't believe myself. I should still be seething over Dad's stunt, or beating myself up over Karl/Ben/Sasha, but here I am doing empathy . . . But it's OK, it really is.

'A *massive* responsibility,' Dino says. 'Anyway, did you know that gerbils can jump about three, maybe four feet when startled? . . . No, neither did I until yesterday. I let him out of his cage and he's running around the living room. I drop a book; it bangs on the floor; Nelson jumps and whacks his head on the dining table. That's it. He's dead.'

'But I saw him in the cage, moving around.'

'That was his replacement. I bought it this afternoon.'

'I think you're being a bit hard on yourself, Dino. Nelson's death was an accident. Coral would've understood that.'

'Oh, she might have, but . . . I had a dilemma, you see?' He looks down now, as if he's ashamed.

'How do you mean?' I ask, resisting the urge to reach out and stroke his hand.

'Tell Coral the truth: Nelson's dead, but here's his replacement, or . . .'

'Or what?'

'Lie, basically. You know, pass the new one off as Nelson.'

'Hang on,' I said, hearing an alarm bell, 'you said Nelson was blind in one eye.'

'I'm sure I could've done it. Human anatomy, gerbil anatomy; there's not *that* much difference. OK, so I'm not a surgeon, but I *know* I could've removed that eye without the animal feeling a thing.'

'What are you saying? You were going to cut out a perfectly good eye so you could fake his identity?'

'Yes, but only to spare Coral from the trauma of Nelson's death. I had everything I needed: the instruments, the drugs. If she hadn't come back and caught me with the scalpel—'

'You were going to cut out his eye?' It hardly needs restating but I can't help myself.

'God, you're as bad as her. I thought I was doing the right thing. You see, as a procedure it wouldn't have been that complicated. The construction of the eye is basically—'

'Whoa, stop right there.' I take a lurching step backwards. All of a sudden I don't want to be so close to *Doctor* Dino . . . Dino the Highgate Chainsaw Massacre-er. 'You are truly one sick fucker,' I gasp. 'I can't believe I was buying into this . . . this sob story.'

'I'm a sick fucker? What about the stupid ruse you dreamed up to come round here tonight? What's that if it isn't sick?'

'That had *nothing* to do with me.'

'You lot, you Charalambouses, you need to sort yourselves out, get some family therapy.'

'God, you're a piece of work. What makes you so

188

fucking perfect? What were you doing with my sister? Eh?'

'That's exactly the point I'm making. Have you talked to her yet?'

'Talked to her about what? What have you done to her?'

'What have I done? Jesus. If you lot weren't so busy faking heart attacks, you might be able to see that your sis—'

The kitchen door flies open and Maroulla falls through. 'Why you shouting, Dino?' she gasps. Dad follows close behind. 'Whass going on?' he yells, miraculously as fit as a fat, hairy fiddle again. I imagine that they've spent the last ten minutes with their ears pressed against the door, straining to listen to their beloved offspring bond (and congratulating each other on the staggering success of their plan). I suppose when we turned up the volume they thought it best to intervene.

Well, fuck 'em. I have had enough of parents – mine, Dino's anyone's – *intervening* in my life. I'm out of here.

I fumble in my pocket for the car keys and head for the door.

'Where you going now?' Dad growls behind me.

'Home,' I snap.

'Whad aboud me?'

'Walk . . . It'll do your heart good.'

The Bit With The SX TXTS

I feel just as crap this morning as I did when I got home last night. I questioned Mum when I got in, but she played dumb. Told me I was completely crazy to think I'd been set up. 'Your father would never do that. These things are a warning, you know. He works too hard. We've got to get him to slow down.' I have to say she was very convincing and it made me question my own judgement for all of five seconds. But, no, I'd been stitched up like a kipper, no doubting it. I stared at her staring at Graham Norton and wondered if she was a very good liar or just extremely stupid. It was late, I was still feeling frazzled and I couldn't decide. So I went to bed.

I was still awake when Dad got home . . . then Emily. I listened to them all come up to bed . . . snore peace-fully . . . and then get up again this morning. I'd have heard the cocks crow too if we had any. No way could I sleep. Amid the churning anger I felt towards Dad were feelings of guilt – how could I forget what I got up to with Karl yesterday?

So much for Mum getting Dad to slow down. He was up and out by six thirty as usual.

And now I'm up too, standing on the landing outside the bathroom. Emily's locked inside, and as I lean on the wall waiting for her to finish, I'm making some decisions:

190

1. Get my facts sorted out. Are Karl and Ben the same bloke? It surely can't be that hard to figure out.
2. Assuming the worst, tell Sasha everything . . .
3. . . . Except for the bit about shagging Karl *after* my suspicions were aroused. So I'm a coward, what can I do?
4. Give Mum and Dad the bottom line: stop interfering in my personal life or else I'm moving out. (Fingers crossed they stop interfering in my personal life, then.)
5. Give Emily an ultimatum. Either she enlightens me as to what Dino thinks we should be talking about or I tell Mum exactly what she gets up to on her 'homework with Alicia' nights (not that I know, but I can guess).

Arse-face. She's doing this on purpose, hogging the bathroom and showing no signs of emerging any time before the weekend. What's she doing in there? More to the point, what's she doing it *for*? I mean, I *have* to spend ages in front of the mirror; I've got to sort out this mess of a face for the poncy gits who come to The Zone expecting to see physical perfection whichever way they turn. My sister, on the other hand, is tarting herself up for what? Double geography and some spotty boys with school dinner on their blazers? I bang on the door and shout, 'Get a move on,' which is a mistake because now she'll add an extra twenty minutes of eyebrow plucking to her routine.

I'm running late. I dash into the kitchen and grab the Coco Pops from the table. The box is empty. I look at the bowl in front of Emily; full to overflowing. Greedy *cow*.

'*Mum*, have we got any more Coco Pops?'

'Not till your Dad goes to the cash and carry again,' she says, not looking away from the portable telly on the worktop.

'God knows when that'll be, what with his *heart trouble* and everything,' I say. Then, in Emily's direction: '*Greedy cow.*'

'It'll do you good to starve, *Thegla*. You're getting fat,' she sneers.

She's right, but I kick her anyway.

'*Mum*, Charlie kicked me.'

'Oh, stop it, you two. I'm trying to watch this,' Mum says. She's watching Nigella Lawson plug her latest cookbook on the breakfast-TV sofa. *Pur-lease*. My mother would only consider buying a Nigella book if it had chapters on frozen burgers, oven chips and Pot Noodles.

I fill the kettle and stick some Nescaff in a mug. I've got a killer headache. Bloody Dad. Bloody Dino. Bloody Karl. Bloody guilt. Bloody . . . This could get boring. 'We got any aspirin, Mum?'

'Not till your dad goes to the cash and carry.'

Mum doesn't do shopping if she can possibly help it. Most groceries come in bulk from the cash and carry. After Dad's trips, our house is more like a warehouse. You can't move for cartons containing fifty of everything so it's amazing that we ever run out of anything, but we seem to regularly.

I sit down with my coffee and rub my throbbing temples as Emily stuffs her face. 'Actually, what I need is a cranial massage,' I say. 'Know anyone who could give me one, Em?'

She nearly chokes – death by Coco Pops – but recovers to glare at me. This decodes as *just remember, if you blab about Sunday, I've got tons of stuff on you*. The fact that we could wipe each other out with the dirt we've got ensures our silence . . . for now.

The doorbell rings and Mum hauls herself out of the chair to answer it. As she leaves the room, I say, 'Dino thinks we should talk, Em.'

She stares at her cereal, looking panicked, but she manages to come back with, 'What would I want to talk to *you* about?'

'I dunno. You tell me.'

She doesn't respond.

'What were you doing with him on Sunday?'

'*Nothing*,' she replies.

'*Liar*.'

'You're only jealous,' she says, getting a little feisty now.

'What have I got to be jealous of? Your pathetic flirting with the stupid doctor?'

'He's not stupid. He's very sensitive, actually.'

'We had a huge row last night because of you. What were you talking about with him?'

'Why should I tell you? You're only interested in yourself. You're—'

'Stop changing the subject. Tell me what you're up to.'

'You're the one who's up to stuff. You're *disgusting*.'

'What are you on about?'

'Who's *Karl*? And what's *I love it when you get star, star, star*, and *I star, star, star all over your star, star, star, star*?'

My face is burning. How could I have been so stupidly stupid? Those bloody texts again. I want to grab her hair – I don't care how thick and shiny it is – and pull it until she screams for mercy, but I can't. Mum has come back into the room and she has company. She's followed by my Soulla-in-law who's cradling her humungous bump in both hands as if it's a bomb that may explode at any minute. Georgina, as usual, is glued to her thigh, and Tony follows behind them looking sheepish.

'Thanks, Mum,' he says. 'Soulla just needs a bit of company. A bit of pampering, don't you, sweetheart?'

She gives him a look. *Hmm*, I sense tension in the Tony/Soulla household. So much for the joys of parenthood.

'Don't worry, we'll look after you, Soulla love,' Mum soothes. 'Charlotte, make your sister-in-law a cup of tea.'

Obediently I get up and put the kettle on. Tony looks at his watch. 'I'd better be going. Is there anything else I can do for you, darling?'

'No, you just go to work. I'll be *fine*,' Soulla says with barely disguised contempt.

He kisses her cheek and tries to hug his daughter, who's making a grab for the empty cereal box and isn't interested. 'There's no Coco Pops,' she pouts. 'I want *Coco Pops*.' He gives up and quickly shuffles off. Can't say I blame him. When your wife's going to explode – both physically and emotionally – and your daughter's an ill-mannered brat, accountancy must seem like the most fascinating job in the world. I know that if I were him, I'd be gagging to escape for a spot of bookkeeping right now.

'Soulla's going to be induced,' Mum announces once Tony has gone.

'What's that?' I ask, though I suspect I don't want to hear the answer.

'It means I'll get an injection to make the labour start,' Soulla explains.

No, didn't want to hear that.

'Charlie was induced,' Mum says, 'but she still took forever to come out.'

'Did they have to break your waters?' Soulla asks, animated now.

194

'Uh-huh. The midwife stuck something like a bloody knitting needle up me and the floodgates opened. It went everywhere. All over the bed, the floor . . .'

Emily and I look at each other. It's one of those rare moments when we see things the same way – we've both turned green.

'You seen the time, Em?' I say.

'God, yeah, we'd better go.'

The Bit Where The World Falls In On Karl

'Daniel, I've decided to promote you,' I say immediately after I've knocked back a couple of extra-strength Nurofen. 'I'm making you Executive in Charge of Zone Check.'

'I'm not going to be your bloody spy,' he moans as I thrust the clipboard at him.

'After yesterday afternoon, you'll be anything I want you to be.'

'I *swear*, I didn't know Ruby was in early. I've said sorry a million times. Anyway, you've got to admit, it was a laugh.'

'Yeah, and the whole fucking place is still in stitches. It's nearly ten; better get on with your rounds.'

'*Jawohl, mein Führer*,' he says, clicking his heels, which doesn't really work with spongy trainers but I get the gist. And I don't care. I've decided that if he's going to hate me just because I'm the boss, then I might as well start acting like one.

Once he's gone I pick up the phone and press the button for Zone Clone. Jarvis picks up. 'Don't even start, Jarv,' I say before he can get a quip in. 'Is Sasha there yet?'

'She phoned in sick, darling. Hey, your workout shorts are in.'

'What shorts?'

'The *Gladiator* ones we had printed up last night. They say *I am Maximus Gluteus* on the arse.'

'Piss off,' I say, slamming the phone down. I dial Sasha's mobile and get her voicemail. I leave a message: 'Sash, it's me. We've got to talk. Can you meet me for a drink after work? Or I can come to yours if you like. Call me . . . Oh, and get well.' She won't be ill. If I know Sasha she'll be floating round her flat on a cloud of candle scent listening to Celine Dion sing the theme tune from *Titanic*. Being as soppy as she is, it's hard to imagine her getting mad when I tell her about Karl/Ben, but she will. How could she do anything else? That's assuming Karl and Ben are the same guy. Whatever. The suspicion alone is doing my head in. We've got to talk.

Now that I've delegated Zone Check to Daniel, I'm at a loose end. It's quiet on the desk. Just me and Rebecca. I'm wondering what to do with myself when the doors swish open and three huge bodyguards stride in. Though I can't actually see the short-arsed chart sensation, I know that they're surrounding Blaize, ready to stop a bullet for her. Her flunkies scurry behind like a bunch of bridesmaids. And then come the dancers . . . Who, of course, include Karl.

He smiles at me . . . and winks.

I close my eyes and swallow hard, but it doesn't make the nauseous feeling go away. I open my eyes. He's just a few feet from the desk and I realise that I still fancy the combat pants off him. *Bastard*. How dare he be so sexy that I start drooling whenever he comes anywhere near me?

Gotta fight it.

Me and him, it's over.

Finished.

For ever and ever.

Or at least until I clear up the Karl/Ben thing.

I turn to Rebecca and say, 'I've got some stuff to do in my office. You OK by yourself?' She goes rigid with fear and starts to protest, but I spin on my heel and I'm outta there.

Must talk to Jamie about extra staff again. I tried to bring it up with him the other day, but all he'd say was that he'd think about it. I just hope he doesn't take too much longer.

'How long can it take to get a couple of coffees?' Daniel sighs.

He's got a point. She's been gone for twenty minutes now.

Must, must, *must* press Jamie about extra staffing.

Daniel and I have spent the time listening to Blaize's next single reverberating through the building. It's only her second day of rehearsals, but I've heard it dozens of times. Sick of it? To the back bloody teeth and then a bit.

The lift door slides open and Rebecca shuffles out balancing three Styrofoam cups in her hands and gripping three bags of crisps in her teeth. Daniel and I watch her as she inches towards us, staring intently at the cups. She's halfway across the foyer when the fire door to the staircase next to the lift flies open and one of Blaize's dancers spills through it. She sprints towards the desk with an expression of utter panic on her face and she clearly isn't going to let a little thing like Becks stand in her way. She shoulder-charges her and we watch three cups of coffee loop through the air and splatter onto the marble floor. To Rebecca's credit, she doesn't drop the crisps.

'Quick, call 999,' the dancer squeals as she collapses panting onto the desk. 'Karl's hurt himself and Blaize is having an asthma attack.'

That wakes us up. Jesus, that's all we need. Tomorrow's *Sun* leading with CHART TOPPER CROAKS IN TOP LONDON HEALTH CLUB. I can hear Jamie losing it now: *'How many more times? It's a TOTAL fucking BODY EMPORIUM.'*

'Phone for an ambulance, Daniel,' I shout as I vault over the desk – quite athletically, I must say – dodge past the frozen Rebecca and run for the lift.

I arrive in Studio Four to find pandemonium. Dancers and bodyguards are in a noisy huddle around Blaize, who's slumped on a chair against the mirrored wall. Those nearest her are passing her water and fanning her with towels. I sprint the length of the polished floor. When I reach her I see that she's ashen and panting slightly. But there's no desperate wheezing, no hands dramatically clutching her own throat as she fights for air. In other words, none of the classic symptoms of asthma, as seen on *ER* the other night.

'Is she OK?' I ask.

'She's in shock,' says Jenna, who's crouched at Blaize's feet and is stroking her forearm with a soothing hand.

'I think I'll be all right,' Blaize whimpers bravely.

'What happened?'

'Your useless bloody sound system – *which I specifically asked you to check, Charlie* – collapsed on Karl,' Jenna snaps.

'Where is he?' I ask, suddenly remembering the other reason I ran up here.

'Over there,' says a dancer, pointing towards the far end of the studio.

I turn round and see him. He's in the corner; lying on the floor, seemingly dead. A large pool of blood is spreading on the pale wooden boards. A short distance away one of the studio's hefty black speakers lies on its side, and close to it is the bracket that held it up on the wall. A few dancers stand around him, apparently at a loss for what to do.

I run towards him and when I get there it's obvious he's out cold. I crouch down and look at his head. *Fuck*, that's what you call a cut. About an inch and a half long, gaping and just above his temple. It's still oozing blood. 'Didn't anyone think to put something on this?' I say to the dancers. 'Quick, someone get me a towel.'

One of them scrabbles around in a kit bag and produces a small white towel. It's damp with sweat, but it'll have to do. I fold it up and press it against the cut. 'How long's he been unconscious?' I ask.

'A few minutes, I guess,' one of them says.

'Have you checked his pulse?'

They look at each other blankly.

I reach down and lift Karl's arm onto my lap. I panic as I remember the first-aid course I did last year and how I could never find my own pulse when the teacher got us to feel for it. But I get Karl's straight away. Relieved (because he's alive and because I'm not going to have to dredge my memory for how to do CPR), I look up and see that Daniel has arrived. 'What happened?' he asks.

'The speaker was making that buzzing noise again and it was giving Blaize a migraine,' explains one of the dancers.

'Karl jumped up and gave it a whack with his hand,' another adds. 'The whole thing just collapsed on him and he went down.'

Daniel gives me a worried look. Like me, he must be picturing the writs, the teams of lawyers, the long days in court and Jamie shoving me into the dock to take the rap. 'Well, the ambulance should be here any minute,' he says. 'What about Blaize? Is she OK?'

We both look to the other end of the studio, where the crowd is now pulling back from her, more out of fear than anything else from what I can see. 'God, isn't there anything other than water to drink?' she says testily. 'Someone get me a tea . . . *Herbal*.' *Hmm*, she seems to be on the mend. She follows up with a shrieked 'Oh my God'. Blaize looks at last towards us. Towards Karl. Oh well, maybe she isn't such a selfish, spoilt princess after all. 'My *bag*!'

I see the bag she's frantically pointing at – a pricey-looking white DKNY number. It's a couple of feet from Karl's head and is in danger of being engulfed by the spreading pool of blood. 'For God's sake move him before he gets blood all over it,' she yells. The dancers nearest me leap into action, crouching down and grabbing Karl by the ankles and wrists.

'Stop!' I snap. 'He might have a spinal injury.' They do as they're told and one of them moves the bag away.

Madness. Daniel and I are looking after a bloke with a serious head injury, while everyone else flies into a panic over designer handbags. But I'm forgetting whose presence we're in and the sacred importance of the hierarchy of grovelling: dancers grovel to choreographer; choreographer grovels to pop star; pop star grovels to studio manager. I *wish*. Then I'd be able to tell her what I thought about her *asthma attack* because – let's face it – it belongs in the same category as my dad's *hutt uttugg*.

At *last*. The door swings open and the ambulance crew trots in, complete with stretcher. 'Tell them I'm fine, honestly,' Blaize protests, but the two paramedics – not being citizens of Planet Pop Star – ignore her and head straight for the real emergency.

'He doesn't look asthmatic,' says one as they reach us.

'He isn't. He was knocked out by that speaker,' I explain.

'OK, you'd better get out of the way, give us some room to work,' he says seriously.

We stand up and move to one side. I look round and see Jenna stomping towards us. As she reaches us I say, 'I'm sorry about all of this,' and immediately regret it because *sorry* is an admission of guilt, isn't it?

'I *specifically* requested that you have those speakers checked, Charlie,' she spits. 'Yesterday, in the café, and I have witnesses.'

Witnesses? Well, Sasha was with us, but she can't remember a conversation two minutes after it's taken place.

'Blaize is rehearsing here on my personal recommendation,' she continues. 'How do you think this makes me look? I'll be talking to Jamie about it, don't you worry.' I can tell that she desperately wants to carry on bollocking me, but she's caught sight of Blaize out of the corner of her eye. Pop star appears to be leaving the building and Jenna, knowing where her priorities lie, grabs Blaize's handbag and runs after her. 'Maybe you should catch a ride to the hospital in the ambulance,' she says. 'You've been traumatised and you really should be checked out, sweetheart.'

'I *hate* hospitals, Jenna. I just want to go home.'

'That's right, let's get you home. You need to put today behind you.'

Blaize, Jenna and the rest file out of the studio. 'Isn't anyone going to stay with Karl?' I ask, but I don't know why I'm bothering. Daniel and I stare at each other in disbelief. I mean, we've seen some prima-donna shit in our three years here, but never anything like this.

The ambulance crew have got Karl onto the stretcher.

A brace is wrapped around his neck and an oxygen mask is strapped across his face.

'Is he gonna be OK?' I ask.

'Probably just concussion, but you can never tell with head injuries,' says the talkative one as they lift the stretcher up and its legs drop to the floor with a clank. 'He'll need a scan when we get him in. Are either of you gonna come in with him?'

Daniel and I look at one another again as they wheel him off. 'I'll handle things here,' he says after a moment. 'You go.'

I look at the disappearing stretcher and feel ripped in two. I want to go with him because he's hurt, possibly seriously, and (I can't believe I'm thinking this) because even unconscious and covered in blood, I still love him. Sorry, *lust* him. But he might also be a total bastard, and until I'm sure there's no way I want him to wake up and see me at his bedside looking like some love-struck idiot. But someone should go, if only to persuade him not to sue when he does come round. We'll have enough on our hands dealing with the inevitable legal shit from Blaize, who looked like she definitely wanted to sue us for something.

God, what to do?

'Go on, Charlie,' Daniel prods. 'You know you want to.'

'OK, I'll call you from the hospital,' I say, and run for the door.

But I've been fannying around for so long the crew has gone. I run to the window at the end of the corridor and look down into the street below. They must already have him in the back of the ambulance because one of them is slamming the back door shut and the blue light has started to flash. I watch it drive away with a burst of its siren.

How sad is that? He was the heart and soul of Blaize's little gang, but now he's on his own. And he reckoned he was close to her. All I can think is that she must be an *extremely* casual shag for all the concern she's shown. This actually makes me feel ever so slightly relieved. Maybe they weren't shagging. Maybe I got it completely wrong and they're not close in *that way* at all. Poor Karl. I've had him down as some sort of monster, and really I haven't a clue.

I head back to the studio and find Daniel looking at the glistening red pool on the floor.

'Too late, they've gone,' I tell him.

'Never mind. He's in good hands. I'll get this mopped up.'

I spot a black leather training bag in the corner – Karl's. I pick it up. I'll take it downstairs to my office for safekeeping, because I'm professional like that and not because I'm a nosy cow and want to root through his belongings.

I'm walking to Covent Garden. Normally I'd catch the tube, even though it's only two stops from work, but this evening I need the walk. I need some fresh air (or what passes for it in London) both to calm my nerves and to get rid of the nasty taste of the day.

Half an hour before I left, Jenna came back in. Well, whatever trauma she's been through, she's a true professional and she had a class to teach. She didn't talk to me. She grabbed Daniel and said loudly, 'Check my studio for me, honey. I don't want anything else falling off the walls.'

I feel bad about what happened to Karl, but I do *not* feel personally responsible. OK, maybe I should have had maintenance check out the buzz in the speakers. But they're not designed to have big, athletic blokes

leap up and whack them. That's just asking for trouble
. . . Isn't it, m'lud?

I phoned the hospital before I left, but they wouldn't
give me any news because I'm not family. 'Can you
just tell me if he's come round or not?' I asked the
nurse.

'I'm sorry, madam, but I can't give out *any* information,' she said, sounding like every person you've
ever spoken to on an information desk.

'OK, you don't have to actually *say* anything,' I said.
'Just cough twice if he's awake.'

She hung up on me then.

I've arrived at The Dome on Long Acre. I didn't want
to meet Sasha at Billy's – a place packed with work
people isn't the venue for the conversation we've got to
have. I'm ten minutes late, but of course she isn't here
yet – Sasha makes the Greeks look punctual. I sit at a
table next to the long windows that overlook the street
and order two beers. I'm dreading this conversation.

Before I left work, I looked through Karl's training
bag – well, there might have been some clues in there
– but came up with nothing. No scrap of paper with
Sash's number on it, no perfumed love letters addressed
to *my darling Ben*. I found his mobile, but it was locked
and I don't know the password. Of course, the fact
that he'd locked his phone got me thinking that he
must have something to hide.

The beers arrive. I take a sip and feel my nerves
calm. I close my eyes and imagine I'm in a beach bar
somewhere exotic, sipping a Technicolor cocktail
stuffed with twizzle sticks and umbrellas. Pelicans are
frolicking on the powdery white sand and—

'Am I late?' Sasha ambles up to the table, killing the
fantasy.

'No, you're right on time.'

'Amazing. I was sure I was going to be late. I was on the phone for ages. Held in a stupid queue for forty minutes. Still didn't get to speak to anyone.'

'Who were you calling?'

'Do you know what? By the time I hung up, I'd forgotten . . .'

Oh to be Sasha, I think as she prattles on about her day. She sails through life like a sailboat with no sails. Permanently going nowhere, but not worrying about it in the slightest.

'. . . and I can't decide whether to do the fun-run thing or not. I mean, I know it's for charity and everything, but it's cancer awareness, which is a bit of a waste of time, if you ask me.'

'Why's that?' I ask. I didn't have her down as the uncharitable type.

'Well, it's like the Madonna of all illnesses, isn't it? Why do they need to do awareness stuff? Who's never heard of cancer? It's like asking who's never heard of spray-on tan. By the way, your hair looks nice today. What've you done to it?'

I've landed in that strange place called Sasha World and if I'm not careful this conversation will drift so far away from the real issue that there'll be no hope of pulling it back. I need to dive in now. 'Sasha, there's something I have to talk to you about.'

'What's wrong? Are you ill?'

'No, it's about Ben.'

'What about him?' she asks, frowning a little.

'Well, you've hardly told me anything about him,' I say, embarking on my fishing expedition. 'What he does, where he lives, stuff like that.'

'Well, he's a dancer.' Knew that much. 'And he's black. *Obviously* . . . Well, white guys can't dance, can they?'

According to the movie they can't jump either. Maybe if Karl was a soppy white bloke he wouldn't have done his high jump to the speaker and he wouldn't be hospitalised now.

'Oh, and he lives in South Ken.'

Ohmygod, I knew it.

'He's got hardly anything in his flat . . . Except he keeps this video camera in his bedroom, which I thought was a bit weird, but he said it's just for training or something.'

Jesus. It's him all right. Karl and Ben are one and the same. All this time – *especially* the time I spent shagging him yesterday – I've been trying to convince myself that it couldn't possibly be so. I feel terrible, like I want to die, or at least crawl away and never come back.

'You've gone white, Charlie,' Sasha says. 'You haven't got the bug I've been pretending to have, have you?' She giggles. 'Sorry I bunked off, but I was supposed to be seeing Ben. Funny, he was meant to call.'

How's he going to call? He's in hospital. But she doesn't know that yet. She doesn't know anything yet. And I've got to be the one to tell her.

'Listen,' I say, 'I've got some pretty awful news.'

'My *God,* what is it? I'm not getting fired for bunking off, am I?'

'Nothing like that . . . but . . . Shit, this is awful. Sasha, we've been screwing the same guy.' I leave it hanging there for a second.

'Who?' she asks, a blank look on her face.

Jesus. 'Well, how many guys are you doing it with?'

After a bit of mental arithmetic she says, 'Just Ben.'

'Right, OK,' I say, limbering up for the big explanation, 'the thing is, I didn't realise that this guy I've been seeing – only I hadn't got round to telling you about him yet – well, his name's Karl, and you see, he and Ben, they're actually the same person.'

There, done it. It was a bit waffly, but it's out there now. Floating up to the stratosphere, messing with the ozone.

And messing with Sasha's peculiar mind. She looks very confused. 'You're seeing someone called Karl? You didn't tell me.'

'No, as I said, I didn't get round to it.'

'What's he like?' She still hasn't got there.

'Sasha, *listen*. Karl's been doing a number on both of us. I'm not sure he knows we're mates, but, what-ever, the end result's the same. He's taking us both for a ride . . . so to speak.'

'What, this Karl guy knows me?'

She may be in great shape body-wise, but she'd really benefit from some mental aerobics. *Deep breath, Charlie, start again. Slowly this time*. 'Karl, who I've been seeing, has turned out to be Karl *Ben*jamin. As in Ben, the guy *you're* seeing. Karl is Ben. Ben is Karl. *It's the same bloke*.'

We have contact. Sasha's eyes have widened, her jaw has dropped; she's there.

'*No!* We're sleeping with the same man?' she screams, causing heads to swivel our way and waiters to stop in their tracks.

'I'm really sorry, Sash,' I say quietly, hoping she'll follow suit and lower the volume. 'If I'd known, I'd never have gone there, I swear.'

She doesn't believe it. *Can't* believe it. He hadn't told her she was the only one, but she'd just assumed, the way you do. I tell her everything (except for the bit about shagging him *after* I suspected). She swears she hasn't seen him at The Zone and I believe her. Sasha has a history of not noticing things. I dyed my hair copper last year (it said Autumn Leaf on the box, but it came out more Sunny Delight Orange). She didn't spot the difference for a week, and only then because I shook my head about like a girl in an Organics ad and shouted, 'Look at my hair, Sash! It's ORANGE!'

After the explanation, silence descends. I look at her, but she's impossible to read. She takes a slow sip of her beer and looks up at the ceiling. No doubt she's trying to get her head round all of this. I can understand that. I've lived with this knowledge for longer than her and can still barely grasp what's happened myself.

'Are you OK? What are you thinking?' I ask after a few minutes.

'Unbelievable,' she says, still staring into the distance.

'I know. I've never met a bastard quite like him. He's—'

'No, *you're* unbelievable, Charlie,' she snaps, slamming her bottle down onto the table.

'*Me?*'

'All this time, I thought you were my friend. Ben is the first good thing to happen to me since, like, *forever*, and look what you go and do.'

'But, but I haven't done anything! Karl— *Ben's* the one who lied to the both of us. He's a serial-shagging bas—'

'Stop trying to shift the blame. You knew I loved him and you just couldn't stop yourself from ruining it.'

'Sash, listen to me, I didn't know any of this until yesterday, and even then I wasn't sure.'

'Yeah? Why should I believe you? Tell me.' She has her arms folded tightly across her chest and she's glaring at me with a look of pure venom. This is shocking because I've never seen Sasha's pretty face do venom before.

209

'Because . . .' I splutter – why should she believe me? 'Because it's the *truth*. And it's not just me he's two-timing you with either.'

'*Huh*? Who else?'

'Blaize.'

There. Said it. And the poisonous look has gone. She actually looks tickled. What is it with celebs? The rules that apply to the rest of us have no bearing on them. If I'd told her Blaize had set fire to her cat she'd be just as starry-eyed as she is now. '*What was she wearing?*' would probably be her first question, closely followed by '*I wonder where she buys her matches?*'

'I'm not one hundred per cent certain,' I continue, 'but I'm pretty sure he's involved with her too.'

'Really?' She sounds sceptical now. 'OK, give me one good reason why I shouldn't think you're making it up to get yourself off the hook?'

'Why would I lie? Look, have I ever lied to you?'

'I haven't a clue, have I? You know, all this time, I thought you were trying to help me,' she spits. 'God, how naïve have I been?'

'But I have tried to help you,' I gasp quietly, the words failing to come out properly. I'm gobsmacked. I fully expected her to be upset, angry even, but I didn't think she'd take it all out on me.

'What, getting me to do those crappy aerobics classes when you knew I hated them? That's *helping*, is it?'

She's raised the volume several notches and the people on the surrounding tables are making no attempt to disguise the fact that they're listening in. I'm not surprised because she's making me sound terrible. God, she's making me sound as bad as Daniel. Didn't I hate him for landing me in the shit with the Batley crew? But it wasn't like that when I persuaded Sasha to go on the timetable. I've got to stand up for myself.

210

'Sasha, you *wanted* to teach. I *was* trying to help you.'

'Teach, yes, but not stupid bloody aerobics. I'm a *dancer*. What did I go through all those years of training for?'

I can't believe she's rewriting history like this. Has she forgotten all those auditions I tried to get her to go to? How nervous she was? I've got to remember she's upset. I mustn't lose it here.

'Sasha, please, I know you're devastated, but I'm upset too. I—'

'*You*? Upset? Did you love him too? Is your precious little heart broken now? Do me a favour. You get every bloke you ever want. You just flutter your eyelashes and they fall at your feet. Even Steve in the gym.'

'Steve? He's always shouting at me. He hates me.'

'Rubbish and you know it. He's not shouting at you. He's just showing off. He told Ruby he wants to get you on the bench one night after everyone's gone because you look like you could take a bit of *pump* action. He's got you sussed, hasn't he?'

Steve? Blimey. News to me. What can I say? She doesn't give me a chance.

'Everyone says you've changed since you got that promotion. Even Maya, and she hasn't got a bad word to say about anyone.'

She's glaring at me through slitty, hate-filled eyes and I want to die. If I were one of the people listening in on this conversation, I'd hate me too. What sort of a cow am I? Have I really turned into the bitch from hell; Lydia's natural successor? Maybe it's true. Maybe subconsciously I wanted to destroy Sasha's career, then steal her man and slowly pick away at the threads of her life until the hole was so big, no patch would ever cover it—

211

What a load of bollocks.

'Sasha, I'm sorry if everyone thinks I'm a cow, but I haven't changed.'

'You're right,' she says, 'you haven't.'

Good, maybe she's calming down, seeing sen—

'No, I think you've always been a scheming, manipulative cow. It's just that we were all too stupid to see it. We all hated Lydia, but at least she only ever stabbed you in the *front*.'

Her face is still filled with loathing, but she's crying now. I realise that I'm about to start too. I've got to try and pull this conversation back to where it started, make her see things for what they are.

'Sasha, I didn't set out to steal your man, I swear,' I say, smearing a hand across my eyes. 'I didn't even suspect him until yesterday and I didn't know for sure until I asked you about him just now.'

'Right. Why don't we see what he's got to say about it then?' she says, pulling her mobile from her bag.

'You can't speak to him now, though,' I say.

'Oh, isn't that convenient? Why not?'

'He's in hospital.'

I tell her about Karl's accident.

'Oh my God, he could've been killed,' she cries. 'No wonder the poor honey didn't call me this morning.'

Poor honey? I can't believe this. Is she somehow so besotted with him that she's going to blame me for everything and let him get off scot-free? 'Sasha, you can't tell me you still care about him?' I gasp.

Her eyes well up again and she takes a defiant last swig from her bottle. 'I don't know any more,' she says, flinging her hair over her shoulder and standing up. 'All I know is that I hate you. How could I ever think of you as a friend? You're a liar, you're selfish and . . . and your hair extensions are crap.'

There are sniggers from the table behind as Sasha walks out on me.

I don't think I've ever felt so low.

Life couldn't get any shittier.

Could it?

The Bit Where Mum Changes Sides
(And For Once I'm Not
Talking About The Telly)

Of course it could.

'*Mum*, what the hell are you saying?' I yell. 'What's got into you?'

'Well, look at the facts, Charlie. You're nearly twenty-five.'

'And that's old, is it?'

'I was married at your age . . . with a kid.'

'Is that when you lost the will to live and turned into a couch potato?'

'Charlie!'

'Sorry . . . Look, all I'm saying is that things go a bit slower these days. This is London in the twenty-first century, not some peasant village where you're engaged at twelve and married at fourteen.'

'Stop being so silly. You're nearly a quarter of a century now.'

'And you stop saying that like I'm ready for meals-on-wheels.'

'You need to act your age, Charlotte, and start thinking seriously about your future. Life just flies by, you know, and you'll be old and lonely before you know it.'

I'm looking at my mum and I don't recognise her. In the olden days – like about a week ago – we wouldn't have had this argument. The old Mum was always the first person to tell me to have fun while I can because life's too short. Her mum, our nan, died two years ago. She was devastated. I remember having a cup of tea with her on the morning of the funeral. We were in the kitchen, just the two of us. 'You start out with all sorts of hopes and dreams, Charlie,' she said, sadder than I've ever seen her. 'You're thinking that they're all going to happen because you're special. You're not like everyone else and your life's going to be amazing. But then you wake up one day and realise that if your dreams were going to come true, they would've by now. You've missed your moment without even realising it.'

It was so moving that I found myself thinking it must be a speech she'd heard on last night's *Corrie*. I was hoping it was. I didn't want her sadness and disappointment to be real. 'Your dreams came true, though, didn't they, Mum?' I asked hopefully.

Dad interrupted us then, bursting into the room with, 'Hey, c'mon, hurrying, hurrying – we gonna be late,' despite the fact that the funeral was still two hours away. Then he said with his usual sensitivity, 'Hey, where my shoes, Maevou?'

Mum gave me a little smile. 'Just make sure you grab life by the wotsits. Don't miss your chance.' Then she went to look for Dad's shoes.

I only heard that speech from her once, but it was typical Mum. Freedom and fun were always what she preached. I don't understand the change. Is it sudden? Or has it been creeping up slowly and I've been too busy to notice? All I know is that right now I want the old Mum back, the one that couldn't give a shit about anything unless it was happening on the square thing in the corner.

215

The *round* thing in the other corner is looking on in quiet approval. He likes his new, improved wife. In the olden days (last week, again), whenever he had a bee in his bonnet, she'd either ignore him or tell him to shut up. Now she's as bad as him and she's not about to let up. 'Charlie, I don't know why you're so upset. Dino's a lovely boy.'

'Look, I don't even *fancy* him.' I spit this in Emily's direction. She looks terrified. And so she should be, sneaking off to bedrooms with my chosen man. OK, so I don't know what she's been up to, but it's obvious something's been going on. She's cowering on the sofa beside Dad and the only thing stopping me from turning the spotlight her way is remembering what it was like to be fifteen. Constantly lying so I could go where I wanted and see who I liked – I'm still at it for God's sake.

'What's fancying him got to do with it?' Mum asks, sounding almost, but not quite, like an old Tina Turner record. 'Grow up, Charlie. You've seen for yourself, he's good-looking, successful. You could do a lot worse, believe me,' she says, looking at Dad then giving me a smile.

She's right. Dino is good-looking and successful, but she's not getting me that easily. 'Look, Mum, he could be Jude Law with a medical degree, but after last night's fiasco I don't think I could ever face him again.'

'Wotchew tokking aboud?' Dad splutters through a mouthful of muesli. (Would you believe it, part of his new be-good-to-my-heart regime.) 'Last night I nearly dying.'

'Oh, spare me, *please* . . . Look, get used to it. Me and Dino: it's not gonna happen.'

Mum smiles at Dad this time. 'Love grows, you know. Look at your dad and me.'

I look at them: the Brad and Jen of Wood Green.

Dad looks torn. No doubt he wants to leap in and shout, '*Wotchew tokking aboud, Maevou? You always telling me you knowing the moment you seeing me I am the one*', but he doesn't want to undermine her now that she's come round to his way of thinking. There's another reason he's keeping his mouth shut. He's got half an eye on RIK, and his favourite soap is reaching one of its climactic moments. The sister thinks she's pregnant by the brother and she's worried that the baby will be a hideously deformed mutant. Well, if it comes out looking anything like her . . .

'Charlie, they're a wonderful family,' Mum says, not letting it rest. 'They've done so well for themselves. You've seen their house. I had a long chat with Maroulla today'

'What about exactly?' I ask.

'Well, even though it was all a bit chaotic round at his, what with your dad's, er, funny turn and everything, Maroulla's convinced Dino took a shine to you.'

'Mum, he was splitting up with his girlfriend and ended up having a row with me! You call that taking a shine?' I sneak a peek at Emily as I yell this. Right now she looks as if she wishes her school uniform were chintz so she could completely blend in with the sofa.

'Stop being so dramatic, Charlie. Maroulla's going to talk to him properly about it and we said we'd talk to you, didn't we, Jimmy?'

He nods. He's got his mouth full and he can't speak. Not that having a full mouth would usually stop him, but he's hooked on the TV. The sister's just walked in and caught the brother doing it with the mother. Well, that's what it looks like, but it's anyone's guess really.

'All we ask is that you give it a chance,' Mum says, going for a pleading tone.

'Yes, you give it the chunce,' Dad echoes, grimacing as he swallows the last mouthful of muesli. Or is it his soap that's offending him? 'How you know you don' like if you don' try?' The way he slams the empty bowl onto the coffee table, I reckon he's talking about the muesli.

I can't breathe. I feel trapped. *I don't want to get married*. Not to anyone, and definitely not to some idiot Greek doctor who thinks nothing of mutilating cuddly pets and needs his mum to fix him up with a marriage partner.

This is madness. I'm Charlie, Funky Manager at a place full of Funky People and Even Funkier Pop Stars. I'm eloquent, articulate and mature enough to sort out my problems in a calm and dignified manner.

'*Aarrrggh*! You're doing my head in!' I scream. 'I mean it. If you try and make me see him, I swear, I'll leave and I'll . . . I'll . . . You'll never see me again. *Ever*.'

I run from the room, slamming the door behind me for effect, which actually has no effect at all because it bounces soundlessly back open again. I hear Dad yelling '*Theglitsa*, you coming back here, but ferst, go gedding me the chizcake in fridge. I'm bluddy starving!'

But he can get lost. They all can.

I AM <u>NOT</u> MARRYING DINO.

Now, am I making myself perfectly clear?

The Bit Where My World
Falls On Me

'Doing you, Theglottsa Charalambous, taking the man, Dino Georgiou, to obeying him, doing him the cooking, clinning and everything else his wanting without comblain till the death is doing you apart?'

'I doing . . . I mean *do*,' I whisper so quietly that the packed congregation can't hear.

'Whad you saying? Spik up,' shouts the priest, who for a short Greek bloke is towering over me – well, I am kneeling. He looks just like Professor Dumbledore. Actually, he is Professor Dumbledore. Only not half as kindly. And out of wizard costume. With a Greek accent.

'I do,' I say a little louder, trying not to choke on the words. Two thousand people are squashed into the church and I can *feel* their joy. I hear the cheer from outside, where thousands more are gathered in the village square. They're watching the action on a thirty-foot screen, erected at huge expense – Dad had to sell the sandwich bar to pay for it. Cyprus has never seen a wedding like it.

'And Dino Georgiou, are you taking the Thegla to be doing your cooking, clinning and ironing and the waiting on your hands and feet until the death is doing her apart?'

'I do,' Dino booms proudly.

Father Dumbledore beams, as does the rest of the hairy congregation – because they all have beards. Down to their knees in the case of some of the older women. 'Good. So I is naming you the man and the wife. Now you doing the kissing.'

Dino reaches over, lifts my veil and unmasks my grief. My face is mascara-streaked, my lips are wobbling and I can taste my tears. I'd run now if the three thousand acres of white silk and taffeta wrapped around my body allowed any movement. Dino leans towards me and puckers his lips. Then a voice behind me bursts into raucous, uninhibited song. Is that? . . . No, surely it can't be. I knew Maroulla hadn't skimped on the invitations, but I didn't think she'd sent one to the Godfather of Soul . . .

'Get up! I said get on upp-ah!'

I jump, banging my head on the marble reception desk where it's been resting. Must have fallen asleep. In front of me I see James Brown in triplicate as he performs on the three TVs. Behind me a groin grinds rhythmically into my bum. Could only be Daniel.

'This is your wake-up call, Ms Charalambous,' he singsongs.

'Sorry, don't know what's got into me. Terrible night last night,' I say, rubbing my eyes.

'Pining for Mr Lover Man?'

'God, no . . . Just some family shit. You don't want to know.'

'You're right, I don't. Anyway, I've done Zone Check. Everything A-OK. Except for Steve. He's a feisty bastard today. Found him bollocking one of the rowing machines for not pulling its weight.'

Steve. Of all the nightmares swilling around my head, all the vicious stuff Sasha threw at me, it's what

220

she said about Steve that's bugging me more than anything. I've got to ask. 'Daniel, has Steve got a girlfriend?'

'Course not. He's saving himself for *you*, honey. He's got your picture on his locker door – well, your head on some porn star's body. Didn't you know? Everyone else does.'

I'm beginning to wonder if there's anything I *do* know about this place. The only two certainties seem to be that Sasha loathes me and Steve doesn't – and I don't know which of those two to be more bothered about. As for Daniel, I can't figure him out. He seems friendly enough, but the shit he's pulled recently, the sly digs . . . God, I'm confused.

But I've got to get my act together and fast. Channel Four will be here tomorrow with their cameras and there's plenty to be getting on with if we don't want to look like complete amateurs – and I'm pretty sure that complete amateurism isn't part of Jamie's vision. The place has gone a bit mental in anticipation. Honestly, it's as if none of us has ever appeared in a prime-time documentary . . . Which, actually, we haven't.

At least one thing I won't have to deal with is a mad-as-hell Sasha. She phoned in sick – again. I really want to straighten things out with her, but today isn't the best time.

Another one who's thrown a sicky is Blaize. Mission Management rang first thing. I immediately panicked, thinking it was the 'See you in court' call. But her flunky only wanted to cancel her rehearsals until further notice. The poor thing is 'resting'. I mentioned that a documentary crew would be in tomorrow. I had a suspicion that this might speed her recovery – we'll see. I also asked if they knew how Karl was. 'Who?' flunky asked.

'So, what's on the agenda today, boss?' Daniel asks me. God knows if the boss thing is a dig – like I said, I haven't a clue any longer.

'The production-company people will be here in an hour or so to do their final prepping. I've got to stick around for them, so, er, do you think you could do me a huge favour? Would you mind going to the hospital and seeing how Karl is?'

'Why?' he says indignantly. 'He's not my boyfriend.'

'Believe it or not, he's not mine either.'

I finally give him the dirt on Karl Benjamin.

'Jesus, he's not just a Nelly lookalike, he's the full Nelly fuck-alike. And I thought I was a horny little bastard,' he gasps when I've finished. Though he's trying to be sympathetic, he can't keep the admiration out of his voice. 'How did Sasha take the news?'

'Let's put it this way. I don't think I'll be on her Christmas-card list.'

'She can't blame you . . . Can she?'

'I don't know, I really don't know,' I say, feeling all the crap I've been trying so hard to keep in check well up inside me.

'What's wrong?' Daniel asks.

I don't know how to put this so I just blurt it out. 'Is it true that everyone around here hates me?'

Daniel squirms awkwardly and the fact that he can't look me in the eye is all the answer I need. After an agonising pause he says, 'I don't.'

'Really?' I say pathetically.

'Course I bloody don't,' he says, putting an arm around my shoulder. 'What's brought this on?'

God, why did I even bring it up? If everyone really *does* hate me, do I really want to hear it? 'Forget it,' I say after a moment. 'So, will you go up to the hospital for me?'

'Do I have to?' He looks gutted, no doubt because he'll miss the chance to schmooze the TV crew. He's got the showbiz bug big-time. He looks gorgeous today. Zone-blue from head to toe with matching blue contacts. He does look pretty damn sexy, as it happens, in a pop-star, hey-look-at-me kind of way.

'Someone has to go,' I say. 'He may be a lying, cheating scumbag, but he did hurt himself pretty badly on our turf. *Please*, Daniel.'

'OK, if I must,' he says.

And then he hugs me and I wish he'd never let go.

Now I'm wishing I hadn't sent Daniel off. The moment he left the phones went mad. Seems word has got out that we're going to be on the telly. Suddenly every class is booked solid tomorrow. Is there anyone in the world who doesn't want to be on television? Yes. My parents. They're only interested in being in front of it. When I mentioned the programme to them, Dad said (without taking his eyes off the telly), 'TV juss rubbish. Why you no doing something useful? Like tegging interest in logol politiggs like me? I thinking I pud myself up for Leader for Hurringey, sort out the bluddy willy-bins once and for oll.'

Talking of Mum and Dad, I haven't spoken to them since my dramatic exit from the front room last night. Our house has never been so quiet. I should have blazing rows more often; I might get a bit of peace. Emily looked terrified at breakfast. I almost felt sorry for her. I can't stop wondering what on earth Dino thinks I should talk to her about. Why doesn't he talk to her, what with him being so *sensitive*?

Stop it, Charlie. I can't worry about all of that now. I've got The Zone to deal with. The phones are going into meltdown, both the clients and the staff have stars

223

in their eyes and every couple of minutes someone from the TV crew gets in my face with another question. Can they put a camera in the women's changing room? Of course they bloody can't.

Where is Daniel? He's taking ages at the hospital. I really must talk to Jamie about hiring more staff, but the last time I saw him he was bollocking me for letting Jacqueline in. As ever, picking the right moment is going to be a problem.

I hear the swoosh of the doors opening and I snap into my smiling, erect welcome-to-The-Zone pose, which is immediately ruined by my jaw dropping as Emily scuttles across the marble floor towards me.

'What are you doing here?' I ask when she reaches the desk. 'Haven't you got a maths lesson or something?'

'I knew I shouldn't have expected you to care.' Her bottom lip trembles and chubby tears appear at the corners of her eyes. 'I'll just go then,' she whimpers pitifully as she turns to leave.

I give in. 'Wait, Emily, *wait*. What's the matter?'

'There's something I've got to talk about and . . . Look, I didn't know who else to come to, all right?'

She must be in trouble if she's come to *me*. We haven't exactly got a track record of helping one another out, so this is freaky. About as likely as Christina going to Pink for singing tips.

'OK, OK,' I say, spotting Daniel trudging up the steps, 'let me hand over here and we'll go to my office.'

Emily plonks herself on a sofa and gazes up at the tellies in a daze. Daniel walks up to the desk, giving her the once-over – well, we don't see many school uniforms in here.

'How is he?' I ask him.

'Bandaged and on a heart monitor, but from the way he's flirting with the big Jamaican mama on his ward,

224

I'd say he'll be spreading his seed around the South East again in no time.'

'*Seriously.*'

'Seriously, he's got five stitches and concussion. They're keeping him in another night for observation, but he'll be home tomorrow. He said thanks for sorting him out and sorry about wrecking the sound system.'

'So he's not going to sue?'

'Shame. I was looking forward to seeing you in the dock . . . Who's the schoolgirl?' He's looking at Emily, who's dabbing at her eyes with a damp tissue. 'She looks suicidal.'

'My sister. She's having a crisis. Probably lost a netball match. Do you mind looking after things for a few minutes while I deal with her?'

'God, I have to do *everything* round here.'

'I can't stay away from the desk for too long,' I say as I close my office door. 'And if it's money you want, you can get lost now.'

'I knew it was stupid coming here,' Emily sniffs, pushing past me. I grab her shoulders and stop her.

'I'm sorry. Sit down and tell me about it.' I try to find my Samaritan's voice the way I did with Dino the other night. But I've never done caring with Emily before and it feels weird. Do I put an arm around her? Tell her *there, there, everything's going to be fine*? This could be another elaborate trick for all I know. Still crying, she sits down in the chair next to the desk and I look at her properly. She doesn't look like the kid sister from hell. She just seems very young and very scared.

'I'm going to be in *so* much trouble,' she says quietly.

What's she done, for God's sake? Has she been caught

bunking off? Cheating in a French test? Smoking crack behind the bike sheds?

'It can't be that bad,' I say. 'Come on, it won't seem so awful when it's out.' I'm trying for a positive tone, but I sound like Mum does when I try to tell her something important and she just wants me to hurry up so she can watch the telly.

'You can't tell anyone, OK?' Emily says. 'If you do, I'll never speak to you ever again.'

Oh, like that would be a bad thing?

But I don't say that. 'I won't tell a soul,' I mumble.

Her face contorts, her mouth opens and a wail spills out. It sounds like *'I'm pregnant!'*. Then she collapses into a heap across the paperwork that's systematically strewn on my desk.

I want to laugh. How sick is that? I want to sing, 'Na, na, na, naaa, na, you're in *trur*-bull!'

But I don't.

Because despite what Sasha said about the world and his wife hating me, I'm honestly not a bad person and I'm going to start proving that right now with Emily.

'Are you sure?' I ask gently.

'Of course I am. Do you think I'd come here to see *you* if I wasn't?'

'Whose is it?' I ask, struggling not to snap at her. I'm truly baffled because I didn't even know she had a boyfriend. Didn't know she had a sex life at all beyond fluttering her eyelashes down the Shopping City.

'I can't tell you,' she sobs. 'Dad'll *kill* me.'

'Well, I'm not Dad. I think it'll help if you can tell me who he is, Emily.' (Though I'm not sure why, apart from it satisfying my nosiness.) 'Does the guy know?'

She doesn't answer; just sobs.

A penny is dropping – clunking like a lead weight. 'You've spoken to Dino about this, haven't you?' I ask incredulously, suddenly realising that this is why he wanted me to talk to her.

'Well, like, *duh*! What else do you think we were doing upstairs?'

'That's not the point,' I splutter, though, until now, what she was *doing* up there was the only thing I was interested in. 'I just can't believe you've gone to a complete stranger rather than your own family.'

'Oh yeah, like I'd come running straight to *you*.'

She's right. I've hardly been there for her, have I? I feel bad now. She must be in a terrible state – well, I can *see* that she is. She's fifteen, for God's sake. What's she going to do with a kid?

'Will you stop looking at me like that?' she says, lifting her head and seeing what I'd hoped was my kindly, understanding face, but what is obviously still my gob-smacked stare. 'Jesus, Dad is *so* going to kill me.'

She's right again, poor kid. Dad is so going to kill her. But I can't say that. I've got to keep the situation calm while I think.

'What am I gonna do?' she whimpers.

'I reckon . . . um . . . I think . . .' Go on, then, what *do* I think? Must pull myself together. 'Look, it's not going to be that bad . . .' What am I talking about? *Of course it is*. 'Actually, it is bad. It's a disaster. If Dad finds out he will kill you.' *Duh*! That is not what I meant to say at all.

'Wha'thefuckamIgonnadoooooooo?' she wails before dissolving into her most helpless, hysterical sobs yet.

I am so *rubbish*. Got to get a grip and handle this properly.

'Have you spoken to the father?' I ask gently.

She doesn't answer.

'Who is he? Do you want me to go and see him with you?'

227

Still no answer, just muffled sobs.

'Why are you protecting him, Emily? Is he older? Did he take advantage of you? Should we be going to the cops with this?'

'*Shut up*!' she snaps. 'He didn't take advantage of me. It was *special* and we *love* each other. And of course I've talked to him. He's shitting himself. What do you expect him to do? He's just a kid.'

Like she's anything but.

'Well, if he loved you, maybe he'd be here by your side, trying to help you through this,' I say.

'I *knew* you wouldn't understand,' she spits. 'You're such a *crap* person to talk to. Anyway, you don't know the first thing about love. Who'd fall in love with an ugly old bag like you?'

I'm about to lose it now – grab her by the arm and march her onto the street – and she must be able to read my mind because she gushes a fresh fountain of tears and says, 'What am I gonna *do*, Charlie?'

She's unbelievable. She comes all this way, insults me and then fixes me with the puppy-dog eyes that have been working on Dad for years and expects me to help her. But she's right – *again*. I do have to help her. I'm her big sister. I may be rubbish at it, but I'm the only one she's got; I've got to be there for her now.

And in my expert big-sister opinion, having considered the options, I've come to the conclusion that she doesn't have any. Well, she has one.

'Emily, calm down, take a deep breath and listen to me,' I say, before taking a deep breath of my own. 'You're going to have to get rid of it.'

'What do you mean?'

'Have an abortion.'

Cue full-blown hysteria. Blimey, I'm going to have to put my arm around her now. I reach out . . . but it

228

doesn't feel right. I stick with it, though, because, well, I'm sure it's what proper big sisters would do. 'Come on, Emily, you're fifteen. You can't have a kid.'

'But what about the father?' she sniffs. 'Doesn't he have a say?'

'He'll thank you, believe me. Besides, there's only one *father* you should be worrying about.'

'You're not going to tell him?' she asks, a look of pure Hammer horror on her face.

I feel a sudden surge of power. It's not pleasant, but it's definitely there. This must be what it feels like to have Killer Instinct. I have the means to get her grounded for at least a year *and* end Mum and Dad's quest to find me a husband, because they'll be too focused on Emily to think about anything else. But something stops me from enjoying the moment. Probably the fact that I don't really have Killer Instinct.

'Don't worry. I won't tell Dad anything,' I say. 'This is bad enough without him getting in on the act.'

'How am I gonna . . . you know?' she asks.

Luckily I've already thought of that. Daniel had to take his sister to a place in Harley Street last year. He gave me the number in case I needed to get hold of him. I kept it because . . . Well, a girl never knows when she might need a number like that herself, right?

'I know a place – a private clinic,' I say.

'But I haven't got any money.'

Should have known she'd hit me for cash eventually.

'I'll lend you it. Just don't ever try to blackmail me again.'

'I don't know, Charlie.'

'Look, just go for a consultation. Get some proper advice and then you can make the best decision.'

'OK . . . If you think so.'

Never – not *once* – has my sister sounded so meek in my presence. I might be feeling a touch triumphant if this weren't such a fucking mess.

'Will you come with me?' she asks.

I can't believe I'm saying this: 'Of course I will. I'll call them now.'

I reach under my desk for my bag and look for my Filofax . . . Which isn't in there. *Shit*. My entire life is in that thing. I can't afford to lose it. God, the shame if anyone were to look inside it. All my personal stuff: period dates, smear-test results, lists of the ten most snoggable Hollywood stars – the kind of things *all* girls make a record of . . . Don't they?

'What's the matter?' Emily asks, registering the anxiety on my face.

'I've lost my Filofax.'

'I haven't got it,' she gabbles – her standard knee-jerk denial.

I glare at her.

'I *swear*, Charlie.'

For once I believe her. But where the hell is it? Think, think, think . . . The last time I had it was . . . *Think!* . . . Karl's flat. Monday night. After we'd shagged, I heard my mobile ring. I remember taking everything out of my bag, my Filofax included, in the rush to answer it. I must have left it on his coffee table.

Bugger.

But I can get it back. I've just spotted Karl's kit bag in the corner. I meant to give it to Daniel to take to the hospital, but I forgot. Karl's keys are in there. I can go to his flat after work. He won't mind, will he? Hang on, what am I worried about? Firstly, he'll never know, and secondly, with all the grief he's caused me, why should I give a shit?

'What are we gonna do, Charlie?' Emily asks.

'It's OK. I left my Filofax round a mate's. I can get it back tonight and call the clinic tomorrow.'

'What mate?'

'No one you know.'

'Is it *Karl*?' she says, her eyes going from puppy to slitty.

'It's none of your business, right?'

'I can find out, you know,' she says slyly, almost as if she's forgotten the mess she's in. She just can't help herself.

'Listen, don't even think about snooping round my life again because I've got the *best* shit on you *ever*.'

I feel so much better now she's reverted to type. *This* Emily I can deal with.

Quietly slip key into lock . . . Turn . . . Click . . . I'm in.

Jesus, who do I think I am? Charlie the cat burglar? Silly. I'm Charlie, Karl's mate (after a fashion), and I'm simply popping round his to drop off his stuff and pick up an essential personal item.

But I still feel sneaky as I close his front door behind me. His hall is pitch black. I fumble for the switch and call out, 'Hi, anybody home?' I know the place is empty, but I have thought this through. I'm being upfront so that if anyone should walk in and catch me, I can hold my hands up and say, 'What do you mean *snooping*? I called out to see if anybody was here, didn't I?'

I walk through to the front room and put the light on. There it is, exactly where I left it on the coffee table. My Filofax. Right next to an empty bottle of wine and two dirty glasses. Funny. Plain old wine. He only ever gave me champagne. Wonder who he had round after me? And why on earth am I feeling jealous, because, if I'm honest, that's what I'm feeling right now. I couldn't have met a bigger bastard than Karl Benjamin – a man who can screw with my head even as he lies concussed in hospital.

Stick with the plan, Charlie. Just get the hell out.

I grab my Filofax and shove it into my bag. Then I turn on my heel and head directly for the door. Except I stop by his bathroom. It's not snooping; it's *peeing*. I'm sticking to the plan: I came, I retrieved, I got the hell out (apart from a quick pee).

But as I sit on the loo I'm tempted. Everyone likes a good snoop, don't they? Who doesn't look through the cupboards when their host isn't in the room? It's why those home makeover shows are so popular. Nothing to do with interior design. They're just a licence to nose around someone else's home. So after I've flushed the toilet, I stick my head round his bedroom door. It's pretty tidy. No sex-tangled sheets. Everything in its place. Move along now; there's nothing to see.

I try the next door. The one that was locked when I was looking for the bathroom on Sunday morning . . . Only this time it opens. I freeze, my stomach doing a guilty lurch. This room was locked. Why? And why is it any of my business? But it's open now, so might as well have a quick peek and then I'll be off. Out of his life. Forever.

I put my head round the door and reach for the light switch. The room floods with light from a bare bulb dangling from the ceiling. I blink and peer inside. I don't know what I was expecting. A spare bed? There isn't one. No furniture of any description. No weights or rowing machines. Or manly toolboxes overflowing with screwdrivers and spanners. Or walls papered with ripped-out magazine photos of Jill Dando. Or whatever it is that single blokes might keep in the spare room with the locked door.

What can I see? Bare, stained floorboards, a TV and VCR and a wall of shelves from floor to ceiling. The shelves are stacked with what look like video tapes. I step into the room and a closer inspection confirms that's exactly what they are. So he's a film nut. Big deal. We like movies in our house too, but our video collection runs from one end of the mantelpiece to the other – and six or seven of those contain episodes of *Dallas* that Mum refuses to let us tape over.

I walk along the shelves and look at the labels, idly curious about his tastes. What does he like, then? Action? Martial arts? Romantic comedies? And who's Michelle Timms? Not a very Hollywood name, but she's made three movies by the looks of it. And Kristin Jenkins? Five tapes have her name neatly written down the spines in black felt-tip. Only one Monica F, but seven Polly Turners. What's going on here? As I scan the shelves, every tape shows a woman's name and there must be a couple of hundred of them. Is he a casting director or something?

I have an unsettling feeling that, actually, he's an *or something* and I'm not quite sure what that *something* is. Suddenly I'm no longer being mildly nosy. I'm now engaged in heavy-duty snooping and it doesn't feel good. I should get the hell out of here. *Now*. And I would if I hadn't spotted a name that makes me stop in my tracks. *Sasha Taylor*. Four tapes side by side with Sash's name on the spines. And – *fuck* – who's that next to her? *Charlie C*. I never made a movie, did I? I'm getting a very strange feeling about this. I reach out with a sweaty hand and pull the tape with my name on it from the shelf. I'm thinking that I know what's on it and the idea makes me want to throw up. Though I don't want to see it, I *need* to, so I take it to the VCR in the corner of the room and feed it into the slot. I press *play* and turn on the TV . . . *Ouch*, that's loud. I grab the remote and fumble for *mute*. Don't think now would be the moment to disturb the neighbours.

I focus on the screen and . . .

I'm so nauseous that I have to suppress the urge to vomit with a huge physical effort. How do I explain how I feel to be looking at this . . . ?

You know how hearing your own voice on tape is a weird and unsettling experience? Like you can't believe you sound that *crap*? Well, try watching a video of yourself having sex and you can multiply the discomfort by at least a billion. And that doesn't even begin to describe the horror I'm experiencing as I watch Karl and my tangled bodies writhe on his bed. I can see – oh my bloody fucking God – *everything*.

I can't watch any more. I lunge for the eject button and grab the tape as the machine spits it out. I sit on the floor, listening to the sound of my desperate panting.

I'm so angry with myself. How could I have been so stupidly, moronically naïve? *He didn't even have a hidden camera, Charlie.* It was there in the middle of his bedroom. In full view. On a great big bloody tripod, screaming *Hey, look at me, I'm a camera* and *Wow, look at you, you're naked*. I remember asking him about it and believing – actually *falling* for – his bull-shit about taping himself rehearsing.

But if I'm mad at me, I'm so livid with Karl that I want to go to the hospital, uncoil the bandage from around his head and reopen that cut of his with a big, shiny axe. I can't believe what he's done. The complete fucking bastardness of it. This has got to be illegal. I didn't sign a release form, did I? What a stupid thing to think. But everything about this is so completely wrong, how could anybody think straight?

But think straight is precisely what I have to do. I try to recall all the times Karl and I had sex. Only twice in his bedroom. Only twice for the camera, then. I stand up on wobbly legs and check the shelves. There it is. A second tape with my name on. I grab it and shove both of them into my bag. Then I take the four Sasha Taylors and stuff them in beside the Charlies. Actually, not all four of them. I hold one back. I may be feeling sicker than I've ever felt in my life, but if I'm going to take these cassettes I've got to be sure. Because you never know, it might not be her – there might be another Sasha Taylor. Weirder things have happened and I wouldn't want to be waltzing off with the tapes of a stranger.

I slip it into the VCR and press *play*. Unless my eyes are deceiving me, oh my God, it's her. And the Sasha that I thought was primmer and proper-er than Mary Poppins, the Sasha that never put-out – not even empties for the milkman – is up on the screen, doing it in full colour. And, what is she wearing? And what's that he's shoving— And, God, that wax must *hurt* when it's poured right onto your— Stop, stop, for fuck's sake press *stop*.

Enough.

Will I ever be able to look Sasha in the eye again?

That's tomorrow's worry. Right now, I've got a job to do. I start at the corner of the top shelf and systematically work my way through Karl's home-movie collection. I'm looking for any more Sashas, Charlies, STs, CCs, or any other combination of letters that may be one of the two of us.

It strikes me now that Karl's entire sexual history must be chronicled on these shelves. And, good God, has he ever been a busy little fucker? What does he do with all these tapes? No, no, *no*, I do *not* want to go there. I'm tempted to take the whole lot, put them in a pile and torch them. Strike a blow for the sisterhood.

No time for that. Gotta get on and get out.

I've reached the bottom shelf and found no more tapes. Just one cardboard box to check. It's sitting on the floor, separate from Karl's porn library, so maybe it doesn't contain more of the same. But I have to make sure. I reach over and lift the flap. Yup, full to the brim with videos. Must be about twenty of them, all labelled with the same name. Just the one. Because there's no need for a distinguishing surname this time.

Not when your first name's Blaize.

THE MIDDLE BIT

The Bit Where Soulla Has A Baby And I Have A Row

I am so *not* in the mood for today.

This must happen all the time. The likes of Ant and Dec, Cat Deeley and Davina must wake up and think *I do not want to be on the telly today*. Well, that's exactly how I feel. Except, of course, this is my one chance – probably ever – of being on TV . . . But I am so *not* in the mood for it.

Even so, I've made the effort. Before I left home I changed outfits four times, reapplied lipstick, eye shadow and mascara ten times and spent an hour putting my extensions into various types of ponytail only to leave it all down.

I check myself out one last time in The Zone's mirrored glass. *Hmm*, slightly overdone. Be natural, Claire told us yesterday. Some hope. I look at the two black-suited security guys on the door. Friends of Stan Lee, the Tai Kwan Do master, so no doubt they can kill a man with just a wiggle of their little fingers. I think that today, however, they'll be fighting off teenage TV-wannabes rather than highly trained ninja assassins.

I take a deep breath and tell myself to put all my shit behind me and get on with it. Then I head up the steps, two at a time, flashing my laminated Zone ID at the bouncers.

Charlie to base, I'm going in . . .

I didn't sleep last night. Again. Virtually not a wink. If I carry on at this rate the bags under my eyes are going to engulf me. I kept going over stuff in my head: Sasha's attack on me, the contents of Karl's spare room, then my sister turning me into an unborn-baby murderer, not to mention the pre-TV tension I was feeling. But last night was no ordinary anxiety-packed night. No chance of that, because last night my Soulla-in-law went into delivery mode.

When I got home from Karl's it was only nine thirty, but Emily was already in bed. I tapped lightly on her door, but she didn't answer. Obviously she didn't want to talk, which I could totally respect because neither did I. Mum and Dad were where they always are, she barely looking up from the TV, he telling me about the row he'd had with the pizza delivery boy. He finally gets a meal delivered and he still ends up in an argument. Unbelievable.

'Why the row, Dad?' I asked.

''Cause I no order no bluddy pizza, thass why. He bringing to the wrong uddress!'

I made my excuses and went upstairs. I did think about calling Sasha and trying to explain again, maybe even telling her about the tapes, but I was too scared that she'd find a way of blaming me for those too, so I just went to bed. But I couldn't sleep. How is sleep possible when every time you close your eyes you see yourself starring in a home-made porn movie with Britain's answer to Seymour Butts?

I finally drifted off at just gone two. That's when I heard the phone ring, followed less than a minute later by Dad battering down my door. 'Geddup, *geddup*!' he yelled. 'We going. Oll of us. Hurrying, *hurrying*!'

240

'I'm not going anywhere,' I shouted back. 'I've got work tomorrow.'

'Your brotha having his baby and you going if I have to dragging you!'

We like to share stuff in our family. Picnics, colds and flu, childbirth. In fact, the most trivial thing can be turned into a major Charalambous Event. A few months ago, Emily's mate Alicia came for a sleepover. She got up in the middle of the night for a glass of water and Dad, a light sleeper who's awake at the merest twist of a tap, was up like a shot. Naturally he woke the rest of us. 'Is OK, Ulisha she juss need the drink of water!' he bellowed, knocking on my bedroom door, then Emily's. 'Is OK, Emily, your friend she juss gedding drink. Go back to slip.'

Unsurprisingly, Alicia hasn't visited since. And a good job she wasn't staying last night otherwise she'd have found herself being hauled out of bed and frogmarched to the car for the journey to North Middlesex Hospital. 'We'll be doing this for you in nine months if you don't get your shit together,' I whispered to Emily, as Dad took a right turn like he was auditioning for the part of Getaway Driver in the next Guy Ritchie movie.

'Piss off,' she whispered back.

The midwives weren't too happy when we tipped up. Understandable, since Soulla's entire family was already there, as well as some of their neighbours, their families and friends and some strays they'd picked up on the journey. It was quite a mob. And, of course, they'd brought food. Greeks do that – take large quantities of food wherever they go (*'Going to the corner shop? Hey, I frying you some chiggen to eat on way'*). I was amazed the hospital didn't evict us. I overheard one of them saying to her colleague, '*Greeks*.' It was all the explanation she needed.

As soon as we arrived, Tony burst out of the delivery room. He was flushed and breathless, but he managed to gasp, 'She's amazing, Dad. She's doing it completely naturally.'

And we could *hear* her doing it. Actually, they could probably hear the screams in Moscow. So that's what my brother meant by *natural*. No need for electronic amplification – kind of *Childbirth Unplugged*. As we sat in the waiting room I looked at Emily. Her face was bleached, no doubt mirroring my own. Looked as if she was finally projecting ahead nine months and wasn't liking what she was seeing. I had the feeling I'd be taking her to the abortion clinic sooner rather than later.

I couldn't sit in that waiting room another second. It was nearly three o'clock and the crowd was acting like it was Party in the Park. I needed some peace. I went off in search of a coffee machine. As I walked along the corridor, I heard screams coming from another of the delivery rooms. I stood outside, listening to cries in what sounded like Arabic. The volume was terrifying and made Soulla sound like a mouse. Poor girl, the pain must have been unbearable. Suddenly, the cries stopped, just like that. Total silence. I feared the worst. Was she dead? Was there something wrong with the baby?

Then a nurse walked out of the room, smiling. Through the crack in the door I could just make out the exhausted, sweat-soaked face of the girl on the bed. She was holding what looked like a bundle of hospital blankets. She looked like shit, but I have *never* seen an expression like the one on her face at that moment and it overwhelmed me. I think that must be what they call love.

I was choked. I walked on a bit, and I didn't notice I was crying till I felt the hand on my shoulder.

'Hey, are you OK?'

I spun round, saw Dino standing there and almost

242

fainted. Not swooning at the sight of him in that sexy white coat, oozing doctorish power and authority. No, not that at all, *honestly*. It was just the lateness of the hour, a lack of food, general stress and exhaustion . . .

'Dino,' I squeaked (I hate it when I squeak). 'Sorry, you made me jump. What are you doing here?'

'It's part of my rotation,' he said, although he may as well have been speaking Greek for all the sense that made. My face must have registered confusion. He smiled. 'Just means that Bart's has to share me with everyone else, that's all.'

He caught me staring at the specks of blood on the front of his coat.

'Don't worry, I haven't been operating on any small rodents,' he laughed. He gestured to the room I'd just been standing outside. 'We had some complications, but I just delivered a ten-pounder in there. Incredible.' He looked high, buzzing on adrenaline.

'Wonderful,' I said and I meant it. 'Just don't expect me to go through anything like that in a hurry . . . *Euurggh.*'

He laughed again. 'Women always say that. But most of them end up doing it. And then, amazingly, they do it again.'

'Must have something to do with you doctors,' I gushed. Blimey. Was I flirting?

We stood awkwardly for a bit. I was searching for something to say; something harmless that wasn't smart-arse or gushy-flirty and wasn't going to lead to any stupid arguments about blind gerbils or whose family was madder. Then he broke the silence with, 'So, what are you doing here?'

'It's my sister-in-law. She's having—'

I stopped because a pretty, grey-eyed nurse had come over to him. 'Nice going, Doctor D,' she said, nodding

243

back towards the room containing the ten-pounder. 'She had me worried there for a while. It's lucky you were around.' She gushed the last bit. Was she flirting?

'Thanks, Molly. Er, I've finished here now. Are you nearly through? I'll, um, I'll hang on for you if you like.'

'Great. I'll be about ten minutes.' She turned and went back to the delivery room, a skip in her step. Who skips at three in the morning?

Dino seemed embarrassed. 'Right, OK, I'd better go,' he said to me.

'*Mmm*. Don't want to be late for *Molly*,' I said, thinking, *What, am I jealous?* and then, *Why the hell am I jealous?* and more to the point, *Why aren't I making a better job of bloody well hiding it if I am?*

'Right, nice to see you again,' he said, shuffling awkwardly from foot to foot. 'Er, by the way, did you speak to Emily yet? I'm sorry we didn't get to talk about it properly the other day, but things got a bit—'

'Don't worry about it, Doctor *D*. Or should that be *Dean*?' I snapped, cursing myself even as the words were coming out of my mouth. 'What are we calling ourselves these days?'

'You shorten Charlotte, don't you?' he said, still trying to sound pleasant, but struggling. 'If people want to play around with my name, that's up to them. I don't mind.'

'Good for you. Anyway, don't worry about Emily. I'm sorting it out, thanks. You don't have to worry about us any more. You can just get back to *Molly* the *midwife*,' were the exact words that came out of my mouth. *Doh!* What did I say that for? What I meant to say was *'Thanks for helping my sister come talk to me so we could sort things out together. We really owe you.'*

'What's your problem?' he asked, a stunned look on his face.

244

I knew exactly what my problem was. I hated him at that moment. So self-righteous and . . . I don't know, but I hated him anyway, just for looking so despicably gorgeous. Actually, I didn't hate him. But from the moment Molly the midwife appeared, my mouth seemed to have become possessed by some evil, jealous spirit and I had absolutely no control over what came out. I didn't tell him that, though. No, I said, 'My problem? I'll tell you what my problem is. You lot have wormed your way into my family, suckered my parents, and all this time no one has any idea what your game is.'

'And what exactly is my game?'

'Oh, come on,' I, or rather the evil spirit, said by taking charge of my mouth again. 'First it was Coral and now you've gone and got yourself a Molly. You men are unbelievable.'

He stared at me, the self-control visibly draining from his body. Then, through very gritted teeth he said, 'Molly has her exams next week and I promised I'd help her with her theory. I have been on a twelve-hour shift, but I'm now going to the staff room to pore over medical textbooks because I happen to think she'll make an excellent midwife one day. I'm fucking knackered and I was going to get myself a coffee and ask if maybe you wanted to join me, but given your feelings on men, I don't think I'll bother.'

I don't suppose I need to tell you that he didn't kiss me goodbye. He spun on his heel and stormed off, white coat flapping. At that exact same moment the evil spirit buggered off too. I was left flapping my mouth and feeling more foolish than I had since, oh, the day I stood in front of a class of forty-six women, convinced I could teach – only that time I was possessed by the spirit of Paula sodding Abdul.

I didn't want a coffee any more. I didn't want anything apart from to find a dark hole and crawl into it for about a thousand years. Humiliation is a dreadful feeling, and there's no humiliation worse than the one you dish out to yourself. I went back to the relative sanctuary of the waiting room, where Soulla's tortured screams provided the perfect soundtrack to the sickening visions swirling around my head. Me on those fucking tapes again, merging in with me shedding all my dignity in front of Dino. I shut my eyes, wanting to fall asleep, but sleep was impossible. Was that Soulla still screaming? Or was it me?

She finally pushed it out at four forty-five. Tony burst into the waiting room and announced in a trembling voice that he had another baby girl. What happened next? Spontaneous applause, whoops of delight, an outburst of Greek dancing? No, the reaction was pancake-flat. Everyone – led, of course, by my dad – had so wanted the baby to be a boy, that they couldn't hide their disappointment.

'She got no hair,' Dad grumbled when we got to see her. She was as bald and shiny as a pink snooker ball; completely different to Emily, his English rose, who came out looking like a seven-pound werewolf. Dad's resentment really got to me. Poor Soulla had been through hell and all he could do was mark her down for producing a baby with the wrong sex and an un-Greek lack of body hair. I couldn't believe I was feeling sorry for her, but I was. 'Well done, Soulla,' I said as warmly as I could manage. I take my hat off to any woman who goes through something that makes her scream like she's starring in *Maternity Ward on Elm Street* and lives to tell the tale.

And tell the tale is exactly what she planned to do – every gruesome twist and turn of it.

'I'm really tired. *Please* can we go?' Emily moaned, echoing my own feelings. Soulla was just getting to the really fascinating bit where the head comes out. Too much information. I've seen *Alien* and know all I need to about heads popping out of ridiculous places, thank you.

We finally got back home at six twenty. Just in time to jump into the shower and begin my exhaustive preparations for the biggest day of my short career.

'You look like shit, darling,' says Daniel, who looks anything but. He's very pumped, as if he's packed six months' worth of personal training into a single evening. He's wearing his shimmering blue contacts and his shiny Lycra vest, the one that's cut off at the shoulders, neck and waist. More of a boob tube, actually. 'You look as if you haven't slept for a week,' he continues. 'Why don't you go home? I can manage here. I didn't want to completely hog the cameras, but, you know, if I *must* . . .'

'I'll be OK,' I say, stifling a yawn.

The Zone opens its doors at nine today. The late start was Jamie's idea. 'Gives everyone a chance to wake up before the cameras roll,' he said. Gives everyone a chance to work themselves into a frenzy of uncontrollable excitement more like. The reception area is crowded with staff, who look like they've breakfasted on E, amphetamines and adrenaline shots, washed down by mugs of coffee (with the coffee taken out and only the caffeine left behind). Amazing that anything can penetrate my fatigue, but even I'm catching the buzz.

Francesca from the sauna is sitting on the desk. Suddenly she flings herself backwards into an elaborate centrefold pose and announces, 'Remember, everyone, *no* playing to the cameras. You've got to act totally normally.'

'*Normal*?' exclaims Ruby the spin mistress. 'What the hell's normal? I can't even remember how to breathe.'

'I don't know what all the fuss is about,' says Maya the yoga queen.

'Don't you *ever* get excited?' Francesca asks.

'Oh, she does when she comes, darling,' Daniel says. 'I hear she drops her nail file and chants *ommmm*.'

Steve from the gym is pacing the floor like one of the tigers in *Gladiator*. Probably spent last night on an intravenous steroid drip. This show of testosterone couldn't possibly be for my benefit, could it? 'I've got a nine thirty one-on-one with a total *wanker* from Coutts Bank,' he snarls. 'Reckons he *personally* handles the Queen's account. Today, I swear, I am going to *slaughter* the cocky little *fucker*.'

'Don't forget The Zone commandments, Stevie babe,' Daniel trills, camping it up a storm. 'Thou shalt not kill; just ever so slightly overexert.'

'Fuck the pussy stuff,' Steve rants as he shadow-boxes the camera fixed on the wall. 'Today, we TAKE NO PRISONERS!'

As they gas, giggle and toss one-liners across the foyer, I look at them – *really* look at them. Do they hate me? If I weren't here, would all the banter be about me? I mean, in Lydia's time, bitching about her was the fuel that got us through the day. It's fun to bitch about the boss – and now the boss is me. But everything seems normal enough. I can't sense an invisible wall between them and me. God, who knows any more?

Obviously, everyone's too excited to do anything other than buzz around excitedly. I should set an example and do some work . . . But sod that. I'm going to the loo to check my lipstick. And while I'm at it I'll work out exactly how much of my knickers are visible when I bend over. This skirt is scarily short. I seem to remember that *revealing* was the general idea when I was getting dressed, but suddenly I'm not so sure.

'No fuck-ups today. Right, Charlie?' Jamie hisses.

'Absolutely,' I hiss in reply, watching the two crewmembers (who are the reason we're hissing) get on with organising their equipment. It's ten past nine and filming starts at ten. Less than an hour to go. The biggest day of Jamie's life. It's no wonder he's giving me that look. God, please don't let anything go wrong. Not today. And while you're at it, God, could you please make sure Jacqueline doesn't come in. Jamie hasn't mentioned her since the bollocking he gave me. That little Platinum card she's got in her wallet will keep Jamie quiet. For a while at least. They go for a fortune and are harder to sell than flat batteries, but every one we get rid of buys him another night's stay at the Sandy Lane in Barbados. He must be at war with himself. The Jamie that hates the sight of physical imperfection and the one that only wants Jacqueline's money must be kicking the shit out of each other.

But – as if any of us could possibly forget – today is C4 day and everything has to be just so. In other words, nobody with spots, bruises, cuts, or a body anything like Jacqueline's should be anywhere near the cameras.

Do you know what? I am so not going to go along with this shit any more. Who does he think I am? Lydia? That I'll just sweep all the misfits under the carpet where he can't see them? Not a chance. And not just because I couldn't find a carpet big enough, either. I said I was going to change things around here, and that's exactly what I'm going to do. Once all this filming malarkey is over. And once I've dealt with the mess that has become my life since a certain bastard with the initials KB walked into it.

Jamie gives me a final menacing look and steps into the lift, as Daniel steps out. I grab him and whisper, 'Do me a favour and get Zone Check over and done with. The mood Jamie's in, if there's so much as a menu out of alignment in the caff, he'll fire us all.'

'Bloody hell, relax, will you? I don't want to miss anything down here. I'll do it later.'

'OK, but promise me you won't forget?'

'Calm down, I won't forget. God, lighten up,' he says, running a hand through his tiny spikes of rock-solid, gel-covered hair. 'Today's supposed to be fun.'

I look at my bag on the floor beneath the desk. I'm thinking about the video tapes squashed inside it. And he wants me to *lighten up*. The fact that they're here in the midst of all this madness is freaking me out. But what could I do? Leave them at home? I don't think so. I feel like the brilliant scientist who's stumbled on a deadly virus that could wipe out the entire planet and she's got it in a test tube in her bag and she's desperate to destroy it before the psycho terrorists get hold of it and . . . OK, maybe my disaster wouldn't be quite so epic – like, say, just my dad annihilating our front room if he found them – but you get the picture.

And Daniel wonders what's got into me.

I need to talk to someone about this. *Now*, before my head explodes. I can't talk to Sasha – I can't face her after what I've seen her get up to. Not that she's talking to me anyway. She's back at work today and so far our paths have crossed twice, but she's blanked me both times. It's going to have to be Daniel.

'Morning everyone, I'm here! Have they started yet?'

It's Rebecca, hyped up, raring to go and only half an hour behind the rest of us.

'You're just in time, Becks. Look after the desk,' I say commandingly. 'Daniel, come with me.'

'What, why, where?' he flaps.

'Executive breakfast meeting in the caff.'

'But the show's gonna start soon.'

'We'd better get a move on then.'

'*Un*believable,' he gasps when I've told him. 'Secret filming . . . That is the *sickest* thing.'

'Too bloody right,' I agree.

'I mean, if he'd been open about it, you could at least have made sure the camera got your good side.'

'This isn't funny, Daniel.'

'Did you at least pull your stomach in?'

'Daniel, *please*!'

'Sorry, sorry . . . So what are you gonna do? Are you gonna tell Sash?'

'Jesus, even if she was talking to me, I don't think I could. We'll both die of embarrassment. Probably literally. You should see what she's like—'

'What, you've looked at her tape?'

I nod and blush.

'And, *and*? C'mon, out with it.'

'She . . . I couldn't possibly say. She's no nun, though.'

'Anyway, never mind her. She's small fry. What about Blaize? Is she a swallower? Does she take it up the arse?'

'*Daniel*! I don't know. I haven't looked.'

He splutters so hard that coffee comes out of his nose. 'Are you *insane*, girl?' he exclaims once he's recovered. 'How could you *not* look?'

Well, I was tempted. But I bottled out because, firstly, what Blaize gets up to in bed is none of my business, and, secondly, I was getting distinctly uncomfortable sitting on Karl's floor surrounded by porn.

'Please, *please* tell me you didn't leave the Blaize tapes at Karl's,' Daniel continues.

That's what I should have done, isn't it? I should have put all her tapes back in the box and walked out. And that's exactly what I did . . . Except for one. You see, I was thinking that if I was going to do the *right thing* and tell Blaize about them, I'd need some evidence. And I was thinking, you know, that I'd have to check it first – make sure it wasn't some boring old rehearsal tape . . .

OK, bloody hell, I admit it. *I wanted to look at that tape.* Who wouldn't? She's a *pop star*. Having *sex*. On *camera*. Isn't everyone naturally curious about celebrity sex?

'I took one,' I confirm for Daniel.

'Only one? Better than nothing, I suppose. Is it here?'

'In my bag,' I whisper.

'Excellent. We can sneak up to Jamie's office later and watch it on his wide-screen. We can listen to her come in Dolby surround sound.'

'No *way*,' I say, even though it sounds like an excellent idea.

'Charlie, have you thought of the money you could make?' he gasps.

'What do you mean?'

'You could sell that tape to a tabloid for a fortune.'

'*Daniel*, I'd *never* do that.'

And I wouldn't. Blaize might be a spoilt, heartless brat, but I'd *never* do a thing like that. Not to anyone.

'I've always said you're too straight for your own good. Only the devious and the unscrupulous get on in this life,' Daniel says. 'C'mon, let's get back to work. I've got a movie of my own to star in.'

*

It's ten to ten when we get back to the desk. We find Rebecca in a state. Apparently, Jenna has just swept through reception and was at her catty finest. The word is she's livid that Karl got the Gurly-Wurly *TOTP* gig after she'd turned them down. Apparently, they looked at his show-reel and felt his particular style of shaking his thing was even sharper than Jenna's shimmying of her thing, and it better suited the image they wish to project to their public (i.e. record-buying eight-year-olds). What gives Jenna the right to be so pissed off? Well, she probably wouldn't have turned the job down if she'd known Karl was going to get it. But as much as Jenna pisses me off, I kind of wish she had taken it – Karl doesn't deserve a break at the moment, unless it's somewhere in the region of his neck.

Jenna is here this morning because the cameras are. As I suspected, their presence has led to Blaize making a rapid recovery from her trauma; her rehearsals are back on and she'll be here any minute.

'Why was Jenna shouting at me?' Rebecca says, her lip trembling. 'I didn't give Karl the flipping job.'

Poor thing doesn't get it at all. 'She picked on you because you happened to be in her line of sight,' I explain, putting my arm around her. 'Tell you what. Go to the loo and splash some water on your face. You don't want red, blotchy eyes for the cameras.'

As Rebecca trudges off, the lift door opens and Jamie saunters out. He's not alone.

So not alone.

'Charlotte, I'd like you to meet Velvet, your new assistant,' he announces as he ushers *Velvet* towards the desk.

'Erm . . . OK . . . Right,' I stutter as my body enters a state of shock.

'You've been banging on about extra staff, haven't you?' he says tetchily. 'I have been hearing you right?'

'Yes, absolutely,' I grovel. 'Hi, er, *Velvet*, lovely to meet you.'

I catch Daniel out of the corner of my eye. His mouth is hanging open. I'm with him totally. There are so many reasons to be slack-jawed here. For a start, when Lydia was here she used to do the hiring. The least Jamie could have done was wave her CV at me – just out of courtesy. Also, *Velvet*. What sort of name is that? Her parents must have been inspired by either a porn star or a toilet roll, and, thinking about it, if you're the one lumbered with the name Velvet, it's hard to know which is the heavier psychological baggage. Finally (and this is the biggie), *check out the tits on that!* Jesus, she makes Claire from Channel Four look positively A-cup. It's perfectly obvious that the credentials that impressed Jamie weren't the ones on her CV. My indignation, of course, hasn't got anything to do with being put in the shade – literally, because the girl's a solar eclipse on legs. No, it's totally to do with my first point and the taking of a professional approach to staff recruitment issues.

'Right, I'll leave you guys to show Velvet the ropes,' Jamie says. 'Oh, and take her to Zone Clone and sort her out something to wear.'

And he's gone. Out of the building, and out of this madhouse. *Velvet*. I look her up and down: a cardigan – so tight it must have come from Baby Gap – is stretched across her torso, and a mini that makes mine look like a full-length ball gown is hugging her hips. Hugging the entire length of her long legs are the highest, pointiest, fuck-me-est boots I have ever seen. Definitely not made for walking, those.

Listen to me. What a bitch. I *am* Lydia's twin sister. I've got to give the poor girl a chance. Maybe she'll be the best thing that ever happened to the place.

'I am *so excited*,' she gushes, sounding *extremely*

excited. 'And isn't it amazing, me starting on the *exact* day you've got the TV people in?'

I look at Daniel. He's giving me the raised eyebrow, which translates as *Yes, a remarkable coincidence, isn't it? And surely nothing to do with a primitive urge on Jamie's part to cast an extremely large-breasted leading lady in his TV documentary.*

Rebecca reappears, her chirpy smile back in place. 'Sorry about that, guys,' she says. 'So not like me to get upset. Anything I can do?'

'Yeah, this is . . . er . . . Velvet—' (*Velvet*. Wasn't it also the name of a Hollywood horse?) '—She's your new . . . um . . . assistant.'

Rebecca swells with pride: she's got an *assistant*. The look on her face really does it for me. Right, I've decided. I'm going to train Rebecca personally until she becomes the best goddamn Fitness Professional this place – this *planet*! – has ever seen. We can do it, I know we can. *Soon*. Right now, though, there's menial work to be done.

'Do us a favour, Becks. Take Velvet to Zone Clone,' I say. 'Help her pick out some work gear. And choose something baggy. She'll be more . . . *comfortable*.'

When they've gone I realise my head is spinning – and the day hasn't even kicked off properly yet. I'm about to sit down, relax and try to get my brain straight when Claire – after Velvet, looking boringly under-endowed – whirls into view. 'Hi, chaps. We're rolling,' she calls breezily, nodding towards the two cameras fixed to the walls. 'Business as usual, though; just relax and pretend we're not even here.'

I instantly go rigid with tension.

Bang on cue the doors swoosh open and Blaize sweeps in, followed by the usual entourage. She must have bat-like hearing and be able to sense a whirring camera from two blocks away. 'Good to see you back,' I say, putting on my best Zone smile as the massed ranks of flunkies and dancers pile up to the desk.

'Oh, the doctors wanted Blaize to take a proper rest, but, you know, the show must go on,' says Julie from Mission Management, putting an arm around her number-one client. Such a *brave* little pop star. We could be in the middle of a nuclear attack and she'd still be here, ready to kick-ball-change.

'Anyway, what happened the other day was like a sign, man,' says a gangly blond dancer.

'Yeah, we're back and we're gonna kick ass for Karl,' whoops another, which gets a cheer. *Hmm*, they're showing a lot more concern for Karl than they managed when he was bleeding to death at their feet.

I nudge Daniel and he jumps into action, herding them upstairs. As they disappear I slump with relief because I was having trouble looking at Blaize without thinking of the tape. Julie has hung back for some reason. She leans on the desk and gives me a twenty-four-carat fake smile. 'Now, darling, a couple of things. The cameras. Blaize is a very private person so the studio is a no-go area . . . Unless, of course, she invites them in.'

Which I'm sure she'll find it in her heart to do at some point.

'Absolutely. Blaize's privacy is of the *utmost* importance,' I say, thinking immediately of the total breach of Blaize's privacy on the video tape and squirming inwardly. 'Was there anything else?'

'Yes, water. Can Blaize have a cooler put into the studio?'

'There's one just outside in the corridor,' I say tentatively.

'It's no good to her outside, is it? She needs it in the studio so she can stay *fully* hydrated.'

Heaven forbid that Blaize should be anything other than fully hydrated. She's the star; if she wants water on tap, who am I to refuse?

'Of course,' I schmooze, 'I'll have maintenance sort something out.'

'Oh, by the way, we're expecting Karl to drop by later. He won't be fit enough to dance, but he's desperate to come along and boost morale. He's been through hell, so please make sure he has everything he— What's wrong? You've gone white.'

'I . . . um . . . No, I'm . . . *fine*. Just a lot of pressure this morning, you know, with the cameras and— *Karl*, yes, don't worry, I'll take care of him.'

'Excellent,' she says, spinning on her heel.

I have to sit down. My legs have gone. That's all I bloody need today. That *shit* showing up, bandaged like a bloody war hero.

Bastard, bastard, *bastard*.

Hindsight tells me it would have been a good idea to bring up the tape with Julie, or at least to have mentioned that I have something delicate to broach. God, I'm so rubbish. What's the point in having brain-waves if I only ever have them when the person I'm talking to has gone?

I look at the cameras on the wall. Both their lenses are staring at me. Better pull myself together. Mind you, I don't know what I'm fretting about. With an A-list star in the building, no one's going to be interested in me. '*Ooh yeah, baby, forget the chart-topping pop diva and gimme a big, fat close-up of the receptionist. Look at the way she's just standing there like a plank. I'm loving that slightly dazed and stupid expression . . . Read the ratings and weep, ITV!*'

Rebecca reappears with Velvet in her new Zone outfit.

'Doesn't she look *amazing*?' Becks sighs, presenting

257

Velvet as if she's Trinny or Susannah. I take in the new, improved Velvet (will I ever get used to that name?). Obviously Rebecca and I have very different definitions for the word *baggy* because what she's wearing couldn't be any tighter if it had been sprayed on with an airbrush.

'Yeah, amazing,' I echo feebly because, in her own way, amazing is exactly how Velvet looks – a bit like a jumbo jet: not exactly pretty, but you can't help being awe-struck by its sheer scale.

'This is *so* incredibly *exciting*,' Velvet says, somehow managing to sound even more hyped than she did fifteen minutes ago. It's a scary thing as well, because her breasts are actually quivering – and I've seen Turkish belly dancers who can't make theirs do that, even after years of practice. 'OK, right. Where do you want me to start?' she splutters.

'By staying away from me with *those,* that's where,' Daniel says, arriving back at reception. Daniel has breast aversion. He's uncomfortable with my 34-Bs, so Velvet's monsters must be completely scrambling his brain.

Daniel's eyes are virtually popping out of his skull. This could get embarrassing. 'Stop staring,' I whisper, but he grabs my arm and drags me to the middle of the reception area, only stopping once we're out of earshot.

'Haven't you noticed?' he hisses.

'*Yes.* Big, aren't they? Let's move on, shall we?' I hiss back.

'Not the fucking tits, what's *on* them. Huge, pink and shaped like a pig's head.'

I peer at Velvet, who's bonding with Rebecca and hasn't noticed us scrutinising her. I look at the vast expanse of cleavage that's squeezing its way out of her deeply scooped top and— *Fuck*, how could I have missed *that*? A huge birthmark, dark pink in colour and definitely shaped like a pig's head. I must have been too busy trying not to look at her chest to notice her chest. At least it confirms she wasn't topless when Jamie interviewed her. He'll go absolutely ballistic when he spots it.

'Shit,' I whisper. 'We'd better find a diplomatic way to get her to cover up.'

As we're heading back to the desk the phone rings. Eager to get stuck in, Velvet picks it up. 'Hello?' she says, moving about as far from the official Zone script as is possible. Then: 'It's for you, Charlie.'

I grab the receiver from her and say, 'Hello, Charlie speaking.'

'Is that what I think it is?' It's Jamie.

'Is *what* what you think it is?'

'That . . . *thing* on her tit. I can see it from the bloody street and it's putting me right off my fucking danish.'

I peer towards the doors and spot him hiding between the bouncers, a half-eaten pastry in one hand and his mobile in the other.

'What the hell is it?' he demands. 'A birthmark? A scar?' I think he's hyperventilating.

'It's a . . . I can't really talk right now,' I say, nodding towards Velvet, who's jigging up and down in time to the Missy Elliott video on the tellies.

'I should've known there'd be a fucking catch,' he says. He sounds (and looks) gutted – like a little boy who's ripped the wrapping off his big new Scalextric set, opened the box and discovered it's full of My Little Ponies. 'She'll have to go,' he sighs. 'Take care of it, yeah?'

'You mean—'

'Fire her, yes. You're a bright girl. You can think of an excuse.'

'I can't do that,' I gasp. 'Not after less than an hour.'

'Look, are you up to this job or not, because I'm beginning to have serious doubts? You've got till the end of the day. In the meantime, get her to cover up. Jesus, it is *gross*.'

I watch open-mouthed as he snaps his phone shut, brushes the crumbs from his lapels and walks in through the automatic doors as if the conversation never happened. He beams at us and calls out, 'Everything swimming along, I hope,' as he strides without pause to the lift.

'Er, Becks,' I say. 'Why don't you show Velvet how we work out the studio schedules? You can do it in my office if you like.'

I watch them disappear. At least I've managed to get her – or more precisely, her birthmark – away from the cameras' gaze for a bit. More than a bit with any luck because, actually, I've yet to show Rebecca how we work out the studio schedules. They could be in there all day.

As I turn back round I see the most despicable, sickening sleazebag who ever walked the earth. No, not Fred West, risen from the dead and interested in one of our tailor-made total fitness programmes. It's *Karl*. He's grinning his golden Nelly grin and a bandage is wrapped around his head looking way cooler than any Nike sweatband or bandanna. In fact, after the Nelly sticking-plasters-on-the-cheekbones fad, it could be a whole new hip-hop fashion thing. But he's *not* cool. He's a perverted sicko and I want to tell him as much right here and now—

Except that one of the production company's roving cameramen has picked this moment to wander into reception. He's nosing his lens up to Karl, obviously drawn towards him by his charisma, just as I was when I was a naïve young thing not so long ago.

'Reckon I owe you some thanks, Charlie,' Karl says breezily. 'Daniel told me you saved my life the other day.'

'Oh, it was nothing,' I say awkwardly, feeling nauseous and sincerely regretting not leaving him to drown in his own blood.

'Come off it, I owe you, *big* time. Oh, and thanks for dropping the bag off at mine. Can't manage without it. My whole life's in there.'

No, you slimy, sewer-dwelling cunt, your whole life is in your fucking spare room, neatly catalogued in chronological fucking order.

But my anger is joined by a rising sense of panic because, of course, *he knows I've been round his flat.* What else does he know? Did I leave the door to *that* room open? Would he have done anything so juvenile as to have taped a hair across the frame, the way I used to on my bedroom door when I was younger? (OK, three months ago when I first realised Emily was snooping for Harvey's texts.) Hang on, why am I scared? He's the one who should be panicking. Sweating. Bloody shitting himself. Not me. Let's face it, on the league table of dirty little secrets, sneaking round someone else's flat trails a long way behind covertly filming every shag you ever had.

Daniel kicks me under the desk. 'I've got to talk to you,' I say to Karl, seemingly involuntarily because I don't want to talk to him at all – I want to re-hospitalise him.

'Nothing to talk about,' he says sweetly. 'I ain't suing. Anyway, the scar will suit me.'

Such confidence.

Such fucking cool.

Does he even know that I know? If he does, it seems he doesn't give a toss. Daniel gives me another sharp kick. I wish he'd piss off. I feel myself burning up and

261

suddenly I'm hyper-aware of the cameras, as if the only thing they've come to film today is me and my humiliation.

'I'd better go. The guys are waiting,' he says, gesturing towards the lift. 'And don't worry, I ain't going anywhere near the sound system. Catch you later, yeah?'

He turns and swaggers off, his long legs flipping along in that apparently casual way that actually requires years of dance training. I'm left flapping my mouth in that dumb way that actually requires no formal training whatsoever. Luckily the cameraman has swung away from me and is tracking Karl as he walks off.

'Well, you've got to admire his front,' Daniel says in hushed reverence as he admires his behind. He looks at me. 'You OK?'

I shake my head, unable to speak.

The phone rings.

'Want me to get that?' Daniel says.

I nod.

He picks up and after the official Zone greeting whispers, 'It's for you. Think it's your sister. Want me to fob her off?'

I take the phone from him. Best deal with her.

'Hi,' I say.

'Well, have you phoned them yet?' she asks frantically.

'Phoned who?'

'The whatsit clinic, *stupid*. You promised.'

'Calm down, will you? I said I'd call them and I will.'

'Can't you do it now? Put me on hold or something.'

'No, Emily, I can't. I'm in the middle of reception, the place is filled with cameras . . . Not exactly an ideal setting for phoning a . . . you know.'

'But you will call them?'

'*Yes*, just as soon as I get a chance. Anyway, where are you? Shouldn't you be in school?'

'I'm bunking off. I can't go in. My stomach is *so* sticking out, *everyone* will know.'

'Look, don't be ridiculous. Go to school and get on with your life,' I snap, unable to hide my irritation.

I hear a strangled little sob at the other end of the line. It makes me forget for a moment how much she winds me up and I feel myself soften.

'Listen, I'm sorry. Emily? Are you there?'

'Do you hear a dialling tone? Course I'm bloody here. God, I *knew* phoning you was the dumbest idea ever.'

'You're bound to be feeling emotional right now,' I say, still – *incredibly* – calm. 'We'll talk properly later and I promise things won't seem so—'

'Do you think you could be any *more* patronising?' she screams.

Now I can hear a dialling tone. She's hung up.

I look up at the TV monitors. Sister Sledge are blasting out 'We Are Family', all loved-up with sickening sisterly-ness. Jesus, those gits at VH1 must be doing this on purpose.

As I grip the marble desktop so tightly that my ten carefully painted nails are threatening to snap, Rebecca and Velvet reappear. 'How's it going, girls?' I ask, trying to put my head back into Zone mode.

'Brilliant, thanks,' Velvet bubbles. 'Becks is such a good teacher.'

Heaven knows what Becks has taught her, but I force myself to think positive. 'Great,' I say. 'You can make a start by typing up next week's schedules then.'

Well, she might as well do something useful in the eight hours she has between now and unemployment.

'Why?' she asks nervously, making it clear that any training tips Rebecca might have given her went in one ear and straight out the other.

'The schedules vary,' I explain. 'We have guest teachers come in, one-off workshops, stuff like that, so we post a fresh timetable on the notice boards each week.'

She's looking at me as if I've slipped into Russian. No ordinary Russian either, but cockney, back-slang Russian just to confuse her should she happen to be one of the world's few Russian speakers (not counting the millions of actual Russians, that is).

'OK. Let's make a start then, shall we? Off you go,' I say encouragingly, pointing at the shiny Mac on the desk.

She's frozen to the spot.

'*What*?' I ask in a voice that I'm sorry to say is pure, icy Lydia.

'It's that,' she says, looking at the Mac. 'I can't use one of them.'

'Oh,' I say, feeling bad because I get it now. 'Don't be frightened of that. It's just a Mac. It works pretty much like any other computer. All you have to remember is—'

'No, you don't understand. I don't use computers. It's my wrists. I've got RSI. My doctor said I'm not allowed anywhere near a keyboard.'

Brilliant, Jamie, absolutely fantastic, I think. *You've hired us an assistant who can't use the computer. And there was me thinking that assistants are supposed to do all the crappy, boring stuff that involves, you know, tapping away at a keyboard.*

Well, there is a small consolation. At least she's presented me with the perfect excuse to *let her go*.

I take a deep breath and say, 'Here's something you can do. Rebecca can take you up to Studio Five. Maya's yoga class will be finishing soon. You can put all the mats away.'

'I couldn't possibly do *that*,' she protests, as if I've just asked her to carry several tons of bricks in from a truck that's parked half a mile down the road. 'I'm not allowed to bend over at the moment, never mind *lift* anything. I did my back in last week. I've got to have weeks of physio to put it right.' She juts out her chest in order to rub her lower back.

'Tell me, Velvet,' I ask tentatively. 'Have you got any experience at all of working in the fitness industry?'

'Don't be silly. I want to be a TV presenter. You know, like Davina. I wouldn't normally get any breaks working in a *gym*, but this is different.' She glances up at the camera, then drops her voice to a whisper. 'I met this bloke at Chinawhite last week and he tipped me off about the telly thing. Timing's everything, isn't it?'

I can't listen to any more of this. I'm in danger of losing it so badly that I'll fire the girl not only in front of Daniel and Rebecca, but also in full view of the entire Channel Four audience. I have to do something . . .

'Where are you going?' Daniel asks. He looks worried. My face must be flashing red-alert.

'To make a phone call,' I shout, grabbing my mobile from my bag. I'm going to phone a certain clinic, and while I'm outside I'm going to take several breaths of soothing fresh air before I explode.

I'm leaning against the window of the newsagent fifty yards from The Zone, feeling the benefits of a sugar rush (a Twix and a king-size Mars bar) as well as slightly sick (ditto the Twix and the Mars). When I was in the shop it was only the fact that I didn't have enough money that stopped me buying fags. As well as the minor, secondary consideration that I don't actually smoke. Yet.

265

I can't believe the day I'm having. In order:

Velvet's breasts.

Seeing Sasha and knowing, even if she does decide to talk to me, it can *never* be the same again.

Velvet's birthmark.

Karl.

Emily.

Velvet.

On an ordinary day any one of the above would push me close to the edge. On the day that the cameras are in . . .

All I can say is that it's amazing I'm not already in a straitjacket. The gulps of fresh air – OK, the car fumes – are working wonders though. I could stay out here forever, living off chocolate bars and never having to face—

'What the hell are you doing out here?'

'*Aaaaaaagghh*!'

That was Jamie asking; me jumping out of my skin.

'Sorry, Jamie. You made me— I was just . . . er . . . getting some air.'

'Do you know how much I spent on aircon at The Zone? It's totally state-of-the-art. Filters out everything except the bloody oxygen – they don't even have anything that advanced on the Space Shuttle. And you want to step out into the smog-filled shite of London for *air*?' He's not in a good mood – I can tell. 'Today of all bloody days you need to be at the top of your game, Charlie. In the fucking zone. Which means, apart from everything else, being *in* The fucking Zone. *Capisce*? I want you back there double-quick. Especially as you've got new staff to handle.'

'Can I ask you, where did you find her?'

'What's it matter? You're firing her, aren't you?' he says defensively, so I guess it wasn't at the Tip-top

Recruitment Agency (motto: *you want a receptionist, we'll send you a rocket scientist*).

'Yeah, I'm firing her,' I say resignedly. I *will* change this body-perfect thing he's got going. Eventually. Just not today. 'I'll get back then. I'll see you la— Where are you going, by the way?'

'To see the fucking lawyers. Lydia slapped me with a writ, didn't she?' he says, somehow managing to talk and grind his teeth simultaneously. *'Discrimination on grounds of physical difference.* What the fuck's the boss-eyed freak on about?'

'I've no idea, Jamie . . . Good luck,' I call out as he dives into a cab.

I set off back to The Zone at a trot, which quickly turns into a leg-pumping sprint. Why? Because I've just remembered my bag. I left it under the desk. Wouldn't normally be the end of the world, but today it's stuffed with hardcore porn starring you know who, you know who and, even worse, you know who.

I reach the steps, brush aside Master Stan Lee's trained killers, plunge through the doors, charge across the foyer, push past Velvet (who's a far more formidable barrier than the bouncers) and dive under the counter, somehow knocking everything off the desk as I go. As I scramble around on my knees, pen pots, papers, an open can of Diet Coke, the master TV remote, a phone and a computer keyboard tumble onto the floor behind me, but I don't care because I've got my bag. I'm clutching it to my chest and looking inside at the video tapes. All seven of them – I count them three times to make sure.

Daniel joins me on the floor. 'That must have looked good on camera. And you didn't even need a stunt double. You OK?'

'I am now,' I pant.

'You're not having a good day, are you?'

I shake my head.

'Let's have a break,' he says.

'We can't leave those two,' I whisper, nodding towards Velvet and Rebecca's legs. 'Or my bag.'

'You can bring the bag with you and those two will be all right. We'll just tell them to play statues for fifteen minutes. C'mon, you need a breather. We'll go to Jamie's office. He's out and it's the only place in the building without cameras.'

He's right. I do need a breather. OK, so I just had one outside the sweetshop, but another won't hurt. We stand up, and as I brush myself off I look at Rebecca and Velvet. They're staring at me like a pair of frightened rabbits. 'Sorry about that,' I say.

'Want us to tidy up?' Velvet asks, looking at the mess on the floor.

'Would you mind? Charlie and I have to do Zone Check together,' Daniel says, taking charge. 'You two will be OK for a few minutes, yeah?'

Rebecca looks panicked. 'What about the tellies?' I look up at the three monitors. They've gone to black. They must have gone off when the remote fell on the floor, which means that so has every TV in the building. Daniel picks the remote up and shoves the batteries back in. 'Stick them back on,' he says, handing it to Rebecca. Then, in response to her freaked expression, 'It's only one button, sweetheart. Press it once for *on*, once for *off*. You can do it, girl . . . C'mon, Charlie.'

'So, Karl's a total bastard perv with the conscience of a serial killer; Sasha blames you for everything and won't speak to you; your schoolgirl sister won't tell you who got her pregnant; and your boss first lumbers

268

you with a pair of walking tits and then wants you to fire her on account of her ghastly deformity . . . Now, do you want to tell me what's really bothering you?' Daniel says, leaning back on Jamie's big leather chair and looking pensively at the ceiling as if he's a shrink.

'*Ha, ha*. I'm being serious, Daniel. I could probably cope with one problem at a time. Why does everything have to happen at once, for God's sake?'

'Look, darling, give it forty-eight hours and you'll be laughing about all of it. I swear.'

He's probably right. It's just that I'm not sure I can make it through the next forty-eight hours.

'Tell you what'll take your mind off things,' he says. 'That exclusive new Blaize vid that's in your bag.'

'Is that the only reason you wanted to get me up here?' I say, hugging my bag protectively. 'And there was me thinking you cared.'

'*Course* I care,' he protests, 'but as long as we're up here we might as well. Anyway, you have to look at it to make certain. It might not be a sex tape. Or she might be completely aware of being filmed, in which case . . .'

He's right. I should look at it, shouldn't I? Just to check. And absolutely *not* to satisfy my burning curiosity to see what Blaize is like in bed. 'OK, stick it on,' I say, tossing him the tape. 'But only for a minute – *no more*.'

He leaps up from his seat, scurries across the room to Jamie's VCR and shoves it into the slot before I have a chance to change my mind. He switches on the TV, presses *play* and settles down beside me on the sofa. We could be a lovey-dovey couple snuggling up to spend a cosy evening watching Meg and Tom in *Sleepless in Seattle* . . .

269

Except that as the screen flickers from fuzz to a picture, I can see that it's very clearly not *Sleepless in Seattle*; more like *Sleazy in South Ken* starring Karl and Blaize. 'Doesn't like to waste any time, does he?' Daniel says as we watch him shove her backwards onto his bed before unbuckling his belt. Then, 'Oh my *God*, he is gi*norm*ous. That thing is completely wasted on women.' I stare at the screen in shock. Not at the size of Karl's dick – well, I've been there, done that – but at the fact that I'm watching Blaize – mega-celeb, regular guest on Saturday morning kids' TV and, according to the *Sun* a couple of days ago, the brand-new face of TeenQueen Cosmetics – rip off her clothes like the world's about to end and she's in Last Shag Saloon.

'Well, it's obvious she doesn't know about the camera,' Daniel says with absolute certainty.

'How can you tell?'

'She's a media pro. If she knew about the camera, she'd undress like she's in a lingerie ad. And do you see her sucking in her stomach? Doing the pop-star pout? No. And look, she's left her socks on. How uncool is that? No, this is the natural, at-home, socks-on-for-sex Blaize.'

He's got a point. OK, we've sussed that she's unaware her boyfriend is filming her, and clearly this isn't an innocent rehearsal tape. We should turn it off now, right?

But neither of us moves apart from to squirm about a bit on the sofa. Daniel must be as uncomfortable as I am watching this, surely? So why are we both still sitting here watching it?

'This is out of order. Daniel, turn it off.'

'We can't stop now. He's making his entry . . . Wow, she's a *screamer*. Must be all that vocal coaching. *Jeez*, you could make an absolute fucking fortune with this tape—'

'Daniel, *pur*-lease.'

'You'd be mad not to consider it. It's really good quality as well. We had this pap in last week, the one who took that topless shot of Prince William's girlfriend. Remember how crap, how grainy it was? Well, he got—'

'Where's the remote?' I demand, forcing myself to my feet. Daniel isn't going to offer it up, so I set off across the room towards the TV. But halfway there I stop. The strangest thing – somehow I'm hearing Blaize's moans in stereo, as if they're coming out of more than one telly. How can that be happ—

'Jesus fucking *Christ*!' Daniel has got there before me. 'How the hell did she get up there?' He's looking up at the other TV high on the wall. Out of its speakers pour Blaize's breathless moans. On its screen one of her legs is locked around Karl's back while the other is flailing in the air, her fluffy pink sock now clinging precariously to the tips of her toes.

'What the fuck have you *done*, Daniel?' I scream – because the second TV in Jamie's office just happens to be the one that's networked to EVERY SINGLE MONITOR IN THE BUILDING.

'Stop yelling,' he yells. 'Turn the fucking tape off. QUICK!'

I dive towards the VCR. I'm fumbling for the *stop* button but my hands have become a writhing mass of fingers and thumbs and won't work properly. At last, I hit the button. Both TVs go black and there's silence apart from the sound of my own hyperventilating lungs. From my position on the floor I look at Daniel. He looks as sick as I feel. Neither of us speaks. After a moment I manage to whisper, 'Do you think everyone saw that?'

He gives me a feeble little shrug.

I'll take that as a *yes* then.

'Aauurrgghh!' Basic English escapes me for the minute.

'I didn't do anything, Charlie, I swear.' He buries his face in his hands, staring at me through the gaps in his fingers.

'No, you didn't,' I say, feeling the light bulb click on above my head. 'It was Rebecca.'

'*Becks*? How do you work that out?'

I tell him. All of the TVs in The Zone are linked. Whatever channel we tune into in reception is what the monitors play throughout the building. Only Jamie's wide-screen isn't permanently hooked into the network. This is so that while the rest of us are bopping around to MTV, The Box or VH1, Jamie can spend his day watching his shares go up on the City channels. Except there is a way of synchronising Jamie's TV to all the others. Lydia tried to explain it to me once. It involved pressing a fiendishly complex combination of buttons on the master remote in reception, and I lost the plot about six or seven steps in. That, of course, is the same remote that Daniel chucked at Rebecca before we came up. *'It's only one button, sweetheart'* – those were his exact words. Now, if you sent Rebecca on a six-month residential course on the mastery of TV remotes, then told her to synchronise Jamie's telly with the rest, she wouldn't be able to do it. She couldn't do it if her fucking life depended on it.

But today, when her life didn't depend on it, when all she had to do was press *one button*, of course she managed it.

'How many tellies did you say were in the building?' Daniel asks when I've finished.

'Forty-three.'

'Fuck, shit, *fuck*,' he gasps.

I know what he means.

'Well, at least there isn't one in Studio Four. Blaize won't have seen it,' he says, spotting a straw and clutching at it desperately.

'Yeah, but what if one of her dancers was taking a leak and saw it while she was outside the studio? Anyway, gossip spreads round this place like disease. How long before she finds out?'

Silence as he watches the straw flutter away in the breeze. Then, 'Do you think we'd better go back downstairs?'

'Do we have to?' I say.

'Well, we could lower ourselves down to the street in the window cleaner's crane, get a taxi to Heathrow and buy two single tickets to Rio, then live out the rest of our lives under false names, eking out a living by selling our bodies to sex tourists . . . Is that the sort of thing you had in mind?'

'We'd better go back down.'

I go to the Venetian blinds that screen Jamie off from the world, prise apart a couple of slats and peer out into the corridor. Calm as calm can be. Just the gentle plinky-plonk of the piano in the ballet studio down the corridor and Philip's voice – 'No, no, no, *no*! I said turn *out*, not in! What is this? The funky chicken?' I'm guessing that Blaize's performance at least passed *him* by. Maybe no one else saw it either. Maybe everyone was so busy exercising, dancing, whatevering that they didn't look up and happen to notice Britain's most talked-about pop singer getting her brains screwed out. And perhaps the people in charge of monitoring the footage from the two-dozen fixed TV cameras (not to mention the two or three roving cameramen) were having a synchronised three-minute sneezing fit and didn't spot it either.

What are the odds of that happening, eh?

The Bit Where I Think Everything Might Just Turn Out Fine

As the lift descends I feel my heart sink with it. Neither of us speaks – what is there to say? *Nice knowing you, see you at the Job Centre,* that sort of thing? We reach the ground floor, the door slides open and—

'Charlie, I'm so, so sorry.'

Sasha – engulfed by the huge Zone puffa jacket she's wearing – is standing in front of me, actually *talking* to me.

'I've been such an idiot,' she gabbles. 'I never should've reacted like that. All you've done is be a friend and look how I've repaid you.'

She's hugging me, almost strangling me and I'm in danger of being suffocated by the puffa jacket, but it's giving me hope. Hope that maybe I was worrying for nothing. Because, after all, if the tape had gone out to the whole building, she wouldn't be standing here now doing Make Up, Make Up, Never Ever Break Up with me, would she? Surely she'd have realised what the tape was and would be a snivelling wreck.

I feel tears well up. 'Sasha, *I'm* sorry. I never meant to hurt you.'

'Please, don't apologise. I've been walking the streets for the last half-hour, trying to summon up the courage to talk to you because . . .'

Didn't Say It Was A Long Bit, Did I?

Oh God. *She's been outside*. Suddenly, my little ray of hope isn't shining quite so brightly.

'. . . now I realise none of it was your fault.' She pauses and looks round at the desk. 'But I think we'd better talk later. Looks like you've got some people to deal with first.'

There's a huddle at reception. People who should have better things to do – like their *jobs* – are clamouring around Rebecca and Velvet. Even from twenty feet away I can tell that there's only one topic of conversation and it isn't the weather. Rebecca's on the phone, shouting. 'No, Steve, I *didn't* turn the TV over. It just finished and— Well, I'm sorry you—' She holds the receiver away from her ear. 'He called me a *prick tease*,' she says, her eyes brimming. Velvet spots Daniel and me and whoops. 'You guys missed the most incredible thing. Blaize's new video was on the telly—'

Blaize's new *video*?

'—and it was *disgusting*!'

Daniel and I stare at each other, our worst fears confirmed. *Please, God, I don't know if you've worked out exactly when I'm going to die yet, but, well, right now would be an excellent time.*

Everyone turns and moves towards us, all of them talking at once.

Ruby: 'You should've seen it, Charlie.'

Maya: 'That willy *can't* have been real. Not on daytime telly.'

Sasha: 'What are you talking about?'

Maya: 'Didn't you see it? Jesus, how could you miss it!'

Velvet: 'Didn't think much of the song. All that groaning. At least her last one had a tune.'

Francesca: 'Maybe it was some sort of new work-out video. You know, like Fuck Yourself Fit.'

I look at Daniel, my eyes pleading *help me out here*.

'Shit, almost forgot, Zone Check,' he gabbles.

'*Daniel*!'

Too late; he's gone. Probably taking the Rio/false name/sex slave option. *Bastard*.

'Listen, I don't know what you're talking about,' I call out as more bodies pile into the foyer. 'Why don't you all go back to work?'

They ignore me, much preferring to mill around discussing pop-star sex. I push through them and go behind the desk. I dump my bag on the floor, bend down and shove it as far as it will go beneath the counter – the further away from me those tapes are the better. When I come back up I see Sasha huddled with Rebecca and Velvet. If her flushed and anxious face is anything to go by, they're filling her in on exactly what she missed while she was outside drumming up the nerve to come and speak to me.

'What's going on, Charlie?' she squeals. 'Rebecca said it was Karl on the video— *Ben*! That it must be some kind of performance-art thing . . .' She drops her voice to a whisper, '. . . but I've got a bad feeling about this.'

'We do need to talk. But not now,' I say, suddenly aware that a cameraman has arrived on the scene. He's not alone. Claire is at his shoulder, nudging him in my direction. Sasha may only just be putting two and two

277

together, but Claire will have sniffed something juicy the moment the first frame went up.

I can see Sasha's brain working faster than it's ever had to before and it looks as if it's causing her severe pain.

'*Aagh*!' she shrieks. 'Velvet said something about black sheets. Ben's got black sheets on his bed . . .'

She's getting there. Slowly but surely she's working it out and there's nothing I can do to stop her. But I just wish she wouldn't do her thinking OUT LOUD. Claire's eyes meet mine and lock for a moment. Her face isn't giving anything away, but I *know* what she's thinking. Just as I'm desperate to keep a lid on this, she's silently pleading for the whole thing to explode while there's still tape in her camera.

'Ben filmed himself having sex with Blaize, didn't he?' Sasha says, coming round to my side of the desk.

'Not now, Sash.'

'He told me that the camera in his room was broken. Did he do it secretly?'

I don't reply. My attention's on Claire, who's virtually dribbling as she makes sure her cameraman is well within earshot.

'Oh, God, he *did*, didn't he?' Sasha goes on. 'The *bastard* . . . Shit, are there other tapes?'

'Please, Sasha,' I beg. 'Let's talk later.'

'*Tell* me, Charlie,' she says, grabbing my arm. 'Did he film you . . . ? *Me* . . . ?'

'*Not now*,' I hiss as two of Blaize's dancers appear at the bottom of the stairs. They take one look at the mayhem and go straight back up again. My body is shaking. All I want to do is scream, but I can't because the camera's in my face now. I want to shove it away like celebrities do when they're filmed coming out of nightclubs pissed and looking wrecked. I feel Sasha's

278

hand on mine, gripping it tightly. 'You've *got* to tell me, Charlie,' she shouts, tears appearing in her eyes.

'*Not now*!' I hiss again, nodding towards the camera – like, *get the fucking hint, please!*

But she doesn't and launches into a hysterical squeak. '*Fuck*, the bastard's been secretly filming himself having sex with me, you, Blaize and God knows who else, hasn't he?'

'NOT NOW!' I shout. But I didn't need to raise my voice because the whole foyer has already fallen silent. I see Claire look away suddenly and nudge her cameraman in the back. I follow his lens as it swings towards the staircase . . . and settles on Karl and Blaize.

'Well, has he?' Blaize asks quietly.

I think a nod from me at this point would be superfluous.

The cameraman is shuffling backwards, trying to get both Blaize and me in his shot. I do the only thing a girl can do in a situation like this. I pray: *God, please make this a different kind of TV show. Please make it* Punk'd. *Then all of this – the Blaize tape, the new girl who's named after a toilet roll, the whole lot – could turn out to be part of an elaborate hoax and we'd fall about laughing hysterically, and everyone would pat me on the back for taking the joke so well, just like they did with Justin Trousersnake that time. Please do that, God, pleeeeeeaaaaaaase . . . Amen.*

God must be otherwise engaged today because (just as a short while ago He didn't strike me dead when I politely asked Him to) there's a distinct lack of people jumping out of the shadows with microphones and saying, 'Hey, Charlie girl, we really had you going there, huh?'

Blaize turns to Karl, who holds up his hands as if he's ready to protest his innocence. He opens his mouth, but no words come out. He makes do with his trade-mark grin, which all of a sudden doesn't seem so cool. She clenches her little fists tightly, as if she wants to hit him. *Be my guest, girl.* But he's over six-feet tall, she's barely five and I doubt she could reach. She must be arriving at the same conclusion because her hands stay by her sides. Jenna's beside her now and her arm goes round her. 'C'mon, babe, let's go,' she says, leading her towards the door. Karl follows a few paces behind, though whether it's to attempt an explanation or to run several miles in the opposite direction is anyone's guess.

Sasha, her body visibly trembling, turns to look at me. Everyone else does too. Gawkers at a car crash, staring as if they can see my intestines spread across the tarmac and bits of bone protruding through my ripped flesh. After a moment the buzz starts up again, but Sasha raises her hand. 'OK, it's all over now,' she shouts, still shaking.

She might as well be invisible for all the notice anyone takes of her. As bad as I'm feeling, at least I've had knowledge of these tapes for a while now. Sasha has always been a good few paces behind me during the unravelling of this nightmare. She's way ahead of me now, though. Her nostrils flare, her eyes flash sparks and she yells, 'I said, it's *over*! Haven't you all got stuff to be getting on with?'

I can't believe this. Of all the people to get their shit together in a crisis, you wouldn't put money on it being Sasha. She claps her hands and the mob actually responds, starting to break up. But now they stop and look at the bouncer striding across the foyer.

What now?

He calls out, 'Is there a Thaglotta here? There's some-one here to see Thaglotta and he says it's urgent.'

I cringe and close my eyes because I *know* what's coming next.

'Hello, sweedy, *surprise*. I cunt forgedding you gonna be on TV, cun I? So look see what I bringing you fresh from fruity veg market.'

Please, God, no, not this, not after everything else.

I open my eyes. Dad's standing in front of me holding a box of plump pineapples. Three years I've waited for him to show the slightest bit of interest in my job, and now that he has I want to die for what feels like the fiftieth time this morning.

'So he's OK?' the bouncer says. 'He's with you, yeah?'

'Course I with her, stoobid,' Dad says. 'She my dotter.'

I give the bouncer a weary nod – I am, indeed, his *dotter*.

Dad's beaming. Not at me, or the bouncer or the still-lingering crowd, but at the camera that's swung towards him as if the star of the show has finally hit the stage. 'OK, where I pudding them?' he asks the camera. Then he spots Sasha. She hasn't moved since her unprecedented show of assertiveness actually worked. She's stunned and I don't know what's shocked her more – her boyfriend's scummy deeds or the fact that she has just acted more like a studio manager than I've ever managed.

'Oh my bluddy God,' Dad gasps. 'Sushou, she walk again. She standing on her own two feet an' everything. Is a *mirigol*!'

What can I say?

Tell me honestly, what can I say?

Dad's elation is cut short as the doors swoosh open. Julie from Mission Management sweeps through them and heads straight for me. 'You have got some serious explaining to do, young lady,' she snaps when she reaches me.

'It was a complete accident,' I say, my voice shaky and feeble.

'Thass right, it was *aggsident*,' Dad says. Her aggression has automatically triggered his defences. He doesn't have a clue what he's talking about, but that's beside the point. Charalambous blood is quite a lot thicker than water – more like treacle.

'Well, your little *accident* has left my client on the verge of a nervous—' She stops herself, remembering the cameras. 'You and I need to have a serious conversation,' she says. 'In *private*. And it might be an idea if your boss joined us. Where is he?'

'He's out . . . at a meeting.'

'No, I'm not. I'm here.'

I look up and see Jamie, briefcase in his hand, look of horror on his face. His eyes are darting from the mob to me to Julie to the camera to Dad's pineapples as he tries desperately to comprehend the mess he's stepped into. 'What's going on?' he asks, trying manfully to keep calm.

'We've got a bit of a . . . *situation*,' Julie explains.

'Look, Jamie, it was a complete accident,' I babble, realising that I won't be making any sense to him, but unable to stop myself. 'I had no idea the whole place was going to see the tape.'

'She having no idea. It was *aggsident*,' Dad reiterates cluelessly.

'Well, I think the police may be very interested to know how a *private* tape got into the public domain,' Julie says, raising her voice now.

'The *police*?' I wail. 'I haven't bloody done anything.'

'She no' done bluddy nothing,' Dad says.

'Done nothing?' Julie yells. 'Don't you realise the *damage*—'

Jamie holds up his hands. 'SHUSH!'

Silence.

He quickly scans the scene, then barks his orders. 'Rebecca, take this young lady to the meeting room,' he says, gesturing at Julie. 'Get her whatever refreshments she needs . . . Daniel— Where the hell's Daniel?'

Yes, where the *hell* is Daniel?

'—Never mind. Sasha, you look after the desk for a few minutes.'

'I'll do it,' Velvet volunteers when Sasha doesn't speak.

'Whatever. Everyone else, back to work. Charlie, my office. *Now*.'

He's about to walk off when Dad says, 'Whadoyoo want I doing with these pineabbles then?'

'The delivery entrance is round the back,' Jamie snaps. 'By the way, who the hell ordered pineapples?'

How long have I been sitting here? Ages. Forever. A fucking eternity and then a bit longer. I'm terrified. And almost certainly dead as soon as Jamie shows up. Where is he? Stupid question. He's with Julie. Schmoozing. Greasing. Promising to do whatever it takes to stop Blaize suing – i.e. promising to fire me. Well, you tell me, which one of us is the A-list pop star whose continuing goodwill is essential to The Zone's profitable future, and which of us is the dispensable nobody with the idiot Greek dad who turns up with bloody pineapples at the most inappropriate moment?

Feeling sorry for myself?

You'd better believe it.

I've been thinking about this mess – well, what else is going to be on my mind? – and I've come to a conclusion: *it's not my fault*. None of it. In fact, *it's everyone else's fault*. All of it. From the top:

The tapes – did I make them? No, that was some sicko, pervy sex-stud's idea.

The Blaize tape – who put it in the slot and pressed *play*? That would be Daniel. He was the one gagging to watch the sodding thing, not me.

The fact that the Blaize tape was broadcast on Zone TV – a shit-for-brains called Rebecca sorted that.

But she's just a kid. I can't blame her. Besides, she's my responsibility, my protégée. I'm supposed to be training her so that when I die (ooh, in just a few minutes from now), she can take on my mantle and wear it with pride, telling everyone about the time and love I invested in her personal growth and development. I can't land her in it.

I flinch as the door opens. Jamie walks straight to his desk and sits down in his big chair. 'You fucking *idiot*,' he says quietly.

'It was Rebecca's fault.' (I know, I know, but sod it, I've got a life to save here – *mine*.) 'She had the remote and she must have reprogrammed—'

'*Stop*! Stop right there. Don't insult my *fucking* intelligence. You're in charge now. Everything that happens is down to you,' he yells, angrier than I've ever heard him be.

'I'm sorry,' I say, because he's right.

'Sorry doesn't even begin to cover it. Now would you like to tell me – from the beginning, please – how the whole of The Zone came to be watching hardcore pornography on a sunny Thursday morning?'

So I tell him – from the beginning.

'Jesus, where do I start?' he says when I've finished. 'Number one, you should not have been in *my* office on *my* time watching a *sex* tape. Two, you should not have left reception in the care of a junior – a junior that you're too busy watching sex tapes to train, I might add. And three . . . I'm sure I could come up with something if you give me a moment.'

I don't respond.

'Today of all days. What the fuck were you think-ing? When this goes out on TV what are we gonna look like? The top London club where celebs come when they want to have their sex lives broadcast to the world?'

I think I know what's coming next.

'I should fire your arse this minute . . .'

Yup, that's what I thought.

'. . . But I don't want to do that.'

Really? Lydia got sacked for a squint. I'm not going to get it for landing him with the biggest PR nightmare of his life?

'This is mad, but I fucking *like* you, Charlie,' he spits. (If he likes me so much, why is he still shout-ing?) 'Can you believe that? I can't believe it myself. You do this to me and I *still* fucking like you . . . And I still happen to think you've got it in you to do this job. Besides, I only promoted you last week. I'd look like a fucking schmuck if I fired you now.'

'Thank you, Jamie,' I whisper, not bothering to point out that by the time Velvet gets fired she won't even have lasted a day, let alone a week, which is going to make him look like a right fucking schmuck indeed.

'You'll do more than thank me. Your soul belongs to me now. You're gonna be working your arse off for me over the next few months.' He takes a deep breath. 'I think I might have straightened things out with Blaize's mob,' he says, calmer now.

'How?' I ask.

'Well, Blaize wants to sue – you, me, everyone – but her manager is taking a more rational view. The last thing she wants is a court case where that tape goes public. No, so long as I can square things with Claire to leave the ruder stuff on the cutting-room floor, we should be OK. I don't suppose Blaize will be rushing back for more rehearsals, but girls like her are ten a penny. Next month she'll be last month and there'll be another two Blaizes fighting for her spot.'

I want to hug him, tell him he's amazing, but now doesn't seem the moment. I make do with another mumbled 'Thank you.'

'Here's what we're gonna do now,' he says. 'You're taking the rest of the day off. I don't want any more cock-ups on camera. First, though, you're gonna give me the tape. I promised Blaize's manager I'd get it straight over to her.'

'OK, fine,' I say. 'It's downstairs in my bag.'

'It's the only copy, yeah?'

I nod, then add, 'There's a whole box of them at Karl's house, though – I only took the one.'

'Not our problem. She'll have to negotiate with him for the rest. Or she can have him arrested. That is one *angry* little diva – wants her pound of flesh. Right, let's go.'

Reception is quiet again and – hey, wouldn't you know it? – Daniel's back behind the desk. I give him my scariest glare and he cowers, knowing exactly why I'm so pissed off with him. Sasha stands next to him, a terrified look on her face. She's still wearing the big Zone puffa jacket she wore to go walkabout. It's boiling in here but she's immobilised from shock by the look of things. She must have used every ounce of willpower for her show of strength earlier and it's left her exhausted.

She manages to smile at me, though, and I want to hug her. But I can't. With Jamie just a couple of steps behind me, I go behind the desk, bend down and pull my bag out from beneath the counter. Daniel shrinks away from me; he looks as frightened as Sasha and so he should. I'm not going to say anything to make him feel better. I root around in my bag. The tapes are in there: four of Sasha, two of me . . .

Fuck.

Suddenly I feel very sick, actually taste it in the back of my throat. I feel my legs weaken and it takes all my strength to stay on my feet. I lift the bag up and empty it out onto the counter. Make-up, Filofax, mobile, keys, all my life's crap scatters across the marble and onto the floor, but I don't give a damn. All I care about is one thing. One tape. It's not there. I check. And check again. And again.

Four of Sasha.

Two of me.

NONE OF BLAIZE.

The Bit Where It Turns Out Jesus Was A Greek Bloke All Along

'Feel any better?' Sasha asks.

'Not at all. You?'

'No, me neither. But let's try and stay positive. At least we're friends again.' She tries to smile, but it isn't working and comes out as a weird little grimace. 'How could we both have been so stupid?' she asks for the hundredth time. She's still hung up on how we didn't twig that he was filming us, but I'm more bothered about the disappearance of a certain video cassette.

'What if the tape doesn't turn up? Or – *Jesus* – what if it does and it's on the bloody Internet? Available to download *free*,' I say. I may appear to have calmed down since we got here – here being the café round the corner – but appearances are deceptive because my insides are mush.

Sasha doesn't reply. She just makes a face that isn't sure whether it's supposed to be communicating *There, there, don't worry* or *Aaaaggghh!* But she's doing her best. And even though she doesn't have to worry about losing her job, I guess she's got as much right to be in a state as I have.

'Look, Charlie, you've got to stay positive,' she says, not sounding especially positive. 'Maybe it's like a set of keys that you tear the house apart trying to find and they turn up somewhere stupid when you've given up looking.'

If only it was just a boring old bunch of keys . . .

We did tear The Zone apart looking for the tape. Well, we weren't exactly like the police, ripping up floorboards in search of a drugs stash, but we were pretty thorough. I wanted to rip up the floors, but Jamie was angry enough already. His face managed to invent several vivid new purples. 'You fucking moron, how could you go and lose it?' he yelled.

'I didn't. The tape was in my bag,' I replied.

'Well it's not fucking there now, is it? Look, just go home. And don't bother coming in tomorrow.'

'What, are you firing me?'

'Yes . . . No . . . I don't fucking know. I just think it's best if you stay away for a day or two while I work out what the fuck to do.'

'Am I suspen—'

'Just *go*, Charlie.'

The tape *was* in my bag when I came back downstairs after watching it in Jamie's office. Someone *must* have taken it. They'd have had their chance while Jamie had me in his office for my bollocking. But who? The world and his wife were in reception around that time. Anyone could have dived under the desk and fished the tape from my bag. Rebecca? Is her complete ineptness a cunning ploy designed to hide a brilliant criminal mind (a bit like that bloke with the limp in *The Usual Suspects*, which, by the way, I *still* don't get)? Too ridiculous to contemplate. Sasha? Come off it – far too traumatised to be devious. Velvet? She's new so she has no reason to be loyal to The Zone or to me, so she has to be in the frame.

But the really depressing thing is that there's only one serious suspect: Daniel. He was the first to know about the tape. He was the only one to know exactly where it was – he watched me stuff it back into my bag in Jamie's office. And look at his behaviour recently. The snide comments about my promotion, setting me up with that coach-load from Batley, getting me to play the tape in the first place – *shit*, perhaps it was *him* who reprogrammed the remote before he gave it to Rebecca. Maybe he was so pissed off that he didn't get Lydia's job that he's been looking for ways to stitch me up ever since. There was me thinking he was my best mate. But look at the way he scarpered as soon as he saw the chaos in the foyer. Is that the behaviour of a mate?

And what was the first thing he advised me to do when I told him I had Blaize on tape? That's right. Make some money, he said, sell it to a tabloid. The more I think about it, the more certain I am that he did it.

When I discovered that Karl was screwing Sasha, I felt *bad*, but not betrayed. It's different with Daniel. Over the last three years we've lied for each other and covered each other's arses countless times – we've learned to trust each other. *Now* I feel betrayed.

'I know who took the tape. It was Daniel,' I say to Sasha as we finish our coffees.

'Really?' She looks surprised. 'But you're so close.'

'He's been different since my promotion.'

'Look, I'm sorry, Charlie, but you're only thinking that because I told you everyone hates you, and maybe, *maybe* I was exaggerating slightly. A lot, actually, because everyone doesn't . . . Well, I did a bit, but not any more because—'

I hold up a hand to stop her. She doesn't have to explain. I know she was only lashing out because her feelings were hurt. She's here with me now; that's all that counts.

'You know, I've never seen you cry before,' she says, referring to the state I was in when we got here. 'You're normally so, oh, I don't know, *together*. I suppose it proves you're human after all.'

What did she think I was? A machine? I feel tears well up again, but I'm damned if I'm going to sit here crying all day.

'Here you are,' I say, blinking madly to keep the tears at bay. 'Your tapes. I'd destroy them if I were you.'

'They're going straight on the fire, don't you worry.'

And when she burns them, I guess that will be that. For her, anyway. If only it would mean the end of my problems too.

As if she can read my mind, she adds, 'And don't worry, Charlie. Jamie's just being Jamie. He'll get over it.'

Her optimism is admirable, and I wish I could buy it. But I can't.

'I'll call you tonight,' I say as I walk out.

'When did we get that?' is the first thing that comes out of my mouth when I walk into our front room.

'Is a beaudy, eh?' Dad says proudly.

'It's a bloody monster.'

I'm looking at the new wide-screen TV that fills a good quarter of the room and doesn't leave much space for the rest of the furniture. It makes the one in Jamie's office seem like a pocket portable.

'The picture is brilliun. Look.' Dad hits a button on the remote and the set comes to life.

'*Aaggh*!' I yelp, jumping backwards. A black-clad Greek mama has filled the screen. She's at least twice her natural size. *Shit*, the picture is so brilliant I can count the individual hair follicles on her top lip.

291

'Is aboud time we gedding a decen' high-tegnical TV, eh?' Dad says.

'It's great, Dad. You could have saved yourself a fortune, though, and just moved into the Odeon.'

'You taking the miggey?'

'God, no. *Never.* Where's Emily?'

'In her room. Doing her schoolwork. She good girl, thad one—'

Hmm, so good she's gone and had underage, unprotected sex with God knows who and is about to make you a granddad again.

'—She won't ending up werking in loony bin like her *sista.* Whass wrong wi' thad place?'

This question is only one of the reasons I've delayed my return home till seven o'clock. I've spent the afternoon outstaying my welcome in various coffee bars in order to avoid facing Emily ('Have you sorted out my unwanted baby yet?') and Dad (see above).

'Hi, Charlotte, you're home,' Mum calls out, walking into the room and saving me from having to find an immediate answer for Dad. She's carrying a bowl of popcorn and four family-sized bags of crisps. 'Like the new telly? Your dad surprised me with it this afternoon.'

Wide-screen TVs, pineapples – full of surprises today is Dad.

'Yeah, it's great. Where did you get it, Dad?'

'The cush and curry.'

Which gives rise to the fear that he may have bought in bulk and I'll find another forty-nine of them stacked floor to ceiling in my bedroom.

'I gedding this an' all. Is for new baby.' He holds up a romper suit, decorated with several fluffy pom-poms. 'You like?'

'It's blue,' I say.

'Coss is blue. My bess colour.'

The sex of his new grandchild must have deeply traumatised him. I know how his mind works. He figures that if Soulla dresses her baby in blue he can at least pretend it's a boy.

'Has she got a name yet?' I ask.

'Aphrodite,' Mum announces.

First Velvet, now Aphrodite . . . Is there no end to this madness?

'Bluddy *stoobid*,' Dad snorts. '*Uffrodite*! She gonna get call *Uff*ro by other kids. *Uff*ro is hairstyle for blagg men. I calling her Bee-unga.'

'Er, do you mean Bianca?'

'ThasswhadIsaying, Bee-*unga*. I'm like the Migg Jugga, me. We liking the *modern* names, no' the bluddy stoobid ones.'

'They're bringing her round tonight,' Mum says.

'She's only a few hours old. Is that safe? Shouldn't she still be in quarantine or something?'

'Don't be silly. Anyway, the Georgious are popping by and they'd love to see the little one.'

God, I'm being ambushed in my own home. No wonder Emily's holed up in her room. Their imminent arrival also explains why Mum is filling the small bit of the front room that isn't already taken up by the new telly with her varied snack selection. It *also* explains the new telly. We couldn't fail to notice the huge wide-screen at George and Maroulla's on Sunday. Mum and Dad came away convinced that our lives would be complete if only we too had a TV the size of an Asda delivery truck.

The bloody Georgious have got a lot to answer for. Think I'll head upstairs and hide out before they—

Ding-dong.

Too late.

Mum and Dad head for the front door and a moment

293

later return with Maroulla, George and a big bunch of flowers.

'Lovely televishon,' Maroulla coos. 'Is like our one. Is bess thing we ever buy. You know—' her voice lowers to a conspiratorial whisper, '—you seeing things you *neva* seeing before.' She smiles, adding, 'And is good for you 'cause you no gedding the headeggs.'

Wow! A TV that relieves tense, nervous headaches. I can see paracetamol being withdrawn the world over as we speak.

'You juss gedding in from the werk, Thegla?' Maroulla asks, looking at the jacket I'm still wearing.

'Yeah, she juss gedding home,' Dad says. 'She very impordant person there, you know. You shou' see the place. I going today with pineabbles—'

I shudder, dreading what's about to come.

'—Is brilliun. Like five-star hotel. *Very* flush.'

I'm relieved he's chosen to tell them it's flash. I should have known he wouldn't let slip that their future daughter-in-law runs a loony bin.

'When's your dad gonna be on the telly, then?' Mum asks – because Dad making his TV debut was what today's visit was all about, after all.

'Next month I think,' I say.

'I can't wait to see it,' Mum says excitedly.

Oh, I can.

'Sorry we late,' George says, finally speaking. 'But the traffig . . . *Gor blimey*!'

'I telling you is going bluddy crazy out there,' Dad says, getting going on a pet subject. 'This congesting charge is stoobid. I paying five poun's every day juss to go to work and the roads is getting *worse* no' better. You know whad the problem is? Is all these Russian drug traffiggers—'

(A word of explanation. Dad thinks the trafficker

294

bit of their job description refers to the fact that they actually sell the actual drugs from their actual cars, which – *obviously* – is the sole cause of all the congestion in Central London.)

'—You think the bluddy Russians paying congesting charge? Course they bluddy not. I telling you, forenners is *ruin* this cuntry.'

'You're right, Jimmy,' George agrees. 'The immigran's is tegging us over. The peoble I got working in my fucdory, I don' know where they coming from no more. Romania, Polakia, Souvlakia . . . Is like bluddy Unided Nations.'

Now, I could really get stuck into them here – I mean, a pair of immigrants sounding off about immigration – but I don't. Time to escape.

'Just going for a shower, Mum,' I whisper.

'Good idea. Be quick and you'll be down in time to see Aphrodite.'

'Bee-*unga*!'

'Can't wait.'

I flop onto my bed and close my eyes. What a day. I feel very strange – this limbo feeling, not knowing whether I still have a job or not. I feel wasted and I just want to sleep. No chance, the doorbell rings signalling the arrival of my brother and his family. I dread the thought of spending the rest of the evening dodging baby sick and talk of Doctor Dino.

It's gotta be done, though. I'm a Charalambous – treacle-thick blood and all that. But before I go down, I've got to hide the two remaining tapes. I take them from my bag and sit with them on my lap, looking at my name on the spines. What on earth am I supposed to do now? Make a little bonfire in the garden? That won't look at all suspicious, will it? I could unravel them and throw them in the wheelie bin, but how can I be sure that some spy won't fish them out when I'm back inside? What *spy*, for God's sake? I'm going mad here.

The door clicks open and startles the hell out of me. I shove the tapes under my pillow, but not quickly enough to stop Emily spotting me.

'What are you hiding?' she asks.

'Nothing,' I say, my voice laden with panic and guilt.

'*Liar*. What is it? You're doing *drugs*, aren't you?'

'Don't be ridiculous. Anyway, what do you want?'

'What do you think I want? I bet you haven't phoned that clinic.'

'I have, actually,' I say slightly smugly. 'You've got an appointment tomorrow at two thirty.'

'I've got double geography then,' she squeaks.

'C'mon, Em, what's more important? Sorting this mess out or being able to find Japan on a map? Anyway, you've bunked off before. What harm's one more day gonna do?'

'I suppose . . . I'm scared, Charlie.'

She looks it too. All white and frail and fighting tears.

'Come and sit down,' I say.

She joins me on the bed, though I make sure that I'm between her and the pillow – I know her too well. She starts to cry and I put my arm round her shoulder. I catch our reflections in the mirror on my dressing table. *Weird*. We look like two perfect, loving sisters. We could be a couple of girls from *The Brady Bunch*. I don't suppose there was ever an episode where Jan fretted about an impending abortion while Marsha wondered how best to dispose of her hard-core sex tapes, but you get the gist . . .

I've got to focus. On my real sister, who doesn't have cute blonde bunches and an adorable gap in her teeth, but who does have an unwanted pregnancy.

'It must be really scary,' I say, 'but it'll be OK.'

'Will you come with me?' she whimpers.

'Yeah, I've got . . . um . . . a *day off* tomorrow. I'll come.'

'When will they do it?'

'They're pretty quick. If you have your consultation tomorrow and still want to go ahead with it, I think they can get you in the next day.'

'I can't go into hospital,' she says, her voice rising in panic. 'What am I gonna tell Mum and Dad?'

'You'll be in and out the same day. I'll give you a cover-story. I'll say I've got you into The Zone on work experience or something.'

We go quiet as we hear someone on the staircase. 'Wotchew doing ub there? Come see your brotha's baby,' Dad yells.

'We'll be down in a minute,' I shout back. Then to Emily, 'Do you reckon you can face them?'

'I dunno. I don't feel well. Must be that morning sickness thing. You haven't said anything to Mum and Dad, have you?' she asks, panicking again.

'Of course not.'

'If this ever gets out, you're gonna have to tell them it was your fault, you know.'

'You're kidding, yeah?'

'No. It *is* your fault,' she pouts.

'How the hell did you figure that out?' I say, pulling away from her.

'Well, *duh*! If you hadn't been so rubbish, I wouldn't be in this mess. Aren't big sisters supposed to look out for their little sisters?' she says as if the logic is so obvious I should have got there hours ago. 'And this whole abortion thing is *your* idea. *You're* putting me up to it.'

'That's the most ridiculous thing I've ever heard,' I snarl, doing my best to keep my voice down. 'I didn't get you pregnant, did I? I'm trying to help you. If you want to go downstairs and tell Mum and Dad that in nine months they'll be grandparents again, be my bloody guest.'

We jump when the door opens and Dad sticks his head round it.

'Wotchew doing ub here so quiet? You tokking secrets?' He's only half joking because he's scanning the room for evidence. I shuffle my bum up the bed until it's on the pillow. If we were playing a game of hide and seek now, my arse would be burning hot.

'We're just coming down, Dad,' Emily says, giving him her English Rose smile.

'Come now,' he gushes. 'This brilliun progrumme juss starting on RIK. Is all aboud old village my fatha coming from.'

He turns and rushes off. Amazing. The new baby, the one he spent months working himself into a lather of excitement about, is here and she's been knocked off top billing by a TV programme. Well, that'll teach her to be the wrong sex.

'What are you hiding under the pillow?' Emily asks, her eyes narrowing.

'Mind your own business.'

Her hand shoots out and tries to worm beneath my bum. She's fast, but I'm faster. I grab her wrist and Chinese-burn it.

'*Aaaaagh*,' she yelps. 'You might have damaged the baby, you know.'

'Sorry,' I say, and mean it.

God, how many times have I said that today?

Emily and I walk into the front room, trying our best to look as if we've spent the last fifteen minutes swapping girly make-up tips. Everyone – except, of course, for Dad and George – is huddled around the baby. They're making a variety of cooing and clucking noises, which are having no effect whatsoever because little Aphrodite's face is purple and she's screaming her tiny lungs out.

'I'm sure it's colic,' Soulla says wearily. 'When she was a baby, Georgina used to cry like this—' (*Used* to?) '—I'm certain it's colic.'

'I thing she hungry,' Maroulla says. 'She too skinny. You need to feeding her ub.'

The Greek mama's instinctive urge to stuff food down a child's throat kicks in very early. If Maroulla were in charge, two-day-old Aphrodite would be off the milk already and tucking into a big bowl of carbs with an olive on the top.

'Maybe she's trying to tell us she's tired,' Mum says, yawning.

Maybe the baby *is* trying to tell us something. Maybe that desperate cry is her way of saying she's just realised what a mad family she's been born into and she wants out. And who could blame her?

'Ah, Theglottsa, you juss in time,' Dad calls out from his position of nose-against-screen. He sounds chirpy as hell. Normally when he's glued to the telly he loses his rag if someone so much as rustles a magazine. Aphrodite's screams should be sending his rage into the stratosphere. Must be the tumbler of whisky that's putting him in a good mood. 'This village is call *Neogorio,* which liderully translading into *New Village* but is ukchewally oldest village in Cyprus,' he explains like it's the most interesting fact we'll ever hear. 'Or the *weld,* even. And in this village, a lot of peoble beliving is where Jesus was ukchewally being *born.* They even huving *proof.* They find this old bid of paper—'

'I think it's colic, Dad,' Tony interrupts.

'Shuddup, Andon*ih*,' Dad snaps, fighting to be heard

299

above the screams, which seem to be growing louder. 'I telling you they find this piss off paper from two thousun years ago. Is like an old birth suddifigate. Is got Jesus' name on and everything.'

Hmm, wonder what it's got next to *father's occupation*. Creator of the universe?

I've got to get out of this madhouse. Away from Dad before he tries to tell me we can now trace our family line back to the Son of God. Away from that screaming baby before someone thrusts it at me, expecting me to do something with it. The phone in the hall rings and Emily and I race for it – she must have the same ideas of escape as me. She's fast, but, again, I'm faster and I make it to the receiver first.

It's Sasha. 'You said you were going to call me,' she says – I can hear the pout forming on her lips.

'Sorry,' I say. 'We've got family round. It's a bit mad here.'

'Sounds like it. What's that screaming?'

'My brother's new baby.'

'*Ahhh*, cute . . . Anyway, listen, what have you done with your tapes?'

'I haven't had a chance to—'

'I trashed mine as soon as I got home. I smashed up the cases, cut the tape into tiny little bits and put them in a . . .'

As much as I sympathise with Sasha for her part in this nightmare scenario, I have to tune out for a moment. I'm not alone. I've been joined in the hall by Mum and Dad who're helping George and Maroulla on with their coats. Driven out by baby screams, I guess. At least it means I won't have to engage in any conversations about Doctor D. Or whatever it is he's calling himself these days.

'Who that?' Maroulla asks. 'Is Dino?'

Aaagghh!

'Why would he be calling here?' Emily asks, looking confused.

'He say he gonna phone me tonide,' Maroulla explains, as if it makes perfect sense that he'd call her here. 'Is him?'

'No, it's for me,' I say.

'What's for you?' Sasha asks.

'Nothing, just talking to— Never mind. We've got a bit of a goodbye situation going on here. Can you hold on?'

'But I'm just getting to the important bit—'

I take the receiver away from my ear while Mum and Dad get on with the farewell. Here we go again. What are they doing? Trying to notch up another record-breaker? Why can't goodbye ever be just one word? *Goodbye* would cover it nicely.

Even with the noise in the hall and the phone on my lap I can hear Sasha. She sounds frantic. I pick it up again and say, 'What is it?'

'I'm trying to tell you. I flushed all the bits of tape down the loo and now it's blocked and I'm too scared to call a plumber in case he starts asking awkward questions. *WhaddamIgonnadooo*?'

Is this really the girl that called for calm when everything was going ballistic in reception?

'Sasha, I'm really sorry but—'

'*Ah*, is Sushou,' Dad cries. 'I di'n tell you, Maevou, she buck on her feet. Walking and everything. I see with my own eyes. Is a bluddy mirigol.'

'What's going on?' Sasha squeals. 'Are they talking about me? God, you haven't told them about the tapes, have you?'

'Stay strong, Sasha,' I say quickly. 'Remember, one step at a time. We'll talk later, yeah?' Then I hang up.

Well, what else can I do?

As Dad launches into the tale of His Dotter The Mirigol Worker, the phone rings again. I pick it up, expecting it to be Sasha, but it isn't.

It's Judas.

I mean Daniel.

'That was quick,' he says. 'I didn't even hear it ring.'

'What do you want?' My voice is icy cold. Friends for years and now I feel as if I don't know this guy. He's probably not even gay for all I know.

'Is Dino?' Maroulla asks, half in, half out the front door.

I shake my head.

'You're mad at me, aren't you?' Daniel says.

'You what? I can hardly hear you.' This isn't a stalling tactic. The noise is deafening now. Tony, Soulla and brats have joined the crowd in the narrow hall. Aphrodite's screams have reached heavy-metal-singer levels and Georgina – never one to be left out of anything – has joined her on backing vocals.

'You going already, Andonih?' Dad yells. 'Programme juss gedding good. They gedding to the bit where they showing real proof. You can see for youself. In all the old paintings Jesus look so Grik, he muss be coming from Cyprus.'

'We'd best be off, Dad,' my brother says. 'It's definitely colic.'

'And Georgina isn't normally like this, are you, baby?' Soulla coos. 'What's wrong, sweetie?'

'Maybe she gedding the colic too,' Dad suggests huffily. 'Reggon I gedding it an' all.'

What's wrong with these people? Isn't it obvious what the problem is? Hasn't anyone heard of bedtime, as in 'It's way past your . . .'? These kids should be tucked up with their teddies, not stuck in our hallway, doing Act III, Scene IV of *The Endless Goodbye*.

'What's going on? Sounds like a madhouse there,' Daniel says.

'It's not a good time,' I say, notching up the chill factor in my voice a touch. 'I'd better be—'

'Please don't hang up,' he pleads. 'I feel terrible. I'm really sorry about dumping you in it today.'

'Why did you do it?'

'I don't know. I just saw all those people in reception and kind of panicked and—'

'I'm not talking about running away. Why did you take the tape?' I say this with my head turned towards the wall while trying to muffle my voice in my sweatshirt – not that anyone will be able to hear me above the tortured baby screams. 'Tell me, is it your idea of a practical joke because I'm laughing my fucking head off here.'

'Is that what you think?' he splutters. 'Jesus, I'd never— I swear, I'd never, ever do anything like that to you. I know I said you could make a lot of—'

'Save it for some mug who'll believe you,' I say before slamming the phone down.

Bluddy poofing bustudd, as I've heard my dad say on more than one occasion.

The Bit Where We Are Family
(I Got All My Sisters With Me)

This place is lovely. Nice comfy chairs. Freshly painted walls. No ancient *Reader's Digests* heaped on the table. And no dog-eared posters warning us not to assault the staff. Wonderful what money can buy. If the NHS were half as plush you'd be happy to queue round the block for your kidney transplant.

Emily and I are in a consultation room at the clinic. The counsellor has left us alone for some quality time. Having gone through the pros and cons, she's giving us 'some space' so that Emily can arrive at a decision that's right for her 'both emotionally and spiritually' in an atmosphere of 'calm and detachment'. In other words, poor old Em has to decide whether to stick around for the op or flee screaming into the street.

'You OK?' I ask.

'I think so. It doesn't seem so scary when you're here, does it? It's a nice place. You didn't have to pay for all this you know.'

She's right; I didn't. But you know what? The weirdest feelings have come over me. Emily looks truly vulnerable today. Normally this would make me want to tip her over the edge by giving her another Chinese burn, but today everything feels different. Maybe a deeply repressed sisterly instinct has somehow fought its way to the surface. Or maybe it's plain old guilt. After all, she was sort of right, wasn't she? If I'd been a better big sister in the first place, maybe I could have passed on some of my learned wisdom. Genius advice, like, oh, I don't know, use a condom.

I feel really sorry for Sasha too. She was crazy about Ben and she's still coming to terms with what a scumbag he is. Even so, she thought to phone me this morning to see how I was bearing up. She even offered to suck up to Jamie on my behalf. I didn't take her up on it, though I hate not knowing whether or not I've still got a job. I've decided that I'm going into work tomorrow to have it out with him.

'I feel so bad about taking it out on you the other night, Charlie,' Sasha said before she hung up. 'If there's anything I can do, just call me, right?' She may swan about in Sasha World most of the time, but she's really trying to be there for me.

And that's exactly what I'm going to do for my sister, starting from now. In fact, I've decided that things are going to change – and given that I seem to be the most useless person I've ever met most of the time, that means an awful lot of changes. I'm going to start with the *inner me*. Forget the hair and nail extensions, the spray-on tan that only takes five minutes to apply, that brilliant Clarins foundation that covers just about everything. I don't care about being a better-looking person. Just a Better Person will do.

Who knows, if it turns out that Jamie has fired me, maybe I'll fly off to Africa, live in a simple mud hut and teach people how to dig wells (after having first learned how to dig wells). But I'm starting with a more manageable project: my sister. She's in a hole; I can dig her out.

She looks at me now with the puppy-dog eyes she

usually saves for Dad, and for once they work on me. I feel a vaguely sugary, slightly yucky feeling well up inside me and I don't fight it. I find myself leaning towards her and before I know it we're hugging. We *are* Sister Sledge. We *are* family. And – *shit on a stick* – we're both crying now.

'I'm really sorry,' she blubs. 'I've been so horrible to you and you've been so great.'

'You've got nothing to be sorry for,' I blub back. 'From now on, I'm always going to be there for you.'

Outrageous.

But I really mean it. And I've got to admit, this Better Person thing feels *fantastic*. As soon as this is over, I'm on the first plane to somewhere hot and dry with simple mud huts.

'I couldn't do this without you, Charlie,' Emily says.

'So you're going to do it then? Have the termination?' (Don't think we're allowed to say the A-word in here.)

'I don't have a choice, do I?'

'Look, Emily, whatever you decide I'll support you two hundred per cent.' As I'm saying this I'm praying she does go for the op because I do not want to be lumbered with babysitting an Aphrodite mark two while Emily sits her GCSEs . . . Though obviously I'd do it without complaining because, you see, I'm a Better Person now.

'I'm only crying 'cause I feel so happy,' she sobs. 'You know, 'cause we're together and everything. Stupid or what?'

'It's not stupid. It's *lovely*,' I gush.

'I've had an idea,' she says, smiling through her tears. 'Maybe we should tell Mum and Dad . . . Well, maybe just Mum.'

'You what?' I say, stiffening slightly.

'Think about it, Charlie. We've never been a close family. But look at us two. Brought together by a crisis.

It's just like a film, you know, with Julia Roberts and Meg Thingy.'

I laugh, but only a little. I don't want to squash her enthusiasm entirely because I'm feeling it myself. 'Let's talk some more about it, yeah?'

The door opens and the counsellor reappears. 'How are you two doing?' she asks sweetly.

'OK, I think,' I say.

'Good, good. Have you reached a decision, Emily?'

My sister looks at me and I squeeze her hand. 'Yes,' she says. 'I want to have the . . .' She trails off.

'The termination?' the counsellor prompts.

Emily nods.

'Are you absolutely sure?' I ask.

She nods again.

'Good, lovely,' the counsellor says, though I doubt it's going to be either of those things. 'OK, right, there'll be some forms for you to fill in, but first we'll pop down the corridor for your blood test.' Emily's eyes widen in alarm. 'Don't worry, it's just routine. Nothing to be scared of. Just a pinprick.' She gestures to Emily, who stands up.

'Do you want me to come with you?' I ask.

'I'll be OK,' she replies, bravely suppressing the wobble in her lip. 'See you in a minute.'

As I watch the pair of them walk off I'm over-whelmed by the emotion of the moment we've just shared. I think about what Emily said before we were interrupted and I'm struck by how wise she is. God, she's just a kid and she's going through hell, but she's so right. If we're ever going to be a close family we have to learn to *share* our problems. If I can be a Better Person, then maybe Mum and Dad can be too . . . Well, maybe just Mum.

I reach into my bag and take out my mobile. Without

hesitating I dial the number for home. I put the phone to my ear and as I listen to the rings I think about the words of Darius. OK, so we all thought he was the world's cheesiest wanker, but (sorry) I'm with him right now – *I can so feel the love in this room.*

The Inevitable Bit Of Any Story Where Everybody Wants To Kill Everybody Else

'I bluddy gonna kill the fuggy bustudd! You just lemme geddin' my hunds on him!'

Mum, Emily and I cower before this outburst. There definitely isn't any love in *this* room right now. Dad is *really* mad. I know this not because he wants to kill – that's a relatively common wish of his – but because he's using the F-word (yes, *fuggy* is the F-word).

'His taking udvunting.' (I *think* he means *advantage*, though I can't be certain – his accent grows more impenetrable when his anger is up.) 'I rip his fuggy head off!'

'Jimmy, for Christ's sake calm down,' Mum pleads. 'I knew I shouldn't have told you, I *knew* it.'

Too bloody right she shouldn't have told him, not least because when I told her I made her swear she wouldn't say anything to Dad.

'You no gonna tell me?' he yells. 'You're my wife. You telling me everything or I bluddy killing you an' all.'

'Stop shouting, Jimmy!' Mum shouts. 'They must be able to hear us in the bloody Shopping City.'

'You don' shout at me. I shouting at *you*!'

'Both of you stop yelling,' I yell. 'Let's talk about this calmly and—'

'Tok? Is no time for tokking. Is time for *ukk*shon. You telling me who he is and I going straight roun' there and I gonna fuggy *kill* him.'

'You're going nowhere, Jimmy Charalambous,' Mum says. 'I didn't tell you so you could fly off the bloody handle. I told you so you could start acting like a proper father. It's no wonder the girls don't talk to you when you spend so little time with them. You're always at work. It's about time you—'

'*Ah*, thass another thing. I lose takings closing shop early to come home an' kill him. I gonna get him reimbursing me first, then I killing him. I going now and you cunt stop me, Maevou. Go and get my shoes.'

Incredible. He's a wild, unstoppable killing machine, but he still needs Mum to fetch him his shoes.

He sets off across the front room, but I'm standing in the doorway, barring his exit.

'Out my way, Thegla, unless you wan' I kill you too.'

'Dad, no one's killing anyone,' I say defiantly, though I feel anything but as he bears down on me. 'You're going to calm down, we'll all sit down and have a good old talk about everything.'

I look – more like glare – at my sister for confirmation.

'Don't you bloody look at me like that, you *grass*,' she squeaks, springing suddenly from the shell she's been cowering in. 'I should bloody well kill you for telling them.'

'It was *your* stupid idea,' I snap. 'God, I wish I'd walked out on you at that stupid clinic and let you come home to all this shit on your own.'

(C'mon, *seriously* now, how long did you expect me to keep up that Better Person rubbish when my sister is a complete and utter idiot?)

'Don' you go shouting at your sista like thad,' Dad

310

booms, trying to barge past me again. 'Is me who is mud as the hell!'

'Sweet *Jes*us, just fecking look at the t'ree of yous,' Mum shrieks, sounding suddenly very Oirish (something that afflicts her only in moments of extreme stress). 'D'you want the entire fecking street to hear this madness?'

The *t'ree of us* are stunned into immobility. We're shocked because Mum doesn't do angry and I've definitely never heard her swear before.

'Right,' she says, her voice slipping seamlessly from Oirish-Irish to its usual London-Irish, 'shall we sit down and talk about this like adults?'

We stand looking at each other awkwardly for a few moments, before shuffling towards the centre of the room. 'That's better,' says Mum the Peacemaker, smartly filling the silence while there's still one to fill. 'Now, why don't we sit down and—'

'Mum, Dad, it wasn't my fault, I *swear*,' Emily interrupts, her voice racing at a hundred miles an hour. 'Going to that clinic was Charlotte's idea. She paid for it and everything. She put so much pressure on me—'

'Hang on, I wasn't the one that *got pregnant*, was I?'

'Yeah, but—'

'No buds,' Dad shouts. 'Juss shuddup! I don' giving the monkey whose idea is it. I juss wanna know why some filthy bustudd *that I gonna kill for definite* is pudding his hands on my baby girl. You telling me, Thaglotta?'

'Don't ask me. I didn't put him up to it. Emily managed to drop her knickers all by herself.'

'Hey, don' you speaking like thad. You got no respegg? Is no wonder she going off the railings when you being such bud influence. You're her big sista. You're suppose to be setting the eggsumple.'

311

'Jimmy, stop shouting for Christ's sake,' Mum says, 'especially not at Charlotte. This isn't her fault.'

'Too right. There's something else that isn't my fault either,' I hiss at Emily.

'What?' she says blankly, as if she's completely forgotten the crucial detail that was the sole topic of conversation on the journey home.

'You know what,' I say.

'What, Charlotte?' Mum asks.

'Yeah, whad?' Dad echoes.

They look at me expectantly, but I'm staring at my sister, willing her to speak. She doesn't.

'Dad, *listen* to me. You're not going to have to kill anyone because there's no reason to. Do you understand?'

'Of course there isn't any reason to kill anyone. Violence is never the answer,' says Kofi Annan – I mean Mum. 'Jimmy, you're being ridiculous. You've been watching too many silly soaps if you ask me—' (*Hello*? Earth to Mother?) '—Whoever took advantage of Emily is an effing gobshite, but that's still no cause to go flying—'

'*Mum*, let me finish. Things aren't how you think,' I say. 'Emily made a mistake . . . didn't you, Emily?' I stop and look at her, giving her a chance to speak for herself like we arranged in the cab (well, like I arranged in between her yelling at me to fuck off).

'I did *not* make a mistake,' she squeals. 'It's all *your* fault. You should've asked me if you could check the result, then we wouldn't be in this mess and Dad wouldn't be standing here now having a coronary.' (Which he does actually look closer to having this time than the last, but let's not go there right now.)

'Whad I huving? I no huving nothing. You giving me his name or . . . '

'*Please*, Dad, stop it. Look, if Emily won't explain, I

312

will. Just because she's too stupid to follow simple inst—'

Emily explodes now – goes off like a petite Irish-Cypriot weapon of mass destruction – and flies straight at me. I didn't see it coming and the next thing I know we're both rolling around on the carpet like two of those WWF blokes, but without the slick moves, the silly outfits or the body hair – well, maybe Emily has the hair.

I'll be honest: we're fighting like women (*obviously*) – all hair pulling and nail gouging, spiced up with some girly screaming. She snatches at my head and her hand comes away with about a quarter of my extensions. That sets me off. I fly at her and we both fall over. As we roll across the room we knock into the lamp, which tumbles onto the vase on the coffee table, which spills faded daffodils and dirty water all over the magazines. Mum screams and it can only be at the horrific sight of her daughters tearing one another apart. But I'm so very wrong. 'Jimmy, get them up for God's sake. That water's gone all over the *TV Times*!'

'*Thegla, you stobbid now*!' he orders (I *think* – it's hard to hear clearly when your head's being crushed beneath your sister's stomach). Mum bends over and tugs at Emily's shoulder, but my sister hasn't finished with me and doesn't want to get off just yet. She plants both hands in Mum's stomach and gives her a mighty shove. Mum stumbles backwards onto the coffee table. Both go over and Mum is left in an undignified sprawl between the upended table legs.

This is too much for Dad, who must be realising that his own plans for murder and mayhem will come to nothing if his daughter gets in first and kills us all. 'Emily, *stobbid*!' he shouts commandingly. So commandingly that she goes right ahead and ignores him. She flails at me with clenched fists and I cover my face with my forearms. Though I can't see, I sense Dad on top of her, trying to get her up. Next, I hear a pained yelp, followed by heavy, stumbling feet, followed by a loud crash, then a dull explosion.

Silence.

Emily has stopped hitting me and gingerly I take my arms away from my face. She's still sitting astride my stomach, but she isn't looking at me. She's staring at Dad, who's crumpled against the wall in the far corner of the room – the corner where only a few seconds ago the brand-new wide-screen telly stood. The TV is now in the centre of the room, screen down, beside Mum and the upturned coffee table.

My dazed dad slowly climbs to his feet and goes to his beloved Sony. He bends down and lifts it upright. It doesn't have a screen any more and its entire innards are visible.

Mum, still on the floor and now covered in shards of glass, lets out a long, agonised scream. 'Look what you've gone and done, you great big fecking *ape*!' Mum snarls, managing to sound more Oirish and, therefore, even angrier than before.

'Whad? I din' do nothing. Is your stoobid dotters, fighting like unimals who—'

'STOP IT, EVERYONE, JUST STOP IT!' Emily shrieks, her face streaked with tears – probably from the frustration of having tried and failed to kill me. 'I'M NOT PREGNANT!'

That's right.

She's not pregnant. That's what the blood test confirmed. And that's when I lost it with her, when she returned to the consultation room, a euphoric beam on her face. Sorry, but I didn't share her joy. Well, I'd just lit the blue touchpaper by phoning Mum with the news, hadn't I?

'For God's sake, those pregnancy tests are made so that even morons can use them. How could you screw it up?' I yelled as the counsellor tried to intervene with some useless tips she must have picked up on an anger-management seminar.

'It wasn't my fault. I thought no blue line meant pregnant,' Emily pouted. 'Anyway, you should have checked it for me. I'm only fifteen.'

I wish I bloody had checked it because it struck me then that where it states 99% *accurate* on the Predictor pack it should add *unless your name is Emily Charalambous and you're so stupid that you couldn't follow the instructions on a pelican crossing*.

To be honest, I wasn't angry with just Emily. I was mad at myself as well. I *should* have checked her test. I calmed down a little on the way home. As I recall, my last words before I opened the front door were, 'Hopefully Mum won't have done anything dumb. Knowing her she'll be flopped in front of the telly, watching *Countdown*, and we'll be able to straighten things out before the shit hits the fan.'

Ha!

Anyway, back to the war zone.

As the four of us sprawl among the wreckage we hear a new voice: '*Hello*. Whass huppening?' It's Maroulla.

What is it with Greeks? Give them a date and a time and they couldn't be punctual if their lives depended on it, but when they're uninvited their timing is impeccable.

'You know, you shou'n't be leaving front door open,' George says, slightly slack-jawed. 'Is very dengerous. Anyone could be coming in.'

I have to say he's dead right about that. Emily and I must have left the door flapping open in the panic of arriving home and hearing Dad threatening World War Three in the front room. And now, thanks to our carelessness, Maroulla and George are surveying the bloody aftermath.

'Hello, Maroulla . . . *George*,' Mum says, climbing to her feet. 'What a lovely surprise.' Her voice is several pitches higher than it should be if normal is what she's trying for.

But tell me, what's *normal* about this situation? I'm still sprawled on my back. I can feel my right eye closing, swollen from the single punch that Emily managed to land successfully. Dad is bent over, purple-faced and panting, his feet still tangled up with the TV cables. Emily stands with her T-shirt ripped and hanging off her. She's still clutching the extensions she ripped from my head – the extensions that cost a small fucking fortune and that bloody Sheena at Hair We Go *swore* even wild horses wouldn't be able to pull out. Emily's own hair is doing a very good impression of an electrocuted scarecrow. Then there's Mum, covered from head to toe in fragments of shattered TV screen and she's doing the *how are you*s like this is just a bog-standard day in the Charalambous household.

And, well, who knows any more, but perhaps it is?

'We coming at the bad time?' Maroulla asks. 'Is juss we passing by and I telling George we pob in and giving you the recibe for the *maccaronia* I telling you aboud.'

'No, no . . . It's *lovely* to see you,' Mum splutters, her voice rising another octave. 'You'll have to excuse the mess . . .'

She trails off and I watch her eyes scan the room in search of a plausible explanation. *Sorry, Mum, but I can't help you here*. I'm usually pretty creative when it comes to lying my way out of a hole, but this one . . . *Impossible*.

'It's the *TV*,' she says suddenly, a spark of something like inspiration flashing in her eyes. 'It just kind of . . .'

'*Eggsblode*,' Dad shouts, seizing on the thread and running with it. 'It juss eggsblode. *Boom*! Bluddy Jabanese rubbish.'

'It was shocking,' Mum continues. 'A wonder it didn't kill someone.'

'*Ah*, I see you gedding the *Sony*,' George says, peering at the small silver badge that's still clinging to the front of the gutted television. 'We buying the *Jay Cee Vee*.'

That, of course, would explain everything.

Mum and Dad visibly relax because it looks as if the Georgious might just be daft enough to buy their story.

'Anyway, drama over,' Mum says breezily. 'Why don't you sit yourselves down and I'll make us all a cup of tea?'

'I giving you the hand, Maevou,' Maroulla says.

'No need. Sit down and make yourselves comfy. Jimmy, Charlotte and Emily can help me, can't you?' Mum says, glaring at the three of us and making it clear that we're wanted in the kitchen immediately for the complex job of sticking the kettle on.

Maroulla and George head for the sofa, where Mum's brushing off some shards of glass with a cushion. They sit down nervously, their eyes darting about the room on the lookout for any more potentially explosive objects. Her guests sitting (kind of) comfortably, Mum ushers Dad, Emily and me into the kitchen.

'Right, not a word from any of yous,' Mum hisses Oirishly.

'I—' Dad butts in.

'I said not a word, Jimmy. This is a fecking shambles

and before we go back in there I want to know exactly what's going on . . . Well, Emily?'

'I made a mistake,' she mumbles.

'You OK in there?' Maroulla calls out from the front room. 'You want hand with the kettlon?'

'Just waiting for it to boil, Maroulla. Be with you in a tick,' Mum yells back. 'What sort of mistake, Emily? C'mon, we haven't got all day.'

Emily can't or won't reply so I do it for her. 'She misread her pregnancy test. She's not having a baby.'

'Well, that's a relief, isn't it, Jimmy?' Mum says, obviously hoping that this will be the bit where we all slap our foreheads and fall about laughing at the sheer silliness of it all. But Dad's still glaring at us. '*Isn't it, Jimmy?*' Mum prompts.

'No, is not. He still a bluddy bustudd. You telling me his name now, Emily, I commending you,' Dad snarls through clenched teeth.

'I'm not telling you *anything*,' she says as she runs from the room. We listen to her feet thunder up the stairs, then a loud slam as she shuts herself in her bedroom.

Both Mum and Dad look at me for an explanation, but all I can do is stare back at them with my mouth hanging open. What can I say? The entire journey home I tried to get her to tell me who it was, but her lips stayed sealed. I'm as much in the dark as they are.

'I go tok to her,' Dad says, but Mum puts a hand on his arm.

'You're staying put, Jimmy. We'll get rid of the Georgious and sort this out la—'

She stops abruptly because Maroulla's head has appeared through a gap in the kitchen door. 'Maevou, you want I clin ub a bit? Is glass everywhere. You giving me the dusspan an' I—'

'Really, it's fine,' Mum says, doing her best to conceal her growing irritation.

'Juss go si' down,' Dad says, not hiding his at all.

Maroulla looks at us suspiciously before shutting the door.

'Right, stick that bloody kettle on, Jimmy,' Mum says. 'And Charlotte, go clean yourself up. Your sister's made mincemeat of you.'

I'm not waiting till the Georgious have gone to have it out once and for all with Emily.

'The truth now, Emily,' I say as I lean on her bedroom door, staring at her with my one good eye. She's curled up in a foetal position on her bed, her face swollen from crying. She doesn't look dangerous any more. Just very young and very tired. She doesn't speak. She won't even look at me.

'Who is it?' I ask.

'Just a boy.'

'How long have you been going out with him?' I prod gently.

She shrugs, but after a moment's silence she says, 'I've got my reasons for not wanting to tell you. He's called—' She stops abruptly.

'He's called what?'

'What difference does it make?'

'I'm just curious. Besides, you've wasted my time and money, given me a black eye and ripped half my hair out. I reckon an explanation is the least you owe me.'

'OK, but if I tell you, you'd better swear you won't tell anyone . . . Or else I'll fucking kill you.' I believe she means it.

'I swear.'

'He's called Mehmet.'

'Excuse me,' I splutter, though I heard her perfectly clearly. 'He's Turkish?'

She doesn't need to answer that. And I believe her now because even in her wildest fantasies, never would my sister invent a lie that involved a Turk. Not even she would be that stupid. Let me explain. With my Dad there's never any knowing how he'll react in a given situation – the word contrary was probably invented to describe him. This holds true when it comes to blokes. One day I could bring home the world's most charming and eligible Greek bachelor and Dad might hate him. On another I could introduce him to the love of my life who happens to be a heroin addict with a criminal record as long as both your arms and Dad could welcome him with the finest Greek brandy. Or he might throw him through the window. That's my point: you never can tell. However, there's one scenario I can be absolutely, positively certain of.

My dad and Turks . . . *Never*. He's not alone. There are thousands of Greek dads who share his view. Likewise, there are thousands of Turkish dads who couldn't handle their daughters bringing home a Greek boy. What can I say? It's history we're dealing with here. The illegal invasion of Seventy-four and all that . . . But now isn't the time for a history lesson. I've got my sister to sort out.

'You're going out with a Turkish boy?' I repeat, still gasping for air. 'Are you mad?'

'I love him.'

All I can think is that she must do, to risk her life so recklessly.

'Why didn't you tell me? Why didn't you talk to me?'

She doesn't have to say anything. She raises an eyebrow and that gesture alone speaks volumes.

I feel weird now. Shocked too. And ever so slightly

relieved. Why? Well, she'll never be able to blackmail me again because whatever I've got up to, I've never committed the crime of going out with a Turk. But that's not all.

'Why are you smiling?' Emily asks.

'I think you've done me a favour, Em.'

'Really?'

'Well, after the shit they've seen today, I reckon the Georgious will be calling off the wedding.'

I can hear them now. Even through the closed door their voices are booming up the stairs from the hall. They must be going.

'Nex' time you gedding the Jay Cee Vee,' George is saying, on the face of it going along with the exploding-telly story. God knows what they're really thinking.

I hear the front door close. A brief goodbye – uncharacteristically short and sweet for Greeks – and no mention of Dino. *Hmm*, think I might just be safe.

'It's clear,' I say to Emily. 'You coming down?'

She shakes her head. Can't say I blame her.

As I turn to go, she says, 'You want these back?' She's holding up the extensions she ripped out a short while ago.

'No thanks,' I say. 'I was getting sick of them anyway. It's time for a change.'

Mum is vacuuming up the last splinters of glass when I get back into the front room. Dad is in his armchair. The TV is back in its corner. Everything could be normal again, except that the bits of wire and circuit dangling from the front of the set are a giveaway.

'So, you tok to her?' Dad asks.

'Yes.'

'How is she?' Mum says, switching off the Hoover and slumping onto the sofa.

'Tired. Very embarrassed. What you'd expect really.'

'Thanks for looking out for her, Charlie,' Mum says gratefully.

'Oh, I did a great job, didn't I?' I reply, stroking a finger along the deep scratch that runs the length of my cheek.

'Well, you did your best.'

'OK, now we tok,' Dad interrupts gruffly. 'Who is he?'

'Just some boy at school. Don't worry. She's not seeing him any more.'

I could tell them the truth – after the beating she's just given me, I don't owe Emily any favours. But I've had enough bloodshed for one day.

'*Hmmph*,' Dad snorts. Looks as if the fight has gone out of him too. He won't be doing any killing . . . Not today at least.

I sit beside Mum on the sofa. No one speaks. We find ourselves staring at the TV. Force of habit, I suppose. This is strange. I've lived in this house for twenty-four years and I don't recall a single TV-free moment. It gets switched on by the first one up in the morning and switched off by the last one going to bed.

What now? No telly. God, that means we'll have to talk to each other. Make conversation. Exchange views on a variety of topics all the way between now and bedtime.

We sit in silence . . .

. . . Until Mum looks at her watch and says, 'Damn, I'm missing *The Weakest Link*.'

'Never mine thad,' Dad says. 'I missing my soap. Is gedding rilly good now. Is the bit where the fatha find out his son and dotter is having the baby and he go mad with shotgun.'

Hmm, I think I see a pattern emerging.

322

'*Corrie*'s supposed to be good tonight as well,' Mum adds ruefully.

Well, it's a start. It's a conversation, even if it is only about the TV they'll be missing. I decide to change the subject. It's a risky manoeuvre, but I need to test the water. 'So, when are we seeing the Georgious again?' I ask tentatively.

'No plans, have we, Jimmy?'

'To be hones' I gedding bit sigg and tire of them,' Dad says. 'They always roun' here, never giving me no piss.'

'I think we'll give them a rest for a while,' Mum concludes.

Oh yes, the wedding is definitely off.

'You back at work tomorrow, Charlotte?' Mum asks after a moment. 'It must be really exciting with that TV show coming up.'

If there's been one good thing about today, it's that it's taken my mind off the nightmare that is work. 'Yeah, I'm going in,' I say. I don't add that I'll probably be coming straight back home again.

But then I think about it. We're talking here. Communicating like families are meant to. Why *shouldn't* I share some of my shit with them? So right here, right now I tell them everything about work . . .

Actually, I give them a version that only vaguely resembles the truth, concluding that Jamie and I have had a 'misunderstanding'.

'Thass terribol,' Dad says when I've finished. 'You doing such a good job. I seeing with my own eyes. You cunt lose it now. Telling you what, tomorrow I coming with you. Your boss remember me with good filling – I bringing him pineabbles ufter all, eh? Don' worry, Charlotta, he foggedding all about stoobid misunnerstanding.'

Damn. I *knew* there was a good reason I didn't talk to my parents. There's an old saying that I've just invented: a problem shared is a problem doubled. Mum senses me squirming beside her and says, 'I'd let Charlotte try and straighten things out by herself, Jimmy.'

'Ukchewally, I cunt close shop again,' Dad says, not feeling up to an argument, but not wanting to miss out on having The Final Word either. 'You going werk withoud me . . . But I sending him some of my bess currot cake for piss offering. Is got real currots in it, you know.'

The phone rings. I don't feel like answering it. Neither, it seems, does anyone else, so I get up and go into the hall.

'Hello,' I say wearily.

'Hi,' says the slimiest two-faced rat ever to inhale oxygen.

'What do you want, Daniel?' I ask with no more friendliness than I showed the last time we spoke.

'I just wanted to see how you were.'

'I'm fine, thanks. Is that it?'

'No . . . Look, I swear I didn't take the tape and I can't bear it that you think I did.'

I don't answer. We listen to each other's breathing for a moment. Then he says, 'You coming in tomorrow? . . . I miss you.'

I still don't answer.

'Hey, guess what. Velvet didn't show today.'

'Yeah, and?'

'Well, it's obvious, isn't it? She must've nicked the tape. She's done a runner so she can sell the story.'

'Velvet didn't show because she probably figured she was going to get the sack, Daniel. Either that or Jamie actually fired her while you weren't paying attention.'

324

'I was with Jamie today and he didn't mention it.'

'Oh, not wasting any time, then. Now I'm out of the picture you're straight up the boss's arse.'

'Come on, Charlie, please. I was talking to him about you, if you must know. I told him we can't function properly without you, that all the clients and the staff love you and that he's got to have you back . . . And I told him it was my fault the tape got played out to the whole club.'

'What a load of old rubbish. The staff don't *love* me. The only person who cares about me is Sasha.'

'You're deluding yourself! How many times do I have to tell you she's got an unhealthy fixation with you? It's jealousy, or something, I don't know, but you're the only person who can't see it.'

I know Sasha can be very needy, but she's like that with all the people she cares about – Jenna, for example. Ben/Karl. It sounds to me like Daniel's just desperate to shift the spotlight from himself. Then again, he did just say that he told Jamie the tape episode was his fault. He didn't have to do that, did he? If he isn't lying, that is.

'Look, Jamie said he's going to let you off with a bollocking,' Daniel continues. 'And since he already gave you a massive one yesterday, he's not even going to bother with that . . . So, you see, you've *got* to come in tomorrow.' Silence from me. 'Please.'

Another bit of my brain – the same bit that only a few hours ago was making me decide to become a Better Person – is screaming at me to give him the benefit of the doubt. And, of course, I'm pleased – more like deliriously overjoyed – that I've still got a job.

But after a long day spent being mentally and physically battered, there's only one possible outcome to this internal battle.

'See you tomorrow, then,' I say as ungraciously as I can manage.

Then the hard-as-nails me hangs up . . .

Before heading upstairs for a good cry.

The Bit Where I Find Out The Sun Shines Out Of Daniel's Arse

I stand across the street and gaze up at The Zone's seven glass storeys. It's only now that I realise how much I've missed it. I feel tears well up and it's a good job I'm wearing sunglasses (on account of my black eye rather than the dazzlingly overcast weather). How long have I been away? A day and a bit. *Crazy*. Must be because I thought I was never coming back. Just goes to show, huh? You don't know what you've got till it's nearly gone . . .

Which is almost a terrific song lyric.

The streets are quiet for the West End. It's that in-between time; after arriving for work but before going out for lunch. Even the trains were empty. I got a seat and closed my eyes – mostly so I didn't have to look at the reflection of my ridiculous, patched-up hair in the window opposite. I ended up sleeping nearly all the way. I could sleep forever, I'm so tired.

What's it going to be like when I go in? Will everyone snigger? Will my authority as studio manager have been fatally undermined by the events of two days ago? Come to that, did the events of two days ago prove that I had no authority in the first place? These and other questions will be answered only once I step through the door.

So I suppose I'd better get on with it.

I'm about to cross the road when my mobile beeps. I pull it from my bag and look at the display. I've got a text . . . It's from Karl.

```
DID U HVE 2 FUCK UP
MY LIFE COMPLETELY?
WOT DID I EVA DO 2 U
APART FRM SHOW U
A GOOD TIME?
WOT GOES RND CUMS RND.
JUST U W8 . . .
```

I feel seriously freaked. I mean, this is the guy with the secret filming fetish. What other weirdness is he capable of? And why has he waited two days to vent his rage at me? What sick, evil plans has he been hatching in his underground (OK, first-floor) South Kensington lair . . . ?

God, enough of the paranoia already. He's just hurt. Damaged. Hopefully beyond repair. Oh yes, he's suffering and so he should be. *Excellent*. I award myself a mental pat on the back. Today's already turning out better than I could have hoped.

I cross the road feeling slightly better. I go up the steps, the doors swoosh open *aaaaaaaaaaand*. . . I'm in.

I stand for a moment and look across the twenty feet of marble towards the desk. Daniel's sitting on it. Rebecca's behind it. Everything's as it should be. But, God, it's only been a day and a bit. It's hardly *Lassie Comes Home*. Daniel looks ashen – like someone died. Shit, he must feel terrible . . . *I feel myself melting . . .* How could I have treated him so badly? . . . *And melting* . . . How could I ever accuse him? . . . *And melting* . . . He's *Daniel*, my best buddy; he just wouldn't . . .

328

I'm more or less a puddle now. I manage to make my feet move across the foyer. Daniel slides off the desk and we meet halfway, falling into one another's arms. Rebecca beams at us.

'Fuck, I'm glad you're back,' he gasps. Then, 'What happened to your face? And, shit, your *hair*!'

'Oh, me and my sis were doing an experiment on *Brady Bunch*-style living . . . Went kinda wrong,' I say. Then (because it's what I've wanted to say from the moment I clapped eyes on him): 'I'm really sorry, Daniel. I should never have accused you.'

'No, *I'm* really sorry. I should never have run away like I did.'

'Forget it. I'd probably have done the same.'

'No you wouldn't. You're the best.'

'No, you are.'

'God, I'm glad you're here. I've missed you.'

'I've missed you too . . . What's up with Becks?'

She's watching us hug and she's gone from beaming to distraught. Almost as bad as she was the time she double-booked Super-chill Tantric Yoga and Wing Chun (Advanced Killing Techniques) into the same studio, and then she was *hysterical*.

'You didn't read the *Sun* on the way in, did you?' Daniel says.

'No, I slept most of the way. Is Becks on page three or something?' I'm joking, but suddenly I feel a deep sense of doom.

'I wish. Charlie . . . you'd better brace yourself.'

'You know I didn't do it, don't you, Charlie?' Daniel asks for the tenth time.

'*Shush*, I'm reading,' I say.

We're sitting in my office, the *Sun* on the desk in front of us. Blaize is on page one. And pages four, five, six and seven. The headline reads 'BLAIZE SIZZLES'. The picture beneath it is grainy and blurred, but there's no mistaking whose legs are wrapped around Karl's sleek back. I flick through the other pages. There's no need to read the words. The pictures – and there are plenty of them – tell the story. Heavy black bars hide the raunchier details but it doesn't require much imagination to fill in the blanks. There are other photos too. One of The Zone, the scene of the tape's world premiere. There's a shot of Jamie leaving the Atlantic Bar with some D-list presenter he was seeing a few months ago. And another of an E- or F-list actor from *Holby City*, who has, the caption tells us, destroyed his Zone membership in disgust.

God, no wonder Karl's text was so pissed off – clearly, he's a *Sun* reader. It's all here, in black, white and full colour, all of it.

'You OK?' Daniel asks.

Good question. Am I OK? The only way I'd feel any worse would be if the stills splattered across the paper were of Karl and *me* having sex.

But that's no comfort whatsoever.

'Jesus, what a disaster,' I say. 'How did this happen?'

'I don't know, but it's all my fault. If I hadn't made you play the—'

'Stop it, Daniel. It really doesn't matter any more. Who the fuck did this? That's what I want to know.'

He shakes his head. 'I've read every word and they don't even hint at who their source is. It has to be Velvet. Who else? She had motive, opportunity and she's done the disappearing act. Bet she's driving around in a pink Porsche Boxster now.'

'*Bitch*,' I mutter, because now I think about it, he must be right.

The door crashes open and Rebecca falls through

it. 'Haven't you heard of knocking?' Daniel snaps, climbing back into the skin he's just jumped out of. 'What do you want, Becks? We're in a crisis meeting here.'

'Sorry, but Jarvis wants to know if you can spare me to go cover in Zone Clone. Sasha's phoned in sick again.'

'We'll try to manage. Off you go.'

She skips off, leaving us alone again.

'Sasha's going to find herself without a job if she doesn't get her shit together soon,' Daniel says.

'Well at least I'll have a mate to hang out with at the employment office. Does Jamie know about this yet?' I ask, looking down at the black bar that covers Karl's naked backside.

Before Daniel can answer, the phone rings. I stare at it as it vibrates on the desk. It's an internal ring . . . Can only be Jamie.

'He knows,' I say quietly.

That was ten minutes ago . . .

When I still had a job.

Jamie was brutal, but at least he was quick. I can't remember much of what he said beyond the odd phrase. Stuff like *appalling breach of trust* and *shockingly unprofessional* . . . Oh, and *devious, money-grabbing* and *bitch* might have come into it somewhere. My pathetic 'But it wasn't me' didn't cut much ice – not sure he even heard it beneath his yelling. He was so enraged that he didn't even notice my shiner, the four-inch scratch on my cheek and the hole in my head where my extensions used to be. On any other day that would have given him three perfectly good reasons to be sick on the carpet and then fire me.

Bastard. Just to freak him out I wish I'd dropped my knickers and shown him the birthmark on my bum.

I'm back in my office, but only to clear my desk.

Since it's only been mine for a couple of weeks and I've hardly had time to personalise it with framed photos of my wonderful family, that should take all of one minute.

I'm not crying. Must be stronger than I thought. Daniel's minding reception. He wanted to be with me (like he's Susan Sarandon, I'm Sean Penn and it's the final scene in *Dead Studio Manager Walking*) but he's on his own out there so it's not an option. He's been wonderful, actually. Everything a friend should be. I'm lucky to have him.

I'm just about done. I sling my bag over my shoulder and head for the door. I stop when the phone rings – external this time. I should just ignore it. Carry on walking . . . But Daniel's on his own out there, so it's the least I can do. I'll take this one. I turn round, pick it up and for the last time ever announce, 'Good morning, you're through to The Zone, Charlie speaking, how may I help?'

'Oh, hi,' says a woman's voice. 'Is Daniel Conrad there?'

'Sorry, he's busy right now,' I say. 'Can I take a message?'

'No, it's OK . . . Oh, go on then. Can you ask him to give me a bell when he's got a moment?'

'Of course. And you are?'

'Jill Simon . . . at the *Sun*.'

THE LAST BIT

(BUT YOU KNEW THAT ALREADY, DIDN'T YOU?)

The Bit Where I Show Off
My Commando Training

Hard to believe all that was only six weeks ago. It feels like years. Another lifetime altogether.

Actually, it *was* another lifetime. I now believe in reincarnation. The reborn Charlie is wearing white polyester overalls, a hairnet and transparent polythene gloves. Her hands are buried up to the wrists in a catering tub of margarine, which she's feverishly slapping onto multiple slices of bread because a round, hairy Greek bloke is yelling, 'C'mon, c'mon, is peoble wanning sun'widges for the *lunch*, not the bluddy tea.'

This is how it happened.

'Stutting Monday, you come werking with me, OK?' Dad said over breakfast the day after I got fired.

'It's all right, thanks. Something'll come up,' I replied.

'Whass gonna come ub thass bedder than werking for your dad?'

Something in the dynamic, fast-moving world of road-sweeping, perhaps, I didn't say.

'I telling you, you're no thinking of nuthing,' he went on.

How about rat catcher, gravedigger, sewage worker, traffic warden . . . ?

'Next wick, your sista back at school, your mum

helping Soulla with baby Bee-unga. Wotchew gonna do at home by you'self oll day?'

Oh, relax, chill out and wallow in big bowls of popcorn and huge vats of self-pity, I should imagine.

'You're coming helping with me. Is gonna be fun.'

'It's OK, Dad. I'm going to try and sort out some interviews. I've got a mate at David Lloyd who might be able to help. There's a couple of other things I—'

'Who this Davey Lloyd? His another pimp like your old boss?' Dad spluttered. Both he and Mum had read the *Sun* – OK, Dad hadn't read it, but he'd looked at the pictures – and he was convinced that The Zone was some kind of high-class brothel. 'I telling you, no dotter of mine is werking in the segs business. No, you're coming work for me. I slizing, you buddering. We gonna be the Richard an' the Judy of the sun'widge bars.'

I'd tried to explain that Blaize and Karl didn't have sex in the actual Zone, but the fact that there was a picture of her doing it on the same page as another one of my old workplace was all the evidence he needed. If you ever find yourself on trial and you see my dad on your jury, well, God help you.

That was the strangest Sunday, as I recall. I mean, only two days earlier his brand-new wide-screen telly had been trashed, his *Inglish Rose* had been deflowered and his other daughter had been unceremoniously sacked from her job in a whorehouse. Yet there he was tucking into a cooked breakfast, happy as Larry. Don't know what Mum had done to put him in such a good mood (and, frankly, I'd sooner not go there). Maybe it was the simple fact that she'd broken the habit of a thirty-year marriage and done him a fry-up.

Unpredictability, as we all know, is Dad's thing, and his attitude towards Emily and me that Sunday was as predictably unpredictable as ever. After our escapades we should have been in the doghouse or worse. But he'd put Emily back on her pedestal and he wanted to make me a partner in the Charalambous sandwich dynasty.

Not that he wasn't sounding off. No, Dad is only truly content when he's spouting truly contentious opinions. As he chewed his bacon and gagged on the yellow stuff that Mum *swore* was scrambled egg, it was the Greeks' turn for Jimmy's wisdom.

My brother and his in-laws: 'Your bluddy brotha, he lucky your poor mum going out of the way to help Soulla. Why *her* mum no go help them? They making me sigg, bluddy stoobid fat Griks.' (Said while scratching his fifty-eight-inch waist.)

The Georgious: 'I shou'n't ledding them coming roun' so much. They jealous of us 'cause they only gedding the crabby Jay Cee Vee. Stoobid fat Maroulla, she giving it the evil eye, you know.'

As he savaged his fellow countrymen, I thought he'd forgotten the job offer, but no. He came back to it as he swallowed his last bit of fried tomato. 'So, Thegla, how you fancying the career in high-cluss sun'widges?'

'Thanks, but no thanks, Dad,' I said firmly. 'I really want to make a go of things in the fitness industry.'

Seems the fitness industry didn't want to make a go of things with me, though. By the end of the week and after dozens of phone calls it was clear that word had spread: Charlie Charalambous was not to be trusted. If someone so much as splits a leotard in class, she'll be straight on to the tabloids with the Polaroids. I was even reduced to phoning Lydia for help. Talk about swallowing your pride – and let me tell you, it tasted awful. 'Sorry, darling,' she trilled, 'but I'm out of that game now. I'm involved in something huge in the music biz. Very hush-hush, so not a word.'

'Don't suppose there's any chance of you taking me with you?' I didn't say, because even at my most desperate (and the fact that I was calling Lydia showed just how desperate I was) there's still a limit to the depths I'll grovel at.

And who cares, because now I'm involved in something huge in the lunchtime take-out biz. Seven days after Dad made his offer I said a weary, worn-down *yes*.

Here I am now: Executive in Charge of Spreading. And, God, will I ever get the stench of curried chicken out of my hair? That's Dad's special today. Curried chicken in a granary bap; East meets West in an explosion of wholemeal curry-ness. It's proving highly popular with the lunchtime trade, let me tell you. The queue is spilling out of the shop and well into Long Acre.

Working for Dad has been quite an eye-opener. There I was thinking that he was the least cool bloke on the planet, but here he is in the heart of Covent Garden, surrounded by more clubbers and fashion victims than I ever used to see in an average Zone day. And you know what? His public adores him. He is charm personified and has a line for everyone. Robbie Williams himself could pick up some tips on working a crowd, and if Dad were to leap onto the counter now and break into the chorus of 'Angels' I'd (a) not be *that* surprised and (b) put money on every one of his customers holding their lighters aloft. Even the confused Japanese tourists who stumble in with their *A-Z*s held upside down, hoping that at last they've found Buckingham Palace, leave with grins on their faces (and more often than not one of his famous *chiz an' piggle hunger-busters*).

There are so many things to laugh about here, and not in a snide, piss-taking way either. I never knew this, but he's got two identical clocks up on the wall with little plaques under them. One says LONDON, the other says WOOD GREEN. He reckons it gives the place an 'indernashonul' feel. He's having a new sign done for the front too. Getting it for free as well because one of the guys from the ad agency up the road thinks it's going to win him awards. Did I ever tell you what this place is called? No, I don't think I did. It's called *Jimmy Chews*. Makes me laugh every time.

All in all, it hasn't been so bad, this . . . er . . . slight career-change of mine. I'm enjoying this new Rock God of Cut Sandwiches side of Dad that I'm seeing. I'm also taking a certain pride in being able to toast a tuna and cheese melt to the perfect shade of beigey-brown while simultaneously mopping sweat from Dad's brow like a theatre nurse as he surgically removes breast meat from a turkey carcass.

I've got to admit, it has been a lot of fun. There is, however, one serious downside. I find myself spending a lot of time on my hands and knees. In fact, I'm on the floor now.

'Wotchew doing down there?' Dad asks. It's not an unreasonable question.

'Oh, I'm looking for that Tupperware thing of cucumber slices,' I say.

'Is no down there, stoobid. Is ub here in chiller cabinet.'

Of course I knew that, but I wasn't going to tell him that, actually, I dropped to the floor with the speed of a fully trained Royal Marine commando coming under enemy fire because I'd just spotted Ruby from The Zone sauntering past the window. That's the trouble with working in Covent Garden. On any given day there's a roughly fifty-fifty chance that I'll spot one of my old workmates. So far – thank God – none of them has spotted me, and with luck they never will because I'm getting really good at the Marine-under-fire thing.

It's not because I'm ashamed. Honestly, why should I be embarrassed about working in a sandwich bar and wearing polyester overalls and a hairnet rather than the latest body-hugging leisurewear and a back-to-front baseball cap? OK, shame might come into it . . . a bit. But mostly it's because I never want to see a single one of the shallow, two-faced, star-fucking, dropped-me-like-a-ton-of-bricks shits again.

Well, there is one of them that I don't mind seeing.

In fact, we're meeting for a coffee after Dad and I shut up shop.

I know it's only Sasha, but I still feel nervous as I sip my cappuccino and wait for her. How do I look? Obviously I've slipped out of my overalls and hairnet, but do I still look like a sarnie-slinger? I check beneath my nails once more for leftover traces of tuna and sweet corn. They're clean.

This coffee date has been put off five or six times. Work stuff always comes up, leading to a last-minute postponement. No, of course I don't mean *my* work stuff. '*Sorry, can't make coffee. Gotta get to Heathrow to catch the red-eye. I'm the keynote speaker at the international sandwich-fillings seminar in Dallas.*' That old one.

No, Sasha's the one who has been putting it off. Always using the same one-word excuse: *work*. If I weren't so grounded and self-secure I could start thinking she's avoiding me because I've become untouchable, a non-person, an outcast, a social pariah, a leper . . .

Must try harder to be more grounded and secure in myself.

I look up and see her standing at the door of the

340

coffee house. She spots me and when she reaches my table we hug warmly – I'm feeling more secure already.

'What's that curry smell?' she asks, sitting down.

'I dunno,' I say, feeling myself blush. 'Must be doing food here now.'

'Your hair,' she says. 'It looks great.'

My hair is lank, currified and in desperate need of a wash, but it's now extension-free, which I guess is why she noticed.

'Well, those rat tails had to go. You said yourself they were crap.'

'I didn't mean it, you know.'

'It's the one thing you were right about, Sash. They were rubbish. One tiny tug from Emily and half of them fell out.'

'So how's it going then?' she says. 'You love working with your dad?'

'Oh, you know . . .' I think about telling her I'm chairing a hugely important government committee charged with finding a non-drip mayonnaise, but I settle for, 'It's fine, thanks. At least it's not as awful as I thought it'd be. What about you? How's The Zone?'

'Oh, you know, the same old same old,' she says awkwardly. 'Everyone sends their love.'

'Oh, really? So you told them all you were coming to meet me?'

It's her turn to blush now and I feel bad – she was only trying to be kind, even if she was talking complete bollocks. 'Well, Becks sends her love,' she says looking down into her coffee. 'I think she might leave. She's finding it really hard to cope with all the changes.'

There's been a lot of those, apparently. Jenna's gone. She was outraged at the treatment of her star client and quit the place in protest. She made a fatal miscalculation, though. She assumed that all her teen groupies

341

would follow her, but, while they might have wanted to, they had exorbitantly expensive memberships to see out. Jamie had to act fast and install a replacement teacher who would, hopefully, be as big a hit with the kids as the Pink Princess had been. Well, he needn't have worried because – as I've known for years – Sasha's a better dancer than Jenna could ever be. Jamie persuaded her to take Jenna's classes as a stopgap and it was the best thing for both of them. Teaching dance rather than aerobics enabled Sasha to find her missing confidence. She discovered that when you can dance as fantastically as she can, all you have to do is lead by example. It didn't take her long to captivate her audience. Now she tells me that she's given up working in the shop completely and she's teaching full time.

Ironic, isn't it? There I was, trying to get her a break when all along all I had to do was leave and let her sort her own life out. I'm truly happy for her. After what Karl/Ben put her through, she deserves it.

She wasn't the only one to come out of the mess better off. You can guess who got my job. Clue: he doesn't kiss girls. He must be quids in too. I don't imagine for one second that he *gave* the tape to the *Sun*.

The story didn't do Blaize any harm either. I suppose she spent a few days thinking that the humiliation might actually kill her, but she's come out the other side a new woman – porn again, you might say. While I've been reincarnated as something fairly insignificant in catering, she's been reborn as the Goddess of Raunch. Hard to believe that a few short weeks ago her appeal was strictly pre-teen because now she's got legions of grown men positively drooling after her, closely followed by armies of grown women who just want to be her.

342

What about Jamie? Far from his day in the *Sun* being the kiss of death, it's been the making of The Zone. He could have spent millions on advertising and not achieved the same effect. Sasha told me they've hired someone whose sole job is to cope with the increased membership enquiries. Now – after I've bloody well left – he hires help.

It's all down to me having the *foresight* to pick that tape up in Karl's flat. And what thanks do I get? Well, fuck the lot of them.

Except for Sasha. She might be looking around like a twitchy bunny, presumably terrified that someone she knows might spot her with the rat that sold out Blaize, but at least she's here. She's the only one that didn't drop me, the only one that *believes* I didn't do it.

She takes a deep breath and says, 'I don't suppose you want to hear about Dan—'

'Don't even mention that bastard-fucker-wanker's name.' I watch her face drain of colour. 'OK, go on, what about him?' I say.

'God, you should see him sucking up to Jamie.'

'He always was a creep,' I say . . . Oh, and I wasn't? Sucking up to Jamie is part of the job. In fact, *kiss Jamie's bottom at least three times a day* is item one on the studio manager's job description.

'I still can't believe he did that to you,' she sighs.

Neither can I. I confronted him straight after the phone call from the *Sun*. He fed me some bullshit about the paper trying to book a studio, but that it was all terribly secret, conveniently explaining why he hadn't mentioned a word of it to anyone. But, *c'mon*, Daniel and I told each other everything, especially – *especially* – when it was supposed to be *terribly secret*. And has the *Sun* been in lately? According to Sasha . . . er, *no*.

He called me a few days after I was fired. What for? To gloat? Mum keeps a whistle next to the phone – someone on *Trisha* said that it's a great way to deter heavy breathers (not that she's ever had one). I don't know about that, but it's the perfect way to deter the bastard who's taken your job and destroyed your reputation. Sasha said he went into work the next day with a wad of cotton wool in one ear.

'How could he?' Sasha continues. 'You two were such a *team*. You were as close as Ant and Dec, I reckon.'

I want to laugh, but feel like crying. I look away just in case.

'I'm sorry,' she says. 'I shouldn't have mentioned him, should I? God, me and my big mouth.'

'I'm OK,' I lie. Again.

'Why didn't you ever say something to Jamie about the phone call?'

'What would've been the point? It would've been my word against Daniel's. Besides, *I* don't do back-stabbing. Look, forget about him. He'll get what's coming to him one day . . . Anyway, I suppose you're going to be watching the telly later.'

Big Boobs' documentary finally goes out tonight. According to the write-up in the *TV Times*, it's 'a revealing exposé of life behind the scenes at a top London health club'. (I can hear Jamie now: *'It's not a fucking health club. It's a TOTAL BODY EMPORIUM!'*) While my dad is hoping there'll be plenty of revealing shots of his fresh pineapples, I should think the rest of the viewing public will be looking out for Blaize's melons.

'Oh, *that*,' Sasha says casually. 'Actually, the whole place has been going mental today. *We're gonna be on the telly, we're gonna be on the telly!* Pathetic. No, I won't be watching.'

Good to see she has some integrity.

'There's a thing about plastic surgery on Channel Five at ten, so I'll tape it instead.'

Oh.

'You're gonna watch it though, yeah?' she asks.

'I don't think so.'

'Don't you just wanna see what you look like on TV?'

'I know what I'll look like, thanks. Something that one of Sharon Osbourne's incontinent dogs left on the carpet I should think.'

'Hey, did I tell you?' she says, suddenly changing the subject. 'Gurly-Wurly fired Ben – I mean Karl. Whoever. They called it *creative differences*.'

'Poor thing,' I say, although obviously I'm glad I'm not the only one to have had their entire life ruined by all this.

'Anyway, guess who's getting the gig.'

'Don't tell me. Jenna bloody Mason.'

'No – *me*!'

'That's great,' I say, a buzz of pleasure shooting through me. 'I always knew you had it in you.'

'And guess what else . . .'

As Sasha sets off on a stream of Zone-related gossip, I tune out. I'm thinking about all those conversations we used to have, the times I tried to get her to have more faith in herself, to believe that she could be anything she wanted. The transformation is amazing and I feel a little glow inside for her. But as she gossips, the feeling fades to be replaced by . . . What? Sadness? Self-pity? It's hard to describe . . . a big, fat, nothingy feeling.

'. . . Anyway, Ruby's really pissed off with Maya because she reckons she always gets first pick of the studios, so now both her *and* Francesca aren't talking to her and . . .'

A sort of numb emptiness. Because Zone life goes on, and while my absence seems to have barely caused a dent, I don't half miss it.

The Bit Where I'm Washing My Hair

'I cunt beliv they saying it aboud us,' Dad mutters. 'If I seeing them I killing them.'

'Change the record, Dad,' I say. 'I can't believe you're still going on about it.'

He was on this rant when I got home after meeting Sasha and there's been no let-up for the best part of three hours. In short, word has reached him via the Cypriot grapevine that the Georgious have been slagging us off. Big-time. We haven't seen them since the, um, *incident*. The gossip is that George and Maroulla reckon we're completely insane. Why on earth would they think a thing like that? Outrageous, eh? Apparently, they're going around saying to anyone who'll listen that we're bad news and to be avoided like the plague.

'Bluddy Griks is oll the same,' he grumbles. 'Gossibbing bluddy peasan's. I telling you, is slunder the things they saying. I got Margus Gristy coming in shop. I usking him for liggle advice.'

'Who?'

'You knowing him. His Phil Midgell's lawyer.'

'It's Mar*cus Christ*ie, Dad, and he's an *actor*. He's only *pretending* to be a lawyer.'

I wonder if the belief that *EastEnders* is a documentary series is a widespread phenomenon or is it just my father?

'You're young, Thaglotta. You no understanding the British justice like I am. I gonna sue the bustudds for every penny.'

'Oh, that's a good idea. Let the truth come out in open court.'

'*Egg-saggly*. Now you gedding it. The *trooth*. Is what British justice system is all aboud.'

'So let me get this straight. You'd be happy for the world to know that the Georgious walked in on your two daughters while they were tearing each other to shreds and annihilating the living room because the underaged one of them had just received the news that her positive pregnancy result was in fact negative?'

'Wotchew on aboud? It was nuthing like thad. Is tiny disagreemen' aboud nuthing wha'soever and they blowing it ub out of every proporshon,' says the man who didn't need a history degree in order to learn how to rewrite it. 'If I seeing them I killing them. And I forbidding you from seeing them, but if you do, you killing them an' all.'

'Jesus, you two aren't still on about the bloody Georgious, are you?' Mum says as she arrives in the front room with savoury snack replenishments. 'Give it a rest, will you?'

'Where's Emily?' Dad says, finally giving it a rest. 'You seeing the time?'

'I told you, Jimmy,' Mum says. 'She's round Alicia's. They're doing their homework together.'

'I pleazed she studying so hard. She making the mends. Is good, eh?'

Studying, my arse – unless you count anatomy class with Mehmet as study. Yes, she's still seeing him, still risking not only her own life but also those of the entire populations of Cyprus, Turkey and mainland Greece. I can only pray she took the hint when she found the

348

ten-pack the condom fairy left under her pillow. Oh yes, I'm playing the good big sister on a regular basis now, even though she never did say thank you.

'Yeah, it's good, Dad,' I say. It's not for me to burst his bubble. My sister may be having it off with a Turk, but I can hardly talk. OK, so I'm enjoying the full and varied sex life of a nun these days, but not so long ago I was doing it with virtual strangers in disabled loos – a memory that still brings me out in a sweat that has nothing to do with sexual arousal.

'Jimmy, quick!' Mum squeals suddenly. 'Have you seen the time? Turn the telly over. Channel Four. It's *starting.*'

Damn, I was hoping she'd forget.

As Dad points the remote at the brand-new wide-screen (another Sony in complete defiance of the Georgious) I get up and tiptoe towards the door.

'You not watching it, Charlie?' Mum asks.

'I'd love to, but I've got to wash this curry out of my hair.'

'I'll tape it for you.'

'Yeah, you do that,' I say as I close the door behind me.

'Come down quick, Charlotte. It's *you*! You're on,' Mum yells up the stairs. 'My God, that skirt's a bit short.'

I'm cringing on my bed. I lift up my pillow, stick my head beneath it and then squash it around my ears.

'Jesus, it's chaos . . . I thought Charlotte was supposed to be in charge . . . What's going on? . . . What are they all standing around watching telly for? . . . I thought they were supposed to be keeping fit . . .'

Mum's bellowed running commentary hasn't let up for half an hour. I've no need to actually watch this

349

programme because even with a pillow smothering my head I can hear exactly what's going on.

'. . . Quick, *quick*, Charlotte, it's your *dad*,' she screams. '*Ahh*, don't those pineapples look *delicious*?'

I grab my Walkman from my bedside table. I stick my headphones on, press *play* and turn up the volume until my eardrums hurt.

I blink in the darkness and gaze at the glowing red digits on my alarm.

4:13

I can't sleep. How can I when I know that tape is sitting downstairs?

As if I'm not going to watch it.

I climb out of bed, put my dressing gown on and step out onto the landing, where three sets of snores are mingling. I tiptoe down the stairs. They creak, but no one stirs.

I reach the front room and turn the TV on. It crosses my mind that I don't have to watch the tape at all. Why should I force myself to relive the worst day of my life? I could just channel-hop for a bit. Or watch this fascinating Open University programme that's starting. It's all about something called metal fatigue.

Arrggh!

Maybe I should just go back to bed and try to get some sleep.

Who am I kidding? Where's the bloody remote?

Play.

My Lootenant Columbo Bit

I stand across the street and gaze up at The Zone's seven glass storeys. It's only now I realise how much I've missed the place . . . *Déjà vu*. Six and a bit weeks ago wasn't I standing in this exact same spot experiencing these exact same feelings? But this time there's a new emotion jostling for attention. *Exhilaration*. It's only faint, but it's definitely there. And if anything is going to get me through what I have to do now, it's that.

I step across the pavement, cross the road and don't stop until I'm up the steps and through the doors. Once inside I can hear music and it's not coming from the TVs. That's new; is it a Daniel Conrad innovation? It's a soft, ambient track, sort of ocean-y . . . And are those whale noises? I guess it's an attempt (by Daniel Conrad, studio manager?) to evoke floaty, tranquil feelings the moment clients step in from the London bustle. The feeling it's evoking in me is seasickness and I'm coming close to throwing up when a voice pulls me clear.

'Charlie!' Rebecca calls across the foyer.

There she is, behind the desk with a couple of new faces. They're both blokes. Young, fit blokes, so obviously Daniel's been in charge of interviewing. And, you never know, maybe they can even use the Mac.

Rebecca's face is illuminated by a huge, toothy smile,

but it's forced and rigid, clearly stuck on to mask her terror. 'Does Jamie know you're here?' she asks, letting slip with a single question that, yes, she's terrified.

'No. Is he around?'

She shrugs. At least some things haven't changed round here. A clueless shrug was Rebecca's stock answer to any question in my day too.

'How's it going?' I ask as I reach the desk.

'Oh, you know, same as ever. *Mad*!' she says, giggling and nodding towards the utter calm of our surroundings.

'Yeah, I can see,' I reply, nodding towards the utter calm of our surroundings. Hang on, why am I being catty with her? She didn't fire me or callously betray my friendship. All she did was launch Armageddon with nothing more than a TV remote.

'You know the programme went out last night?' she says.

Yes, I know.

'Well, we've had over two hundred calls just this morning from people wanting to join,' she gushes. 'Absolutely *mad*!'

'Terrific,' I say flatly. 'Shame I can't help out with the rush.'

She looks down, her face reddening. Damn; now I feel *guilty*.

'So, what's your new boss like?' I ask, trying to soften my tone.

'Daniel? Oh, he's great,' she bubbles. This means either (a) *he's great* or (b) *he's got the whole place bugged so I'd better say he's great*. 'I really miss you, though,' she adds in a whisper clearly intended to avoid electronic surveillance.

I don't get a chance to reply because the lift pings behind me, causing me to freeze. I hear familiar footsteps striding towards us. I swivel round just as Jamie says, 'Hi, Charlie, come for your P45?'

'No, actually, but I suppose I could pick it up while I'm here.'

We stare at one another in silence for a moment. His face is blank, not betraying a glimmer of whatever it is he's feeling. I wonder if mine is making as good a job of hiding the nerves that are churning inside of me.

'This purely a social visit, then?' he asks finally.

'Not exactly . . . I came to see you . . . If you've got a minute.'

'Definitely not social, then,' he says, gritting his teeth. As he glares at me I hope he's feeling at least a pang of something regretful on account of how fantastic I look. I'm wearing an eighty-quid hairdo, a forty-quid facial and a seventy-quid DKNY top – all acquired on the basis that if I didn't actually *possess* the courage to go through with this, then maybe I could *buy* it.

Feelings of regret? In Jamie? Not a chance and he proves it by saying, 'We've got nothing to talk about. I'm going for lunch. Rebecca can stick your P45 in the po—'

'I don't care about my P45,' I force myself to say because all morning I've been promising myself that *I would not be intimidated.* Just to reinforce the point, I fling my hair over my shoulder, the way you can when you've just spent a small fortune on it. 'I need to talk to you, Jamie. It's really important . . . really, *really* important.'

He stares at me. Contempt oozes from his pores, making my insides turn to mush. Then he snaps, 'OK, upstairs. I'll give you sixty seconds.'

*

'What's this all about?' he says angrily as he closes his office door. 'You got more porn tapes? What are you going to do? Try blackmail this time?'

I know I said I wasn't going to be intimidated, but the way I feel, maybe I should leave right now.

'I *trusted* you, Charlie,' he spits. 'I *liked* you. Have you any idea how much you *hurt* me?'

God, this is bit melodramatic, isn't it? Especially the way his hand is clasped over his heart. (Take note, Dad. At least he knows where his heart actually is.)

'How could you do that to me?' he continues. '*Sell me out.*'

His resentment is tangible and he looks ready to sling me out, using force if necessary. Sixty seconds, he said – I'd better get a move on. I take the deepest breath I've ever taken – probably my subconscious calculating it may be my last – and plunge in. 'Number one, Jamie, you've got no right to be outraged because whoever flogged that tape to the *Sun* did your business a huge favour—' (Crucial point, this. Jamie might not enjoy being betrayed any more than the next bloke, but money is his overriding priority – he'd happily take a knife in the back so long as it came with a six-figure cheque.) '—and number two—'

I don't get a chance to hit him with number two because the door bursts open. Daniel and Sasha spill through and they're giggling so hard that they don't register Jamie and me until their momentum has carried them to the middle of the room.

'Jamie!' Sasha splutters, her face crazed with shock. 'I thought you were at lunch.'

'Charlie!' Daniel gasps simultaneously. 'Your hair . . . It looks great.'

So fucking *gay*. The atmosphere is crackling with high-voltage hostility and he notices my hair. But after

354

his bright start he collapses in on himself, fear getting the better of him. He must be recalling the whistle-blast I gave him the last time we spoke.

'What are you two doing up here?' Jamie yells. 'You always treat my office as a playpen when you think I'm not around?'

I watch them squirm. I'm ashamed to admit it, but I'm enjoying their discomfort . . . *Pah*, I'm not ashamed to admit it at all.

'No,' Sasha says defensively. 'Well, not really, not at all . . . Er, I'm teaching in five minutes, so we were just, er . . .' She looks at Daniel for help, but right now he's a rabbit caught in some very big, very bright headlights.

'Whatever,' Jamie says, not wanting to hang around until they've come up with an excuse. 'You two had better get lost. Charlie and I were in the midd—'

'No, Jamie, they should stay,' I blurt. 'They should see this.'

'See what?'

I reach into my bag and (with only slightly trembling hands) whip out a video tape . . .

Iiiiiiiiiiiiiiiiit's showtime!

Daniel and Sasha look confused. Jamie looks pissed off. 'I haven't got time for this, Charlie,' he says.

'*Please*!' I beg. It does the trick because Jamie collapses onto his sofa, followed by Daniel and Sasha.

I set off towards the wide-screen telly and slip the cassette into the slot on the VCR, ignoring Jamie's 'God, I knew it. It's another bloody sex tape.' I'm just about to press *play*, but I stop. It's dawning on me that this is just like *Columbo*. You know, the final scene that's the same in every single episode. Everyone is gathered together and Lootenant Columbo reveals the crucial clue before fingering . . . the *culprit*. And doesn't he always make a little speech of some kind?

I turn round and survey my audience. Daniel (looking v. scared), Sasha (looking v. baffled) and Jamie (looking at his watch). Then I clear my throat and . . .

Bollocks to all that. I press *play* and watch the opening titles roll.

Damn, shit, *damn*! And while I'm at it, *fuck*! Because if this were an episode of *Columbo*, you can bet the lootenant would have cued up his tape before his big climax. He wouldn't have rewound it to the bloody beginning, thus lumbering himself with having to faff around in search of the *right bit* while his audience looks on impatiently . . . But what can I say? It was late when I finished watching it – well after five in the morning, for God's sake. I was exhausted. I wasn't thinking straight.

Jamie loses his rag now. 'Jesus, girl, what are you playing at? Do you honestly expect me to sit through—'

'Jamie, *please*,' I say again. 'It won't take long – I know exactly what I'm looking for.' And I'm hoping I do as my fingers fumble for the *fast-forward* button. I find it and the picture races forward . . . Past Daniel virtually mugging the camera like a man who knows his destiny is to have his own daytime TV series . . . Past Fenton whipping his dancers into a frenzy of Justin Timberlake-ness . . . Past Daniel again, coming on a bit too Graham Norton for his own good . . . Past Steve flexing his biceps . . . Past Master Stan Lee halving a breeze block with his bare hand (never got the point of that. Isn't B&Q full of tools for that sort of thing?) . . . Past Daniel . . . *Again* . . .

'I'll give this another ten seconds,' Jamie says. 'If you haven't made your point by then, I'm leaving. And you're leaving with me.'

'I think I'd better go now, actually,' Sasha pipes up nervously. 'My class will be waiting.'

I turn and give her a pleading look and she reluctantly

settles back into her seat. 'We're nearly there now, guys,' I say.

And as I look back at the TV screen I can see that we very nearly are. We've reached the bit where Blaize is going out on Zone TV. And credit to the Channel Four people, the way they handled this was brilliant. They didn't show it. Not a single frame of shagging went out on telly last night and that somehow made it more powerful – like a horror movie that holds back on revealing the monster until the finale. You could *hear* the sex, all right. Blaize's grunts and moans (which some smart DJ is bound to sample and work into an Ibiza club anthem soon) were all there in glorious stereo. What they *showed* were people's reactions. The bloke in the caff dropping his Mars into his Coke. The girl in the swimming pool stopping mid-stroke. The jogger in the gym falling off his treadmill . . . And at last we're in reception – my old home from home – where Rebecca's and Velvet's jaws are dragging round their ankles as they stare up at the monitors.

Next it's the clamouring mob in the foyer. Daniel and I walking out of the lift to find Sasha waiting; Daniel fleeing for his life; Blaize and Karl arriving, then departing; Sasha calling for calm; my dad coming in with his fruit delivery; Jamie's return from the lawyer.

My back is turned to the others as I study the TV, but I sense them shifting around awkwardly. I can hear their bums squeaking on the leather sofa. At last, this is the bit I've been looking for.

I press *play* and the picture slows to normal speed. I'm no longer in the scene, having been sent upstairs by Jamie. My dad's centre stage – another man who *knows* his destiny is to have his own daytime TV series (it'll probably be called *An' Another Thing I Telling You*). He's holding up a pineapple and saying, 'The way you knowing is perfec' is when you squeezing it juss here an' is feeling a bit soft . . . Here, you having a go.'

'Right, Charlie, your time's up,' Jamie says. 'Let's—'

'It's coming, it's *coming*,' I say frantically. 'Watch really carefully because if you blink you'll miss— *There*! Did you see it?'

'See what?'

I hit *pause*, then *rewind*. I take the tape back about thirty seconds and this time I play it frame by frame. 'Look carefully,' I say. 'Not at my dad. Look at what's going on in the background . . . at the desk.'

As the TV picture nudges forward v-e-r-y s-l-o-w-l-y, it's easier to focus on the chaos going on behind Dad; much easier to spot Daniel returning to the foyer after his disappearing act and then—

'This is it,' I say. 'Hang on . . . *There* . . . You saw it that time, yeah?'

Silence behind me. I daren't look round . . . But eventually Daniel speaks. 'You *bitch*.'

Oh yes, he's spotted it all right.

It's at this point that I thank God for giving us humungous wide-screen televisions. What was it Maroulla said when she first clapped eyes on our set at home? *'You know, you seeing things you neva seeing before.'* I never thought I'd end up crediting Maroulla Georgiou with any insight, but there you go.

'What the hell am I supposed to be looking at?' Jamie demands, annoyed now because he hates to be the last one to get the punch line.

I hit *rewind*, then *play* again, and this time I take them through it with a commentary. 'Right, look at Daniel walking across the shot behind my dad . . . Look at Rebecca, Velvet and Sasha behind the desk . . . Daniel crosses in front of them . . . And now there are only *two* girls . . . Where's Sasha? . . . Oh, there she is, popping back up. She must've bent down to tie her shoelaces . . . But what's that?'

I stop talking and point at the screen. At the black rectangular object – the shape and size of a video cassette – in Sasha's hand. It's not there for long. No, it soon disappears into an inside pocket in her over-sized Zone puffa jacket.

'Fucking hell,' Jamie says, finally up to speed.

Now I turn round. No one is looking at the TV any more. Jamie and Daniel are staring at Sasha, whose eyes are clamped shut. Jamie opens his mouth to speak/shout/scream, who knows, but before he can say a word, she's out of her seat and out of the room.

I don't have to search hard for her. She's in the staff changing-room, emptying out her locker, carelessly chucking her gear into her big kit-bag. She heard me come into the room, but she won't look at me. She's crying and I can't quite believe that after what she's done I feel sorry for her.

When I made my discovery at five this morning I was angry. I mean, I was really, *really* angry, and if Sasha had been in the room with me then I wouldn't have been held responsible for my actions. I still feel hurt, but I can't stop the pity that's welling up inside me. So much for Jamie's Killer Instinct – I don't even have the Kick-on-the-shins Instinct. But from the first time I ever saw Sasha, all nervous and quivering outside her audition, I've felt an urge to look out for her.

I walk up to her and say, 'Stop, Sasha. Talk to me for a minute.'

She ignores me, angrily throwing her gear into her bag as if she's the one with the grievance.

'Why did you do it?' I ask, reaching out and touching her shoulder.

'Oh, get lost, Charlie. What do you care?' she says, shrugging my hand away. 'Don't you see what you've done?'

'What *I've* done?' I gasp.

'Humiliated me in front of Jamie. It's all over for me. *Finished*.'

Protective isn't quite what I'm feeling now. 'Oh, but it was OK for me to lose my job and have my name blackened, was it?'

'That is just so you!' she shouts. 'It isn't enough to nick my boyfriend. You have to ruin my career as well. You're such a selfish bitch.'

My mouth opens but I force myself not to speak. I know my track record with saying smart-arse things I always end up regretting later. To be on the safe side, I decide not to say anything for a minute. Try to calm down a bit first.

'I didn't take the tape on purpose, you know,' she says after a moment's silence.

'So why did you take it?'

'I took it to . . . I was just looking after it for you,' she says quietly.

'Well, why didn't you give it back when you saw me tearing the place apart looking for it, then?'

'I couldn't,' she whimpers. 'It was too late. Everyone would've thought I'd taken it on purpose.'

'But we went for a coffee straight after. You sat with me and listened to me accusing Daniel. You saw me going through hell, Sasha.'

'It was too late,' she whispers. 'I was going to post it to you anonymously.'

'But you gave it to the *Sun* instead. What for? Safekeeping? How much did they pay you?'

360

'You've no idea what they're like.'

'You're right, I haven't. I've never sold out a mate to a tabloid.'

'They really pressurise you. And I wasn't selling *you* out, was I? Blaize was the one spread all over the paper. I didn't know Jamie was going to fire you.'

'Didn't it even cross your mind?'

'He loved you, Charlie. I thought he'd just . . . I don't know. I thought you'd be all right, the way you always are.' She's getting her second wind now, launching into a fresh attack. 'Nothing ever hurts you, does it? You just seem to breeze through life, always getting what you want without even trying. You know something? After you left, I realised how it must feel to be you. I got all Jenna's classes, just like that. Then the Gurly-Wurly thing. Everyone loved me. They greased up to me the way they always did to you.' She picks up her bag and slings it over her shoulder. 'I should've known it couldn't last. Congratulations, Charlie. You win again.'

'But, Sasha, we were never at war,' I say as she turns and walks out.

I sit down on the bench between the two rows of lockers, feeling more dazed than I did the day I went five rounds with Emily.

I hear the door open and look round, foolishly hoping it might be Sasha coming back to . . . What? Do kissy-kissy-make-up? It's not. It's Daniel. He looks at me, relieved.

'Thank fuck for that,' he says. 'I saw Sasha stomp out and I thought I'd find your corpse in here. Everything OK?'

'Is that what everyone thinks of me?' I ask, still stunned.

'What?'

'That I'm some kind of spoilt, selfish bitch who just snaps her fingers and gets what she wants?'

'Of course not.'

'Sasha's just making it up, is she?'

'You're gonna accept a personality appraisal from a flaky fuck-up like her?'

'What, they *never* bitched about me when Jamie promoted me?'

'Yeah, the rumour was that you'd given him a blowjob to get it, but that was just stupid gossip. Meaningless. The day I got promoted, the rumour went round that I'd given him one too. Everyone gossips about the boss. That's life. Doesn't mean they don't *like* the boss . . . Unless she's called Lydia.'

He's sitting down beside me now and his hand has crept along the bench until it's on top of mine.

'I can't believe she did it,' he says. 'My money was always on Velvet.'

I feel a bolt of guilt shoot through me.

'Look, I'm sorry, Daniel.'

'What for?'

'Accusing you of—'

'Give over,' he smiles. 'I'd have done the same in your shoes. Everyone accuses me of everything – it's just my bad-boy rep. But if you really want to make up, you can do me a *huge* favour.'

'Yeah?'

'I've got twenty-five wannabe street-dancers in Studio Three and no fucking Sasha. You don't fancy sticking on a tracksuit and—'

'Get lost, Daniel. But I'll buy you a drink . . . If you want.'

'*Moi*, drink with a sandwich-bar skivvy?' he screams. 'OK, gimme five minutes.'

The Absolutely Last Bit
Of The Last Bit

Philip twinkle-toes into reception and stops by the desk. He's got his indignant face on. He gestures snootily towards the builders who're smashing up concrete outside. 'Charlie, if I'd known I was going to have to teach ballet in a building site, I'd have worn a hard hat and a tool belt.'

'Ooh, the Village People look, you retro scamp, you,' Daniel coos, causing Philip to mince off huffily.

'He's got a point,' I shout over the noise of the pneumatic drill. 'It's hardly a haven of peace and tranquillity, is it?'

The builders are installing a wheelchair access ramp. *Honestly*. You really wouldn't believe how much things are changing around here.

The biggest one is that I'm back, though that probably doesn't seem like much of a change since I wasn't away for *that* long. A couple of days after I'd shown him the tape, I was sitting in Jamie's office again, though at his invitation this time.

'I'd like to bring you back into the fold, Charlie,' he said.

'Life moves on, Jamie,' I said with a flick of my zillion-quid hairdo. 'I've got a new career now. Fresh ambitions, new horizons—'

'I'm begging you. The place barely functions without you. You, Charlie, *are* The Zone.'

'O . . . K,' I said after an agonising (for him) pause. 'I've got a few conditions, though.'

'Name them.'

'I want double the salary . . . And eight weeks' holiday, your office, a car – maybe a little red Porsche . . .' I watched the colour drain from his face and figured I could hit him with one more before the coma set in '. . . and a £500-a-month wardrobe allowance.'

'Done. When can you start?'

What, you believe that? Only the bit where he said 'I'd like to bring you back into the fold' is true (and even then, I'm paraphrasing. I think his actual words were 'I suppose you'll be wanting your old job back then'). I didn't care. All I wanted was for him to know I *didn't do it*. I did make one condition, though, which he accepted. Reluctantly. And the staff meeting where he stood up and gave me an unreserved apology is a memory I'll take to my grave. To his credit he did slip me a brown envelope on my first day back. 'What's this?' I asked.

'A little something for the time you were . . . um . . . on sabbatical. It's cash so for fuck's sake don't tell the taxman.'

So what's new, then? I'm back; Daniel and I are pissing about; Philip's having pouty fits; Rebecca's getting the coffees in . . . everything is exactly as it was, isn't it? Well, there's the wheelchair ramp. After the TV programme, which showed nothing but perfect tens, a bunch of disabled-rights campaigners camped outside in their wheelchairs, blocking the entrance. Jamie wasn't going to give in, though – 'Look at the scruffy fuckers,' he sneered. 'Do you think they could even afford the membership here?' But after it had gone on for two days and we'd been in all the papers again, I made some calls and discovered he could get council *and* EU grants for installing disabled facilities. Jamie loves grants. He knows exactly the right builders to help him scam the system and come out ahead.

The ramp's just the start. Soon there will be disabled changing-rooms, extra-wide studio doors, lift signs in Braille, and I really, really can't wait for Ruby's first paraplegic step class.

Sorry, I'm lying again. The ramp is just the start, or so it said in the press release. In reality, that's also where it's going to end. Basically, the disabled are welcome to wheel themselves in and take an admiring look at the foyer before wheeling themselves straight back out again. Jamie told me he's putting it in to shut the campaigners up, but if people imagine he's going any further they can dream on. I nodded and didn't say much. One step at a time, I'm thinking – well, for those of us lucky enough to be able to walk, that is. As for those less fortunate, just give me time.

Actually, apart from the ramp, I can report one other small change.

Quite big, as it happens.

'Brace yourself, Daniel. Here she comes,' I say as the automatic doors swoosh open. We watch Lydia sweep into the foyer as if she's never been away.

'Morning,' I call out. 'Great to see you again.'

'You look fantastic,' Daniel adds, the world's smarmiest grin plastered across his face.

'Don't give me that,' she says, one eye on me, one on Daniel. 'I can see flannel when it's being rubbed in my face. Now, is everything ready?'

We nod like a pair of noddy dogs.

'You've checked the sound system? The water cooler's in place? And towels? We'll need about two dozen. And are there fresh flowers? Oh, and dough-nuts. The girls like doughnuts.'

Daniel mutters, 'I bet they fucking do,' as we exchange glances. We haven't had a list of demands like this since Blaize was in. But then, Lydia is in the diva business now too. She's a partner in Crisis Management and she's booked the basement studio for one of their acts. They haven't had a record out yet, but, believe me, you'll be seeing plenty of them . . . *Plenty*.

After what Jamie did to her, why is Lydia back? I mean, London's got loads of perfectly good studio centres – you know, ones that didn't fire her for having squiffy eyes. She's here because of the settlement she and Jamie reached. She agreed to drop her wrongful-dismissal claim in return for free rehearsal facilities for all Crisis Management artists. Jamie thought he was getting a great deal – no negative PR, no hefty legal bills, no even heftier payout to Lydia when she won (because, as he well knew, she would have). And on top of all that, he'd have a regular supply of pop stars tripping through The Zone's doors. But when he signed on the dotted he wasn't aware of the kind of pop stars Lydia's company represents.

When she was selling them to me on the phone the other day (like I'm the head of A&R at CBS) Lydia said, 'Darling, these girls are going to be mega. Believe me, large frames are going to be the new black.'

Daniel and I have seen the photos, but nothing could have prepared us for the reality. Here they come now, in the flesh as it were. Powering up the steps, squeezing through the doors, pounding towards the desk: The Next Big Thing. There are three of them and Lydia is pitching them as the twenty-first century Spice Girls. Daniel has christened them already: Lardy Spice, Even Lardier Spice and Fucking Monumental Spice. There's no denying it, they *are* huge, but I did kick him when he said it. You haven't seen my dad's half of the family, have you? I know I'm more like my mum, body-wise, but things could easily change. I could look something like these girls a few years from now, and if large frames are going to be the new black, I'm behind them all the way.

They reach the desk and Jacqueline (wouldn't you just know it, she's one of them – and massive though she is, she's only Lardy Spice) leans across and gives Daniel a truly sloppy kiss. And he deserves it. He is, after all, the guy that spotted her MTV potential all those weeks ago when he signed her up for Platinum membership.

'Right,' says Lydia with a managerial clap of her hands, 'let's get this show on the road. Daniel, when are the guys from the *Sun* here?'

'In about half an hour,' he says, surreptitiously wiping the mixture of slobber and lipstick from his cheek.

Yes, yes, yes, that call I took from the *Sun* the day I got fired . . . well, Daniel wasn't bullshitting me. It was to arrange this . . . erm . . . *earth-shattering* event. The reason it's been delayed for so long is that one of the girls (Even Lardier Spice, I believe) had secretly gone on the Atkins Diet and it's taken a few weeks to get her back out of shape.

I turn to Rebecca, who's back with the coffees, and say, 'Becks, would you mind taking the girls to their studio?'

'They're in Two, right?' she says, putting the drinks down without spilling them and flashing a dazzlingly confident smile.

As Rebecca leads away The Next Big Thing, Daniel turns to me and says, 'How did you get her to remember this time?'

'Easy,' I reply. 'I made her memorise *Studio Two, Lydia's a poo*.'

That's another thing that's changing around here: Rebecca. I'm keeping the promise I made to myself to train her *properly*. And we're getting there. Simple rhymes work with kids, don't they? All the best teachers know that. I bet even Einstein once sat in a classroom and recited *I before E except after* C. OK, I don't expect Rebecca to solve the mysteries of the universe, but she *will* become the best fitness professional on the planet, *goddamnit!*

We watch the lift doors close on TNBT and I say, 'Thank God Jamie's in LA. I couldn't cope with him seeing this.'

'You haven't explained things to him?' Daniel splutters.

'I thought you were going to.'

'You're the fucking studio manager.'

'No, *you* are.'

The fact is we both are. When Jamie re-hired me, he could hardly demote Daniel, could he? This might be a problem if it weren't Daniel's last week. He's moving on to bigger and better things. He really is a man destined to have his own daytime TV series. After his camera-hogging performance on Channel Four he was inundated with calls from producers. Well, he had one. He got an offer from ITV. He co-presents his first Saturday morning kids' show in a couple of weeks. Daniel doing kids' TV. I ask you. He's promised to keep his shagging-cameraman-type antics to a minimum and not to do it in front of the children. It's a start.

I'll be gutted to see him go, but at least he's leaving something behind: Carlton, Curtis and Rod. They're the three guys he hired to cope with the extra work-load. They're absolutely gorgeous, but – God *almighty*

– three tents in a row couldn't be more camp. They're already squabbling over rights to the seventh-floor broom cupboard. I'm going to have to sort out some kind of rota for them. I really like them, actually; it's like having Daniel in surround sound.

Daniel isn't the only one moving onwards and upwards. Jamie's in America setting up the deal for The LA Zone, Blaize is at number one for the fourth consecutive week and even Sasha's headed for exotic climes. Right now she's probably somewhere between Lanzarote and Tenerife.

She's working on a cruise ship, scraping her feather headdress against the ceiling, probably recalling those happy days when she had two people in her aerobics class. I only know this because I called her. My mate at David Lloyd said they were looking for teachers and I thought she might be interested. Daniel couldn't believe I was helping her – he'd wanted to phone every dance studio in London to get her blacklisted. But I was still stunned by the bitterness she'd felt towards me and I guess I needed to prove that I'd only ever wanted to help her. I was too late, though. When I rang, her flatmate told me she'd left already. I'm not expecting a postcard.

Weirdly, I miss her. At least, I miss the Sasha I knew before the Karl/Ben madness kicked off. As for old snake-face himself, he's disappeared without trace. A bit like the tapes of us shagging. No, I haven't lost them. Just disposed of them very carefully – think scissors and hammers and lighter fuel and matches and you're there.

It's brilliant to be back. I love my job. I'm going to love it even more when The Zone opens in LA and Jamie spends most of his time over there, leaving me in sole charge here. Though, knowing him, he'll install

CCTV cameras with a satellite link to the States just to keep an eye on me. Whatever, it's great to be back.

My mobile beeps and I pull it from my pocket. I've got a text:

STILL OK 4 2NITE?

'Will you cover for me later?' I say to Daniel. 'I have to leave half an hour early.'

'You're not really going to meet him, are you?'

'I have to,' I say because I've already keyed *yes* into my phone.

'Of course you don't *have* to. You're playing a dangerous game, young lady. Just remember, she who plays with matches ends up getting more than her fingers burned.'

'Yeah, yeah, and he who takes it up the arse ends up talking out of it. Right, should my mum or dad call, tell them I'm taking Rebecca through spreadsheet training.'

'Ah yes, spreadsheets. Your speciality. Honestly, why don't you just tell them about him? He's so fucking eligible. And he isn't the type to secretly film you while you're giving him a BJ . . . You hope.'

'Daniel, you're never going to be able to understand my dad. I've known him for a quarter of a century and I still don't get him.'

'But it wasn't so long ago that he wanted you to marry the guy.'

That's right. I'm seeing Dino/Dean/Doctor D – I seem to be developing a thing for blokes with multiple names. I didn't intend to go out with him, really I didn't, but you know how these things just take on a life of their own . . . don't you?

After that night at the hospital, when I managed to

stick both feet in my mouth, I'd been dying of embarrassment every time I thought about it. And I'd been thinking about it a lot – something about the white coat he was wearing. Anyway, I decided to phone him to apologise. You don't know the trouble I went to. I called one hospital which put me through to a department which suggested I try a different department which transferred me to another hospital which put me on hold before connecting me to . . . It took ages, possibly days – I completely lost track of time. If it had been a genuine medical emergency I'd have been dead and buried. But all I wanted to do was say sorry.

When I eventually got hold of him, I was so nervous – not to mention suffering from severe phone fatigue – that I didn't even manage to say that. As I recall, my opening line was, 'I shouldn't even be talking to you. My dad wants to sue your entire family.'

'So why are you calling me then?' he asked, not unreasonably.

I managed to prise my foot from my mouth and say, 'Er, I think I owe you an apology. I was rude to you at the hospital . . . Very rude . . . Indeed. Sorry . . .'

I listened to the deafening silence from his end of the line, then started gabbling. 'It was so not like me, I was just, you know, under pressure and it was three in the morning and—'

'Mmm, I know what you mean,' he said, not sounding as if he knew at all. 'Look, I'm sorry, but I'm kind of in the middle of something at the moment . . .'

At that point I could have killed myself for having had the *brilliant* idea of calling him. Blush? The bloody receiver was melting against my ear.

'Yeah,' he continued, 'it's quite a tricky procedure. I've got this kitten strapped down and I'm about to take its windpipe out.'

Boy, did I laugh. Probably out of relief. And because it was funny. Mostly relief, though.

'Our families have made a bit of a dog's dinner out of things, haven't they?' he said.

'Rubbish, aren't they? But just because they're not talking doesn't mean we can't be friends. Does it?' I had my fingers crossed behind my back.

'Friends sounds good. I suppose that means you'll want me to buy you a drink then?'

Honestly, I hadn't anticipated having to answer that question, but it took me . . . oh, about a tenth of a second to say yes.

I suppose an analyst would say it was something to do with rebellion, only wanting what I can't have, shoving Dad's contrary tendencies right back at him. But I'm sure that would be mostly bollocks. I'm seeing him because I fancy the pants off him. I've never denied that he's gorgeous, but now I know he's clever, funny and kind to animals as well. Except for gerbils, but that's fine with me. Well, they're just rats with a fancy name, aren't they?

No doubt the same analyst would recommend I tell my dad about him – something about forging closer family bonds through openness and honesty. That would be mostly bollocks too. No way am I telling Dad. He isn't just off the Georgious. He's got a major downer on all Greeks – 'bluddy peasan's the lot of 'em,' he says, his mouth crammed with food and his feet up on the furniture.

Not that he's abandoned his plans to marry me off. Last night he said, 'Theglottsa, this man, his coming in shop. Very nice block. His only young, but his very suggsessful. In combuders. Got his own combany an' everything. Anyway, I thinking you should mit him.'

I didn't respond, which he took as a sign of unbridled enthusiasm.

'So I inviting him for lunch then? His called Nathan Stein.'

'He's Jewish?' I said, my eyebrow curving upwards.

'How come Charlie gets to go out with *Jewish* boys?' Emily said. I could see her mind whirring – *if Charlie's gonna marry a Jew, I'm telling them about my Muslim.*

'I'm not bloody well going out with anyone,' I snapped. 'Jewish or otherwise.'

'Why not?' Dad argued. 'Whad's wrong with Jewish peoble? They more like the Griks than anyone. We huving the same beliefs an' everything.'

'But they don't believe in Jesus,' Emily said.

'*Egg-saggly*! They don' beliving in Jesus 'cause is oll wrong the way it say in the Bible. You see, Jesus, his not Jewish, his *Grik*.'

'Jimmy, shut up and eat your tea.' Mum had evidently heard enough. Besides, she hadn't slaved away for two minutes putting the pre-cooked turkey roast in the microwave just to have it go cold.

'Is *true*,' Dad protested. 'You seeing the programme where they showing his birth suddifigate.'

'Yeah, and I heard they found a piece of bread in Larnaca,' I said. 'It had his fingerprints on the crust and it's almost certainly a leftover bit from when he fed the five thousand.'

'Ah, shuddup. You don' knowing nothing . . . I inviting Nathan for lunch on Sunday.'

'Well, I won't be here,' I said, getting the last word in. Funny, but he didn't argue.

I look at my watch. He'll be here soon.

'Jesus, look at you,' Daniel splutters. 'You're like a

373

dog on heat. Will you pur-lease tone it down. It's infec-
tious, you know. I'm going to have to shag someone
soon. Anyone.'

As he says this, three very large and very tearful girls
tumble out of the lift, followed by a stressed-out Lydia.
Surely not musical differences already? Steve appears
at the bottom of the stairs, clearly ready to add to the
mayhem because he's got his *when the fucker who's
late for his fucking seven o'clock shows up, he's fucking fucked*' face on. Oh yes, it's just another typical
day at The Zone.

'Anyone?' I ask Daniel as Jacqueline runs past us.

'*Yeeuurgh*! I'd rather shag *you* and that's saying
something.'

'Come on, you know you want me.'

I lick his ear and he runs away from me, screaming
like a girl.

He's gorgeous even without the white coat. Even more
gorgeous now he's off limits, if I'm honest. What can
I say? I'm my father's daughter.

He kisses me on the cheek. I can smell him – Polo
Sport mixed with something vaguely medical – and it
makes me want him even more.

'Where do you fancy, then?' he asks as we walk away
from The Zone.

'There's a bar round the corner that does pretty good
food,' I reply. 'And it's got this really cool disabled loo
in the basement.'

No, I just *think* that last bit.

Acknowledgements

I'd like to thank Susan Sandon, and of course every-one else at Arrow, the Best Publisher in the World. Next up, thanks – as always – to Lavinia Trevor; the Best Agent in the World.

I'd like also to send a very cryptic type of thanks to John. He's a builder and a very special bloke because he achieved something (not at all to do with home improvements) that I failed to accomplish. If you need any work done around the house contact me and I'll give you his number. He really is good. And he likes it white with no sugar.

I have to thank Michael Buerk for being the inspi-ration behind the gerbil story. Michael Buerk and gerbils, eh? Who would have thought it?

And finally, to Matt, who is brilliant in every single way. Except for maybe when he's supposed to be doing something really urgent and important and decides to read the paper instead. Oh, and also when I'm trying to mouth something secret about someone and he can't lip-read and goes 'What?' really loudly so that the person looks round and realises they're being whispered about. Apart from that, he's the best. Except for massage. He's useless at that too, but really, apart from all those things (and a few others that aren't worth mentioning at all), he's my total hero.

Marsha Mellow and Me

Maria Beaumont

She's written a dirty book, now she's got to come clean . . .

Amy's written a bestseller. The ultimate shopping and shagging novel only without the shopping.

She should be enjoying the money, the fame, the eight-page spread in *Hello!* And maybe she would be if only she could tell her mother. But the woman's so over-bearing and puritanical, Amy hasn't even told her she smokes.

So instead, Amy does what she does best, she hides, protected by her pseudonym. But for how long, now that the tabloids have launched a crusade to uncover Marsha Mellow's true identity?

Being found out isn't her only worry. There's the sex-crazed ex who inspired this mess in the first place, the boss that she'd hate if he weren't so irritatingly gorgeous and the growing realisation that everyone else in her life seems to have a dirty little secret of their own.

Marsha Mellow and Me shows that keeping secrets can be really painful and painfully funny.

'This month's must-read: the girly wit of Kathy Lette meets lashings of raw sex.'
B

arrow books

Bringing Down the House

Ben Mezrich

How Six Students took Vegas for Millions

Liar's Poker meets *Ocean's Eleven* in Ben Mezrich's riveting story of a team of brilliant card counters who developed a system to take some of the world's most sophisticated casinos for millions of dollars. *Bringing Down the House* is a real-life thriller, utterly gripping and a fascinating insight into a tightly closed, utterly excessive and utterly corrupt world.

'In this high-octane tale with rich, sharp dialogue, bordering on Elmore Leonard turf, the plot races by at a Nascar pace and the characters on both sides of the table are as real as an inside straight . . .
Bringing down the House is a can't-miss deal.'
Lorenzo Carcaterra

'An extraordinary story . . . [I read] this thrilling book in almost one sitting - it is, to use that cliché, "unputdownable". . . a book that will surely become a classic of its genre.'
Sunday Express

'The tale laid out in *Bringing Down the House* is so beguiling, so agreeably reminiscent of, say *Ocean's Eleven* or *House of Games* that you find yourself mentally casting the parts as you read along . . . A fine yarn'
Sunday Times

arrow books